A DANCE FOR THE DEAD

NUZO ONOH

STYGIAN
S K Y
MEDIA

This is a work of fiction. All of the characters, organizations, and events portrayed in this novel are either products of the author's imagination or used fictitiously.

A Dance for the Dead

Published by Stygian Sky Media, LLC

30011 Commons Royal View Dr.

Huffman, TX 77336

ISBN 978-1-63951-082-5 (paperback)

ISBN 978-1-63951-100-6 (hardcover)

ISBN 978-1-63951-099-3 (ebook)

First U.S. Edition November 2022

PRAISE FOR NUZO ONOH

"Nuzo Onoh's A DANCE FOR THE DEAD is a thrilling, creepy, and moving novel about betrayal, sacrifice, redemption, and the weighty but necessary cost of reconciliation and restitution. Very powerful. A story I won't soon forget."--**Paul Tremblay**, *author of A Head Full of Ghosts and Survivor Song.*

"Nuzo Onoh's novel, A DANCE FOR THE DEAD is a mesmerizing and terrifying thrill-ride from start to finish. I haven't read anything really like this before. Crafty plot twists, brisk pacing, and multi-dimensional characters bring the story to life and will keep readers turning the pages well into the night." - ***Jeremy Bates,*** *author of SUICIDE FOREST and THE SLEEP EXPERIMENT*

"When a man's penis grows too big for his loincloth, he shouldn't be shocked when a monkey mistakes it for its banana"

(An African idiom)

Dedication

Dedicated to my brother, Ken Josef Umunnakwe Onoh,
the original *Agu-eji-ejemba*.
Our Warrior and Our Pride.

GLOSSARY OF IGBO TERMINOLOGY

Agu-eji-ejemba – The great Tiger that leads us into the battle front.

Ajo-ofia – The evil/bad forest where the accursed dead are buried.

Amadioha – The god of thunder & lightning, belonging to the Igbo community in Nigeria.

Aná – The earth goddess, also of the Igbo Community.

Chei – A common exclamation of surprise, shock, impressed.

Chi – One's personal protective spirit or god.

Egbe belu, Ugo belu – May the hawk and the eagle both perch on the tree when their wings weary from flying.

Ekwensu – A Demon spirit, Satan, usually a curse against an adversary.

Igede – An Igbo ancient dance reserved for exalted peers and freeborns

Igba drums – Big drums made from cow-hide or leather.

Ile-nwanyi – *A w*oman's Tongue, an incorrigible gossip.

Ise! - So be it.

Jigida – String of beads worn around the waist by Igbo women, sometimes charmed to offer protection from harm, or just as a fashion accessory.

Juju – Powerful magic or hex.

Kachifo - May morning come, goodnight.

Ndewo – Hello, good-day, goodbye.

Ngwutree – A sacred tree in Igbo culture that signifies greatness. It is not to be cut down or planted, and supposedly, grows on land or homes that will produce great sons.

Nna-anyi - Our father, a respectful greeting for one's father or a respected elder.

Nsibidin – Ancient writing, usually in symbols; found amongst the Igbo, Calabar, and Efik communities.

Nwanne – Womb-siblings, a brother or sister sharing the same mother, even if not the same father.

Ọgba-Ama – Treachery or traitor.

Ọjị Ìkéǹgà - The special kola-nut of bravery, nobility, and luck.

Okpala - The first son.

Ọnodu Ugo – The exalted status of the eagle, which is usually a source of envy to the Hawk and lesser birds.

Osu - A slave to the gods, usually an outcast, a victim of discrimination and prejudice.

Ọzo – Titled peers, leaders of their communities, recognised for good and honourable deeds

ONE

— • —

A DANGEROUS REJECTION

THE WITCH DOCTOR OBSERVED the young girl as she approached. The large clay pot on her braided head was heavy with water, and her exposed breasts were decorated with white-black drawings in intricate patterns. The girl's long, thin legs seemed too fragile to bear both her broad hips and water-laden pot as she navigated the steep hill that jutted out of the desolate landscape like a mottled boil. The witch doctor had followed her along the dusty trail that led to the murky stream reserved solely for the unclean, the village slaves and outcasts.

He smiled as she began her descent from the hill towards his hiding place by the cluster of bushes. His knife-scarified face glistened with sweat under the sun. Overhead, the vultures and hawks soared, fighting over sky-space, occasionally diving low to snap an unwary lizard or rodent for their meal. He slunk deeper into the thick bushes, breaking several dry twigs with impatient hands. The heavy beads around his neck rattled as he laid down his raffia bag on the ground and withdrew his wrapped bundle of chalk paste and charcoal. With hurried flicks of his fingers, he smeared his face with the paste, weaving patterns of black and white on his skin, paintings designed to strike terror into the hearts of even the bravest of warriors.

When he was done, he replaced the bundle inside his bag and straightened his back, pushing out his bony chest like a rooster inside his hen-harem. The bloodied chicken feathers on his head contrasted sharply with the age-whitened hair covering his small skull and jawline. A quick left and right glance assured him no one else apart from the young slave-girl traversed the pitted grounds of the narrow trail.

As if she sensed his presence, the girl suddenly paused, turning her head to survey the deserted path. The circular mark stamped on her forehead—the symbol of her slave status—marred the delicate beauty of her face. A dark shadow clouded her eyes. The witch doctor knew what the girl was thinking. It was the same thoughts that went through the mind of every villager that found themselves in a deserted place at noon when the sun boiled the skies and roasted the earth to dusty brownness. *Ghosts! Malevolent spirits!* Everyone knew that at noon and midnight were the favourite times for haunting spirits to inflict their mischief on the living.

The slave-girl is right to be afraid, not just of the dead, but also of the living, he thought with a smug smile. He wiped the sweat from his face as he watched her draw closer, feeling the sudden quickening of his heart, a thudding of desire.

With a loud shriek, the witch doctor stepped out in front of the girl, hopping around her in a manic dance of terror. The girl's scream pierced the air, her clay pot crashing to the ground in sharp pieces. She turned to run but he grabbed her arms, his fingers hard on her skin. His arms around her were like steel bands as he screeched relentlessly into her ears, filling her heart with terror. It was his tried and effective method of conquest, one he had used on countless occasions to subdue young and

2

nubile girls from the poorer clans. His full witch doctor regalia, coupled with the terror-shrieks, were sufficient to get the girls to give in to his lust without threatening them with a *Juju* curse of infertility and early death. He'd never needed to exert much force to achieve his desires, not when his reputation served as his weapon.

The slave-girl fought him. For several stunned seconds, the witch doctor stared in open-mouthed disbelief as the girl returned his shrieks with louder screams and a powerful push that sent him stumbling to the ground. He lunged forward as she tried to run and grabbed her left leg, sending her crashing to the ground. He threw his weight on her, pushing her face into the ground. They wrestled together on the wet earth, made muddy by the spilled water.

"Are you mad?" his voice was hoarse, breathless, and ugly with fury. "Do you know who I am? How dare you fight me, a useless slave like yourself? Are you suicidal? Are you the foolish fly without wisdom that follows the corpse into the grave? Do you not wear the stamp of slavery on your forehead? You belong to the gods and I command you to lie still and do your duty to your deity, whose priest I am."

"I belong to the king, not your deity," the girl cried, heaving him off her back with a strength that surprised him. Her foot connected with his face as he tried to grab her again, bringing a shout of pain to his chalk-coated lips. A red colour replaced the white chalk on his mouth, a warm colour that tasted of blood. He wiped his lips with the back of his hand and stared at the blood with stunned eyes. Sudden rage turned his eyes as red as his bloodied mouth.

"You...you...stupid...." he spluttered, struggling to restrain his fury as spittle sprayed the air. "You non-being, daughter to no human, worm of no soil! You dare...you dare to spill the blood of the greatest witch doctor in the ten villages and beyond?" He struggled to his feet as the slave-girl stumbled away from him, running like one chased by a pride of lions. "Hear this! You will remember this day and rue the day you were brought into this world!" his voice was pitched like a girl's, fuelled by rage. "You will beg your ancestors for death by the time I'm done with you. You will crave for the solace of the grave-soil and wish that your accursed foetus was aborted by your mother when I come for my revenge. Hear this! Hear this!"

His hoarse shriek followed her fleeing back like the faint echo of dying thunder, while his malice shadowed her soul like the dark cloud of a locust plague.

Two

—·—

A RELUCTANT GROOM

IFE FELT HER eyes boring into his back as he danced. The familiar unease pricked the back of his neck, causing him to miss a step in the dance sequence. He swore both at her and himself. With steely resolve, he forced his mind to focus on the drums and the intoxicating pulse of the famous *Igede* dance beats.

Softly, with tentative taps, the wooden gong joined the metal one, gently inviting the beaded and clay instruments into the undulating rhythm. Finally, the instruments were joined by their king, the leather-clad Igba drum with its throbbing, seductive beat.

Ife's feet flew with the joy of the rhythm. The dust was a brown cloud underneath his hopping legs. His body gyrated and twisted as he allowed the magic of the Igede to transport him to breathless ecstasy. He stooped and rocked his waist, executed a perfect twirl and jump, in sync with the thunderous pounding of the drums.

The crowd gasped and roared their approval with loud claps and hoots. Ife paused, held his body still, allowing their adoration to wash over him and infuse his limbs with renewed energy as he prepared for the final sequence.

"Ife! Feather-Feet! Killer of Sorrows! Ife! Feather-Feet! Dance for us!" The crowd cheered.

Ife was the youngest son of their king, Ezeala of the Oma clan and nothing excited the crowd more than seeing the prince dance. Their praise infused his heart with intense joy, same as the countless occasions he had entertained them at the Ukari village square during various festivals.

He smiled and lifted a hand to wave his gratitude, calm their excitement and ready them for his next dance, The River Dance. The crowd roared their approval. They knew what was coming. They had watched Ife perform that famous dance in the past and each time, the magic remained, fresh and astonishing as ever.

Ife raised his right arm to invite the slow taps of the wooden Ekwe instrument. His tall, lithe body glistened with oiled sweat. A virgin screamed and fell to the ground in a swoon, overcome by passion. The crowd around her inched away, ignoring her prone body as they jostled for a better view of the slender, ebony-skinned youth, famed as the reincarnate of Mgbada, the greatest dancer in the ten villages and beyond.

With a shout of unbridled bliss, Ife freed his body for the famous River Dance that demonstrated the flexibility of his body, the fluidity that turned his bones to elastic as he executed it, mimicking the undulating flow of the River Niger, meandering and twisting along the dusty village square like a beautiful, magnificent sea creature.

The crowd followed his movements with hypnotised intensity. Soon, they were cheering wildly once again, dazed by his prowess. Ife completed the final loops, raised his arms over his head and swung them down with the final crash of the manic drumming. The ground heaved as the crowd rushed at him, shoving and fighting to get to their idol. They lifted him in their arms, swung him up in the air, and passed him across the multitude with frenzied bliss, their voices shrill as they screamed his name.

Ife's warm tears merged with his sweat as he was cloaked with the love of his people. Save for the sweetness of fresh Palm-wine, nothing else beat the thrill of surrendering his body to the tempo of the drums. As the crowd finally set him down, he felt strong arms wrap him in a tight hug, lifting him off his feet again.

He laughed, a loud shriek of joy. He didn't need to turn around to know who it was that held him with such strength. He would know those arms even in death, recognise the distinctive body scent that smelled of smoke, dust and clean sweat. *Diké!* His older brother, heir to their father's royal stool and leader of the fearsome *Ogwumii*, the deadly warrior cult whose exploits struck awe and terror in the hearts of their enemies.

"Nwanne! Womb-Brother from my mother's womb!" Ife returned his brother's hug, smiling into Diké's face, his bony features wreathed with happiness. "I prayed you'd be here to watch me dance, and my prayer's been answered. Tell me, was it good? Did I do well?" He searched his brother's piercing, deep-set eyes, seeking his verdict. Diké's approval mattered more than that of the entire ten villages, even more than their father's.

"Do I need to tell you how wonderful you were?" Diké laughed, releasing him and ruffling his hair affectionately. "Can't you see all the women still lying on the ground, thanks to your handsome face and nimble feet? I tell you, at the rate you are going, our population may soon die out, what with all these besotted virgins resisting marriage in the hope of snaring you."

Ife laughed. As long as Diké liked his dance, all was well in his world.

"You flatter me, big brother. You know it's you that fills the dreams of every village maiden. What woman doesn't love a hero, eh?" he punched Diké's arm playfully.

"You forgot to mention Iruka Big-Bosom as the one woman whose heart will never belong to me." Diké's eyes teased his. "Talk of the devil, here comes your biggest admirer in the world, Iruka Big-Bosom of the breasts to die for. I swear, Ifekandu, I don't know why you have not taken what she's been offering you all these years. Most men would die to sink their heads into those big, soft buns on her chest."

Ife groaned, retreating hurriedly towards the crowd.

"Distract her while I make my escape, please. She hasn't stopped stalking me ever since our father announced my betrothal to Ada of the Nightingale Voice. She's threatened to kill herself the day I marry Ada, and Ada's promised to douse my feet with boiling oil and put an end to my dancing days if she ever discovers I've succumbed to Big-Bosom's charms." Ife sighed, a frazzled frown on his taut features. "Amadioha in His high heavens! Why can't women be like dancing? Easy and joyous. Why do they have to make everything so complicated?"

"Because they're the pesky flies twirling around the cow's tail, created solely to torment men." Diké laughed, pushing Ife aside and turning around to grab the bright-eyed teenage girl with the fulsome figure in a tight hug. "Big-Bosom! What a delight your lovely face has brought to these tired eyes of mine."

Diké swung her around in his arms, laughing as she squealed in mock fright. Her full, naked breasts pressed against the hard plane of his hairy chest, bringing a sudden hardness to his groin and a tug of regret to his heart—*If the girl weren't so besotted with his little brother, he'll readily place a bowl of assorted meats*

8

outside her late father's hut to indicate his desire to make her his second wife.

On the other hand, perhaps it wouldn't be the wisest course. He didn't fancy having Big-Bosom's repulsive snake of a brother, Emeka, as an in-law. Save for Ife's insistence on calling Emeka his best friend, Diké would have since banned the man from their compound—*After all, what good can one expect from the son of a traitor?*

"Where's Ife? I thought I just saw him with you. Let me go. I've got to find him before he disappears. Diké, let me go." Big-Bosom's large, dark eyes flashed her impatience, shining as bright as the *Jigida* beads encircling her neck, waist and wrists. Her long braids were decorated with colourful shells that mirrored the short red and yellow raffia skirt she wore, and her round face glowed with youth and health. Though she lay no claim to great height, she carried her curvy body with a confidence that made her appear several inches taller. Even without her magnificent breasts, hers was a face that caught and held the attention of all that met her, despite the perpetual ill-tempered frown that furrowed her brows.

Diké held her tight, resisting her squirming attempt to escape till he was sure Ife had vanished into the crowd.

"Come now, Big-Bosom; I thought we we're friends, you and me? And here I am, foolishly believing you'll be as happy to see me as I am to see you." Diké chuckled.

She eye-balled him and kissed her teeth in frustration before dashing off into the crowd, calling out Ife's name. Diké shook his head, a wry smile on his face. Sometimes he wondered whether the dance-drums had burst his little brother's head, allowing his brain to flow out of it. Any man that would run away from that luscious bundle of young, fertile femininity must be crazy. Even at nineteen years of age, Ife was still a young fool ruled by the Igede drums and Palm-wine.

Despite the eight-year gap between them, Diké always felt more like a father than a brother to Ife. Their mother's early demise while giving birth to Ife, coupled with their father's re-marriages, meant the responsibility of protecting him fell on Diké. His nine half-sisters from their father's three wives were distant strangers with whom he had minimal interaction. Their tender ages and his demanding life as a warrior made it impossible to forge an intimate relationship with them, not counting the fact that they were all girls. Even his wife, Mgboye, hardly saw much of him on any given day, a fact she blamed for their childless state.

He had hoped to one day induct Ife into the exclusive Ogwumii warrior cult. There would have been deep satisfaction in fighting side-by-side with a womb-brother, but he had given up that dream at the realisation that Ife was a dancer and a dreamer, a boy-man who would never know or appreciate the thrill of a sharp machete against an enemy's neck.

Worse, while most of the boys his age's age-grade were happily married with wives, multiple children and thriving farms, Ife was happy to devote his life to his drums and the Igede dance. His betrothal to Ada of the Nightingale Voice was now into its third year and still the boy showed no signs of carrying the final pots of Palm-wine and cowrie coins to the girl's father to seal the marriage pact arranged by their father.

While Diké didn't particularly fancy having the air-headed beauty as a sister-in-law, it was clear to him that it was a case of Ada of the Nightingale Voice or nobody else. That was how determined their father was to seal the pact with Ada's father, despite Ife's reluctance. It had taken Ezeala years of sustained threats and intense bullying before Ife finally caved to the pressure and consented to the marriage. Big-Bosom and all the other love-struck virgins would need the intervention of a thousand powerful witch doctors to thwart their father's will.

Diké re-joined the rowdy throng, who were now enjoying the colourful display of the masquerades with their carved masks and beaded bodies. The air was filled with the aroma of cooked foods and fresh Palm-wine as the people celebrated the annual New Yam Harvest Festival.

Without warning, a shrill, male voice pierced the air. "Look who's here. It's Diké, first son of our great king, Ezeala of Oma clan! *Agu-eji-ejemba*, the great Tiger that leads us into the battle front. Our warrior and the people's protector. We salute you!"

The praise-singer's voice drew the crowd's attention to Diké. Within seconds, he was surrounded by his own adoring crowd, a crowd double the size of his brother's fans and made up mostly of grown men and young boys, unlike Ife's predominantly female admirers. He allowed them to hug him, shake his hands, and raise his strong right arm in brotherhood. Their voices were a raucous chorus as they chanted impromptu songs in praise of his glorious deeds on the battleground.

Diké raised his arm for silence. The crowd stilled, almost to a hush.

"My treasured possessions, my people, I salute you all," Diké called out, his deep voice reverberating in the vast village square. His piercing dark eyes glinted in the fierce noonday sun. "My owners, whose humble possession I am, I salute you! The right hand needs the left hand to function fully, while the tongue would be useless without the teeth. Nature is synchronicity and together, we thrive."

The crowd roared their approval, almost killing his eardrums. Like all Igbo people, they adored humility in the mighty. Diké raised his arm once more, and a hush descended again in the square. Ears pricked and eyes glittered, as the crowd surged closer to him, eager to catch his words.

"Brothers and sisters, I'm proud to join you today in this wonderful celebration of our bounteous harvest. The Earth Mother, *Aná*, has been kind with her soil this year and our sky father, *Amadioha*, has been generous with his rains. But best of all, our great deity, *Ogu n'Udo*, he of the two faces of war and peace, has blessed us with prosperity and security. The deities are clearly happy with the sacrifices we've offered them, and we pledge our faith, our loyalty and our undying gratitude to them. Let the celebrations continue, my people. *Ndewo!* I greet you all!"

THREE

— • —

BIG-BOSOM

BIG-BOSOM PUSHED through the crowd, her eyes darting everywhere, left and right, front and back, in search of Ife. She cursed Diké with loud expletives as she combed the crowded square for the man whose handsome face filled her every thought. Earlier that morning, she had visited Dibia-Nene, the village root-healer and love-witch. The old woman had coated her face with charmed oils after making some incantations to the love-spirits. She assured Big-Bosom that her face had become a love-magnet which would bewitch Ife once he laid eyes on her. The facial oils smelled right, spicy and strong, like something infused with supernatural powers. Dibia-Nene had warned that for the love-charm to work, Ife's eyes must behold her face before the sun gave way to the moon.

It was now almost sundown and she was still to look into Ife's face directly. Several times while he mesmerised the crowd in the square with his magical feet, she had been tempted to rush over to him, grab him in her arms and scream her passion into his face. It was only the fear of the collective wrath of the ecstatic villagers that had kept her glued to her spot at the front of the ring of onlookers.

Big-Bosom hissed, her brows furrowed—*She can take any of the stupid villagers one at a time, even two or ten!* She wasn't afraid of anyone, but as her late father used to say, 'a clan can eat up the dish served by a single man, but a man cannot eat up the banquet served by an entire clan'. She wasn't a fool. She knew when to pick her fights and it wasn't before the entire ten villages gathered at the square. Instead, she had expressed her frustration with vicious shoves and loud curses at the people nearest to her and happily gave one of the idiot fainters a good kick when the girl collapsed close to her feet—*Idiot girls have no right fancying Ife. He's hers and hers alone!*

She had known it since the fateful day of her very first monthly curse, when she felt her legs cramp underneath the deep river. The currents had dragged her away from the safety of the shore and her mouth filled with salty water that choked her lungs and stole her breath.

Big-Bosom had known that her destiny lay with the owner of the strong arms that had pulled her from the greedy claws of death. The arms had not belonged to her three brothers, or her father and uncles, but to a prince and her brother's best friend, Ife, the great Feather-Feet, whom she'd always worshipped from afar. She didn't believe for a second it was all a coincidence. Out of everyone gathered on the beach on that fateful day almost five years ago, it was Ife that had risked his princely life to pull her to safety.

People had hailed him a hero. They said he had used the awesome skills of his River Dance to outwit the waves. That was in the days when her father was still a respected member of the village community and it was considered a good thing to save his only daughter. *Not anymore, though.* Her father's name was now a cursed name, synonymous with treachery. Save for Ife and Diké, everyone in the ten villages probably wished he

14

had let her drown that day, that the river had swallowed the bloodline of the traitor to the last son and daughter.

Big-Bosom exhaled loudly, cursing under her breath— *What does she care about the villagers when the people that matter, Ife and Diké, wish her well? It isn't as if she had forced her late father to do what he did.*

Suddenly, she spied Ife underneath the great Iroko tree that fanned its broad branches across the vast village square. He was surrounded by the members of his dance troupe and his age-peers. They were drinking Palm-wine, their voices raucous and drunk-merry.

Big-Bosom paused. She could see no females in the group and knew it was taboo for females to join the dance cult when they were gathered under the Iroko to drink. She pulled her braids with restless fingers, debating her options— *She isn't afraid of them. What's the worst they can do to her for barging into their midst? Hit her? Curse her? Who cares! At least, Ife will have no choice but to look her in the face and seal his fate to hers. If he's love-hexed, it'll give him the courage to resist his father's pressure to marry Ada of the idiot Nightingale Voice.*

Big-Bosom quickened her steps, her brows dipped in determined will— *The sun mustn't go down on her or the magic potion is doomed. She'll risk the displeasure of the wretched men to achieve her dreams. Fists and harsh words never killed anybody. She should know. She's still walking and breathing, isn't she?*

Just as she drew to within twenty leg-strides of the Iroko tree, she spied her elder brother, Emeka, amongst the group and her heart sank. Dismay brought a soft groan to her full lips. She had lied to herself when she said she wasn't afraid of anyone. What she should have said was that she wasn't afraid of anyone –except Emeka. Of her three brothers, Emeka was the one that brought the thuds of terror to her heart whenever his small, black eyes rested on her. Yet, he was the brother that loved her the best, the one she knew would commit murder for her sake... *had committed murder for her sake.*

Everyone believed their father had taken his own life three years prior, unable to live with the shame of his treasonous crime. Even as his corpse was carted away for a disgraceful burial in *Ajo-ofia*, the evil forest of the accursed dead, Big-Bosom had watched her brother's face with intensity, searching for the smallest sign that might reveal the cold murderer she knew him to be. But Emeka had wept the loudest, grieved the deepest till she began to believe his pain was genuine, even though she had caught him out in the unspeakable deed with his hands stained with their father's blood.

Emeka had grabbed her with the same bloodied hands he'd stabbed their father with, shaking her violently to stop her hysterical sobs. He told her their father's crime was a curse on their entire clan, especially for Big-Bosom, the only girl in the family.

While the sons were insulted and demeaned in the ten villages, no man wanted her as a wife, even with her famed bosom. It would require paying a bride dowry to the clan of the vile traitor, something no self-respecting suitor would do while their father lived. The snake tattoo branded on his torso by the witch doctor marked him as a traitor wherever he went. An honourable exile would've gone a long way towards ameliorating the consequences of his actions, but their father had been too much of a coward to do the right thing by his family.

So, it had been left to Emeka, his first son, to salvage the family's honour by ending their father's life with a speedy death. It was a shameful death, no doubt, since no suicide could be given a good burial in hallowed ancestral grounds to re-join the ancestors for a good reincarnation. Emeka had done everything for Big-Bosom, for his great love for his little sister—*Did she for one moment imagine that he'd enjoyed what he did, that he wasn't living in pain and guilt with every breath he took?*

Big-Bosom tried to be grateful to her brother for what he'd done for her sake, but her eyes could never forget the brutality of his hand as he plunged the sharp blade into the neck of her sleeping father, already drugged by the herb-infused Palm-wine Emeka had offered him that evening before they retired to their beds. All these thoughts raced through Big-Bosom's mind as she observed her brother and Ife enjoying their Palm-wine in the company of their peers. She sighed wearily and turned away.

It isn't meant to be after all. She would rather forego Ife's attention for the evening. than risk Emeka's ire. Her brother's anger was long and vicious, just as his love was possessive and fierce. Yes; Emeka would kill for her without batting an eyelid, but he would also kill her without a second's thought should she ever provide him with a good enough reason to do so. She knew that hard truth as she knew the features of her face. Her only escape was through marriage. Marrying Ife, a prince and someone that Emeka loved was the perfect solution. She wished Ife's will was as strong as Diké's. Then he would defy the King, and dump Ada of the Nightingale Voice for her—*It isn't even as if the girl's voice is anything to talk about. She's heard her sing a couple of times and in her opinion, the vain tart should really be called Ada of the Crow Voice, huh.*

With another deep sigh, Big-Bosom dragged her feet away from the village square and trudged her slow way back home—*Today might not be her day after all, but the sun will rise again for another day of hope.*

FOUR

–·–

MOUSE IN A TRAP

IFE'S HEART PLUMMETED to his tired feet as he stumbled into his father's vast compound with its multiple red-mud huts and fruit trees. As always, his instinct was to return to his Palm-wine, his friends and his drums, but the moon was riding high in the sky and the celebrations had petered out to drunken stragglers and randy couples in search of dark nooks to hump their hips.

From the interior of one of the mud-huts, Ife heard his father's voice raised in rage. The sound brought a sudden ache to his head—*Please, don't let the King use the double F-word,* he thought, as he lurked by the large Ngwu tree located close to his father's house, the only house built of stone-bricks in the ten villages. He prayed none of his little half-sisters would find him behind his sanctuary, revealing his presence to their father. The King's fury was notorious, scorching the guilty and innocent alike. The rest of the compound was shrouded in an unnatural stillness, as the various wives and children quaked in silence inside their huts, waiting for the king's fury to abate.

"As for the useless Feather-Feet, just wait till I get my hands on the fool," his father's voice thundered. "I've

18

been too soft with the boy and see what it's brought me—nothing! No grandsons and no yam barns. Just the humiliating title of father of wretched Feather-Feet."

Fear wiped the alcohol haze from Ife's eyes. He prayed his father would forget his existence while he raged, or at best, call him by his good name, his ancestral name, Ifekandu, meaning '"child that is more precious than life". Feather-Feet was a title he usually wore with pride except when spoken by their father. On the King's lips, the name 'Feather-Feet' became a shameful slur, an embarrassing silliness, a fool's crown.

"Great King, calm yourself. Don't allow the insignificant ant to attract the attention of the mighty elephant." Diké's voice floated through the dusk, its deep burr calming Ife's racing heart. As long as his brother was around, he knew he would always have a protector from their father's wrath. "Let me talk to Ifekandu. I'm sure I can get him to see the sense in sealing the marriage pledge." Like their father, Diké was the only other person that called Ife by his full name, Ifekandu, meaning, 'child that is more precious than life'. This was customary for sons, so as not to lose the power and blessing behind the name.

"Nothing can get that boy to see anything but his drums." Their father's voice was calmer. When he wanted to, Diké had that effect on people—even the angriest of fishwives calmed in his presence. Yet, he was the most fearsome of warriors, a born killer who dispatched enemy souls to their ancestors' hell without blinking a lid.

"I blame you as much as I blame myself," the King's voice dripped bitterness. "That boy is fast becoming a bad debt owed to the dead ancestors, just like a spinster daughter. You've raised the boy like a prized egg from the day he killed your mother in childbirth and I've let you get away with it. That's why he has no sense of responsibility and spends his time dancing away his sperm rather than breeding strong sons and accumulating great yam barns," the King's voice plunged so low Ife skulked closer to catch his words.

"By our ancestors, I'm done with being patient with your brother. First thing after the Ritual of The Soul-Eaters in the next couple of days, I want you to make a journey to the homestead of Ezugo of Okoh clan, the chief of Abuọ village. Inform him that we're coming in a week's time to deliver the final kegs of Palm-wine and dowry for his daughter, Ada of the Nightingale Voice."

"Father forgive me, but aren't you being rather harsh?" Diké cut in, his voice pleading, a tone never heard except when he spoke to their father about the welfare of his little brother. "Let us give the lad some time. If we rush him, he could flee and where will you be then? Let me speak to him first, please. I know I can make Ifekandu see sense."

"Stop! Enough!" the King barked, his voice the thunder that had cowered many a rebel in the ten villages he ruled. 'Am I still the head of this family and the king of Ukari? I will not be ruled by a foolish boy. By our ancestors, you will go to the Okoh clan in three days from tonight and you will deliver my message. Get your Ogwumii warriors ready to kidnap the wretch and carry him to his betrothed's compound to do the final marriage rites. Once he's there, he'll be too cowed to do otherwise. I know him; he's my son after all. He's not one to make a public fuss before his elders. This marriage must happen to cement my alliance with the Abuọ village chief. The head that wears the eagle's feathers must fight to keep the vultures from plucking them off his head."

The King sighed. "Nothing we discussed tonight may leave your lips. I know how much you love your brother, but this is one time I demand total loyalty and silence from you. It's in his best interests and the progress of this family."

Silence oozed from the hut for several seconds, as if the men had sunk into the sudden *Tsetse* sleep in the middle of their chat, except it was night-time and the sleep-inducing *Tsetse*-fly was prone to seek victims in daylight. All Ife could hear were the hard thuds of his heart. He prayed for oblivion to wipe away the dire words spoken by the King, for some miracle to make Diké reject their father's demands.

"It will be as you wish," Diké eventually said, his voice weary.

"Good; that's settled then. Now we have to get down to the real business of the New Yam Festival." The King's voice was suddenly hushed. "Has the oracle named which of the captured slaves will be sacrificed to Ọgu n'Udo, tomorrow?"

"Not yet; for some reason, the oracle is taking its time this year. Whatever happens, come dawn in two days' time, we will know for sure whose heart we'll be eating."

"May it not be the heart of the slave, Ezekiel Fat-Head," the King said. "I've grown used to having the man around. He's great with the goats and livestock. The man's *Chi* must be a strong one for him to have escaped the attention of the oracle all these years."

"Indeed; we can only pray the oracle picks one of the other slave boys we've captured in recent wars so Ezekiel Fat-Head can survive for another year. If I am not mistaken, this will be his third year with us, isn't it?"

"Ha! Son, I think the Palm-wine you drank today has dimmed your brain," the King's laughter rang with indulgence. "You forget Ezekiel Fat-Head came with the same batch as Teresa Chicken-Legs, which was almost six years ago. Talking of Chicken-Legs, how time flies, eh? The girl was barely into her first monthly curse when

NUZO ONOH

you brought her as a house slave and now, she's ripe enough to make someone a wife. I'm thinking I should wed her to Ezekiel Fat-Head, seeing as they both seem to have the shy-eyes for each other. What do you think?"

Ife didn't think any marriage was a good idea. The king was a marriage addict, and would marry off the entire human, animal, and insect world if he could. He swore silently, creeping closer to catch the rest of the conversation.

"I think what you propose is a good thing. Chicken-Legs has proved a good risk, especially in the home front. She's been amazing with all the children in our hamlet. They love her even more than they love Ifekandu, a real miracle, since we know how that boy enthralls all." Diké chuckled, his laugh echoed by the King. "And I must confess, I prefer her cooking to my wife's. I believe if you give Ezekiel Fat-Head a farmland of his own and build him his own separate hut, then he'll be more than happy to build his future with Chicken-Legs. She'll no doubt present Ezekiel Fat-Head with healthy sons in no time and ensure his bloodline is not wiped out should anything happen."

"Which is more than we can say for your wife, Mgboye, or any of my three useless wives, whose wombs can only harvest female children," the King snarled. "By the way, what has the latest oracle said about your wife's inability to conceive?"

"Nothing more than what you already know," Diké's voice was terse, indicating his reluctance to continue the conversation. "We've performed all the rites and sacrifices demanded by the witch doctor, so hopefully, my wife should be able to conceive within a few moon-cycles."

From his crouching position outside the King's house, Ife felt sudden pity for his brother's plight. He knew Mgboye's childless state was a source of worry and shame to Diké. Their father, the incorrigible marriage broker, was already talking of marrying a second wife for him if a son didn't materialise by the end of the year.

"Hmm, we'll see," the King said, his voice equally terse. "We have to hope your brother will bring more sons into our clan. Our enemies are many and their ambitions strong. As our people say, the flight of the great Eagle is of great envy to the lowly Hawk. Go now; let it be as we've planned. Organise your warriors for the task at hand. In the meantime, we'll meet at the shrine-grove at cock-crow to learn the will of the oracle. *Kachifo*, may morning come, my good son and pride of his father's heart. May your sleep be free of the bad dreams."

"Same to you," Diké said. "May your sleep be free of the bad dreams too, and may the morning find you well and strong."

Ife listened to the familiar greeting exchanged by every Ukari villager at bedtime with scant attention. Their people had long been known to dream nightmares, from the oldest man to the youngest child, a dark legacy inherited from their ancestors. Nobody knew why the villagers were plagued by nightmares, and each family continued to offer sacrifices to appease the ancestors for some unknown wrongs.

Next, he heard the scrappy sound of Diké's chair and the heavy fall of his feet walking towards the entrance of the house. He quickly dodged, running to the rear of the building, clinging close to the stone-brick walls where the deep shadows kept him safe from the glow of the full moon. His legs were so shaky he feared they would collapse under him. His groins pressed heavy, full of fear-piss. He dashed over to one of the cassava farms to relieve his load. His head pounded and his heart quaked—*By Amadioha in His great heavens, he isn't getting married! No way... not*

23

yet. Please great-ancestors, don't let the King force him to carry the final keg of wine for Ada of the Nightingale Voice.

Ife shuddered as the full ramification of the conversation sunk in. In just under a week, he would lose his freedom forever, never again to fly to the beat of the drums. He'll be yoked in married servitude to Nightingale Voice, breeding and raising sons for the clan, working in the numerous family farms and losing the warm camaraderie of his Igede dance-mates. No more exciting travels to various villages, entertaining large crowds and basking in the adulation of the admirers.

He liked Ada of the Nightingale Voice—*of course he does*. He loved listening to her melodious singing voice. He admired her tall, slim contours and polished dark skin. He would marry her —*eventually*, when he was old enough and his legs were too old and tired to fly to the beats of the drum; when age brought its own realities of mellow acceptance to one's fate.

But not now; dear Amadioha *in his vast heavens, not now.*

Ife stumbled towards his hut, his heart beating as loud as his drums earlier that day. He entered his hut and collapsed on his raised mud bed, but the hut felt claustrophobic, stealing his air. He jumped to his feet and stumbled out again, heading out of the compound, fighting the rising terror in his heart—*Perhaps, he should go to Diké and beg him not to carry out their father's orders?*

Ife paused, turned around and started walking towards Diké's large hut—*But what if Diké says no? What if the king orders the rest of the Ogwumii warriors to abduct him all the same with or without Diké's co-operation?*

Ife stopped, wild thoughts racing inside his head like frightened ants—*Think... think!* There had to be a way out, something that would change the King's mind and spare him the eternal doom of married misery.

From one of the huts, a shrill voice pierced through his muddled thoughts. One of his three stepmothers was screaming at her daughter who had come home late from the moonlight games.

"How many times do I need to remind you of *Onodu Ugo*, that the Eagle's glorious flight will forever be a source of envy to the Hawk and lesser birds?" his stepmother scolded the child, parroting the king's favourite mantra. "Don't you know there are enemies who envy your father and his power and will relish the chance to do harm to any of his children? One of these days, you'll be kidnapped or worse, you'll be fed witchcraft in the peanuts offered by an evil witch and become infected with the witch-virus for eternity, you silly child."

Ife heard the hard sound of his stepmother's palm on her child's body and the loud wail that accompanied the smack. But he was no longer paying attention to them. A bright light was flashing inside his head, before his pupils, right across his heart—*Salvation! Finally, a solution to his troubles.*

Suddenly, Ife's legs picked up strength. He scowled at the moon, wishing it away, willing morning to rush in. His plan was one that would get him some reprieve, buy him time to come up with a permanent solution to his troubles. He stifled a giggle as images flashed across his mind. It was a brilliant plan. Genius, even—*Who was it that said all his brains lay crushed beneath his Feather-Feet? Just wait till he shows them.*

By the time he hit his bed for a second time, Ife's eyes were already half-closed in slumber. That night, he slept the deep sleep of pure innocence and joy. If he had the bad dreams, he couldn't remember them and even if he did, they wouldn't have dented his bliss.

FIVE

—·—

THE PLOT IS HATCHED

EMEKA WAS WAITING for him under the Iroko tree at the village square early the next morning. Ife called out a loud greeting and clasped Emeka's arm. The gourd of Palmwine he carried gushed thick foam from the open lid, and several flies hovered around the gourd, drawn by the pungent odour of the beverage.

"Brother-friend, I hail you. May the rooster forever crow in your dawn."

"Feather-Feet! May your mighty feet remain forever light on the soil and firmly attached to your legs," Emeka returned Ife's greeting with a chuckle.

Emeka was almost the same age as Ife's older brother, Diké, though his slight stature made him appear no older than a teenager until one looked closely into the knowing blackness of his small eyes.

"Come, let's share this Palm-wine and talk. By *Amadioha*, there's something that's chasing the tortoise from the safety of its shell," Ife moaned.

"*Tufia*! May the heavens forbid such an evil!" Emeka spat out the curse into the sandy soil and swung the evil over his shoulders with his arms. Ife arranged himself on the ground, with Emeka sat across from him. He filled his mug with some Palm-wine from his gourd and leaned

26

forward to pour the drink into the soil in solemn libation to the ancestors.

Emeka watched him, a smirk on his face as he held out his cup for some Palm-wine

"So, tell me, what's happened?" Emeka's close-knit eyes were bright with curiosity. His small, wiry frame quivered with anticipation. He was known in the village to like a good story and to share numerous bad stories with reckless enthusiasm, hence his nickname, *Ile-nwanyi*, meaning 'Woman's Tongue.' It was an alias Emeka detested and which Ife only used when he was displeased with him.

"It's my father," Ife said, his voice as glum as his face. "He's ordered the Ogwumii to abduct me and force me into immediate marriage to Ada of the Nightingale Voice. It's to happen two days from now."

"Chei! That is terrible," Emeka exclaimed, his eyes wide with shock. "My sister will die if she finds out your marriage will finally take place after all this time." Emeka tried to make light of things but there was an underlying hardness to his voice which surprised Ife. Ife glanced at him with a frown and Emeka smiled, raising his palm in a disarming manner.

"Just joking. But seriously, what are you going to do about this terrible news? You know you don't want to marry yet. You've said so yourself, over and over. Surely, your brother can talk your father out of it? Ask him to help you. We both know the almighty Diké would annihilate the entire world for you if you desired it." Emeka's voice was laced with sarcasm. His dislike of Diké was no news to Ife. It saddened him that the two people he loved the most, his big brother and his best friend, couldn't abide each other.

"I can't talk to Diké about it," Ife replied with his brows furrowed. "It was to Diké that father gave the order. He must obey our father and organise my abduction with his warriors."

"So, what will you do? Go along with them and allow yourself to be married off before you're ready? You're aware you can never dance with us again once you become a married man, don't you?"

"You don't need to remind me," Ife snapped, his voice terse in unfamiliar anger. "I'm not a fool despite what a lot of people might think. Actually, I've got an idea which I think will scupper my father's plans."

"Okay then; tell me what it is," Emeka's voice was sullen, his face aloof. Ife topped up their cups once again, feeling the slight trembling of his hands. He wasn't sure if it was as a result of his renewed terror or the potency of the Palm-wine.

"I've been thinking; what if I disappeared? I could come to your house and hide out for a while and you can spread the word that I was abducted by some enemies from an unknown village. Father will be so busy searching for me and so troubled by my abduction that the last thing on his mind would be a marriage rite to Ada of the Nightingale Voice. By the time I miraculously escape and find my way home, I can pretend to be so traumatised by everything that the marriage will be delayed indefinitely. So, what do you think of my plan?" Ife's eyes gleamed with both excitement and anxiety.

Emeka stared at him goggle-eyed.

"*Chei!* Have you lost your mind, or is it the Palm-wine speaking?" Emeka sneered. "Hasn't it occurred to you that the first place they'll search will be *my* house, just to be sure I haven't harmed your precious body?" Emeka barked a harsh, bitter laugh. "You know how people hate our friendship. Your brother loathes the very ground I walk upon. No one understands why the son of our King would stoop so low as to befriend a pauper's son like me; and not just any pauper, but one whose father is buried in *Ajo-ofia* for the abominable crimes of treason and suicide."

Emeka shook his head, his eyes hard as cold pebbles. "Has it even occurred to you that such a stunt would put the lives of innocent people at stake? Do you think your brother will just sit down and twiddle his thumbs, offering useless libations to rubbish ancestors in the hope you'll come sauntering home unharmed some day? Ha! You clearly don't know your brother. Diké will march his deadly warriors against the ten villages and beyond. Heads will roll and the soil will muddy with the blood of countless innocents before Diké and his warriors are done searching for you. *Chei!* I swear, sometimes your selfishness astounds me. I don't know why I even bother with you."

Emeka refilled his cup by himself this time. He drank up the Palm-wine in one long gulp.

Ife's face broke out in hot sweat. Shame wilted his heart. Emeka always had a way of making him feel unworthy of his friendship. He wanted to shout at Emeka that he wasn't stupid, that he was aware all the villagers viewed him with affectionate contempt because he was neither a warrior like his brother nor a successful farmer like his age-peers, even as they enjoyed his famed dancing. But he kept his peace, stilled his frustration underneath the helpless demeanour he had perfected through nineteen years of living with his father's disdain.

"So, what d'you propose I do?" Ife turned over his problems to Emeka as he'd always done. "If you think my plans are stupid, why don't you come up with something better?"

Something flicked in Emeka's eyes, an expression Ife couldn't define, but one that brought a sudden sense of unease to his heart. His friend turned and spat into the ground.

"To kill a tree, you must reach deep into the soil to its roots. Cutting the branches will not destroy it, as it will only sprout new ones; are you following my logic?" Emeka's voice was hard, his features like granite.

Ife nodded, slowly. He wasn't sure he understood what Emeka meant, but he was confident it would be revealed in time. Like everyone else, Emeka liked to speak in riddles when speaking to Ife, as if to reinforce his stupidity.

"You can kidnap yourself all you like, but the marriage will always hang over your head until you kill the idea for good. Let me tell you a sad truth that has so far eluded you. Your problem is Diké. He's the leader of the Ogwumii. What he tells them to do is what they'll do. Not even the King has as much influence over them as your brother. So, listen carefully. The person we need to kidnap is your brother."

Ife gasped, shaking his head violently. "Are you crazy? Have you lost your senses completely? And you accuse me of being stupid! You can't kidnap Diké, you foolish goat; and I for one, won't be party to such a fool plan. You forget who you're talking about. Diké's machete will dispatch you and whoever else that's stupid enough to try anything against him."

"Calm down! You should let me finish before declaring my plan a stupid one."

"Because your idea is beyond a lunatic's imagination it makes no sense exploring it further," Ife took another gulp from his cup. Beads of sweat dotted his forehead. Emeka's words had brought the trembles to his body.

"You're right, of course," Emeka's voice was reasonable, even gentle. If Ife's words offended him, he neither showed it in his words nor his expression. "But, have you forgotten that some of the greatest ideas are from the minds of the hopelessly insane? So, be patient and hear out the ideas of this particular lunatic, and when I'm done you can either call me the son of a lunatic or the son of a genius, okay?"

Finally, Ife nodded, slowly, reluctantly. Emeka took a sip from his mug.

"Who is the leader of the Ogwumii warriors, tasked with abducting you?"

"Diké, of course, you fool. What's this game you're playing? I thought you were taking my troubles seriously, instead of wasting precious time playing silly riddle games."

"Believe me, I'm taking your troubles very seriously, so permit me to continue. Tell me, who has your father instructed to visit the clansmen of Ada of the Nightingale Voice to declare your impending marriage and oversee your abduction?"

"Diké," but ... Ife was slow in responding. A frown furrowed his forehead.

"Who does your father value more than his own life? Who does the entire village look up to? Depend upon to protect them? Whose loss would plunge everyone and everything into total chaos?"

"Diké." This time, Ife's voice was firmer. A dim light was starting to sparkle inside the fuzziness of his drink-muddled brain.

"Exactly. Everything boils down to your brother," Emeka's voice was raised in triumph. "Do you think if Diké goes missing, even for one day, that your father would remember a person called Ada of the Nightingale Voice exists? Or that his good-for-nothing dancing son needs to get married without delay? Of course not!" Emeka leaned closer. "We will kidnap him and hold him hostage inside my late father's empty hut. Everyone knows how much Diké loathes me, so that's the last place they'll look for him. He'll be safe here. By the time we release him, everyone will be so relieved that the celebrations could well last for several moons. The matter of your marriage will be forever forgotten."

"Except that Diké'll never forget or forgive. He'll kill us both and rightly so."

"Only if he knows we're responsible. Believe me, I don't harbour a death wish and would never enter a lion's den while it roams free." Emeka lifted the gourd of Palm-wine, shaking it vigorously. He peered into the open lid to see how much of the drink was left. The grimace on his face told Ife their treat was almost finished. Emeka filled Ife's cup to the brim and poured the remnant into his cup. It was barely enough for a mouthful.

"*Chei!* This Palm-wine is sweet. No sane person ever refuses an offer of Palm-wine from Feather-Feet because they know it will be the very best in the land."

Ife couldn't resist the brief flush of pride Emeka's words brought to his heart. Emeka was right; he owned the best Palmwine kegs in the ten villages and beyond.

"Ok, now you're done praising me, what's all that got to do with my brother and his abduction if I'm stupid enough to go ahead with your plan?" Ife asked, fixing alcohol-blurred eyes on Emeka's face.

"Because I have some special sleeping herbs which I got from that old hag, Dibia-Nene, after my father died and I struggled to sleep. You remember how it was with me then." Emeka shook his head at the memory. "Anyway, I still have loads of the herbs, which we can mix into Diké's drink. My two brothers and I will wait inside your hut and once he's drugged, we'll carry him to our hamlet."

"Uh-uh; I'm not sure—" Ife started to shake his head.

"Don't worry, we'll feed him and keep him safe," Emeka hurried to assure him. 'We'll wear masks, so he won't recognise us even if his blindfold gets undone. He'll be so out of it from the sleep-herbs that he won't know or care about where he is until we sneak him back to his hut. He'll wake up happy and safe and no one will be the wiser. All Diké will recall is that he shared Palm-wine with you, and you left him to return to your hut and the rest is history. Let him and the villagers break their heads trying to figure out why he was kidnapped, who kidnapped him and why he was returned unharmed. The anxiety will keep them busy for the next twelve moon cycles and you, my Brother-friend, you'll be as free as a bird to dance away your feather-light feet in our village square for as long as your little heart desires."

Emeka downed the last remnants of the Palm-wine and smashed his calabash mug on the ground, simultaneously releasing a loud belch and a louder fart with a giddy smile.

Ife stared at Emeka, his heart racing with excitement. A sudden rush of adrenaline sent his senses reeling, temporarily clearing the fog from his brain—*Oh, sweet ancestors! This could just work! This might really work!*

"Brother-friend, you're the son of a genius!" Ife shouted, clasping Emeka's hand fiercely. "I hail you! I bow my head to you," Ife bowed oleaginously in Emeka's direction.

Emeka laughed. "Don't let anyone see you bowing your head to a nobody like me," Emeka said, his eyes black orbs of ice, alcohol-free, unlike Ife's drunken glaze. "We have to strike fast. We must ensure that journey is never made. Everything must happen tomorrow night latest if we're to stop Diké. I'll leave you to arrange the Palm-wine while I get my brothers ready. I'll send my little sister to you to confirm everything. Don't worry, she won't know a thing. You can never trust women with secrets. All you'll need to tell her is 'The Palm-wine is ready.' If it's not ready, we'll know the plan is aborted and our friendship is ended. I won't go through all this trouble for an ungrateful friend,"

Emeka's laughter did not reach his hard, dark pupils. He got to his feet and brushed the dust off his loincloth. His small, wiry frame glistened with the sweat of the mid-morning sun.

"Till we meet again, Brother-friend," he said.

Ife stumbled to his feet, his limbs weakened by the Palm-wine. He grabbed Emeka in a tight hug, his face wreathed in a sheepish grin.

"I'm lucky to have sh...such a wise owl and cunning tortoise as my Brother-friend." Ife hiccupped, burping loudly before breaking into teary giggles. "Promish... promise me on your life that you'll take very, very good care of my brother. Promise by Ọgu n'Udo, that not a single hair on Diké's head will be hurt while he's in your hamlet."

"Of course, I promise," Emeka snapped. "I know how precious the mighty Diké is to you and the entire village. I'll treat him like the prized guinea-fowl egg he is. Satisfied?"

Ife smiled, nodding as he stumbled away, clutching his empty Palm-wine gourd in his hand. His life is beautiful indeed, he thought. With a Brother-friend like Emeka, a wonderful big brother like Diké, the great camaraderie of his dance cult-mates and the sweetness of fresh Palm-wine, what else could a man ask of his personal *Chi*?

Ife's voice raised with drunken cheer as he stumbled and danced his way back to his father's hamlet.

Chi'm di mma, eh, eh, eh! (my guardian spirit is good to me)

Chi'm amaka, oh, oh, oh! (my guardian spirit is wonderful)

Six

—·—

THE SOUL-EATERS

DIKÉ LOOKED AT the silent group of men gathered inside the secret shrine of Ọgu n'Udo, the village deity of the two faces of war and peace. The air was cool with the early dawn breeze and above them, the moon was still to complete its journey and give way to the sun. Its pale shadow hovered over the greying skyline like the blind eye of a nameless god, piercing through the broad branches of the trees to dapple the ground with dull, silvery rays.

There were ten mighty, mystical Ngwu trees set in a semi-circle. They were said to represent the ten great warriors of the Oma clan, who in their lifetime possessed the secret of transmogrification, the ability to shape-shift into terrifying lions in the battleground, devouring enemies in a bloody orgy that ensured the security and perpetuity of the Oma clan's rulership.

A clattering sound from above caused Diké to glance at the trees shrouding the shrine-grove in perpetual gloom. He took several steps backwards, putting some distance between himself and the nearest tree. The dreadful rattling sounds from the hundreds of white human skulls dangling on the branches of the trees sent a slight shiver to his exposed skin. Despite the numerous

NUZO ONOH

times he'd visited the secret grove, the sight of so many bone-fruits glaring down at him with hollow sockets never failed to tease the hairs at the back of his neck with chilly fingers.

With hooded lids, Diké surveyed the various people gathered with him inside the shrine-grove. The King stood out in his royal resplendence. His broad shoulders were draped with a heavy leopard-skin shawl, while three Eagle feathers circled his head. Several rows of large beads hung heavy around his neck, beads from different rare stones from carnelian to multi-coloured garnets. A wide ivory armband covered with intricate designs clasped his upper right arm, silently proclaiming his elevated status to the world. The rest of his visible body was a patchwork of sacred and protective *Nsibidi* symbols, inscribed in black and red ink.

Around him stood Diké's five warrior-leaders, the witch doctor, Dibia Okpoko, and the members of the Ọzo peer group who were the leaders of the ten villages that made up the Okoro territories. Each of the ten chieftains represented the most prosperous families in the villages, and the distinctive Ostrich feathers on their greying heads, together with the ivory bands around their ankles, proclaimed their high status.

"Ezeala of Oma clan, our great King, may the bad dreams never harm you and may your house never fall," Ezugo of Okoh clan said. He was the father of the famous village beauty, Ada of the Nightingale Voice.

"Ise! So be it!" Everyone chorused.

"May your son, Diké, continue to bring more greatness to your name and our ten villages," offered a second peer.

"Ise!"

"May the gods continue to bless your bloodline with the greatness of the Ngwu tree."

"Ise!"

36

"And may your wives do right by you and bring more sons to your household, who will enjoy the blade more than the dance-drums," called out a humorous voice.

"Is...." The response this time was muted and unfinished, hesitant.

All eyes turned to the speaker, Ọzo Agwọ of Uba clan, to gauge his expression for signs of mendacity or mockery. Everyone knew how touchy the King was about his dancing son, and numerous wives whose wombs only yielded female harvests.

Rage flared briefly in Diké's heart as he studied the plump features of the obese chieftain, Ọzo Agwọ, whose tongue eternally licked his fleshy lips as if they were made of honey. The kingship used to reside with his clan, the Uba clan, till the deity, Ọgu n'Udo, proclaimed Ezeala's great ancestor as King.

Ọzo Agwọ was the richest of all the gathered men, even richer than the King. It was rumoured he made his money by selling slaves captured at war to the white men located at the distant Calabar shores. Some even said he had started selling his own people, but no one could prove the stories. What was clear was that the man now harboured aspirations to the kingship stool and had been vocal in demanding a rotational system of leadership amongst the ten families that comprised the Ọzo peer group. His idea had so far met fierce criticism and strong admonition from the rest of the chieftains, who reminded him that the current King had been ordained by the ancestors and the great deity, Ọgu n'Udo, in whose shrine they were now gathered.

As Diké observed the icy humour on Ọzo Agwọ's face, he knew that the old jealousies still festered in the man's heart like a poisoned wound. The chieftain would never rest till he wore the leopard shawl and the eagle feathers of kingship on his head. Diké knew his command of the military might of the Ogwumii was the only thing that ensured the safety of his father's throne. It was only a matter of time before the wealthy chieftain made his move.

The king raised his royal staff and silence descended on the gathered men.

"Esteemed chieftains and my warrior-leaders, we await the voice of the oracle to guide us in our secret rites today," the King said, turning to the witch doctor.

Dibia Okpoko stood apart from the group, watching the gathering in ominous silence, his close-set eyes hard as coal. The king called the witch doctor by his secret name, inviting him to initiate the ceremony. The knife-scarified man raised his withered arm in silent acknowledgement and with a grim nod, stepped forward, bearing two live white chickens, a *Juju* sacrifice to the ancestral spirits of the trees.

Dibia Okpoko consecrated himself with the sacred oils and chalks, then, with a brutal stroke, sliced the throats of the chickens, spraying his exposed chest with the blood of the dead birds. Next, he circled each of the ten mystic trees, spraying chicken blood at their crawling roots while mumbling secret chants to the ancestral spirits. When he was done, he sat cross-legged before the tallest of the trees and reached into his raffia bag with a bloodied hand. He pulled his sacred gift to the ancestors, *Ọjị Ìkéǹgà*; the special kola-nut of bravery, nobility, and luck. He broke the red nut into ten equal pieces and started shouting praises to the ten great lions, the ancestors' spirits residing inside the *Ngwu* trees.

Diké and the assemblage joined in the loud obeisance to the ancestors till Dibia Okpoko raised his arm for silence. For several minutes, all was still in the gloomy grove save for the harsh breathing of the men and the insistent wild rattles of the hanging skulls atop the trees. Suddenly, Dibia Okpoko began convulsing, his body thrashing on the dusty ground like one suffering a demon attack.

It had begun.

The oracle was speaking its message into the mind of their witch doctor. The ancestral spirits of the Ngwu trees were naming the slave whose blood they would drink and whose heart would be devoured by the warriors, imbuing them with supernatural strength in the battleground. Again, Diké said a silent prayer for the protection of their house-slave, Ezekiel Fat-Head, that his name be once again bypassed by the oracle on this occasion.

"Theresa Chicken-Legs! Theresa Chicken-Legs! Theresa Chicken-Legs!"

Three times the witch doctor shrieked the name of the chosen sacrifice as was directed by the oracle. And for the first time in the known history of the gathering, the men gasped. In fact, Diké screamed, his shout drowned out by his father's own.

"Dibia Okpoko!" Diké exclaimed, running to the witch doctor and grasping his arm. "Surely, you misheard the oracle! The spirits cannot demand the blood of a woman. How can a woman's heart imbue warriors with courage and strength? I request you speak again to the ancestors to get their correct message."

"Theresa Chicken-Legs! Theresa Chicken-Legs!" the witch doctor repeated, his voice louder, harsher.

Murmurings broke out amongst the gathered men. The chieftains, egged on by Ọzo Agwọ, demanded that the gathered warrior-leaders go without delay to abduct the slave-girl and bring her to the shrine for the sacrificial ritual, as was the custom. They accused the King and his son of challenging the oracle's decision because the girl had become a valued slave in their hamlet.

"Come, *Agu-eji-ejemba;* surely, you'll not set your selfish desires against the wishes of the oracle and the great ancestors!" Azo Agwo exclaimed, his hard eyes glinting with spite.

"This has nothing to do with our family! I refuse to defile myself by eating the heart of a woman, and I command my warrior-leaders to reject this Ritual of The Soul-Eaters till a man's heart is offered," Diké shouted, his voice a menacing thunder that brought the quakes of terror to the hearts of the gathered chieftains, even the conniving Ozo Agwo.

They all knew how fearsome Diké's machete and his fighting arms were. His warrior-leaders in their midst would obey his commands without hesitation should he order them all dispatched to their ancestor's hell. Already, they could see their grips hard on the bronze hilts of their war machetes, even as they struck a casual pose.

"Great warrior, iron man of valour, I greet you and ask for your indulgence," Ozo Agwo's voice was now oily, warm with flattery, the dangerous voice of reason. His massive body trembled with rolls of fat as he made his way towards Diké, his arms gleaming with multiple ivory arm-bands. "I ask you, brothers, has Dibia Okpoko ever been wrong in the past? Did he not foretell the coming of the locust plague and the great drought that almost ruined our crops? Did he not identify the witchcraft possession that occasionally infected some of the young girls in our village, exposing them to immorality and unwed pregnancies until we sacrificed them all to the ancestors to prevent the birth of their witch-infected foetuses? As you all might recall, those witches were so incensed with Dibia Okpoko for revealing their wicked natures that they even sought to smear his good name by accusing him of defiling them!"

40

Ọzo Agwọ's voice suddenly rose to deafening decibels as he struck a combative pose, his legs wide apart, arms akimbo. "You are a great warrior, Diké. But I challenge you to try and withstand the might of our ancestors when they possess your human flesh and spirit. Then you'll find that what Dibia Okpoko endures for our good is not something to be questioned or treated with the disrespect you've shown today."

Ọzo Agwọ turned to the King, his brows raised in cold arrogance. "Ezeala, you are our King and he is your son. I leave it to you to decide whose will shall prevail today—yours or our ancestors."

Even before his father spoke, Diké knew that Ọzo Agwọ had won and the poor slave girl, Chicken-Legs, was doomed. A tight knot grew in his neck, choking his speech and his breath. Guilt poisoned every vein in his body. *He's to blame. Everything's his fault.* But at the time he had captured the girl, he'd thought he was bringing a domestic slave to his father and not a shrine slave. Chicken-Legs had enjoyed all the privileges of their wealthy hamlet as if she were a daughter of the clan. How was he to know the oracle would demand a female sacrifice?

Diké stared long and hard at the overweight chieftain, reading the malice in his dark pupils before turning his gaze at the witch doctor, where he still lay prostrate on the ground before the blood-soaked, crawling roots of an *Ngwu* tree. Diké's hands reached for his two bronze machetes, his action involuntary, an unconscious habit. A cold glint flashed in his eyes. The urge to swing his arms in a double murder was strong and it took every ounce of military discipline he possessed to resist annihilating the treacherous chieftain and the false witch doctor. With slow reluctance, he allowed his hands to release their grip on his machetes. A sudden

41

hush descended amongst the watching men as they followed his movement with tense wariness.

"Dibia Okpoko, you say the oracle has spoken and it shall be as you have said," Diké said. "Let it be known to all gathered here that I, Diké, first son of the King, Ezeala of Oma clan, declare that my hands shall not be tainted with the blood of the slave-girl, Theresa Chicken-Legs, neither will I defile my soul by partaking of her heart at the Ritual of The Soul-Eaters. I have never doubted the oracle till today and I will not challenge the will of our ancestors. But, Dibia Okpoko, mark my words. If you think you misheard the ancestors and refuse in your pride to seek clarification from them, then may that innocent girl's blood be on your head and on the heads of all gathered here who sanction her death, right to the tenth generation and beyond. I am finished."

Diké plunged his machetes into the soil with a violence that brought loud gasps to the lips of the chieftains. As he turned to leave, he heard a rustling sound as Dibia Okpoko struggled to his feet. He turned and met the burning hate in the dark eyes of the blood-splattered witch doctor.

"Diké, son of Ezeala of Oma clan; hear this! I demand you recant your words immediately and apologise to the high priest of Ọgu n'Udo, for your insults and provocation or face my terrible curse," Dibia Okpoko's voice shrilled at him.

"You'll receive no apologies from me unless you agree to seek clarification from the oracle and confirm that it is indeed the heart of a weak woman the ancestors want their warrior-leaders to eat."

The witch doctor stared at him for several seconds before spitting tobacco-browned sputum into the soil. His eyes were red-rimmed, wild with the mania of hate.

"Today, you have insulted the priest of the gods and the mouthpiece of our ancestors. In your foolish pride, you have dared question the will of the oracle. Hear this, Diké, son of Ezeala of Oma clan; I, Dibia Okpoko, the high priest of the great deity, Ọgu n'Udo, hereby pronounce the curse of The Shadow Crows on your head! I have spoken, so it shall be. Hear this!"

Everybody gasped. Even the five hardened warrior-leaders shouted, their scarred faces stunned. The King bellowed, grabbing Diké's arm with fingers of steel.

"Son, recant your words now," the King urged, his voice holding an unfamiliar tremor. "Beg Dibia Okpoko's forgiveness and the forgiveness of our ancestors, that this evil curse may be lifted from your head."

Diké shook off his father's hand, deep furrows ridging his forehead.

"I will not apologise, not when he refuses to admit he misheard the oracle," Diké snarled, spitting into the soil to show his contempt. "Are you all blind? In the history of our existence, when have our ancestors ever demanded the heart of a woman for the Ritual of The Soul-Eaters? I will not defile myself by eating a woman's heart and if Dibia Okpoko wants to curse me for it, then that is his prerogative and my prerogative to reject his curse. I believe in my Chi."

Another gasp filled the air. Everyone stared at Diké as if he had suddenly sprouted horns, tails and claws.

"Ezeala, you have bred a son whose penis has grown too big for his loincloth," mocked Ọzo Agwọ, turning to the other chieftains for confirmation. They all nodded their heads vigorously, giving Diké accusing looks. His warriors quickly flanked him, linking their arms as in combat.

A terse silence hung in the air, a silence of screeching hate. The witch doctor stared coldly at the gathered warriors.

43

"Diké, son of Ezeala of Oma clan, hear this!" He pointed a blood-reddened finger at Diké. "I once again pronounce the curse of The Shadow Crows on you! A dark cloud now hovers over your head, a cloud of crows, the shadow of misfortune and pain. You have become the foolish chicken that walked out of the protection of its mother's wings and became food to the preying Hawk. Even as you stand before me today, your body has already become meat-feast to the grave worms."

Dibia Okpoko turned and faced the stunned warriors, his eyes blazing. "Hear this! Any of you warriors who refuses to abduct the slave-girl for the sacrifice, shall also be burdened with the curse of The Shadow Crows. Your foolish leader has commanded that you reject the heart of the slave-girl and I will not punish you for obeying your leader. That is the law of your cult, after all. But you must obey the laws of the land by performing your duty to the gods, which is to bring the human sacrifice into the shrine. Go now and bring the slave-girl that you may all live. As for your leader, he is doomed. I, Dibia Okpoko, have spoken, and the words I sow have never failed to harvest crops!"

He turned back to Diké and spat into the soil. "As for you, proud prince, upon your foolish head be your doom. The black birds have spread their invisible wings over you and the clouds above you have turned to night in the middle of the day. Start counting your days, proud prince, and remember to count backwards, not forward."

For several terse seconds, the two men glared at each other, hatred blistering like an inferno between them. Finally, Diké picked up his machetes and turned and walked away from the shrine-grove. He waited to hear footsteps behind him, the fearless feet of his warrior-leaders and his father.

He heard nothing. No one followed him out.

A sudden shiver layered his skin with goosebumps. He shook it away with a loud curse as he stalked away from that place of death.

Every man has his own palm-lines, his own lines of destiny, he thought. He could not fight Chicken-Legs' doomed destiny. He could only fight his own. He didn't believe that the decrepit witch doctor had any powers over his destiny, regardless of his threats. Should misfortune come, he would handle it with the fortitude of a man. Should death come instead, he would face it like the warrior he was and fight it without fear, without mercy and with great respect.

SEVEN

—·—

THE ABDUCTION

IRUKA BIG-BOSOM KNEW that something was brewing in their hamlet. All day, she had watched her three brothers huddled in deep conversation inside Emeka's hut, something that rarely happened. In fact, the last time she recalled seeing her brothers together was after their father's death, when they divided his possessions amongst themselves, leaving her nothing.

Just before sunset, Emeka summoned her to his hut. Her heart dropped to her feet, fear quaking her limbs—*Amadioha have mercy! What does Emeka want with her this time? What's she done to deserve his anger?* Frightened thoughts raced in her mind as she entered Emeka's hut.

"Get yourself to the King's compound and ask Ife if he has some Palm-wine to share with me," Emeka said, fixing his hard little eyes on her.

Instantly, Big bosom's heart soured at the prospect of seeing Ife, even as a small prickling of unease dampened her joy. She stared at Emeka, thoughts whizzing through her mind. The message was so unimportant that it raised her suspicions—*Why is Emeka sending her on such a useless errand?* After all, the men simply met and drank together whenever the mood took them, which was almost every hour of the day, a habit that left Ife permanently sozzled when he wasn't dancing.

"What? Why are you staring like a fool? Are you deaf?" Emeka shouted at her. "Get going at once and make sure you tell no one about this errand. Return as soon as you've spoken to Ife, or else..." Emeka didn't complete his threat. He didn't need to.

Big-Bosom sighed, turning away. She'd be a fool to invite his brutal fists on her body, even for all the beancakes he gave her after each beating. Emeka never used to threaten her while their father lived. Their mother's sudden death a few moons after Big-Bosom's first woman's-curse, had made their father even more protective of her as the only daughter. But their father's absence had released a demon in Emeka's soul. These days, it took nothing to trigger his rage, and there was no one to protect her from his beatings. Her two brothers had tried their luck on her body after seeing the liberties Emeka took with his fists, but Emeka had thrashed them till they almost met their ancestors. After that, none of them dared hit her again, neither would they intervene when Emeka pummeled her body.

She had considered confiding in Ife, especially at those times he noticed her bruised eye or swollen lips and cracked a joke about her clumsiness, but she knew that Emeka would kill her if she ever told. Ife's friendship was the one thing he valued above everything else.

Ife wasn't happy to see her when she arrived at his hut with Emeka's message. He frowned at her with the familiar impatience she was used to, coupled with a new look she couldn't decipher. She guessed their compound must be grieving over the death of that nice slave-girl, Chicken-Legs. Everyone in the village was talking about it, shocked by the strange voice of the oracle. Never in the history of the ten Okoro villages had Ọgu n'Udo demanded the sacrifice of a woman.

Big-Bosom adjusted her voice to mirror the sombre mood in the King's compound as she delivered Emeka's message.

Ife listened to her message with ill-repressed irritation before he said, "Tell Emeka the Palm-wine is ready."

That was it; nothing more. She waited for further instructions and when nothing was forthcoming, she asked, "Do you want me to carry the wine gourd back?"

"No, it's okay. I'll see Emeka later."

Ife ushered her out of his hut as if she were an annoying fly, and withdrew back inside, shutting his narrow, wooden door. She felt tears prickle her lids and forced them back. There was nothing new in Ife's rejection, but it always hurt as if it were the first time—*If only Emeka hadn't been around on that day Dibia Nene gave her the love hex! Then, by now she'll be the one engaged to Ife, and not that rubbish Nightingale Voice.*

She trudged back to their hamlet with heavy limbs to deliver Ife's message. Emeka was so happy with the message that he gave her a big hug, something he only did when anything bad happened to one of his numerous enemies. His reaction confirmed her suspicions that something else was afoot apart from the mere prospect of drinking Palm-wine with his best friend. More curious were the reactions of her other two brothers. They both seemed as excited as Emeka—*Something is definitely afoot. If only she can hear their whispered conversations or read the gleeful furtiveness in their eyes.*

A strong instinct told her that whatever it was bringing such looks to their faces signalled evil for some unfortunate person. She shrugged—*What does she care who they hurt or what they do?* After all, it wasn't as if anyone cared about their welfare in Ukari village apart from Ife, and her brothers would never plot evil against Feather-Feet in eternal moon cycles. With a shrug, Big-Bosom withdrew into her hut and closed her door, shutting out her brothers and their mischief.

Ife's heart pounded as he made his way across the large compound towards Diké's hut, carrying a small jar of Palm-wine. His hands leaked with the same hot sweat that dampened his brows. Beneath the exposed smoothness of his chest, his heart pounded so loudly he feared the whole hamlet would hear the treachery in its thuds—*It isn't too late to back out, abandon the whole kidnap thing and just resign himself to their father's wishes*, he thought, desperation dizzying his vision. Emeka would be furious. The man had threatened the end of their friendship should Ife back out of the plan, and he had seen the hard glint of resolve in Emeka's eyes—*But can he truly go through with the plot? Can he possibly deceive his hawk-eyed brother who can read him with the precision of a mother's gaze?*

From the various huts dotted across the vast hamlet, Ife heard the muted cries of the children—an occasional loud wail hurriedly hushed by a mother's rebuke. The tragedy that had befallen the homestead that day, the death of Theresa Chicken-Legs, the kind and cheerful slave-girl that had been the surrogate mother to all the hamlet children, still hung heavy in the air.

Ife had heard from one of his stepmothers that the Ogwumii had stormed the hamlet that morning and dragged the screaming girl away to the shrine, where she was sacrificed for the New Yam Festival. He'd been away at the time, purchasing the very Palm-wine he now carried in his trembling hand when the abduction occurred.

There had been an air of mourning in the compound throughout the day and Ezeala had raged against everyone, beating even his favourite wife and throwing a bowl of hot soup at another one, almost scalding the woman. Ife had made himself scarce, staying away from the hamlet till the rooster crowed in the hens for the night and the sun finally gave way to the moon. The last thing he needed was his father's attention.

Now, as he stared at Diké's hut, a new resolve filled his heart. Diké would need cheering up after everything that had happened. He would likely be too distracted to notice the trembling in Ife's hands or the twitches of his eyelids. It wasn't easy being the leader of a cult of killers entrusted with the terrible task of abducting a young girl for a ritual sacrifice, especially one like Theresa Chicken-Legs, whom he knew Diké had cherished like a little sister, despite being her enslaver.

Diké was stretched out on his raised mud-bed when Ife entered his hut. His large, muscled body glistened with sweat brewed by the hot humidity of the hut. He raised his head as Ife entered and laid back again, a weary smile on his chiselled face.

"'Little brother, what brings you here so late in the night? You should be sleeping instead of disturbing the sleep of others," Diké teased.

Ife laughed, a sound that was overly loud and hearty. He stooped to place the jar of Palm-wine on the floor before reaching for the bronze mugs hanging on the metal hooks nailed into the mud wall.

"I heard about what happened to Chicken-Legs and thought you could use some cheering up with some of my special Palm-wine," Ife said, reaching for his Palm-wine jar and noticing an empty one on the floor by his brother's mud-bed. "But I can see you got started already. So, I guess I might as well go drink mine all by myself."

"Hey! Not so fast." Diké scrambled up from his bed, reaching down to adjust his loose loincloth. "You're in such a hurry to escape with your Palm-wine that I'm starting to suspect you didn't want to share it with me in the first place, you stingy tortoise. Come! Pour your womb-brother a cup of your special brew and let us share a chat."

Ife lowered himself onto the hard, red-mud flooring of the hut, his movements fluid and graceful. His heart started racing once more, bringing stronger shakes to his hands. He shook the jar vigorously as Emeka had instructed, to ensure the herb-drug mixed in well with the wine. Then he poured the drink, filling Diké's cup to the brim and his own cup to half.

Diké poured a small amount into the floor as libation to the ancestors. Ife almost emptied his mug as he imitated Diké's actions. It killed him to have to waste such good Palm-wine, but Emeka's instructions had been explicit—he mustn't drink more than half a mug of the Palm-wine to avoid getting himself drugged. He waited as Diké praised and thanked the ancestors before taking a long and satisfying drink, emptying his mug in one go. Ife refilled Diké's cup and raised his own to his lips, taking a small sip. The urge to drink it all was almost irresistible, but he forced himself to hold his breath, to avoid inhaling the intoxicating aroma of the brew—*Later, after everything, he'll indulge in as much Palm-wine as his heart desires.*

"So, you heard about Chicken-Legs?" Diké's voice was low, morose. "Ezekiel Fat-Head is almost inconsolable, the poor man. He was quite close to Chicken-Legs and in fact, Ezeala had planned to marry them before all this happened."

Diké held out his mug for another refill. Ife quickly complied, setting his own mug on the floor. He had no need to continue the ruse. Diké was too preoccupied to notice anything and it was best to avoid temptation.

"You know, little brother, I used to wish that you would join our warrior cult, stand side by side with me at the battleground and share all the joys and sorrows of a true warrior. But after what happened this morning, I'm glad... yes, very glad that you're not a warrior. Today, my men were forced to carry out a dishonourable task for that worthless piece of dog shit, Dibia Okpoko," Diké downed his drink in one go and held out his mug again.

Ife noticed the slight trembling of Diké's hands with mixed feelings of fear and elation—*Ancestors! The herbs are starting to work!*

"How can the ancestors demand a woman's heart? I ask you, how can warriors be expected to eat a woman's heart for courage and strength in the battlefield?" Diké's voice rose as his rage built. "I refused to eat Chicken-Legs' heart and told the heads of the Ogwumii to reject it as well. They obeyed me and none of them partook of the ritual after Dibia Okpoko gored Chicken-Legs' heart from her chest. But they caved under the witch doctor's threats and abducted Chicken-Legs for the sacrifice; all my warrior-leaders, even my bravest, Igwulube. I know that our father and the rest of the Ọzo peers drank her blood as custom demands, and all because they feared the witch doctor's curse." Diké swore softly, a word so vulgar Ife's ears burnt. "I tell you little brother, I never knew I would live to see the day that such abomination is sanctioned; but who can doubt the voice of our ancestors, eh? Up until now, I've never doubted the oracle, but today, I doubted the hearing of our witch doctor. The wretched man misheard the oracle; I can swear that fact on our beloved mother's grave. But his pride will not let him admit it. Yet, he dares to accuse me of pride, even went as far as casting the curse of The Shadow Crows upon me."

"No!" Ife's shout startled Diké, causing him to spill some of his wine. "Please tell me you're not being serious?" Ife's voice held the same tremor as his limbs.

But for the fact that he was already sat on the ground, he doubted his legs would have held up his body. "You must take some white chickens and Palm-wine to Dibia Okpoko without delay to apologise and request the lifting of the curse. I beg you, Womb-Brother. Please don't delay."

"Are you crazy? Apologise to that worm? Never!" Diké jumped from his mud-bed in rage and promptly collapsed back on it. His face had a startled look like a child bitten by a snake he mistook for an earth-worm. He shook his head violently and moaned softly. "Ifekandu, that is some very potent Palm-wine you brought," he laughed, downing the remnant before setting down his mug on the floor. "That's enough for me, I think. You can finish the rest." Diké yawned, long and deep, before stretching out on his bed. "I think I'll call it a night now. I need sleep for the important work I'll be doing tomorrow."

His abduction!

"What work?" Ife's voice was sullen, yet urgent. He wanted Diké to tell him the truth about his plan to abduct him and force him into marriage to Ada of the Nightingale Voice. If Diké could open the line of communication, it might enable Ife to plead his case, convince Diké to abandon the abduction and call off Emeka's plan. It wasn't too late yet to back out.

"It's a secret, little brother, but you'll find out tomorrow, I promise you. And you must promise not to be too upset with me when you find out, okay?" Diké giggled, an uncharacteristic laughter, a drunk's titter. He yawned and rolled over with his face facing the wall. "I'm tired. Go away to your hut and let me sleep. Kachifo, and may your sleep be free of the bad dreams."

"Kachifo," Ife repeated, his voice dull. "Sleep without bad dreams too."

He pulled himself from the floor, his movements sluggish, like one recovering from a long illness—*He has tried; by Amadioha, he's truly tried.*

Ife picked up the empty jar of Palm-wine and walked out of Diké 's hut. Thoughts darted inside his head like startled cockroaches—*Diké has brought it all on his own head. If he can defy the powerful witch doctor and refuse to eat Chicken-Legs' heart, then he can easily refuse to abduct his own brother for a forced marriage. He's right in going along with Emeka's plan. No one can blame him for protecting himself. In a couple of days, Diké will sleep off the effects of the drugged wine and return safely to his hut.*

Within the silent gloom of Ife's hut, Emeka watched his friend's dragging feet returning and a cold smile spread across his face.

EIGHT

—·—

THE CURSE OF THE SHADOW CROWS

DIKÉ AWOKE TO a chill beyond anything he had ever experienced. The noisy chattering of his teeth was as violent as the shivers that wracked his naked body. He tried to stretch his arm and find his goatskin cover on his mud-bed, but his limbs were like stone—heavy and dead.

A voice whispered in his ear, a whisper like none he'd ever heard. An icy air numbed his right ear into which the voice spoke, a voice that was both a whisper and a shriek, worse than the wild howling of *Ikuku*, the fury-wind demon.

"Wake up, our warrior! Wake up, wake up!" There was something familiar about the voice, something that brought an inexplicable dread to his heart. With superhuman will, he pulled his heavy lids apart and looked into a face that had no business above the warm soil of the grave. It was a ghastly visage that glowed with a pale light which revealed the hollow sockets where living eyes should have nestled.

The spectre drifted away from him like a feather blown by a gentle breeze. He followed its gliding movement with eyes goggled with terror. Even before his gaze settled on the ashy body, Diké knew he would find a black hole where its heart should have lodged.

Theresa Chicken-Legs! Ancestors save his soul!

Diké's head swelled to the size of the full moon. Skeletal fingers crawled a chilling path across his back and up to his neck. He opened his mouth to shout, but a silent scream remained trapped behind his lips. The pale shade of the murdered slave-girl drifted back to his side, leaning close into his face. He tried to scramble away, put in as much distance between himself and Chicken-Legs, but his limbs rejected his will and trapped him on his bed like a stone statue.

Except he wasn't on his familiar mud-bed as he had thought. His eyes carried out a frantic scan of his surroundings. It was a strange room illuminated by the pale glow that shrouded Chicken-Legs' mutilated ghost. His mind registered that he was stretched out on the hard floor of an unknown hut. That was as far as his thoughts went before the killing chill rattling his body brought his gaze back to the glowing terror before him.

"Our warrior, you must leave this place at once. Leave now before the rooster crows in the morning and he finds you here," Chicken-Legs' voice had a hollow quality that layered his skin with goosebumps.

Again, Diké tried to speak. He wanted to ask her why she sought him, where he was and how he got there, but his body and lips refused to work with him despite the pressure of his will. It was as if some demon had stolen every bone in his body and left him with a clothing of soft, melting skin.

"Look; the night is starting to leave the sky. Soon, he'll be here. You must leave before he finds you. Come with me, please; come now. I'll show you the way out of this place," Chicken-Legs started to drift away from him in a ghastly, gliding motion that filled his heart with icy terror.

What is this place? How did he get here? Who is it that mustn't find him here? Questions ran around in his mind like cockroaches blinded by a housewife's lamp; but his legs refused to obey his will. He was a prisoner of his own body, cursed into a living statue by a malevolent spirit.

Fight! Fight! Diké shouted the words into his head, a command fuelled by fury and desperation. He sent frantic commands to his limbs, calling on his ancestors to infuse his flesh with living, moving bones. His toes began thawing, one at a time, till his two feet were moving freely, released from the dead freeze that had killed their motion. The thaw continued up the long trunks of his muscled legs to the hard contours of his thighs. *He can walk! Praised be the ancestors!*

"Oh no! I hear him! All is lost! It's too late now! Our warrior, you're doomed!" Chicken-Legs' screech reverberated in the room like a graveside dirge. Then her cries turned into a raging shriek that filled his heart with numbing dread. The glow shrouding her spectre flared briefly, intensely, like an exploding moon. Then it dimmed, growing fainter till it winked out completely, leaving nothing in the space she had occupied before.

A new light illuminated the room, the light from a wick-lamp held by one whose face sent Diké's heart racing with sudden blinding fury.

"Dibia Okpoko! What is the meaning of this?"

The raspy sound of his own voice stunned Diké, as did the violent movement of his body when he finally staggered up from the hard floor. He saw the same stunned look on the witch doctor's eyes just as a wave of dizziness fogged his gaze. He pressed his hands on his head, seeking to steady himself.

"Ha! What is this my eyes see? Look who's here! If it isn't the great warrior-leader himself, Diké, son of Ezeala of Oma clan, the proud prince himself!" Dibia Okpoko raised his lamp higher, closer to Diké's face. His small eyes glittered with unrestrained glee and his feet were almost hopping in excitement. "Let me get a better look just to reassure myself that my eyes are not deceiving me, that this is indeed the great warrior himself here," the witch doctor leaned in closer and Diké pushed him away with a force that sent the diminutive man crashing to the floor.

The lamp fell and winked out, plunging the room in gloom. A pale light trailed the open doorway of the room, a doorway that resembled an opening to a cave. Diké stumbled towards the exit, his limbs still heavy and unsteady. He heard the witch doctor's shout behind him, a piercing scream that halted his steps. He turned and saw Dibia Okpoko almost at his elbow, his eyes blazing with rage.

"Do not step outside this shrine! Not until the oracle sets you free!" Even as he spoke, the witch doctor was pushing past Diké, his voice raised in a shriek.

"People! Ukari People! Come and see the evil my eyes have seen!" Dibia Okpoko yelled, running out into the shrine-grove. This was the same grove whose sandy soil Diké had stood upon with his warrior brothers and challenged the witch doctor's divination only the day before—*How in his ancestors' name has he ended up in the forbidden shrine of all places?* The last thing he remembered was sharing a drink of Palm-wine with Ife.

Before he could ponder over the riddle, Dibia Okpoko ran across the grove and grabbed the great Igba drum and started to beat it with frenzied hands. His voice rose over the drums, shrill and terrible as he ran out of the shrine-grove towards the village.

"People and humans, hear this! An abomination has occurred in our land today! A great tragedy has befallen us! Gather in your multitudes and witness the evil that has come upon you today! Human feet have today stepped into the forbidden shrine of Ọgu n'Udo. Gather beyond the shrine-grove of our great deity and witness the fall of a mighty tree!"

As he listened to the witch doctor's words, Diké felt waves of dizziness assail him all over again. His head expanded and contracted over and over till he thought he would collapse on the floor like a child. Diké turned around and stared into the room behind him where he had seen the terrible spectre of Chicken-Legs, and heard—*too late*—the warning she'd desperately tried to give him.

He was indeed in the forbidden shrine of Ọgu n'Udo, the two-faced deity of war and peace. He, a mere man, had entered a place where no human feet should tread save the sanctified feet of the witch doctor and the sacrificial victims of the gods. Somehow, without conscious awareness, he had walked the bone-littered trail leading to the shrine-grove and ended up right inside the deep cave that housed the mammoth statue of the deity of war and peace.

But how? How?

The questions raged inside his head even as he heard the multitude of voices and footsteps beyond the dawn-greyed shrine-grove. His eyes returned to the grove, to the ten Ngwu trees arranged in their supernatural circular formation, their crawling and bloated roots nurtured and coated with the congealed blood of countless humans sacrificed to the fearsome god they guarded.

He had stood underneath those very trees only yesterday, and had stormed away but later, lurked in the shadows as his Ogwumii warrior-leaders abducted

59

poor Chicken-Legs and brought her to the shrine. At one point, her ear-piercing screams had almost forced him to attempt a rescue. But he had known that such an action would have been foolhardy, even dangerous. No one could interfere with the sacrifice to the gods, not even the King. Without their annual sacrifice of flesh and blood, neither the ancestors nor the gods would reward the villagers with fertile soil, fertile wombs and powerful sons to protect the people from their enemies.

His warrior-leaders had spoken with him afterwards, their eyes reflecting their rage and helplessness. Never before had they had to abduct a woman and deliver her to the shrine. It was a duty that filled them with shame for the first time in their lives. Together, the warriors had sat underneath the great Iroko tree at the village square and drunk endless gourds of potent Palm-wine to drown the shame defiling their honour. And much later, Ife had arrived with his familiar easy charm and potent jar of Palm-wine. That was all he recalled until the ghost of Chicken-Legs woke him up from his deep sleep inside what he now knew to be the forbidden shrine of Ọgu n'Udo— *What in Amadioha's name happened? How did he end up in this accursed cave?*

Dibia Okpoko ran back into the grove, still beating his drum, shouting his dire message like a demented demon. The voices of the villagers beyond the shrine-grove were like the thunder of a demon's storm booming his doom.

"Come with me, so that the people may see you branded as the slave you've now become," Dibia Okpoko ordered, dropping his drum and pausing in front of Diké. "But go no further. Do not attempt to leave the shrine-grove or you risk instant death."

The witch doctor's voice broke into Diké's thoughts, sending his heart racing afresh. He looked up to the skies as if seeking escape in their vast infinity. The skies remained dull and overcast, even as the morning grew stronger and brighter. A small drizzle began to shower the grounds like the cold tears of invisible grieving mothers. The witch doctor withdrew the metal branding iron from his raffia bag and motioned Diké to follow him, waving his arm impatiently.

Diké's heart rebelled, rooting his feet to the entrance of the shrine. Cold fury blazed from his eyes.

"You will not brand the first son of a king, you wretched demon. Not now, not ever!" Sudden strength returned to his voice. He wanted to tear the wizened old man to shreds, dispatch the charlatan to his ancestors' hell for eternity. But the lethargy that had gripped his body since he awoke inside the shrine kept him rooted to the cave's mouth.

"Do you think that by refusing to be branded you can avoid your fate? Are you still so full of pride even now? I warned you, didn't I? I told you that the dark shadows of the death crows hung over your head, but your foolish pride deafened your ears and killed your reason. Now, you're doomed. You have become an unclean, an untouchable and an outcast, a prisoner of the shrine. You, that was once the mightiest warrior in the ten villages, a prince and the first born of a King, have today become a slave, a non-citizen who shall never be accepted into the community again or recognised as a human."

Dibia Okpoko paused to look into Diké's stricken face with glee, rubbing his hands together. "Permit me to explain your situation to you, dear prince, just so you understand how things now stand for you. You are now an *Osu*, a slave to the gods. To the tenth generation and beyond, any child you bear henceforth, shall also be *Osu*, cursed with your fate. In a few hours, you will be permanently ghosted and will walk in invisibility amongst the sons of humans and the daughters of men. You will be taken to The Pool of Dead Memories by the slave stream, where the sacred water will wipe out your pride and condition you to humble servitude, just like every other slave. Your wife will now belong to your brother, and your wealth shared amongst your kinsmen. Your old compound is forever barred to you and your old name and your mighty deeds will become extinct, wiped from the history of our lands. When you walk amongst the people, including your old family, none will see you or acknowledge your presence. Tell me, don't you now wish you'd heeded my curse and apologised while you still had the chance? Ha! The stubborn chicken has indeed learned its lesson too late, right inside the steaming casserole pot of a wretched widow!"

With a loud bark, Dibia Okpoko turned and ran off to address the crowd gathered beyond.

The next time the witch doctor returned to the shrine-grove, he was accompanied by the King, a few Ozo peers, and the five warrior-leaders of the Ogwumii. On seeing Diké at the mouth of the forbidden cave, the King gave a great scream and staggered backwards. He would have fallen to the ground save for the strong arms of the warriors that held him up.

"Who did this? Who committed this abomination on my son?" the King shouted, lunging at the witch doctor, murder blazing in his eyes. His warrior-leaders drew their war machetes. Dibia Okpoko backed away from them, waving his arms frantically.

"Stop! I order you in the name of Ogu n'Udo to stop!" He ran towards Diké and dashed into the shrine for sanctuary in the assurance that no sane person, King or warrior, would risk entering that forbidden cave. "I did not do this to your son. How could I? I came here at dawn as is my habit, to do my divination and confer with the oracle, as well as feed our god. My shock was greater than yours when I beheld our great warrior within Ọgu n'Udo's forbidden shrine. Perhaps, he wandered into the shrine in a drunken haze; who knows? Perhaps, he was even possessed by an *Amosu*, night-hag, who lured him into these forbidden grounds. Or perhaps, this is the curse of The Shadow Crows wreaking its devastating magic on a proud soul." Dibia Okpoko paused to survey the stunned men as he inched slowly out of the shrine.

"I warned him yesterday, didn't I?" the witch doctor continued, his voice growing stronger, his swagger more assured. "You all heard me curse him. You begged him to apologise, but he didn't listen. Now, see the result! He has refused to present himself to the people for the final time as a human before I proclaim him an *Osu* and brand him with the stamp of slavery. But you have all seen him. So, you will become the eyes of the people and report what you've seen. Say your goodbyes for the last time to he that was once the greatest son of our land, before he forever becomes a ghost to you all."

Dibia Okpoko strutted back into the grove, no longer fearful for his life. The stricken looks on the faces of the gathered men imbued him with renewed confidence as he walked out to the crowd beyond the shrine-grove to address them.

Finally, Diké's feet moved, uprooted themselves from the ground as he stumbled out to the grove and into the waiting arms of his father. The King held him as if he were fighting *Owu*, the Death-Lord himself, for the life of his son. His hot tears dampened Diké's face as something hard finally thawed in Diké's heart, drowning him in a sorrow beyond any pain he had ever known.

"My son, my pride, the Eagle's feather on my head! That my accursed eyes should live to see this day of great evil!" The King's voice was a dirge, fed by the loud sobbing of his warrior-leaders, rock-hearted men whose eyes he had never seen shed a tear.

63

Together, the men came to Diké and held him, hugged him harder than they had ever done in their happiest victory on the battleground.

His second-in-command, Igwulube, spoke for his men.

"*Agu-eji-ejemba*! The Tiger that marches before us as we go into the battle front! Our eyes shed blood instead of tears on this cursed day of sorrows. Diké, son of King Ezeala of Oma clan, may your soul be reborn in freedom and greatness! In our next incarnation, may we be brothers and warriors together once again. *Ndewo*, goodbye brother-warrior till we meet again."

The warriors stepped away from Diké to form a line of honour. They held up their war machetes high in the air and bowed low to him. For the first time in his life, Diké wept in front of his men. His heart became un-manned, his pride in tatters as he allowed the weak tears of the womenfolk to flow unheeded. His body shuddered like a mountain quaked by a fiery eruption as he clung to his father, once again the little boy he was in the idyllic days when his mother still lived.

The enormity of his plight hit him like a fist in his gut. He wanted to speak, to beg them not to let this terrible evil befall him, but all he could do was cry, hard, wracking sobs that echoed his father's wails. Even the three Ọzo peers in their midst, stoic old men with scant emotions to spare, struggled to stifle their sniffles.

"We are done here, and we will now pronounce his fate," Dibia Okpoko announced as he laid down his raffia bag and withdrew the black and white paints of his art. With deft fingers, he smeared his face with the terrifying patterns of his profession, circling his eyes with white chalk and painting his lips with the same white paste. The fine, ground charcoal powder coated his hair and his chest, turning his grey hairs a dusty black. On his body, the *Nsibidi* sacred symbols inscribed in black ink, were stark and foreboding. He grabbed one of the numerous white chickens strung up beyond the entrance of the forbidden shrine and sliced its throat, allowing its blood to drain over his head and his body till he reflected the full terrifying visage of his ancient craft. When he was done, he broke some kola nuts, which he offered with some Palm-wine to the ancestors lodged within the ten Ngwu trees.

"I am ready. Come, follow me. As our King, you must make the proclamation to your people," the witch doctor said to the King, malicious glee in his voice.

The King looked stricken, shaking his head, holding tighter to his son.

"You must pronounce your son a slave, just as you would pronounce others. As the King, it is your duty which none other may perform for you save your heir and first son, who sadly, no longer exists." Dibia Okpoko was almost crowing.

The warrior-leaders quickly surrounded the King, their faces devoid of emotion, as they prepared to do their duty to their people and escort their King into the midst of his subjects.

Diké eased himself from his father's arms and stepped away, bowing deeply to him. When he rose, his face was remote, taut, as he began the permanent soul-separation from his closest kin.

"He is right, father. You must now go and perform your duty to our people. Your son bids you farewell and asks your forgiveness for this shame he has brought to your house. I thank you for the honour of having been your *Okpala*, your first son. May our ancestors and Ọgu n'Udo keep you and your house safe from evil for eternity. Please keep my war machetes safe till they can be held again with honour by a son of your loins." He bowed low again to the King.

"This is not over, my son. I promise you that I will not rest till I find the vile vipers that perpetrated this evil on you and my house. And when that glorious day comes, they will rue the day they left their mother's womb and entered the soil of humanity. I promise you this as both your father and your king. You will be avenged. May our ancestors watch over you, my good son, till we meet again in freedom and greatness."

"Ise!" chorused all gathered, save the witch doctor.

Diké watched as Dibia Okpoko led his father and the rest of the gathering out of the shrine-grove. His gaze followed the unfamiliar stoop of his father's shoulders as he prepared to face his anxious subjects and explain the impossible to them. Above him, the skies suddenly broke out in glorious sunshine as if sharing Dibia Okpoko's joy in his downfall. Beyond the grove, the morning breeze carried the deep and shaky voice of his father to his ears, sealing his doom.

"My good people, indigenes of Ukari village and the nine Okoro villages, your king salutes you. *Egbe belu, Ugo belu!* May the hawk and the eagle both perch on the tree when their wings weary from flying. And should any of them deny the other the branch, may its wings break and render it land-bound for eternity. Live and let live."

"Ise!" the crowd shouted, cheering their king with vigour. After a few minutes, Diké heard his father's familiar voice rise over the crowd's din once again.

"My people, today, your King brings you the worst news in the history of our lands. Hold your hearts and prepare yourselves for great sorrow. A mighty tree has fallen. Today, Diké, son of Ezeala of Oma clan, the people's protector, great leader of the Ogwumii warrior cult, was struck by the curse of The Shadow Crows!"

A loud gasp interrupted the King's words, followed by the keening wails of the women and the disbelieving shouts of the men.

"It is my pain as a father and my duty as your King to pronounce today, the ghosting of my first son, your warrior, Agu-eji-ejemba. From this day onwards, he has become an *Osu*. Should any person come upon him and acknowledge his existence as a citizen, that person and their family shall be excluded as citizens for twelve moons. It is done. Return to your huts and mourn the loss of he who was once the greatest son of the lands of the ten Okoro villages. There will be a three-day mourning period in the village after which you will all wipe out the memory of Diké, former son of Ezeala of Oma clan, from your memories to the end of your lives."

As Diké listened to his father's voice proclaim his doom, a clawing pain gripped his heart—*The impossible has become reality. He is now truly an* Osu, *denied every freedom including the freedom of suicide and the choice of an honourable death.*

Diké shuddered, struggling to keep breathing, to not give in to the dizziness that threatened to knock him out. He would have asked any of his warrior-leaders to end his wretched life with a single stab deep in his chest and they would have obeyed him without a second thought. But he was not a slave to man, but a slave to the gods and only the gods can kill that which belong to them. He dared not ruin the chance of an honourable reincarnation by cursing himself with the easy, earthly route of suicide.

Diké staggered back into the forbidden shrine and collapsed on the floor underneath the towering stature of the deity, Ọgu n'Udo. Cold chills once again layered his body in goosebumps as he lay curled up on the hard red-mud flooring of the shrine. The fierce frontal face of Ọgu n'Udo, the war-face of the deity, dared him to cry and disgrace his manhood with the weak wails of a woman. Its burning red eyes sent his heart pounding with terror.

Diké scrambled away and stumbled to the rear of the statue, the part that held the second face of the deity—the smiling face of benevolence and love, the peace-face of the god of war and peace. He fixed his gaze on the gentle dark eyes on it and wept.

For the first time in his life, he knew the true feeling of helplessness and despair. He understood how that poor slave girl must have felt before her death. From a place deep in his bowels, sudden rage surged to his heart, a fury that burnt with hatred and vengeance—*He'll find the person responsible for his plight. By his ancestors and all the gods, he will find the traitorous viper if it takes his whole miserable existence to do so.*

He had no doubt that Dibia Okpoko was involved, but the man must have worked with somebody else to execute his plan and ensure his curse came to fruition. The witch doctor was already a dead man walking as far as Diké was concerned. He would bury him when the time was right, after he'd found out the identity of the unknown person that helped him execute his dastardly plot.

A sudden weariness overwhelmed Diké, a weariness of the soul. He tucked his hands between his thighs and closed his eyes, shutting out the world and his thoughts as a deep sleep wiped away his pain with the sweet nothingness of oblivion. And for the first time in his life, he slept a sleep devoid of the bad dreams.

NINE

—·—

POISONOUS HANDS

IFE AWOKE TO absolute chaos. The piercing cries of the women and the angry shouts of the menfolk were like a hail of rocks on his alcohol-poisoned head. No hangover had ever felt as deadly as the one he now nursed. But then, never had he drank as much as he'd done last night. But now he was awake, he realised it had all been in vain: The guilt and shame he had hoped to drown out had accompanied him into his drunk sleep and awoken with him like the foul smell that followed a putrid corpse.

Just as he was about to stumble out of his bed, his door crashed open to reveal his father, dressed in his full kingship regalia. The King stared at him for several silent seconds with reddened eyes filled with contempt and something else Ife couldn't define—*Fear? Pain? Confusion? Surely not! It's just the Palm-wine putting stupid thoughts into his head.* His father was born devoid of every human emotion save those of ruthlessness. He should know. He had never heard a kind word from his father or felt his touch in affection.

"Get up now!" The King spat the words. "Tie up your loincloth and come into the compound without delay.

Your father's house burns to the ground in noon-day while you sleep away your drunken life."

The King shook his head several times as he stalked out of the hut. Beyond his door, the cacophony in the compound rose to such a pitch that sudden knee-weakening terror overwhelmed Ife. Panic sent all kinds of thoughts to his head—*Diké has returned and told all! The kidnap plot has failed after all. No, no, it can't be! Didn't he see Diké carted off to Emeka's compound the previous night; watched as Emeka and his brothers tied him up and secured the hut where he was hidden?*

Ife had stumbled away from the place, unable to bear the sight of his brother being manhandled by Emeka and his brothers. There was something repulsive about their hands on Diké's unconscious body, a wrongness that brought a lump to his throat, especially seeing the uncharacteristic helplessness of his fearsome brother—*But he'd had no choice, had he? It was either that or be kidnapped himself by Diké and his Ogwumii warriors for the enforced marriage to Ada of the Nightingale Voice.*

Ife took several deep breaths as he re-tied his loincloth with trembling hands. Then, he pulled out a hidden jar of Palm-wine and took a long drink straight from the jar. Several mouthfuls later, he squared his shoulders, pasted the familiar smile on his face and stepped out of his hut, praying his eyes would hide the terror in his heart. The midday sun almost blinded him. He raised his hands to shield his eyes as he stared around him with stunned eyes.

The compound was full like the village square on festival celebrations. Except this festival looked more like a funeral than a party. Everywhere he looked were people, all wearing faces of misery. An air of mourning hung over the place with women and children wailing, while the men were split between the shouters and the morose.

The sight calmed some of his earlier terrors. He heaved a deep sigh of relief—*Diké hasn't escaped after all. All is okay.* He figured the King had finally discovered Diké's disappearance, hence the outpouring of grief from the people. It was exactly the scene Emeka had envisioned when he came up with his brilliant plan. The chaos in the compound had surely killed all plans of his abduction and forced marriage.

Ife pushed his way through the crowd—*It mightn't even be necessary to keep Diké away for the three days they had agreed on. No need prolonging their father's agony even though the old bully has brought it all on his own head.*

With legs and heart now strengthened by his summations, Ife walked towards the high throne underneath the Ngwu tree, where the King usually received large crowds or delegations from the other villages. Hands tugged at his arms, lots of little hands. He looked down and saw several of his little half-sisters staring up at him with tear-stained grubby faces.

"Big brother! Here you are," They fought over his hands, blocking his path and halting his steps.

"Why are you all crying, eh?" Ife crouched till he was at their face level. "Come; tell big brother and he'll go and tell the naughty people to behave themselves otherwise Feather-Feet will never dance for them again."

He waited for them to laugh as was usually the case, but it was as if the cries of the women in the compound had infected the children with their sorrows. Their little shoulders shook harder with their sobs as they crowded closer to him, seeking the comfort he couldn't seem to give them. His memory suddenly recalled the other event, the sacrifice of Theresa Chicken-Legs the day before. The slave-girl had been greatly loved by both the children and the womenfolk of the compound. Little wonder the poor things were still grieving her loss.

"There, there; don't cry, okay?" Ife pulled the children closer and wrapped them in his arms. "I know you all miss Chicken-Legs, and I miss her too but, she's at a happier place now. I know she loves you all and will send you good fortune if you ask Ọgu n'Udo to bless her."

To Ife's shock, the children broke into louder wails and broke from his arms, running from him as if they were being chased by the terrifying *Mmaa* masquerade of the three crocodile heads. He followed their flight with a perplexed frown, before heading off towards the King's throne underneath the broad Ngwu tree.

"*Nna-anyi,* our father, I greet you." Ife bowed low before his father, one knee on the ground.

After waiting in vain for several uncomfortable seconds for the King to return his greeting, he straightened up and smiled sheepishly at the clansmen and Ọzo peers surrounding him.

"First son of our king, we salute you," greeted the gathered men. Their faces were like stone.

Huh?

"Brothers, why d'you mock me so and dishonour my brother by calling me first son when the king's first son, your mighty warrior, still walks above the grave-soil?" Ife asked, forcing the smile on his face even as he seethed at their mockery.

"It would be only you in the entire kingdom who remains ignorant of the plight of your father's house," the King finally addressed him, his voice, flinty. "The person you once knew as your brother has ceased to exist. You are now my first son for my sins. But then, as our people say, 'the rooster that crowed was once an egg.' Life begins from somewhere and I will accept the hand that fate has dealt me."

The King sighed deeply before fixing a hard gaze at Ife. "As soon as the three days mourning is over, you will marry Mgboye, your former brother's widow, to honour him as is our custom. However, since we all know that Mgboye's womb is cursed by the river goddess, you will equally take Ada of the Nightingale Voice as your second wife within a week of your first marriage. Your days of silly dancing and Palm-wine drinking are over. Managing two wives should keep you busy enough. You may never be the warrior that your former brother was, but I pray to Ọgu n'Udo that you'll be more fortunate than he was in breeding sons for your father's house."

"Ise!" chorused the gathered men, beating their chests with their fists in the traditional sign of mourning.

Ife stared at them, his heart pounding so loud he thought the whole world could hear it.

"But... but, Diké is not dead," he stuttered, his eyes wide, goggled by guilt and confusion.

"Had you been outside the shrine-grove this morning like the rest of the villagers, you would have heard your father pronounce his son an Osu," The King's voice was bitter.

"A what?" Ife's scream pierced through the crowd's clamour, bringing a sudden silence in the compound. People began to surge closer to the Ngwu tree. "*Nna-anyi,* our father, what in *Anả*'s earth would make you commit such an abomination against your own blood, especially a son like Diké?"

"Sshh!" The clansmen quickly hushed Ife up. "You have no brother by that name. Do not mention that name again for as long as you live."

"What d'you mean by such nonsense?" Ife shouted, stunning both himself and the crowd who had never seen the affable young prince raise his voice. "Shut your rotten-teethed mouths before *Amadioha*'s thunder strikes out your remaining teeth for you! How dare you say that I have no brother or that I can't call my brother by his name? Go fuck your mothers! My brother's name is *Diké* and after all he's done for this village, I can't believe you can all sit here in your righteous ingratitude and disrespect him with shameless impunity."

Ife turned to his father, holding the King's glare with equal fury, his normal fear vanquished by his rage. "And you, Diké's father, the great King himself, you sit here while these people disrespect your first son's name; yes, your first son, Diké. D'you hear me say his name? Diké! Warrior-leader of the Ogwumii. He deserves much more honour than you've all given him today. I hope Ọgu n'Udo punishes you all for this day," his voice broke as he spoke. Tears spilled from his eyes and trailed his bony cheeks. "And for your information, I'll never marry Mgboye, not now, not ever!" He glared at the king before taking his leave as the clansmen shouted after him.

"Leave the boy, let him be," the King said in a voice Ife had never heard, the weary voice of an old man, the voice of defeat.

Not that Ife cared. He was going straight to Emeka's house to release Diké and return him to his hut. He didn't care if he was disowned by their father for abducting Diké, or if Diké strangled him for his stupidity. Enough was enough. Let the bastards dare repeat their vile words to his brother's face and see if they lived to see the next dawn.

He was halfway to Emeka's house when he heard his name called by a voice he recognised.

Big-Bosom! Ife stopped and turned around to see the girl running towards him. A frown of irritation furrowed his brows. He didn't have time for Big-Bosom and her infatuation, not on a day like this one.

"Big-Bosom, is your brother at home? I need to see him at once." He heard her loud breathing as she struggled to catch her breath.

"I know what you did, you evil, horrible man!" Big-Bosom pulled his arm with a hard tug. Her words stunned him, halting his steps.

"What did you say?" Ife asked in a low voice. "What d'you mean you know what I did?"

"You betrayed him! How could you do that to your own brother who loved you more than his own life?" Big-Bosom's voice broke, tears filling her eyes, big dark eyes that looked at Ife with an expression he'd never seen before, one that stunned and horrified him.

She looked at him with pure loathing.

"I didn't betray my brother, you little idiot," he snarled. "If you want to know the truth, we were just hiding Diké in your compound for a couple of days to stop him from taking me to the hamlet of Ada of the Nightingale Voice for my marriage. All I did was give him some sleeping herbs Emeka gave me to keep him sleeping for a few days before we return him to his hut, satisfied?" he hissed and resumed his journey, driven by sudden panic to hasten his brother's release.

"So, that's how you did it; that was why Emeka sent me to your house with that stupid message. I wondered how you people were able to abduct Diké without losing your necks in the process." Big-Bosom's eyes were wide with wonder, quickly replaced with suspicion. "Okay, if you only planned to hide him, why did you take him to the forbidden shrine and turn him into an Osu, eh? Answer me, why?"

"What did you say? What forbidden shrine?" Ife shouted, glaring at her. "Diké is locked in your father's old hut. I took him there with your brothers last night. I'm going there now to free him. Whatever gave you the stupid idea that I took Diké to the forbidden shrine? I wouldn't do such an evil thing to a viper much less my own womb-brother." Ife shook his head, exasperation cloaking his eyes as he turned away from her.

Big-Bosom grabbed his arm once more, with such force that he almost stumbled. Her eyes stared up at him, filled with horror. A cold chill began to crawl up the back of his neck, creeping, slowly, till his heart rattled with terror.

Suddenly, he was truly afraid.

"You don't know, do you? Oh, my ancestors in their blessed realm! You have no idea, do you?" Big-Bosom slowly started backing away from him. "He deceived you, you drunken fool! My brothers did not keep Diké in my father's hut. They dumped him at the forbidden shrine of Ọgu n'Udo and the witch doctor discovered him there this morning, although I wouldn't be surprised if the bastard plotted it all with Emeka. But you, you stupid, stupid man, you let them do this to your own brother!"

Big-Bosom turned and ran, racing back towards the King's compound instead of her own home.

Ife's legs gave out beneath him, as he collapsed on the sandy soil in the middle of the path, holding his head with his hands, howling at the sky, the earth, the air. The truth he had refused to face from the time he heard the words of his clansmen that afternoon finally pierced through his armour, stabbing his heart with countless sharp knives.

Diké!

Diké!

Diké!

Over and over, his brother's name rang in his head. He howled till people surrounded him, lifted him from the ground, and led him away from the sandy path. Eventually they had to carry him, as his legs refused to bear his weight. He moaned, wishing for the escape of death. He heard voices shouting for the crowd to give way, that Feather-Feet had collapsed, that the grief of the family tragedy had proven too much for Feather-feet to bear. Other voices said to call the king, as the young prince might be seriously ill.

He's ill alright; ill with shame and sick with guilt. Amadioha help him! He's dying from a soul-pain beyond any pain any human has ever endured. He has betrayed his own brother and been vilely betrayed by his so-called best friend.

Again, Ife groaned, his stomach churning with bile, the bitter pill of betrayal—*Emeka! The viper under the sleeping mat, the benevolent friend that shakes hand with poisoned palms.* Diké had seen Emeka for the snake he was, had tried over and over to warn Ife about him. But, like a fool, he had closed his ears to his brother's warning. Now, Diké was paying the cost of Ife's ignorance and stupidity—*And for what? For the King to still impose the same marriage that he's sacrificed everything to avoid? Ancestors pity him! His life is truly ruined. Palm-wine; he needs a drink desperately. If only the ancestors will take pity on him and call him home without delay...*

His helpers left him shivering on his bed as they sought the help of the herbalist, Dibia Nene—*It's only a matter of time, just a matter of time to the next Palm-wine and the blissful oblivion from this killing pain attacking every pore in his skin with relentless fury.*

TEN

—·—

THE HANGING SKULLS

THE SMELL OF blood was strong inside the cave, the rank odour of countless years of human sacrifice to the deity of the shrine. Diké marvelled that it had taken him so long to notice the odour of death, a smell his nose should have been familiar with after the numerous wars he had fought in blood-drenched battlegrounds.

The bowl of rice and drinking water brought to him by the witch doctor, Dibia Okpoko, remained untouched. Diké didn't trust the demon not to poison him in his bid to prove the efficacy of his wretched Shadow Crow curse—*Later perhaps, he might feed the food to the shrine chickens and see if they live or die.*

He was fast reaching the conclusion that the witch doctor was responsible for his plight, that the demon had somehow hexed him into entering the forbidden shrine in a stupor of the mind. There was no other explanation for the glee the man took in his ruin.

In the dim light cast by his wick lamp, Diké surveyed his new home with eyes devoid of sleep. He had slept his day away and would have willingly slept his life away if he could. At least, inside the forbidden shrine his sleep was strangely free of the bad dreams. Now, he found himself companion to the owls and the bats, together with other evils that made the night their day.

Deep in his subconscious, one particular night creature plagued his peace. *Chicken-Legs!* Diké shuddered. He knew she meant him no evil, but nonetheless, he didn't think he could cope with another visitation from Theresa Chicken-Legs' ghastly spectre. The sightless, gliding ghost with the gaping hole where her heart should have been, wasn't a sight he wished to witness ever again.

His stomach growled, protesting its starvation. Diké cursed under his breath. The last time he recalled having anything was when he shared Palm-wine with Ife, just the night before. And yet, in that brief spell, more damage had been wreaked on his life than would have happened in a hundred moon-cycles of hard fighting in the battleground.

Ife! Poor, poor boy! Thinking of his little brother brought fresh tears to his eyes—*Who will take care of the boy now that he's gone?* Diké held his head in his hands and groaned. The thought of Ife abandoned to his fate was like a knife stab in his chest. He hadn't even said a proper goodbye to the boy before his *Osu* status was declared, and all because of his stupid pride.

Dibia Okpoko was right; he was indeed a prideful fool who should have gone out to see his people for the last time before he was ghosted. At least, he would have had the chance to see Ife, hold him as a brother for the final time and say his goodbyes in the proper manner, with sound advice, good wisdom and great affection. Only the ancestors and the gods knew when next, if ever, he would see his brother again. Ife's tall and slender beauty flashed in his mind, the fluid, dancing elegance of his walk, his laughing eyes and gentle voice that matched his easy and happy disposition. And again, Diké wondered how such beauty could have come from the loins of their father, a man more respected for his strength than for his looks.

Diké wiped his face with his hands, a face wet with both his tears and sweat. His head pounded harder than ever and his stomach cramped, gnawed raw by hunger fangs. He thought he should eat Dibia Okpoko's bowl of rice after all, but first, he must carry out the chicken test to be sure. He dragged himself up from his mat and re-adjusted his loincloth. He scooped a handful of cold rice from the bowl and lifted the wick lamp from the floor. He cat-pawed his way out of the dark cave with its jagged walls and rough floor. Outside, the night air was stagnant, yet cool, and it quickly diluted the powerful scent of stale blood that clung to his nostrils. The moonless night plunged the shrine-grove into a darkness that was almost impenetrable, with the broad branches of the Ngwu trees blocking out the occasional star that might have winked through their leafy armour.

He shuffled his way towards the wooden pole where several live shrine-chickens hung upside down, awaiting their turn to sample Dibia Okpoko's sharp blade. He lifted his lamp high and picked out the plumpest of the lot and force-fed it the rice—*Now to wait and see if the chicken survives*.

Diké wasn't sure how long he waited before he realised that he didn't need the lamp anymore to see the chicken. The shrine-grove was lit up so brightly that the sky must have given simultaneous birth to five full moons. The sudden cessation of all sounds, night sounds, crickets, frogs, bats, and owls, hit him like a giant's fist. Even the hanging skulls on the trees were ominously quiet, their familiar clattering swallowed by the unnatural silence that shrouded the shrine-grove.

Without warning, an intense brightness illuminated the shrine-grove, a glow that seemed to come from the direction of the *Ngwu* trees. Diké lifted his head to look at the trees, and his blood curdled. Suddenly, it didn't matter anymore if the fat chicken survived or died from its poisoned rice. Nothing mattered but his life, and his sanity. His scream pierced the night, sending the chickens into a frenzied cacophony of clucks and flaps. The wick lamp in his hand crashed to the ground, winking out its light. Diké's goggled eyes remained glued to the trees as he stumbled back.

On the hugging branches of the Ngwu trees, a multitude of lamps glowed with a misty light that resembled a sky-litter of sickly baby moons. Except these small moons had hollow eyes and cavernous mouths, skull-moons that leered with malevolence and fury.

The hanging skulls of the sacrificed slaves!

The skulls pulsed with shimmering life, as if the moon had given each skull an infusion of fire. They glared down at mankind with empty sockets blazing with hate. Even before Diké's mind could accept the terrifying vision, a sudden sound shattered the silence, the horror shrieks of countless raging skulls. They were screams like nothing Diké had ever heard, not even in the bloodiest battleground.

A great wind rose from nowhere, its fury swaying the branches and their bone-fruits into wild frenzy. Even as he struggled to stay on his feet, a new sound arose beyond the grove, a wave of grinding clatter, surging relentlessly towards where he stood. Diké's head swelled; his body shook, and his mouth dried out in a blink—*Ancestors and the deities save his soul! He doesn't want to see whatever it is headed towards the shrine-grove, or imagine what new horror might be making such a ghastly din.*

Diké turned to run, to escape into the safety of Ogu n'Udo's cave. Even as he cursed himself for the shameful coward he had become, he knew he would be a fool to face the unknown horrors from beyond the realm of the living. He would battle a thousand warriors over this—*At least, they're human, and not the supernatural terror he's witnessing.*

A movement to his right caught his attention and Diké wished he hadn't looked. From the crawling roots of the Ngwu trees, shadowy bodies materialised, headless spectral torsos formed of phosphorous paleness, with black holes where their hearts should have been. They glided in a silent wave, seeking their missing skulls and skeletal limbs. Diké saw the white bones pouring into the grove from the shrine entrance in a deluge of clattering, confused lunacy. They were the skeletal bones of the sacrificed slaves that layered the pathway to the shrine, forming a jagged carpet of hard whiteness.

Diké froze as the bones crashed into the grove in an avalanche of white terror, filling the air with a terrifying clatter. Above the trees, the hanging skulls shrieked their fury. All was madness, a horror that almost stole Diké's sanity. His sight blurred, blinded by the sudden dust-storm whipped up by the multiple twisters dancing on the ground. He blamed his damaged vision for what he saw next, the impossible that became terrifyingly real as he fought the enraged wind hampering his escape.

What he saw was a horrible building project, a macabre assemblage of body-parts. The pile of white bones scattered and regrouped, seeking the parts of themselves, the femur that joined the fibula, the ribs that clung to the sternum, phalanges to radius, till the headless skeletons emerged, tall and near-complete in their terrifying boniness. Their numbers were great, at least over five scores by Diké's estimation. With blind intuition, they staggered to their glowing, ghostly twins spewing from the tree roots for a terrifying re-joining of spirit and bones.

In seconds, the grove was overrun by the animated headless skeletons of the sacrificed slaves. They surrounded Diké, blocking his escape. Above him, their hanging skulls shrieked and damned him for the enslaver he was, their hearts he had devoured, and their lives he had stolen. They bellowed at their headless skeletons, urging them to annihilate the person responsible for their demise.

In the sudden freezing air of the grove, Diké's body dripped with sweat as he tried to escape the outstretched arms of the headless skeletons. The downbursts of the dust-storm choked his breathing and stole his sight. He was pleading to his ancestors for salvation even as he fought the punishing wind. Each way he looked, a sea of gliding white bones drew closer to him, as if drawn by the magnet of his living warmth, his pounding heart, his raspy breathing and low groans.

As he felt their cold claws on his body, something inside Diké snapped. A burning rage filled his heart, competing with the terror that held his body hostage—*Amadioha curse his soul! Is he a warrior or a wife? He'll be damned if he lets himself, he a warrior-leader and a prince, be cowered by a bunch of slaves, ghosts or no ghosts,* Osu *or no* Osu.

"Cowardly slave bastards!" Diké shouted, punching the nearest ghoul into a scattered pile of white bones on the ground. "Even in death, you're nothing more than cowardly slaves my ancestors subdued in war. Like the worthless chickens you are, you attack me in your multitudes because you cannot fight a warrior man-to-man; ha! Ghost-to-man! Come on! Do your worst. Just know that if I go down, your souls will be less than an ant's life by the time I'm done with you. Pain and misery exist everywhere, even in death. I'll dish out more agony to you in death than you ever endured in

NUZO ONOH

life. I swear this to you on my ancestors' souls. Come on!"

Diké punched and kicked with blind recklessness, shrugging off chilly claws and bone-bodies that threatened to swamp him. Just when Diké thought his skin would freeze to death from their chilly talons, a sudden silence descended on the grove. The cacophony from the skulls ceased as abruptly as it had started, while the fury-wind died out, sucking the multiple twisters into the ground. The area around Diké cleared and the skeletons surrounding him clattered away from him, their bones rattling in the sudden stillness.

A dazzling light lit up the grove. Diké turned to look in the direction of the light and gasped, a gasp that was more a whine. Cold terror trapped his voice behind his throat, quaking his limbs.

Before his stunned gaze, five young women materialised out of thin air, five women whose glowing bodies formed a line of horror inside the grove. As they glided closer, Diké felt his head swell up—*Amadioha have mercy! He knows them; he witnessed their trials and their executions for demon-pregnancies after they falsely accused Dibia Okpoko of squashing their bodies in lust. The witch-sisters!* Diké shuddered, struggling to rein in his terror.

In their midst stood Chicken-Legs, her hollow eyes sending cold chills to his spine. Hers was the only face without eyes in the gathering of blazing ghosts. Her eye-less gaze must have had the same effect on the hanging skulls because their glows winked out with their shrieks. The skeletons collapsed back into piles of disjointed bones as they flowed out of the shrine-grove in a frenzied wave to resume their previous occupation of bone-carpeting along the pathway. Their headless spectres, now devoid of skeletal support, crowded

84

together in a pale huddle underneath the trees in a phosphorous circle of silent dread.

The blazing women glided deeper into the grove in a trail of light till they stood within arms' reach of Diké. He remained rooted to the ground, all strength sapped from his limbs. He was beyond any feeling, beyond fear and pain. Even the voice inside his head, the one that had told him to escape the shrieking skulls into the safety of the forbidden shrine, the one that ordered him to fight the bone-ghouls or die with honour, had stilled. The only voice he now heard was the one in his heart, the weary voice telling him to yield to an inevitable death without struggle; that it was better to be dead than to endure another second of the night's horrors or continue a cursed existence as a slave.

Diké shut his eyes, took a deep breath and bowed his head low into the ground to receive the burning touch of death.

"Slaves of the shrine, lost souls with the devoured hearts. We come to you again with pity and sorrow, we the blameless ones with undevoured hearts."

Diké heard the words from a distant place beyond his space, words that sounded like the howling of winds. They layered his skin with countless tiny bumps.

"We, the falsely accused, cleansed of our defilement by the ancestors' fire of purity, bring our peace to you and share your rage," the witch-sisters shrieked. "Rage, brothers! Rage until your voices touch the sky and reach the ears of your ancestors. Stand with us, whose hearts seek the same vengeance as yours. Rage until our day of freedom comes and evil pays its dues. Rage! Rage!"

And the skulls raged.

The ground shook underneath him and the clattering on the trees merged with the rattle of bones beyond the shrine. Diké moaned and crouched low, shielding his head with his arms. He heard Theresa Chicken-Legs scream louder than all the other ghosts, and his body trembled. For some reason, her rage terrified him more than any other. It was an alien sound from a gentle slave-girl, who in life had spoken only in soft tones of servitude. Now, she was a fury of death. He prayed her fury wasn't also for his life.

In the chilly air of the shrine, an unexpected warmth spread over Diké's exposed skin. He opened his eyes and stared with a feeling of wonder and awe. The witch-sisters had ceased their shrieks. As he stared, they glided into the centre of the grove, and with their arms spread wide, released a blanket of intense light that covered the trees like the burning rays of the sun. In the shimmering haze, the headless ghosts floated, swayed and swam like moths basking beneath the warm glow of a lamp. Their skulls howled mournfully into the night, a cry of inconsolable pain.

Diké's throat tightened; sudden pity overwhelmed him, drenching his heart with regret—*Amadioha forgive him! He had failed to understand how they felt or appreciate their pain. But he's... was... a warrior, obeying the laws of their land, laws that require slaves to be sacrificed to the gods, and their hearts devoured by the warriors for strength and bravery in the battleground. The custom existed before the birth of his great ancestors. Other warrior-leaders before him had captured slaves and devoured their hearts in countless Rituals of The Soul-Eaters. Why should he feel guilty for obeying the demands of the gods and the ancestors?* Thoughts ran through Diké's mind with panicked frenzy.

Diké heard the witch-sisters speak once again. Their synchronised voices returned the terror-chill to his pounding heart.

"Sad souls, we ask you now to hold your rage. Let us save our hate for the one whose dish it is. This man before you has also caused us pain, just like his ancestors before him. But we ask you to let him live, just for a little longer. He now shares the same fate he had given you—a common slave, whose fate is even worse than ours as his soul will never be free, in life or in death. One day, one glorious day, our souls will be free and our vile killer, the false witch doctor, will be stripped of his charmed protection which prevents us from harming his person. Return to your tormented sleep till the time is ripe. Our day will come. Vengeance will have its day. Sleep deep, brothers. Sleep still and wait; wait..."

As their voices faded, the trees rattled with the familiar clack of the hanging skulls hugging their curved branches. The warm light flowed back into the outstretched arms of the witch-sisters, and the air was again icy on Diké's skin. He shivered, wrapping his arms around his body. He saw the horde of headless spectres vanish underneath the bloated roots of the Ngwu trees, from where they had risen. Above them, the skulls returned to their dirty white tint, devoid of light and life.

"Quick, come with me, our warrior." Diké looked up into Theresa Chicken-Legs' hollow eyes. "You shouldn't have come out at this time to disturb our communion. Follow me and say no words. We have little time. Even now, the vile one is on his way, alerted to the night's events in the shrine. You must be prepared when he comes. I cannot help you in the daylight, only by the power of the night. Hurry; there's no time to waste."

Diké stumbled to his feet and followed the gliding spectre of the slave girl back into the forbidden shrine, his hunger forgotten in the terror and confusion that fogged his mind. Chicken-Legs glided soundlessly past the towering statue of Ọgu n'Udo, till she hovered by his mat, waiting for him. When she motioned him to his mat, Diké obeyed her as if she were the master and he the slave. And when she spoke, he listened to her words

87

with the intensity of an apprentice and the terror of a haunted child.

Eleven

—·—

DAYS OF THE VULTURES

I FE STUMBLED OUT of his bed, holding his head like one carrying an egg. Sunlight streamed through his open door, blurring his sight. He bumped his big toe on one of the stone sculptures of his ancestors arranged in the customary circular formation in his personal shrine.

"*Ekwensu!*" he cursed loudly, stooping to nurse his injured toe. He almost toppled from the intense dizziness that clouded his vision. The two young men in his room caught him before he hit the ground and lowered him back to a sitting position on his bed. With silent efficiency, the men assisted him into his loincloth, even as he demanded more Palm-wine from them.

"Our prince, do you think it's a good idea to drink at this time? The king and the clansmen are all waiting for you and if we don't get going now, fear your father's reaction," one of the men said, an older man whom Ife recognised as one of his favourite clansmen, Ogbodo, a good drinking pal. The fear in the man's voice was palpable—*Ancestors save his soul! He's been discovered! Why would the clansmen be waiting for him with the King if not to confront him with his crime against his brother? Death, where the shit are you when you're needed?* The thuds returned to his heart, fast and hard.

By the time he had drunk his third mug of Palm-wine, the deadly headache plaguing him suddenly became easier to bear. He stood up without aid and adjusted his loincloth. He cleaned his teeth with his finger, using the ash and chalk blend in the copper jar, before rinsing out with salt-water. Finally, used his fingers to fluff up his lush, black hair.

"Feather-Feet, perhaps you might wish to change into a ceremonial loincloth," Ogbodo suggested. "It's just that we have strangers amongst us today."

Ife groaned silently. *That's all he needs—the entire village coming to witness his disgrace!* He reached up an arm for one of several loincloths hanging on his metal railing, the one washed in red dye.

Diké has one just like it.

Ife quickly pushed the thought and the loincloth away and pulled out another one, a yellow-dyed one—*He won't think of Diké now.* The rage started to rise, the unfamiliar fury that had become his companion since the day he discovered the mendacity of the snake he had once called 'best friend.' The urge to stick several knives into Emeka's chest was strong in his heart.

He straightened his shoulders and walked out of his hut with as much dignity as the dizziness allowed him—*Well, here goes nothing.* The group of men sat underneath the broad umbrella of the Ngwu tree with the King watched his graceful steps with overt admiration. In fact, several of the men called out, "Feather-Feet" with loud enthusiasm before the king's glare shut them up. They quickly rearranged their smiling faces with stern frowns. Ife's heart sank to his toes, slowing his walk.

"*Nna-anyi.*" Ife bowed low to the King. He prayed the King wouldn't keep him waiting too long before acknowledging his greeting. He didn't think his dizzy head could cope with a prolonged stoop.

"The king greets his first son." his father finally replied, his voice icy.

"I'm not your first son," he shouted, forgetting protocol, forgetting the strangers in their midst who stared at him as if seeing an entity from a different realm. "How many times do I have to repeat myself? Your first son is Diké, my brother Diké, whom you're determined to forget. I refuse to suffer from your amnesia. I refuse, d'you hear me?"

He heard the gasp of the clansmen, the shushing sounds, as they tried to stop him from repeating the forbidden name. He glared at them, hating them, hating himself even more. He plunked himself on the space to the King's left side, ignoring the chair placed at the right side of the king—the heir's chair. Over his dead body would he usurp his brother's chair and status, curse or no curse.

"Clansmen, honoured guests, I implore you to ignore my son's impropriety," the King voice was hard, anger repressed behind the low tones. "Our people say that the calamity that brings down a great man will annihilate a pauper. Even I still struggle with the tragedy that has befallen my house, so it's little wonder this boy is weighed down by it. Let us break Kola and thank our ancestors for their goodness."

The King picked a red kola nut from a bronze bowl and passed it over to the guests to share. Ife picked his own Kola nut with a sweat-dampened hand and stared at it. His eyes saw nothing and his ears heard nothing, not even the long prayers made to the ancestors by the oldest clansman in the gathering, or the sudden, loud gasp of the clansmen, until he heard his name called out several times by the King.

"Ifekandu, what is the matter with you?" the King roared, jumping to his feet as if to strike Ife. He jerked back from the King's fist. "Your house is on fire and

91

you're busy chasing the rat you found under your chair! Are you deaf? Did you not hear what these people from the Okoh clan just said?"

"My apologies, *Nna-anyi*," Ife mumbled. "I missed their words. I'm nursing a bad headache."

"How surprising, with the amount of Palm-wine you've guzzled in the last three days," the King sneered. Some of his clansmen tittered. The King glared at them before turning back to his guests "Visitors from Okoh clan, please do us the favour of repeating what you just said to us, just so *all ears* hear your words."

Ife forced himself to listen as the leader of the delegation from the Okoh clan, spoke.

"Great King, we salute you again. As we said, we are only messengers and do not have any hand in the decisions reached by our leader, Ezugo, head of Okoh clan and chief of Abuọ village. So, please keep your rage from the messenger."

The man addressing the gathering was small in stature with some sprinkling of grey hairs on both his chest and his beard. When he spoke, he avoided the King's gaze and instead, looked at Ife. "Our leader, Ezugo of Okoh clan, has asked us to return the betrothal jars of wine you gave him when you claimed his daughter's hand in marriage to your son, Ife of the Feather-Feet acclaim."

"My first son has no acclaim as Feather-Feet, and I will ask you to address the King's heir with the respect that status deserves," the King snapped.

Ife opened his mouth to challenge his father, but thought better of it—*No need riling the old man. His throbbing head won't cope with his rants. They're all welcome to their collective amnesia. His heart knows the truth and that's enough for him.*

"I apologise to the King." the messenger bowed low and remained there until the King grunted his acceptance of the apology. He waved an impatient hand to permit the man to continue with his speech.

"I thank the King for his graciousness. Our leader, Ezugo of Okoh clan, is sorry to state that his daughter, Ada of the Nightingale Voice, is now betrothed to Ọzọ Agwọ of Uba clan, chief of Atọ village. Their final marriage rites will take place in seven days. Ezugo of Okoh clan says we should convey his apologies to the King for the disappointment. He hopes the king will understand his position, the fact that no daughter should be made to wait for three years to be married to the man who pledged his hand in marriage. He feels his daughter has waited enough, but he hopes the friendship that has existed between your clan and his clan will remain as strong as always. Finally, he prays that the ancestors continue to bless your house despite the tragedy that has recently afflicted you. *Ndewo*, I greet you all."

Ife gulped with disbelief and head-giddying relief—*He's free! Free! Praise be to his ancestors and his personal Chi!* But the faces of his clansmen reflected the king's own—fury and shock.

"Delegates from Okoh clan, I greet you," the King's voice was dangerously low. Ife's nerves tightened. He knew that tone only too well. "Our people say that a wife seeking to end her marriage will claim that she saw a rat in her kitchen and cannot stomach a second longer in her marital home. It is my belief that Ezugo of Okoh clan would have found any reason, no matter how trivial, to break our agreement."

The King's eyes turned a red hue as his anger sizzled. Ife noticed the terror on the faces of the delegates from Okoh clan and felt a kinship with them, having himself been on the receiving end of his father's fury.

"We all know the saying that when the lion is away, the hyenas will come out to play. The news of my tragedy has spread, and the cats are showing their claws. But what are the claws of a kitten to the paws of a tiger?" the King glared threateningly at the delegates from Okoh clan. "Go; return to your chief. Tell Ezugo that I have received his message. Tell him that I wish his daughter happiness in her marriage to a man old enough to be her grandfather. Tell him that I am well and that my memory is long and strong; and tell him to choose his alliances wisely. May his ancestors remain awake and watch over him and his house." The King rose to his feet. "Let us all enjoy some wine and food before you begin your long journey back to your village."

The dark threat in the King's words brought soft gasps to the lips of the visitors. Ife hurriedly followed his father into the house, smiling his gratitude at the quaking delegates. The startled look they gave him almost brought loud laughter to his lips. He wondered if he would ever laugh again, if that joyful expression was lost to him forever.

Inside the King's house, Ezeala took to his throne and motioned Ife to the nearby chair. Ife sat down, feeling the rapid thudding of his heart. He wished he could be anywhere but here. Worse, the Palm-wine brought by the visitors would be guzzled up before he got his share.

The King took several deep breaths, striving to cool the anger still simmering in his heart.

"Tell me, do you know our people's saying that, 'the one-eyed man is king in the land of the blind?'" the King asked. Ife shook his head. His father grimaced. "It means that mediocre always flourishes in the absence of genius. The message brought by the delegation from Okoh clan is proof of this saying." Ezeala paused and stared at Ife for several terse seconds. He tried not to show his nerves—*Whatever he does, he must avoid riling their father today*.

"These are the days of the vultures, the time our enemies sense our injuries and swoop low to devour our crippled bodies. The great flight of the eagle has always been a source of envy to the hawk and lesser birds. The other village chiefs have always envied our clan for our good fortune. Now, with our tragedy, a rebel leader has grown amongst them, he whom I refer to as the one-eyed man that is King in the land of the blind—Ọzo Agwọ of Uba clan, chief of Atọ village"

The King stared into space, seeing pictures Ife could only imagine—*perhaps, images of Diké, in his full warrior-paint and bronze machete, leading the fearsome Ogwumii into battle. Who knows?* Ife shrugged inwardly. He knew he would never be the man his brother was, the protector and advisor their father needed. Even listening to the King's words was a strain on his mind. All he wanted was to drink Palm-wine and forget the world.

"I know you resent the new responsibilities thrust upon you. Ọgu n'Udo knows I feel the same, but no man can fight his fate." The King returned his flinty gaze on Ife. "You've heard the message from the Okoh clan. This is only the beginning. Our enemies, especially Ọzo Agwọ, sense our weakness now. They are forming alliances in preparation for a big confrontation and we must be prepared. You have so much to learn and we have so little time, so I've instructed that no one brings you Palm-wine henceforth. I need you lucid and prepared to face the troubles coming to us. For good or bad, you are now my heir, and we must mould you into that position without delay."

Ife gasped. His eyes widened with disbelief. "You can't do that... you just can't ban me from drinking Palm-wine," he stuttered, leaping out of his chair.

"I can, and I have," the King said with grim satisfaction. "Sit down and wear your listening ears. We have completed the three-day mourning period for the one we lost. Tomorrow, we purify both you and the widow,

Mgboye, so that you can live as husband and wife and provide heirs for the clan. You—"

"Never!" Ife shouted startling the King. "I'll not touch the flesh of my brother's wife, not while Diké breathes and his heart beats. I don't care about tradition or your wishes or our enemies. I'll not marry Mgboye."

The first blow from the King's staff almost knocking him out. He cried out, nursing his injured left shoulder. The next blow caught him on his arms as he shielded his head. Soon, his stooped back suffered countless hard strikes of the King's staff until Ife's howls brought in several clansmen. They held back the King, pulling Ife away from the room.

"Useless boy! I curse the day you were born, you mother-killer!" the King shouted after him. "See the insult I just received from the Okoh clan? Had my true son still lived, would they have dared step into my compound to spill their filth? Instead, I am cursed with a drunkard who would rather dance away his seed than populate his father's house with sons. Let me go, so I can finish him off and know I have no sons. Let me go, I command you!"

Ife could still hear the King's screams as he was helped into his hut by the clansmen who quickly asked the hamlet wives for their soothing *Abuba-Eke*, python-fat balm. In no time, Ife's bruised skin was covered with the cool salve, as he groaned softly, wishing for death and oblivion. The men helped him into his bed with gentle hands.

"Palm-wine, please," Ife gasped. The men looked at each other and shook their heads.

"The King has instructed that no one gives you Palm-wine or sells you the wine either," one of them said, avoiding his eyes.

"Go then, leave me alone." Ife waved a feeble hand at them. The men shuffled out of his hut, shutting the door behind them.

Ife tumbled to his feet, groaning with pain. He reached blindly for his jar of Palm-wine, hidden inside the wick basket, and took a long gulp. He sighed deeply, blissfully, despite his pain. *Amadioha be praised!* It was a good thing he always kept spare jars of wine for emergencies. He gulped several mouthfuls before lowering himself on his mud-bed again, wincing as his cut skin connected with the hard surface.

It had been ages since he felt their father's staff on his skin. Diké had kept him safe, forbidding their father from hitting Ife as soon as he became the Ogwumii warrior-leader. That was the only time Ife had seen their father back down. Having been an Ogwumii leader in his younger days, the King knew that he daren't challenge the new leader, despite him being his own son. In frustration, he took every opportunity to humiliate Ife. The more the people loved Ife and his dancing, the more the King cursed him for the worthless son he was. Ife knew that nothing he did would ever please their father, not even if he married five Ada of the Nightingale Voice and produced a hundred sons. The King would still find fault somewhere and a reason to abuse him. He would never forgive him for killing their mother in childbirth and denying him all the sons that would have secured his legacy.

Now Diké was gone, and Ife knew the beatings would become regular occurrences again. He didn't think he could live with it, not when he couldn't defend himself against the King's violence. The laws of nature and their lands forbade a son from raising a hand against his father and a citizen from touching the King's body in violence. The way things were, taking his own life was starting to look like a better option, even if it meant being rejected by the ancestors and having his corpse dumped at Ajọ-ọfia as a cursed suicide—*But not before he takes that bastard son of a traitorous dog with him and dispatches the vile snake to his own ancestor's hell.*

He hadn't set eyes on Emeka since the night he led him into Diké's hut and unwittingly betrayed his brother to the demon. He knew it was just a matter of time before he confronted him. Ife wasn't a fighter and would have little hope of besting Emeka in arm-to-arm combat. So, he must plan his strategy and play the fool Emeka and everyone took him for—*Yes, that's what he'll do. Hide his hate and pretend friendship with the dog—until he gets him to relax his guard. Then he'll drug the bastard with the same herb he had betrayed Diké with, cut him up, one toe at a time, one finger at a time, one ear at a time, till he's completely dismembered him like the vile snake he is.*

Ife grunted, grim satisfaction warming his heart. First, he must rest and sleep away the pain, get strong for his revenge. He took another long drink from the jar till he emptied it. He shut his eyes, took several deep breaths and allowed the darkness to lure him into blissful oblivion.

TWELVE

— • —

THE COUP

A WEEK TO the day following his father's attack, Ife awoke to his latest rage. His heart leapt into his mouth, bringing the shakes to his limbs. He wondered if the time would ever come when his heart didn't quake at the sound of his own father's voice. With slow deliberation, he adjusted his loincloth, wincing from the pain which still tortured his swollen left fingers where the King's staff had hit them. Just then, his door yanked open and Ogbodo entered his hut.

"Our prince, the King wants to see you immediately," the clansman said.

"Ogbodo, do you have any Palm-wine? I must drink something or die... Come, help your favourite kinsman, please," Ife smiled. He saw the flicker in the man's eyes, an anxious spark, quickly followed by a resolute grimace.

"Ok, wait. I'll tell the king you're dressing up." Ogbodo dashed out. Ife tried to make himself decent. The constant lethargy that clung to him like a second shadow made his every action a drag. Even running his fingers through his hair took all his strength—*Ha! So much for Feather-Feet. He'll be lucky if he doesn't pass out at the sound of a drum, much less raise his legs in dance ever again.*

To Ife's surprise and relief, Ogbodo returned with a small jar of Palm-wine. Even before he drank it, he already knew it was good brew. The smell hit him with welcome bliss, filling his nostrils with its potent aroma. He drank straight from the jar, long and greedily like a man starved of water for days.

Ife followed Ogbodo out of his hut, squinting his eyes against the intense noonday sun. He felt a lightening of his mood, buoyed by the Palm-wine he had consumed, but the unrest in his heart remained, with tiny flutters and rapid beats. By the time they arrived at the Ngwu tree, it was almost impossible for him to drag up his customary smile. Thankfully, the faces of the men underneath the tree told Ife a smile was the last thing they needed. Several of them wore the distinctive Ostrich feather of the Ozo peers, and Ife counted ten in total. He realised with a sinking feeling that this meeting was more serious than he had anticipated. It was rare to see all the ten chieftains gathered together at one sitting.

"Ezeala; come, my good friend. How can you say I insult you when I say that a kitten is not a lion even though they're both of the cat family? Your late son was a warrior and the other, a dancer. It is clear that one son cannot perform the work of the other despite both springing from the same loin." Ife heard a man's voice speak.

There was something wrong about the its dulcet tones, something not quite as respectful or sincere as one should be when addressing the King. Ife found himself detesting the voice even before he met the owner.

"Ah! This must be the famous Feather-Feet! Young prince, it is my honour to finally meet you. Your feats on the dance floor has reached my ears and many ears far and beyond our ten villages."

The tall and over-fleshed man who had been speaking took Ife's hand in a grip so tight it seemed as if he were testing the strength in Ife's hand. The man licked his lips over and over as he smiled, a habit Ife found repulsive. In fact, he found everything about the huge man rather gross, from his excessive beads to the garish paintwork on his obese body. In fact, as far as Ife could see, everything about the man was bigger and more expensive than the rest, as if the peer was determined to shout his wealth to the world. Even though the man's smile and words were friendly, Ife detected a slight contempt in them—*What's new? He finds himself equally contemptible.*

Ife smiled at the man, the disarming smile that won him universal friendship and goodwill. Before he could respond to the man's greeting, the King motioned him over to the chair by his side, the right side—*Diké's side!* Ife's heart rebelled once again, but the look in the King's eyes made him pause; 'This isn't the time for your foolishness,' they warned. With a frown, Ife perched himself on the edge of the offered chair and clenched his hands tightly between his thighs.

"I want you to listen to the insults Ọzọ Agwọ has deemed fit to speak to the King," his father said. "I want you all gathered here to see that I still have a grown son who is capable of taking on any task that his King demands of him."

Ah! So, this is Ọzọ Agwọ of Uba clan, the man that married Ada of the Nightingale Voice! Ife looked at the obese peer with renewed interest.

"But, forgive me for repeating the obvious," Ọzọ Agwọ said with the same oily voice and disdainful smile. "Your son is a dancer, *not* a warrior. I just shook his hand and

101

believe me, that is not the hand of a killer, a hand that can dispatch our enemies and protect our people. It is—"

"What enemies?" the King interjected. "Right now, the only enemy I see before me is you. First, you go behind my back and steal the bride reserved for my son. Then, you swoop down like a vulture the minute you hear of my tragedy to demand your son takes over the leadership of the Ogwumii, a role reserved solely for the first son of the King!"

"I beg to differ," Ozo Agwo said, the smile finally leaving his face, his eyes icy. 'Our custom is that the first son of the King, who has proved himself in the battleground, can wear the mantle of leadership of the Ogwumii. Should that son die in battle, then the leadership will fall on the second son of the King, if *again* that son is a recognised warrior. Should no sons from the royal family be available for the role, then it falls in rotation on the first adult sons of the ten village peers who have also proven themselves in the battleground," Ozo Agwo said. "The second village peer after yourself is my father-in-law, Ezugo of Okoh clan, whose daughter, Ada of the Nightingale Voice, I recently married. We all know that Ezugo has no grown sons, just little boys still running around without loincloths. Ezugo, I bow to you, my father-in-law, and pray our ancestors grant your young sons long, healthy lives and prosperity,"

Ozo Agwo bowed towards the general direction of the seated peers. Ife heard a soft voice acknowledge the blessings. He saw a small man with a gentle face he immediately recognised as Ezugo of Okoh clan, the father of Ada of the Nightingale Voice. Like his face, his voice was gentle, and Ife nodded respectfully at him.

Ozo Agwo was speaking again.

"As you all know, I am the third peer from the third village. My son Ikenna is already an Ogwumii warrior and has fought numerous battles under the leadership of both your late son and his immediate group-leader, Igwulube. My son is qualified to become the new leader of the Ogwumii, and I demand that you ratify his appointment in accordance with our custom. Is my request unreasonable, brothers?" Ozo Agwọ turned to the gathered men with an injured look on his face, like a man unreasonably persecuted by a troublesome mother-in-law.

Several of the men chorused their agreement, but curiously, Ife noticed that some of the peers kept silent, neither agreeing nor disagreeing, a thoughtful frown on their faces. Their silence sent Ife's heart racing—*Please ancestors, don't let them appoint him as the new Ogwumii leader! He isn't a warrior like Diké; he's only a useless dancer who wouldn't know what to say to an enemy wielding a machete. Yes, he deserves this punishment for what he's done to his brother. In fact, it would serve him right to take on Diké's role as a warrior and suffer for his misdeeds in the battlefront. But, still ancestors, have pity and spare him from this horror.*

Ife mumbled the silent prayers frantically, glancing around wildly in search of an escape route. He felt a hand grip his wrist and the King yanked him up from his chair, his eyes blazing, daring Ife to contradict him.

"This is the King's first son, an adult with a sane mind," the King roared, raising Ife's arm high in the air. "He will learn and perform his duties with the standard expected from his people. I say that we place him in intense training with Igwulube, the best of the Ogwumii leaders. Then, we shall gather here again in a few moons for him to demonstrate his skills and prove his readiness to lead the warriors."

"And what happens in the meantime while he's learning?" Ozo Agwọ asked, not bothering to hide the sneer in his voice. "If our enemies attack, do we tell them to come back later after the young dancer has finished learning how to kill them? Come, Ezeala, you know I am right. There is no time to waste. But I'm a reasonable man and I am willing to work with you in this matter. So, this is my proposal. You will send the dancer to train with Igwulube, but in the meantime, my son becomes the temporary leader of the Ogwumii, till your son proves to us that he can lead our warriors into battle. What do you say?"

The King's grip on Ife's wrist weakened before he let go. He slumped back into his chair, staring into the distance as everyone awaited his answer. Ife remained standing, debating if to bolt or faint—*Either way, he's ruined.*

"Great King, we hail you," one of the chiefs wearing an Ostrich feather stood up, Ezugo of Okoh clan, the father of Ada of the Nightingale Voice. His voice was calm and wise. "I have always supported your house and even though the union of our children didn't occur, I still retain the warm affections I have carried in my heart for you and your house. So, please believe me when I say that the words I'm about to speak, come from a place of friendship and respect." Ezugo paused and took a pinch from his snuffbox, stuffing his nostrils with brown tobacco powder and inhaling deeply. He waited a few seconds for the nicotine to hit his head before continuing his speech.

"Having listened to everyone today, it's my belief that Ozo Agwọ's proposal is the best compromise we can reach today. It is a reasonable one, and I'm sure that your son will prove himself as skilled with the sword as he is with his feet. After all, a good warrior must be flexible, full of dexterity and able to move swiftly in the battleground, an advantage your son already has as a dancer." Ezugo turned to smile at Ife, a warm smile that brought a reciprocal smile to Ife's face. "Once the young prince is trained then we can gather for the ceremony to initiate him into the Ogwumii and declare him the new leader. Brothers, are we agreed?"

Ezugo turned to face the other chiefs and elders and they all chorused their agreement with loud cheers, hailing Ezugo for the wise and peace-loving man he was. Ezugo bowed low to the King and returned to his seat. The King heaved a deep sigh before standing to face the group. His face wore a weary look. He cleared his throat and began to speak.

"Our people say that the coward lives a long life to show the brave man's children where their father is buried. A good leader is he who knows never to sacrifice his entire group of warriors in a war he may win on another day. I will bow to your collective wisdom and declare Ikenna, son of Ọzo Agwọ of Uba clan, the new temporary leader of the Ogwumii. It is done. So be it."

The King sealed the edict by spearing the soil with his royal staff. A wild cheer went up in the air as the men bumped their *Nzu-Iyiya*, horsetail fly-fans and clasped arms. People were shaking Ọzo Agwọ's hands, praising him with lavish words better suited for the King. A stranger stumbling into the compound would have been hard pressed to state who, between Ọzo Agwọ and Ezeala, was the king; such was the arrogance with which the peer carried himself and the fuss made of him by the gathered men.

"I now demand that the King surrender the two bronze machetes of the Ogwumii leader that we may return them to my son," Ọzo Agwọ's eyes glinted with victory.

"Never! The machetes stay here," the King shouted, jumping to his feet and pushing his face into Ọzo Agwọ's own. His eyes blazed with a dangerous glint that warned the peer he was walking a very thin thread. "Until

Ifekandu completes his training and a permanent leader is declared, those sacred machetes will remain in the King's compound and that's the end of the matter."

Ọzọ Agwọ smiled, a grin that didn't reach his eyes. "Okay, we shall wait; there is no rush. What flies up must fly down eventually. Come, my friends, let's drink the sweet wine we brought and celebrate the day with our gracious King."

The group fell on the drinks with the ravenous greed of starved hyenas. The king remained seated on his high-chair, waving away the endless cups of Palm-wine offered him, his face set like granite. Watching the events unfolding before his eyes, it suddenly dawned on Ife that something greater than just the position of the Ogwumii leader was at stake. He recalled the King's words on the day he was thrashed viciously with his staff, words he had dismissed with the cool indifference he reserved for everything their father had to say— *'These are the days of the vultures, the time our enemies sense our injuries and swoop low to devour our crippled bodies.'* That was what the King had said and what Ife was suddenly witnessing in the vast grounds of his father's compound that afternoon. A sudden shiver layered his skin, a prickle of unease and uncertainty. If there was ever a time he needed his brother the most, this was it.

By the time the third delegation arrived at the compound a few days later to demand that the King secede a disputed piece of land to Ọzọ Agwọ's village, Ife knew that his prospective training with Igwulube were now the least of his problems. A new era had dawned on the house of King Ezeala of Oma clan, a dawn of misfortune that shrouded them with the dark curse of The Shadow Crows. And, he knew with a sense of doom, that he was as unprepared as a new-born infant to fight the crows of death.

Thirteen

—·—

THERESA CHICKEN-LEGS

IF ANYONE HAD told Diké that his sanity would one day depend on the ghost of his female slave, he would have laughed them out of his sight. But Chicken-Legs' nightly companionship was fast becoming the highlight of his existence inside the accursed place of death and soul-weariness. The sightless holes of her eyes and the deep gorge in her heart still filled him with dread. What helped was clinging to the memory he had of her in their previous lives, the picture of the cheerful and helpful young woman with the ever-smiling face. In his own way, he knew he brought her some solace too. These days, she raged less and talked more

Their friendhip had started on the terrible night of his attack by the skeleton ghosts of the hanging skulls. Diké still shuddered each time his memory took him back to that night of horrors. He had thought he had finally escaped when Chicken-Legs led him to safety inside the forbidden shrine, but his horror was only just starting.

"Our warrior, you must promise never to enter the shrine-grove deep in the night," she said, her voice urgent. "You might not escape the vengeance of the hanging skulls again and even the ones the villagers call the witch-sisters, might not be able to save you

107

again. You have to understand that you enslaved and consumed their hearts, not forgetting that you come from the long bloodline of those who had done the same to them. So, their anger against you is great,"

"Good friend, you don't need to tell me twice not to pull the lion's tail," Diké said fervently. "Believe me, the horror of what I witnessed tonight will bring back the nightmares to my sleep."

"You don't need to worry about the nightmares, our warrior. As long as you're inside Ọgu n'Udo's shrine, you're safe from the bad dreams that plague your people,"

"I've wondered about that. Tell me, how is it that I'm free of the nightmares here?" Diké asked. "I did think it strange that ever since I became enslaved, my sleep is no longer tormented by the bad-dreams our people are cursed with."

"That's because the dreams are sent by the hanging skulls," Chicken-Legs explained. "Their hearts were consumed and they have lost all humanity and seek vengeance. It's only the witch-sisters that stand sentinel and keep them away from the village, otherwise by now, your people would have been dealing with greater evils than just the nightmares, believe me. The witch-sisters and I have undevoured hearts, so we still retained our human emotions. As a result, they're able to keep the evil of the scarified slaves away from their loved ones. As long as they sooth the restless souls of the hanging skulls, no harm will come to their loved ones and the rest of the village. All they can do is haunt the villagers with poisonous dreams, but Ọgu n'Udo keeps you safe here."

Diké's jaw dropped as he stared at Chicken-Legs with eyes glazed by horror. The villagers had long believed that their dream-plague was a dark legacy inherited from their ancestors. Discovering the truth filled him with icy terror. He struggled to cope with the terrible realisation that they were all victims of a supernatural attack by angry and malevolent ghosts.

"But why don't they vent their rage at Dibia Okpoko as well? Surely, if anyone deserves their fury, it's him. I know I'm guilty but I think he should also pay,"

"Nobody can touch Dibia Okpoko," Chicken-Legs hissed, her temper flaring. "The demon-man is immune to their vengeance. He's bound them with his powerful charms and sealed himself from their touch. It's the same thing he's done to me and the witch-sisters too. He plucked out my eyes to ensure I never find his soul when he traverses the spirit world, where my powers are stronger than his own. Even though our hearts were not devoured, Dibia Okpoko has hidden them so well that we're no better than the doomed ones whose hearts were devoured. We are all prisoners of the shrine, and we can't touch him as long as he holds our hearts in bondage. Still, one day, one blissful day, I'll find a way to touch Dibia Okpoko. He'll feel my touch, and will himself rue the day he left his mother's womb to enter the realm of womankind." Chicken-Legs kissed her teeth furiously.

Listening to Chicken Legs' hollow voice, Diké knew he had been incredibly lucky to escape with his life on that terrible night.

"Our warrior, there is something else I think you should know," Chicken-Legs said, coming closer to him with the familiar chill that followed her. "I know the people that brought you into the shrine on..."

"What?" Diké jumped to his feet, his heart pounding. "Who was it? Who did this to me?"

"Emeka and his two brothers. They carried you in unconscious. I heard their laughter as they gloated about your ruin. I did not see them till they had dumped you here. I showed them myself and watched them flee the shrine screaming their heads off. I tried to wake you up before Dibia Okpoko arrived and found you, but you were like one drugged and would not wake up till it was too late."

Diké listened to Chicken Legs with a growing sense of horror. *Oh, ancestors have mercy! He was drugged! There's no other explanation for the state he found himself in on that terrible morning. But how? By whom? He's never had any close contact with Emeka and his brothers. So how on earth could they have spiked his drink?*

"Did they mention Dibia Okpoko's name at all? In any way implicate him in my ruin?" he asked, his voice hard.

Chicken-Legs shook her head. "No, they never mentioned his name. I loathe the man but I don't think he had anything to do with your kidnap."

Her words killed the suspicion he had initially nursed in his heart that the witch doctor was behind his misfortune. But that didn't mean Dibia Okpoko was blameless—*After all, it all started with his curse. Had the demon not hexed him with the curse of The Shadow Crows, none of it would have happened. What it means is that there's a deadly traitor he has to unearth, the vile one that drugged his drink for Emeka and his brothers.*

Diké's thoughts were everywhere as he tried to piece together the events leading up to his ruin. He remembered sharing Palm-wine with his fellow Ogwumii warrior-brothers at the village square. He would stake his life on their loyalty and innocence. So, the harm must have been done by the person who had supplied them the Palm-wine on that day, maybe someone who had been bribed by Emeka—*Ancestors! How he wishes he could find out from his warrior-brothers who it was that had supplied their drink on that accursed day!*

110

But he was trapped by shame within the gloomy confines of the shrine. Yes; he had the right to leave the shrine and reside anywhere at the edge of the village, away from normal humans. But he would still be invisible to all, even to Ezekiel Fat-Head and all the men he had enslaved. They were now superior to him, with more freedom than he, their enslaver. Diké shook his head violently—*Never! He'd rather die than live openly in the village as a slave, where he had once ruled as a prince.*

Diké ran into the shrine-grove and screamed until his voice went hoarse. Hatred burned in his heart, loathing such as he'd never felt in all the moons of his life. His hands itched for his inherited bronze machetes imbued with the spirits of his ancestors and the strength of the lion-spirits of the Ngwu trees. He yearned to spill blood, to hack down bodies till he had dispatched all those involved in his betrayal to their ancestors' hell. He had craved for death to release him from his curse. But that was before he discovered the truth from Chicken-Legs' ghost.

Now, he prayed for sanity and strength, for a healthy life, long enough to exact his vengeance on the people responsible for his destruction—*Emeka and his two brothers are dead men even though they don't realise it yet, together with the repulsive snake they bribed to drug his drink, the unknown enemy whose identity he'll extract from Emeka before dispatching them all to their graves for the grave-worms to feast upon their fetid corpses.*

Diké spent endless nights in wakeful discussion with Chicken-Legs' ghost, dissecting his situation and her life as a slave and a ghost.

"Why did you decide to take me as a slave, our warrior?" Chicken-Legs asked him one evening as they chatted, the hollow sockets of her eyes fixed on his face.

"You usually capture only male slaves for the shrine and I always wondered about it, but never dared ask while I was a slave in your hamlet. Don't get me wrong; you were very kind to me. Everyone in the King's compound was kind to me, even the King himself, but you were not my family. For many moons, I cried through the nights, missing my old life and hoping the day might come when I would get myself home again. I think what I hated the most at the time was knowing I would never be a free-born again even if by some miracle I made it back to my village alive. They would know that I'd been a slave, you see, and they would never accept me into the community again. The humiliation would have been worse for me in my village where everyone knew me. I thought it was better to be a slave amongst strangers, and luckily, when I was old enough and finally taken to The Pool of Dead Memories, I woke up the next morning and found that my memories of my past life had started to fade until one day, I realised that I was happy, that I was at home with my family, which was your family."

Chicken-Legs paused, a small smile playing at the corners of her lips. "I really miss the hamlet children and Feather-Feet's stories and dances. But that's another change that will get easier for me to bear, in time. Time is a great healer, a gentle stream that flows over rough stones till they are washed into clean smooth pebbles. You too will soon find a rhythm that works for you eventually, and in time, this new life won't be as unbearable for you as it is now. Maybe, you might consider visiting The Pool of Dead Memories? It will help you forget and make everything bearable."

The Pool of Dead Memories. Diké knew it well, the circular pond by the stream whose glistening, black water oozed a sinister and hypnotic pull that was both alluring and terrifying; the place all slaves were taken to complete the cycle of enslavement. While he would never demean himself by killing his very soul at that terrible pool like a common slave, he knew Chicken-Legs' advice came from a place of affection and good intentions.

Listening to her, Diké wanted to reach out and hold the ghost of the girl whose life he had ruined. A tight band gripped his chest, rising to the back of his neck as he tried to keep the tears trapped behind his eyes.

"I am so, so sorry, Chicken-Legs," he whispered, the tears breaking through his lids to curve a wet trail down his cheeks. "Please, forgive me for the pain I brought to you. I thought I was doing you a favour. Your village was empty, we had killed almost all your warriors. You were found alone, wandering in the village, little more than a child. I thought I would bring you home to my father as a hamlet slave and give you a home where you would be cared for. I swear, I thought I was helping you and never in my wildest thoughts did I imagine the demon, Dibia Okpoko, would name you as the sacrificial offering to the gods. Never in our history had the oracle ever demanded the heart of a woman. Which was why I refused to consume your heart and ordered my warriors not to either."

Theresa Chicken-Legs hissed, her face suddenly a ghastly visage that chilled his bones. He shrunk back despite himself, fearing a return of her raging. But she held it in, her body flashing a brief fiery blaze of fury before fading back to its murky glow.

"Dibia Okpoko is a wicked man who hides his evil underneath his witch doctor's loincloths. He tried to squash me in lust, just as he did with my spirit-sisters who share the shrine with me, the five innocents whose hearts were never devoured." Chicken-Legs hissed again. "When they got pregnant, he accused them of witchcraft and demon-possession and had them sacrificed. I rejected him and fought him off when he tried to squash me, so he cursed me. He told me that I would rue the day I left my mother's womb and entered the realm of man." Chicken-Legs flung her arms wide in despair, gliding away from Diké to stare at the statue of Ọgu n'Udo. When next she spoke, her voice was low, almost a whisper.

"Dibia Okpoko was right. I regret the day my mother gave birth to me. That wicked man ruined my life. Look at me now; see what I've become, a wandering soul, eternally restless because my heart is trapped in this shrine."

She glided away from him, staring at Ọgu n'Udo's statue for several seconds before turning back to face him. Her face looked desolate, her empty sockets bigger and darker. "You do not know this, our warrior, but your stepmother, the king's youngest wife, is trapped in the witch doctor's power. He's convinced her that he has the magic to give her the son your father so desperately desires," Chicken-Legs continued. "But first, she has to agree for him to squash her body in lust. Now, she's his prisoner. She cannot escape his touch, neither can she reveal her shame. She fears that any son she gives the king may bear the witch doctor's blood."

Chicken-Legs scowled again. "I've seen her sneaking into the shrine-grove and heard her begging him to set her free. I've seen several other entrapped and blackmailed village women brought into this supposedly sacred shrine by the demon and ravished on the very ground we stand. You have no idea the number of women that would be declared Osu like you if anyone ever learns about their visits here. But, who can I tell? I fear that more women will fall prey to that demon's evil lust before his ancestors call him home; more innocent girls will yet lose their lives, accused as witches like the poor witch-sisters once Dibia Okpoko points the death-finger at them."

Diké couldn't believe what he was hearing. His mind was whirling like a churning river—*Dibia Okpoko has done the unforgivable by having carnal knowledge of the King's wife!* It was high treason punishable by death. Should his father hear of the deed, the witch doctor would roast in his ancestors' hell before the rooster crowed in the next dawn—*But who will tell the king? More importantly, how can he warn the king without getting his stepmother killed?* Diké was fond of his stepmother, a young and gentle woman who always treated him with great respect and deference. He would hate to have her blood on his hands.

Diké's body trembled with helpless fury. He wanted to avenge his father's honour, strangle the witch doctor and give him a slow death for the evil he had perpetrated against Chicken-Legs and the other innocent women whose ghosts were trapped in the shrine-grove—*He'd been right after all when he questioned the oracle's message at the Ritual of The Soul-Eaters.* He knew that should the story reach the ears of the Ọzo peers and Ogwumii warriors, the witch doctor would be torn to shreds by the entire village.

Diké felt a sudden burden lift from his heart. Now, he knew the truth, he was starting to think that his plight might perhaps, have a positive outcome. Had he not been ghosted, he would have never discovered the extent of the man's corruption and evil.

"I will search for your eyes and your heart for you, Chicken-Legs. I promise you that," Diké said, reaching out a hand to pat Chicken-Legs' arm, resisting the urge to gasp when his hand went through the icy, pale glow of her arm. "I will watch Dibia Okpoko and learn as much as I can from him. I know I'm a warrior and not an occultist, but if it's the last thing I do before I enter the grave-soil, I shall give your spirit the freedom I stole from your body when I enslaved you. This I promise you on the free-born souls of my ancestors and in the name of Ọgu n'Udo. I shall give you and your spirit-sisters your justice."

Fourteen

—·—

GHOSTED

DIKÉ WRINKLED HIS nose with disgust. He got up from his musky sleeping mat to seek the freshness of the shrine-grove. It had been over a week since he last had a wash and enjoyed the male camaraderie at the village stream. His body odour filled him with revulsion and the wild growth of his beard made his fingers itch for his hair-cutting blade. His loincloth stank to the skies, and despite his demands, Dibia Okpoko had refused to provide him with water for his ablutions.

"You can't hide here forever," the witch doctor had said with the mocking glee Diké had come to expect from him. "Sooner or later, you must make your way to the slave-stream like all the other slaves in the village. You refuse to go to The Pool of Dead Memories to kill your pride. You're still bound to your glorious past, still cloaked in your high pride. You refuse to realise that this is your new reality, that your days of glory are gone, vanished like consumed food, never to be re-lived." Dibia Okpoko shrugged. "Oh well, when you're desperate enough, you'll find your way to the slave-stream."

The man was right, and Diké now found that he couldn't live a day longer with his own stench. He made plans to visit the stream at dawn when most villagers were still in slumber in their beds. The humiliation of going to the slave stream was bad enough without having his downfall witnessed by all. It shamed him to admit he was a prideful man who refused to accept his fall as Dibia Okpoko always taunted, but he could not —*would not*— control the journey of his emotions. His pride was all he had left to him and he would value it the way he'd failed to value his freedom till he lost it.

Diké looked up at the rapidly-lightening sky as he started his journey to the stream. All was still and the dawn air crisp and cool on his skin. The moon was like a fading giant dandelion in the sky, shedding bits of spores in a ritual cycle of suicide and rebirth. He felt strange leaving the shrine-grove, almost like an infant leaving the warmth of its mother's womb. Yet again, he felt a joyful exhilaration, like one breathing fresh, clean air after several moons trapped in a shit-pit.

Soon, he found himself facing the bone-layered path leading out of the shrine-grove. *Their bones! Amadioha have mercy!* Diké shivered, clenching his fists. He had walked that bony path numerous times in the past without thinking twice about the hard, dirt-white path, striding boldly on crunchy ground, his feet cruel on *their* dead bones.

Now, he knew better. He knew the bones lived, that they could rise again and inflict horror and death. Only a fool with a death wish would disrespect the dead by trampling their bones with impunity.

With intense concentration and care, he navigated the path with terror-jellied legs, straddling the grassy edges and avoiding the scattered bones, hard, raspy breaths escaping his open mouth. His body was tensed for another attack, his mind running wild with imagined sounds—*clattering sounds of wakened bones flowing behind him, poised to drown him underneath their vengeful hardness.* He kept glancing behind, all the while running as fast as the thick shrubs bordering the path allowed. When eventually he stepped on bone-free soil at the edge of the village, he felt like a drowning swimmer pulled into breathing safety.

Diké paused, stooped till his head almost touched his knees, inhaling deep gulps of air. Soon, the weakness left his legs and the trembling, his body. He didn't want to think about the journey back after his ablutions at the stream—*Uh-uh! He'll face that terror when the time comes.*

The route to the slave stream went through the heart of the village. Diké knew he would have to navigate that section of his journey with stealth—*He prays no slaves arrive at the stream before he completes his ablution and escape back into the safety of shrine.* Lush Cassava farms and mud-hut homesteads mapped the landscape, together with multiple family shrines harbouring various statues of their ancestors, surrounded with all manner of offerings and gifts. Here and there, a live chicken hung upside-down on the doorpost of a shrine, while the occasional dog barked away the moon for a new dawn, competing with the morning rooster for the noisemaker-of-the-day award. The air had the familiar smell of burnt wood, fresh grass, Cassava farmland, stale foods, and fermented Palm-wine—*the fragrance of freedom and normality.* It brought a lump to Diké's throat.

The old woman stumbled into his path before Diké saw her. He had been so busy looking behind that he failed to see the danger in front. Her loud gasp coincided with his hushed apology as he instinctively reached out to steady her, forgetting his slave status. She stared at him, her rheumy eyes wide with fear and an emotion he couldn't read.

Then, she began to wail. She fell on the ground and clasped his right ankle with both her gnarled hands, wailing so loudly that shut doors hurriedly opened. Multiple voices released from deep slumber shouted panicked questions. Diké tried to hush her, to release her trembling hands from his ankle, but she clung to him with the tenacity of a dog to its bone. Her wails turned into the familiar sing-song dirge practiced at funeral wakes, her trembling voice shrill, sending chills to his spine.

"Doomed soul, I mourn for the unborn ones who never knew your name, Ewooh!

I cry for our people who will never speak your name again, Ewooh!

I wail for the fall of the tallest tree and the death of a lion, Ewooh!

May the gods love best the unfortunate one rejected by men, Ewooh!

Nameless one, I remember you; I remember, I remember! Ewooh!"

Diké felt her warm tears on his foot, tears that raised his own tears. He was ashamed of the weak slave he had become, a fake man that now cried with the ease of a woman. Yet he could not hold in his tears. He felt the eyes of countless people—men, women and children—as they lined the entrances to their hamlets wailing his doom with the old woman.

The air shook with the howls of the women and the shouts of the men as they tried to bring order and calm, spare their families the forbidden sight of the ghost. Still, the occasional male voice defied the law and called out a prayer to the ancestors, asking that they protect the nameless one and remember his great feats.

Diké read the pity in their eyes, pity for him by the ones he used to pity, the housewives and elderly, even the incomplete men with limbs lost to wild animals, accidents, and cursed reincarnations. Yet, in their wretched misfortune, they pitied him, where once they had looked at him with awe.

Diké turned and ran. He tore his leg away from the old woman's gnarled hands and fled down the winding route back to the bone-littered path that led to the shrine-grove. He did not stop running till he stumbled into the gloomy cocoon of the forbidden shrine and collapsed on his mat.

The tears that followed his flight refused to stop when he stopped running. They ran down his cheeks till he thought his body would melt and turn into a salty river. When Dibia Okpoko arrived to carry out his daily divination with the oracle, Diké ignored his usual taunts with weary indifference. Instead, he curled up on his mat with his knees up to his chest.

"Ha! I hear you finally showed your face in the village today and yet I smell your stench like the fart of an old woman," the witch doctor wrinkled his nose. "Did you think they would welcome you into their homes, eh? That they would dance and chant your name like they used to do? I hear the villagers shunned and shamed you, that they cursed your name and spat at you. You now appreciate your place in the world. I pray your pride is as dead as your name. Come, eat the food I've brought and get yourself into the grove to clean it like the good slave you are," Dibia Okpoko walked away to begin his divination with the oracle.

Diké remained on his mat, ignoring the food. Dibia Okpoko's insults washed over him like water on oiled skin. Over and over, his mind played out the scene in the village that morning, the pity in the men's eyes and the wailing of the women. Dibia Okpoko was wrong. No one had cursed or spat at him. But then, no one had called him by his name, not one of them. They, who had once called him their warrior, *Agu-eji-ejemba*, praised him as their protector, hailed him as the King's heir, yet they could not bring themselves to call him by his name.

Even the old woman, the one who mourned his doom, keening with the pain of a newly-made widow, had called him 'the nameless one.' Diké's chest tightened so much he thought he would pass out. The pain spread from his head to his heart, soon engulfing his entire body with burning anguish.

He stretched out and shut his eyes. Within minutes, warm heaviness returned to his eyes, plunging him into the welcome darkness of sleep-land and dreamless peace.

Fifteen

––·––

REVELATION

BIG-BOSOM THOUGHT she was going to die, that her heart would literally pop out of her chest. She shifted deeper into the shadows, hugging the tree trunk, hoping he wouldn't see her, that he would pass on without hearing the loud thuds of her heart or her harsh breathing.

Diké! It's him! She would know that muscled body anywhere, despite the lack of its former straight-backed assurance. He walked as she'd never known him to walk, his shoulders stooped, his feet gentle on the ground, like a cat unsure of its paws. He glanced about him with frequent turns of his neck, as if fearing detection or an unexpected attack from some wild animal.

Ever since she heard from the villagers that he had been seen, she had yearned to catch a glimpse of his face, just to assure herself that he was fine, that her brothers' treachery hadn't destroyed his soul. She knew her best chance would be by the route that led to the slave stream and suspected he would make the visit in the night, when he was least likely to run into the villagers again.

For several nights, she had waited in the dark, but she had started to doubt she would ever see him again—till now. Big-Bosom's heart quickened as Diké came close to her tree, so close that she heard his breathing which was as harsh as her own—*Don't speak! He's Osu. They'll kill you if you speak to him. The gods and ancestors will curse you if you speak to an* Osu. *You've seen him and he's all right. Just go home now. Don't speak! Don't spea...'*

"Diké! Our warrior!" Her lips betrayed her before her mind could stop them. Her voice was no louder than a trembly whisper, but he heard her and stopped. He turned around, saw her and gasped. In the clear light of the full moon, his face reflected a shock as great as hers.

"Big-Bosom?" his voice was hushed. "Big-Bosom?" He seemed unable to say anything else.

"Our warrior, I'm s-sorry... so sorry for what happened to you," her voice was wobbly from the unfamiliar tears that filled her eyes. "It's not fair! How can they treat you like this after all you've done for them? Are you okay? You don't look well. I would have visited you if I knew where to find you. I've thought about you every day, every minute, I swear. Tell me how I can help you and I'll do it."

The words tumbled from her lips and he reached out an arm and touched her face. He ran his fingers lightly over her arm before pulling her into his arms in a tight hug that almost squeezed the breath from her. He held on to her, saying nothing. His body shook like one crying. But she knew he wasn't crying, he would never cry—*not Diké, not the people's warrior.*

She smelled the unfamiliar rank odour of his skin and felt his shame as if it were her own—*She must never let him know that he smelled bad, he who was always so clean. The humiliation will be too much for him to bear.* She held her breath and stayed still in his arms, till gradually, her nostrils became inured to his smell and her breathing came easier. After what seemed like a lifetime, he released her, stepping away from her and turning his face away from hers.

"I am sorry, I shouldn't have touched you. Just that it's been such a long time since I spoke to anyone apart from Dibia Okpoko. It felt so wonderful to see a friendly face again. But you shouldn't be speaking to me, dear girl. Go quickly before anyone sees you." He started to walk away from her.

"Our warrior, stop; please," she ran after him, grasping his arm with desperate fingers.

"I am not your warrior anymore," his voice was dull. When he looked at her, his face was haggard.

"You'll always be our warrior. I don't care what anyone says. You're the greatest warrior in the ten villages and beyond and this stupid *Osu* thing can never take that away from you. Surely, there must be a way out? Can't the King reverse it?"

"What a sweet girl you are," Diké said with a tired smile. "You don't quite understand our traditions, do you? But that is understandable, seeing as you are just a girl—"

"I'm not 'just' a girl," Big-Bosom said sharply. "My age-peers have all married. I'm the same age as that stupid one they call Nightingale Voice, who Ife almost married till her father married her off to that old, rich peer."

"What did you just say? What old, rich peer?"

"Ọzo Agwọ. You didn't know? You heard no gossip at the slave stream?" Big-Bosom returned his look with wide eyes that mirrored his own. "No one told you about it?"

Diké shook his head. "No, you're the first person I have spoken to since..." His voice trailed as he glanced about them, a nervous look in his eyes, fearful of discovery. "When did Ada of the Nightingale Voice marry Ozo Agwo? How is the King taking it? Tell me everything you know."

Big-Bosom shrugged. "All I know is what I heard from my brothers." She proceeded to tell him everything, from the marriage to the Ogwumii leadership contest, to Ife's training and the expectation that he would become the warrior cult's new leader.

Diké's stared at her as if she had sprouted horns overnight. His eyes looked through her without seeing her. She started to get worried by the prolonged silence, the pained look in his eyes and the way his chest rose and fell, just like his fists, which kept clenching and unclenching.

"Diké, are you all right?"

"I'm fine, it's all right." He tried to smile, a ghastly smile that hurt her heart. "Anyway, what are you doing walking around the village at this late hour? Shouldn't you be at home?"

"I hate our hamlet and can't stand my brothers."

"Your brothers are bastards," Diké spat, fury clouding his face. "They are vile snakes." Diké heaved a deep sigh. "Sorry, Big-Bosom, I forget myself. Ignore my words. Go now and thank you, my dear, for talking to me. I will never forget it or your kindness."

"You know, don't you?" Big-Bosom's eyes were like saucers, her voice, hushed. "Oh merciful ancestors, you know about my brothers?"

"What?" Diké suddenly grabbed her arms, squeezing her so tight she cried out in pain. "You know what your brothers did to me? Were you in on the plot too? I should strangle you right now, you evil...."

"I didn't know, I swear. I didn't know anything," she cried, her eyes filling with tears. "I only found out afterwards and I haven't spoken to Feather-Feet since then. I hate him almost as much as I hate my brothers for what they did to you."

Diké stumbled back. "Ife? Ifekandu? What has he got to do with it? Speak girl; what do you mean by your words?" He was shaking her as if she were a piece of loincloth. Terror filled her heart—*He doesn't know about Feather-Feet! Oh ancestors have mercy! Why did she have to open her big mouth and spill evil?*

"I'm sorry our warrior, so sorry." She shook her head, fighting her tears. "I shouldn't have spoken so rashly. If only I could take back my words and..."

"Stop babbling, girl, and explain yourself," he was almost shouting, his eyes wild. "Speak now. What does Ifekandu have to do with my ruin?"

"It was him that drugged your Palm-wine," she whispered, watching the sudden violent trembling of his body, the mercurial shifts in his eyes which raced through shock, horror and a terrible pain she never wished to witness in another human's eyes ever again. "He didn't know what they planned to do—I swear. He was a fool, you know how easily he trusts and my brothers tricked him. They told him they were going to keep you in our hamlet, that was why he went along with the plot."

"Liar! All of you are liars, as treacherous as your father. Oh ancestors have pity! See how they've gone and corrupted my brother with their vileness! I warned Ifekandu, but he wouldn't listen and now this. Get away from my sight before I strangle you," Diké's eyes glazed with fury.

"I didn't do anything; It's not fair. I was tricked and I..."

But Diké had heard enough. He turned and began to sprint. Big-Bosom stared at his fast-retreating form and started running too, stretching her shorter legs to match his long ones. She clasped the weighty roundness of her breasts in her hands as she chased after his fast-disappearing form. Her breath was raspy, her body hot, tears blinding her sight. She followed him till they reached the path leading into the shrine-grove and she saw the gleaming white carpet of human bones layering the path.

Big-Bosom froze, terror sending chills to her spine. She stared at the narrow bush-bordered path lined with a cobbled patchwork of disjointed bones and felt her legs weaken underneath her dyed raffia-skirt. Suddenly, the bright light of the full moon wasn't enough anymore. Only intense sunlight could chase away the badness she felt all over her body.

She turned and ran, back towards the route leading to her hamlet. She sobbed as she ran, crying for herself and for him, for all of them and the end of her happiness and hopes. Diké hated her now and her heart was no longer a slave to Feather-Feet. Every tender emotion for him had died on the day she discovered his complicity in the destruction of his brother. She knew he had been deceived by her brothers, but that didn't stop the contempt that grew like wild weed in her heart, together with a strong critical spirit that never existed in the past.

What kind of man will agree to betray his own brother in the first place, especially a brother like Diké, who loves him beyond his own life? What kind of man can't even stand up to his own father even if said father is a king, and instead, just allows himself to be led along like a goat towards some idiot marriage? Will a real man drink and dance away his life the way Feather-Feet does, rejecting all responsibilities that'll make him a good husband and a good father? He doesn't even own a yam barn, has never held a hoe or rake in his pampered life. Even her vile brothers, as useless as they are, each has a full barn of yam and cassava, including Emeka, who now drinks almost as bad as Feather-Feet.

Big-Bosom sighed deeply. She had wasted her life on a shadow man when she should have been searching for a Diké, a true man with his own mind and an honourable spirit that would protect and provide for his family.

Suddenly, Big-Bosom gasped as someone grabbed her arms, male fingers digging painfully into her skin. She would have lashed out with her fist and given the person pain in their groin for touching her with disrespect, but she recognised the touch and felt a different kind of fear throb her heart.

Emeka!

"Where have you been, you little slut?" Her brother's voice was harsh in her ears.

She tensed as Emeka grabbed her long braids in a painful yank. She moaned softly, resisting the urge to cry out. The last thing she needed was to draw attention to them or have curious villagers witness their fight and mock them with their habitual spite. Emeka would give her an even greater pain afterwards for the humiliation.

"Did you think I wouldn't notice that you were not in your hut, eh? Do you think your brother is a fool? Talk, girl and tell me who it is you've been meeting in the night, you *Mbarama*, loose-moral girl."

Emeka's open palm connected with her face and this time she cried out, nursing her stinging cheek with a trembling hand.

"I was alone. I wasn't meeting anyone," she tried to keep the tremor from her voice, loath to let him see her fear.

"You lie!" He raised his hand to slap her again but this time she deflected it with her arm. The blow didn't hurt as much as it would have done on her face. "I thought you only wanted to open your thighs for that fool, Ife. Not that he can do anything for you or any woman in the state he is now." Emeka spat into the ground. His breath reeked of Palm-wine.

"No thanks to you." the words were out before she could hold them in.

129

"What do you mean by that? Speak up before I break your head." There was an ugly look in Emeka's eyes, suspicion making them smaller than they already were.

Big-Bosom shook her head. "Nothing, just that you also drink like him and it's no surprise he's always drunk if his best friend drinks as much."

She saw a flicker of relief in Emeka's eyes, and felt the same relief in her heart. Emeka would kill her if he discovered she had spoken to Diké. His hatred and envy for the warrior was like a festering wound poisoning his blood.

"You know nothing about it. So, shut up and start walking home with me before I break your stupid head." Emeka said, pulling her by the arm.

She allowed herself to be dragged home like a wayward child instead of the woman she was. Until a man placed Palm-wine and assorted meats at her brother's doorstep and asked for her hand in marriage, she was stuck with Emeka's brutality. Even if there was a man in the ten villages brave enough to risk marriage to the daughter of the village traitor, she couldn't be sure that Emeka would agree to release his hold on her freedom, not when his laundry, housework, meals, and errands depended on her.

Big-Bosom's throat tightened with suppressed tears. She had been a fool to waste her affections on Feather-Feet, believing him to be the one person her brother would allow her to marry. Now, her dreams were dead, as dead as Diké was inside the forbidden shrine—*Life is so unfair! How can the best of men end up an outcast while the vilest worms like her brothers, walk as free-born citizens? Now, she's gone and made Diké's plight even more unbearable by opening her big mouth and blabbing about Feather-Feet. Amadioha in his heavens! The pain in his eyes! Worst of all, he now believes that she's involved in his ruin. She'll kill*

130

Feather-Feet with her bare hands, that's what she'll do, alright. But that will require finding him sober and awake, the idiot.

Big-Bosom cursed under her breath. The whispers in the hamlets were that Ife had finally succumbed to the drink and would be lucky to dance again, if ever. A dark shroud now wrapped the entire village in a sickness of the soul. They were all like lost goats waiting for directions, for something to happen. No one knew what it was they were waiting for except it wasn't something good. Good luck had gone from the village on the day the people's warrior left.

Big-Bosom heaved a deep sigh. Thoughts ran through her mind with the restlessness of confused ants—*She must find a way to help Diké and make up for what her brothers have done to him. She must convince him of her innocence in her brothers' evil actions. There must be a way to free him from that curse and return normality to the village.* She had no idea how she would achieve both, but if it took her a lifetime of beatings at the hands of her vile brother, she would find a way to bring the warrior back to his people and atone for an evil and grave injustice.

Sixteen

—·—

VISITATION

CHICKEN-LEGS' SPECTRE hovered close to Diké, watching his heaving chest with sightless detachment. After he had shared what Big-Bosom told him, Diké lay on his mat, staring sightlessly into the roof.

Ifekandu! Over and over Ife's name ran through his mind like the repetitive hoots of the night owl, together with the questions. *Why? Why?*

"Our warrior, you must hear the truth from your brother," Chicken-Legs' hollow voice pierced through his grief. "You must give him the chance to explain himself. We both know Big-Bosom is not the wisest of girls and tends to be rash with her words at times. Feather-Feet has no evil in his heart, that I can swear to on my eternal doom. Don't let hate build the grave on your brother's name without letting him speak in his own defence."

"What defence can he possibly have?" Diké shouted, jumping to his feet from his mat. "What in Ana's earth could that snake, Emeka, have said to make him betray his own blood? Haven't I loved him better than a father and as gentle as a mother? Yes, I may not have spoken the words enough times to let him know how dear he is to my soul, but I showed him. I showed him my heart with every breath I took."

He leaned close to Chicken-Legs, searching for her eyes within their dark, empty sockets. "Chicken-Legs, you knew us like you knew your own family. You knew how much the boy's happiness mattered to me. Ifekandu owned my life. He knew that nothing, not even my wife, mattered more to me. Yet, he turned on me like a viper against an exposed ankle, stealing my future with heartless brutality! If he wanted to be heir, I would have prepared him for the role and happily handed the eagle feathers to him when it came my time to wear them. But I knew he had no interest in being King. All he wanted was the freedom to dance and enjoy Palm-wine in the company of his friends. So, why would he plot my doom with those sons of a treacherous snake? Why?"

Chicken-Legs reached out a glowing arm and placed it on Diké's head. Immediately, he was enveloped in the same soft warmth he'd felt on the night of his attack in the shrine-grove, the healing glow of the witch-sisters. He felt like a baby swaddled inside its mother's back-pouch. The throbbing pain drained from his head and a deep calm descended inside his mind, removing all thoughts and worries. His limbs grew weak as he collapsed back on his mat with a soft sigh.

"Rest your soul, our warrior." Chicken-Legs' voice was like the soft lullaby of a loving mother in his ears. "How long can you continue fighting and hurting without losing your mind? I have no answers for you, but I can give you peace. Sleep now and sleep deep. When you awaken, you will be rested and stronger. May the ancestors watch over you."

Diké slept; and he dreamt.

In his dream, Diké was inside the forbidden shrine, sitting on his mat. The smell of stale blood was overpowering, and he knew it was night-time by the

133

complete absence of light. He had grown used to the glow from Chicken-Legs' ghost which lit up the shrine-cave during the long hours they spent together reminiscing on their past lives. This time, the kindly ghost was absent, and the darkness was solid. Even so, he could still see the mammoth statue of Ọgu n'Udo towering over him, its shape blurred in the dense blackness. Everything appeared normal except the total absence of sound.

Diké listened out for the incessant clattering of the hanging skulls on the Ngwu trees, the nightly hoots of the owls and the noisy clucking of the shrine chickens. But all was soundless, like the eardrums of a deaf man. Diké felt an unease in his body, a crawling of bony fingers along his spine, that icy feeling that told him that even the air he breathed was all wrong.

Diké felt a crawling of bony fingers along his spine. Something moved inside the forbidden shrine. He heard no sound and saw nothing in the darkness but he knew he was no longer alone, that something else was in the shrine with him, something that stole the warmth in the air and plunged the room into a freezing chill.

He hugged himself, wrapping his arms around his body. His teeth started to chatter and goosepimples spread a prickly path on his skin. He tried to rise from the mat, but his limbs were weighted as if with rocks. The terror was building in his heart and the urge to scream was strong. But he held his voice locked behind his throat—He's a warrior regardless of his plight. By Amadioha, he'll not scream from an unknown terror like a virgin bride confronting the turgid rod of a well-endowed husband.

He heard a sound like running water, at first, a gentle flow, then a loud gush. His mat quickly soaked with the wetness and soon, his legs were covered with the liquid which was oddly warm and sticky. Again, he tried to move but the invisible force held him down on the soaking mat. Without warning, the great statue of Ọgu n'Udo began to glow, a dim light that quickly exploded into dazzling brilliance. In the sudden brightness that illuminated the shrine, Diké saw the source of the damp.

He screamed after all.

The shrine wept blood; from the jagged roof, down to the circular mud walls of the cave, thick blood poured like red sludge. Already, the level of the red flood was rising quickly on the ground and Diké could barely see his knees in the blood swamp. But the greatest horror was the glowing mammoth statue of the deity of war and peace. The black eyes of the statue glowed with fierce awareness, while the benevolent smile seemed to grow wider, turning the hard granite of the effigy into the soft plaster of living skin. As Diké stared in frozen terror, the statue began to rotate, slowly, like an awakened corpse learning to walk. Its movement was sluggish, yet, filled with a terrifying intelligence that brought icy dread to his heart.

As the smiling and benevolent rear-face of the god slowly disappeared from his view, Diké shut his eyes, unwilling to see the front face of Ọgu n'Udo, knowing the animated fearsome face of the deity would blind him with terror. With his eyes shut, the horror grew with the insidious scratching sound of the deity's heavy motion. Diké thought his heart would explode underneath his pounding chest. He was mumbling prayers to the deity and his ancestors, begging their forgiveness for his transgressions, known and unknown. His voice was a babble of hushed horror.

Then, new sounds replaced the gravelly sound of the deity's crawl, sounds that made him wish he had been born deaf. From the exterior of the forbidden shrine, the hanging skulls shrieked a cacophonous fury, banging their branches and each other so violently that Diké thought they would break free of their strings and crash to the ground in angry, bony pieces. Something was stoking their rage, something Diké was too terrified to see. But his eyes had their own curiosity which defied his fear. They opened of their own will and Diké gasped, struck by awe and shock.

Before him stood nine fierce and muscled men that looked just like him in the days he wore his warrior paints. They stood tall before the deity of the shrine, their black bodies glowing like polished ebony beneath Ogu n'Udo's dazzling light. Each of the men had bushy brows under piercing black eyes, and the hairs on their broad chests were lush and black, just like those on their heads. Their bodies bore multiple scars from machete and spear cuts, similar to his own body, the souvenirs of countless fights in bloody battlegrounds. Their loincloths were covered in the ancient abstract symbols of the sacred Nsibidi writing of their community, scripts that would have been visible on his own loincloth save for the filth coating them in shameful invisibility. Even without the symbols, Diké would have recognised the visitors for who they were. He cast his eyes wildly, searching for the tenth warrior, but he only saw nine.

Diké scrambled to his knees in the blood-flooded ground and bowed his head low, greeting the silent ghosts of the dead warrior-leaders by their true names, names he'd learned in the secret initiation ritual that preceded his induction into the Ogwumii warrior cult. He had hoped that his own name would one day join that list of exalted heroes immortalised in the village lore for their bravery and great feats; that he would become the eleventh warrior-leader to join the "lucky ten" whom the ancestors favoured.

Now, he was nothing, just a ghost; but not the kind of ancestor-ghost that would bring honour to his clan. Instead, he was an outcast, whose memory would be wiped from the village annals for eternity. Seeing the *great warrior-leaders of the past emphasised his ruin. The agony of his loss was like countless deep stabs in his chest. He held back hot tears*—By Amadioha, he'll not unman himself before these great men!

"Agu-eji-ejemba! *The Tiger that marches before his people in battle! Arise, great warrior-brother and son; rise and shake the hands of your peers." The nearest warrior-ghost reached out a hand and helped Diké up.*

Diké's body trembled as he fought to stay on his feet on the blood-soaked floor of the shrine. One by one, the dead warriors each clasped his arm in the familiar greeting of their Ogwumii cult. Diké was in a daze; his eyes filled with the tears he fought to suppress—They've acknowledged him by his name! The great warriors have welcomed him as their peer despite his wretched situation!

He felt his shoulders straighten and his face wreathed in a smile that stretched to his ears. The wild raging of the hanging skulls was like the roar of thunder and war, but Diké was deaf to their ire. A small voice within told him to think on the pain and fury of the sacrificed slaves, who were now witnessing the unprecedented presence of almost every single warrior-leader that had enslaved them and eaten their hearts at countless Rituals of the Soul-eaters.

Diké dismissed the voice like an annoying fly, shutting his ears to their shrieking fury atop the Ngwu trees.

"Machete-brother, we heard your pain and we wept blood tears for your ruin," *said the tallest warrior, the leader of the nine, he that was known by the name of Ikolobia in the days of his glory. He was the very first Ogwumii warrior-leader of the ten Okoro villages and Diké's great-ancestor several times removed.*

Again, Diké sank involuntarily to his knees and bowed low, reaching out both hands to the great warrior, seeking his comfort, his heart pounding with gratitude for his words.

Ikolobia took his hands. His touch was chilly, and Diké shivered.

"Even now, the shrine floods with our tears, for the great tragedy that has befallen our bloodline. You don't remember us, do you? Yet, we have clasped arms and shared wine with you in your past life and watched the three suns of our realm together. We've reminisced over our exploits in the battlefield before you left the ancestors' realm for your latest reincarnation. Since then, we've been waiting for the day you, the tenth warrior, would return to the realm of the ancestors to complete our numbers again and release the spirit of the lion in us so that we may ride the lands of humankind in our true forms, the spirits of the great cats, just as we once did in the glorious days of old."

*Diké's mouth was a wide O, just like his eyes. His heart pounded so hard he thought it would explode—*He was the tenth warrior! He, Diké, an *Osu* and outcast, was once the tenth warrior!

"That's why you returned to this incarnation, to fulfil the prophesy and return our glory," Ikolobia continued. "The oracle prophesied that the tenth warrior would be the greatest warrior of all, he that would be made an outcast, yet, walk into the dead realm of the ancestors while he still lived. It is prophesied that he would charm The Old Ones *into revealing the secret words of our feline transmogrification and glorious rebirth. We wondered when that would happen and despaired of ever fulfilling our destiny, until word came of your ruin and we knew that you were the one, our lost Machete-brother, the tenth warrior! You may have forgotten us, but we recognise your spirit even in this new body you wear."*

Again, the warrior-ghosts chorused their assent with deep grunts.

"Brother, prepare yourself for the greatest journey of your life. We thank the gods that you have not bathed in the cursed pond of the slaves, a water poisoned with the willows of forgetfulness, as your soul would've been truly enslaved, and you would be useless to fulfil your great destiny. We thank our great deity who has protected you in his shrine and spared you from that evil curse."

The warrior-ghosts all bowed deeply to the glowing statue of Ogu n'Udo, whose fearsome front-face now appeared less threatening to Diké, even friendly.

. "In the next few days, you will prepare yourself for your journey to the realm of the ancestors. Listen carefully to my words and follow them to the letter," Ikolobia continued, his gaze intense. Diké leaned in closer.

"Firstly, you must observe a ritual of purification. Your body must be bathed by a woman with water infused with menstrual blood and salt. This will ensure that your passage into our realm is pure, and that you arrive in the womblike state of your original birth. Remember, you cannot bathe yourself. You must be purified by a woman's hands. For a full day and night before your journey, you will fast and eat nothing save the pure honey from the beehives. This will sweeten your mien and make you more endearing to The Old Ones. *It will also cleanse your body of all the impurities of your curse. Finally, you must bring* The Old Ones *a gift that will thrill their hearts beyond anything they have in the realm of the dead. Only then will they release the secret of our transmogrification."*

Diké's heart skipped, panic thudding his heart.

"Great warriors, what gift could I possibly bring to The Old Ones *that would thrill their hearts sufficiently*

to influence their minds? Please advise me, blessed ones, you who know them well and dwell in their midst."

*"That, we cannot tell you, good son and brother,"
Ikolobia said. "Nobody knows the hearts or minds of
The Old Ones. Their ways are as mysterious to the
dead as they are to the living. You must come up with
a suitable gift all by yourself. Now, for the final step of
your journey."*

*Ikolobia paused for several seconds staring at Diké
as if judging the health of his mind.. His grip on Diké's
hand tightened and his eyes gentled once again. When
he spoke, his voice was the voice of a mother, devoid of
the steel of the warrior.*

*"Good son, to journey to our realm, you must sleep the
death-sleep, one of the most painful sleeps known to the
living. You will die the three deaths of water, fire, and
earth before* The Old Ones *will open the gates of our
realm to you again. The witch doctor of the shrine is the
only one that can oversee this ritual and guide you into
the final sleep of the black herb. He will also guide you
back into this shrine if* The Old Ones *allow you to leave
our realm. For, know this; you may never return to the
land of the living once you have made this journey into
the land of the dead. Even so, you will be in a better place
than where you are now, amongst your peers, living in
freedom and peace. For the minute you cross the realms,
the curse of* Osu *is lifted and you will become a freeborn
again."*

*Ikolobia turned to the other ghosts and they all
crowded around Diké, embraced him and hailed
him with his true name,* Agu-eji-ejemba. *As each
warrior-ghost stepped back they were pulled into the
blazing conduit of Ogu n'Udo, one after another, taking
with them endless streams of blood sucked from the
shrine. Finally, only Ikolobia stood in the shrine with*

Diké. The old warrior-ghost reached out a fading arm and took Diké's hands in his cold ones again.

"Be strong, great son," he said. "Trust in your strength, believe in yourself and remember that you are the tenth lion, the greatest warrior in our lands, whose destiny it is to awaken the lion spirits of the ten Ngwu trees and return us to eternal glory. Do not fear your journey into the land of the dead. Every battle is fought and won in the mind. Conquer your mind and you own your destiny. I await you, great warrior, in the realm of The Old Ones. May your light blaze till eternity."

And like the others before him, Ikolobia winked into the blazing deity and the shrine went black. Ogu n'Udo lost his glow and the shrieking skulls finally stilled.

When the ghost of Chicken-Legs came several hours later to wake Diké, he resisted her hollow whispers until the chill of her dead breath finally pierced through his dreams and woke him up. Diké stumbled out of the shrine, fleeing both his dreams and Chicken-Legs' ghost in blind disorientation. His body was freezing, right to his bones. In the shrine-grove, the skulls were white and still underneath the full moon, and their familiar rattles were devoid of threat or rage.

He felt a presence beside him and turned. Chicken-Legs glided in silent introspection at his side, her face pale and sad in the moon-glazed shrine-grove. Once again, he felt a warm feeling of comfort in her presence and within minutes, started to narrate his strange dream to her. She listened to him in, nodding a few times as he spoke.

"Our warrior, what you had was no dream," Chicken-Legs said, once he was done. "It was a visitation. I felt their presence and it scared me away from the forbidden shrine. Every soul in this shrine felt their arrival, and I won't be surprised if all the villagers slept for the first time without nightmares this night—that's how disturbed the lost souls in the shrine were tonight. You've received a sacred message from your ancestors, one that will set you free from this accursed place and return you to your former glory. But you cannot do this task by yourself. You must seek your brother and enlist his help. I know your heart angers against Feather-Feet, but let him speak and maybe the truth will finally be known and the two of you can come up with a solution to this great task."

Diké knew that she spoke the truth. Even though the fury still burnt in his heart against his brother, he knew that he had to get to the truth and bring peace to his soul—*He must find a way to speak to Ifekandu.* Diké squared his shoulders and nodded his head—*He'll not fail his ancestors; not this time. He'll not fail himself.*

SEVENTEEN

_._

THE SNAKE'S TONGUE

IFE WEAVED HIS way along the dusty path that led to Emeka's hut with two large jars of Palm-wine clutched tightly in his hands. His sleep-deprived eyes were the red hue of the habitual drunk, yet a cold clarity in his mind observed his clumsy steps, heard the twitters of the villagers as they watched him from their hamlets. Their thoughts were almost as loud as the pounding in his heart—*There goes Feather-Feet. Poor King Ezeala! One son dead and the other, a pathetic drunk.*

Ife called out and waved at them and even managed some rowdy songs, the glazed fool's smile pasted on his face. The urge to drink from the jars he carried was almost irresistible but he needed to have his head clear when he came face-to-face with Emeka. Ife raised one of the jars to his nostrils and inhaled—*Maybe sniffing the heady aroma might curb the craving, Amadioha spare him this torture!*

His mouth watered and his steps stumbled. He put the jar in his right hand to his mouth and took a long drink. It was potent stuff. It hit his head in an instant, filling him with the familiar giddiness. He took another mouthful and soon, his steps had turned into dancing hops, another loud song bursting from his lips.

Several minutes later, Ife paused outside Emeka's hamlet, forcing his heart to slow its frenzied race as his eyes caught sight of the mud-hut where he'd last seen Diké on that fateful night of his eternal shame. He quickly looked away, unwilling to resurrect his anger—*Not yet, not till the time is right to vent his fury*.

He called out Emeka's name, his voice hearty and loud.

"Brother-friend, are you there?" The old affectionate name galled Ife.

A door opened in the biggest hut in the hamlet and Emeka came out. He looked like a man caught by his mother-in-law giving money to his mistress. Guilt and fear drenched him in hot sweat as he stared at Ife from his doorway. Then his face hardened, devoid of a welcoming smile. Suspicion glinted in his shifty eyes.

"Why do you stand there moping like a frog, eh?" Ife called out with merriment, waving the jars in the air. "See, I brought us the best wine in the village to drown our sorrows. Come, the sun's growing hot and we don't want this wine to go stale on us." Ife took another drink from the jar in his right hand before stumbling towards the mango tree. He plonked himself against the trunk and stretched out his legs. "Bring some cups, will you? I forgot to bring them with me."

Emeka soon joined him under the mango tree, taking longer than usual. When he smiled, Ife noticed a tightness to his features, a wary intensity in the way Emeka's eyes studied his face. Ife met his gaze with a disarming smile and waved him down by his side.

"I decided since you don't want to come and see me, then I'll come to you." Ife laughed, raising an arm for a handshake. Emeka hesitated before accepting it. Ife resisted the urge to snatch back his hand and wipe off the repulsive contact. "Don't worry, I'm not too angry with you anymore," Ife said, bestowing a hazy smile as

144

he shook one of the jars to stir the wine, the same jar he had been drinking from. He kept the other jar to his side, close to his thigh. "I can't blame you for my brother escaping your hut and wandering into the shrine while drugged. After all, I fed him the drugged wine, didn't I? So, we're both guilty. How were we to know that Diké would end up inside the forbidden shrine, eh? Come, let's drink away our sorrows. What's done is done and I'm now the King's first son. If Igwulube can train me enough, I might even end up the leader of the Ogwumii!"

Ife tittered and Emeka joined him, his laughter sudden, loud, and long.

"I know, I know. I mean, can you imagine me as a warrior-leader, I ask you? Me with my dancing legs and feeble arms?" Ife hooted.

Emeka shook his head, his shoulders shaking with intense mirth. Ife bent his head to pour the wine, shielding the hate burning in his heart—*Let the viper laugh at his expense—as always.* Emeka's contempt fed his loathing and steeled his will. He felt the cold blade of his knife against his skin, concealed inside his loincloth. Before the day was done, its blade would be stained with Emeka's blood.

He handed Emeka a full cup of wine and topped his own cup, before pouring some on the ground for the ancestors.

"Brother-friend, you have no idea how happy I am to see you," Emeka said, slapping Ife's shoulder with a sweat-dampened palm. "See how you already have me laughing when I haven't even cracked a smile since our great warrior wandered away. *Chei*! I haven't stopped blaming myself for the tragedy and of course, I've never once blamed you for your role, even though I did it all as a favour to save you from marrying Ada of the Nightingale Voice, who is now married to Ọzo Agwọ.

Chei! How fate toys with us. If only we had waited a few days more, all this would have never happened. My heart aches when I think of what has become of your late brother." Emeka drank his wine, not stopping till he had emptied the cup and raised his cup for a refill.

"Diké is not dead," Ife snapped, instantly cursing himself for revealing his anger. He pasted the fool's smile again on his face and topped Emeka's cup. "I mean, we all know he's still alive inside the forbidden shrine. It's just this stupid Osu thing that insists that he's dead."

"But we can't disregard our customs, Brother-friend," Emeka said, looking at him with pity, the look that madmen still covered in loincloths reserve for worse-off lunatics running naked in the marketplace. "To every Okoro citizen, your brother is dead, and his name must never leave our lips again. It's terrible what's happened to him, but you're now the King's heir and I rejoice for your good fortune. Here, let's drink to your future success and our continued friendship. May your nights be free from the bad dreams."

Emeka raised his cup to his lips and Ife followed his lead, forcing the drink down his constricted throat. He quickly poured another cup for Emeka, noticing the absence of suspicion in his gaze. The fool felt confident in his deceit, assured of Ife's stupidity. A few more drinks would be enough to carry out his plan. Ife resisted the urge to reach for his knife inside his loincloth.

"Where are your brothers?" he asked Emeka, peering with squinted eyes around the hamlet.

Emeka laughed loudly. "They're at the far-farm." He hiccupped. "You're lucky you found me here, I was just about to join them when you arrived." Emeka reached over and poured himself more Palm-wine without waiting for Ife to refill his cup.

"Where's Big-Bosom?" Ife asked.

"Ha! Now he asks about her because Ada of the Nightingale Voice has gone and married someone else." Emeka leered. "*Chei*, this crafty man, eh? I always suspected you liked my little sister more than you let on, you randy goat. Well, if you want to make her your wife, you know I won't protest. Her hips are broad, and she'll bear strong sons for the King's compound now your brother is gone."

"I'm not interested in marrying anyone." Ife said with an impatient wave of his hand. "I only asked where Big-Bosom was since I haven't seen any of you since Diké's tragedy."

"Ok, ok. She's inside her hut. I've banned her from leaving the compound for a while since she's been sneaking out at night. I sush-suspect she must be meeting some man even though the little whore denies it. Here, fill my cup again. *Chei!* This Palm-wine is the best, ever."

Ife frowned. Big-Bosom was a complication he hadn't expected. He knew the brothers went to the farm every market day. Big-Bosom sold foodstuff at the market table on the last market day of every moon and he had timed everything accordingly—*How was he to know that the mad dog will hold his sister hostage inside their hamlet?*

Ife wanted to scream out his frustration, throw away every caution and just kill Emeka and himself and be done with life. It didn't matter if Big-Bosom was a witness and the entire ten villages knew about his crime. At least, he would meet his ancestors knowing he had avenged his brother and redeemed his own heart.

He reached into his loincloth for the knife, just as Big-Bosom came out of her hut and waved. Ife groaned and released the hilt, moving his hand in a pretend groin-scratch.

147

"Big-Bosom." He waved back. "I was just asking about you and telling your brother that I haven't seen you since our tragedy." Ife saw fear flicker in her eyes before she smiled. She was as eager to hide their conversation from her brother as he was.

Emeka waved her away as if she were an annoying fly. "Go away, girl, and leave us men alone to enjoy our wine," he leaned forward to top up his cup. He picked the jar and frowned. It was empty. He reached for the second jar and Ife stalled him, pulling the jar away. It was the jar with the poisoned wine.

Ife cursed silently—*Now, he'll have to dispose of the wine and rethink his strategy. Damn the wicked fates and the snake's good Chi.*

"This wine's not for us, it belongs to the King," Ife said. "I was on my way home after picking up the jars but decided to pop in and share my own jar with you before heading home."

Ife struggled up from the ground, feigning inebriation with clumsy foot-work. Emeka didn't need to pretend. He was as drunk as Ife himself planned to be once he returned to the seclusion of his hut. Emeka used Ife's leg to hoist himself up from the ground.

"*Chei!* Why did you tempt me with two jars and then deny me the treat, eh?" Emeka grumbled. "Come, I'll walk you home so the people will see that we're still friends."

"Is there any reason why they should think we're not friends?" Ife asked, looking Emeka in the eyes.

Emeka frowned before glancing away, but not before Ife caught the guilt in his eyes.

"No, no, you misunderstand me, Brother-friend," he laughed, shoving Ife with a playful fist. "I meant to say that the villagers have never been happy with our friendship, and now that you're the king's heir, they'll be even more upset. For myself, I'm so happy that you don't hold it against me for your brother wandering away from our hamlet that night. Anybody else would hate me for that fatal carelessness, but not you. Instead, you bring me Palm-wine and shake my hand in friendship. Feather-Feet, you're a good friend, a very good man." Emeka had tears in his eyes.

Ife read them as the tears of the drunk and the tears of the traitor. The man had the tongue of a snake, one that crooned sweet words that hid the pure evil of his bite. Save for his conversation with Big-Bosom, he would've never known the truth behind Diké's tragic fate.

Ife maintained his fool's smile as he clasped Emeka's arm as they began to walk—*He'll play along till the time is right. The patient frog gets the juicy termite, as the saying goes. Soon, very soon, his time will come, and his bite will be more poisonous than a Black Mamba's venom.*

Ife had barely made it back to their hamlet when Big-Bosom accosted him outside his hut. Her face dripped with sweat, her breathing was harsh.

"Feather-Feet, I must speak with you urgently while Emeka is still under the drink."

She dashed into his hut before he could respond. An irritated frown furrowed his brows—*What does the blasted girl want this time?* He had always found Big-Bosom's passionate fixation on him both a source of amusement and annoyance, but since the bad business with her brothers, he now found the entire family loathsome. A rational part of his mind told him that Big-Bosom was innocent. But his heart acted without his mind and what his heart felt was hatred against her entire clan.

"What do you want?" Ife asked, standing by his open door, his body taut with impatience. Big-Bosom returned his frown with a fiercer frown. Her big eyes flashed at him with a contempt that took him by surprise. It was a look he had never seen in her eyes before.

"I saw Diké two nights ago and spoke with him," she said.

Ife's heart leapt into his mouth. His legs weakened and he staggered to his bed and collapsed on it.

"How?" Ife's voice was hoarse, hushed. "Where did you see my brother? How was he? What did he say? Does he know? I mean, does he know who was responsible for his ghosting? Speak, Big-Bosom. Tell me everything, quick!"

"He knows… I told him but I didn't mean to. I thought he knew and I was only trying to let him know how sorry I was. But now, he thinks I'm as guilty as you and my brothers and he hates me and it's not fair. Why should I be the one to blame when you're the one that betrayed your own brother?"

Ife saw red, a hue so bloody it seared his reason.

"May Amadioha strike you dead, you wicked gossip!" He lunged towards Big-Bosom, intent on smashing her head into the ground till she was a bloody pulp of brain and bones. She screamed and ran out of his hut, standing a safe distance from his doorway, her face drenched with tears and sweat.

"I hate you!" she shouted, not caring who heard her voice in the compound. "You'd better go speak to Diké and tell him that I'm innocent, do you hear me? You should be the one cursed inside that horrible place, you shameless worm. I heard everything you said to Emeka today and I think you're despicable. To want the King's throne so badly that you're willing to betray your own blood in such a vile manner is not only cowardly, but evil."

"Shut up, Big-Bosom, and get in here now,"

"No!" She hissed and shouted a vile curse he preferred to forget.

Ife took a deep breath. "Listen, I'm sorry I lost my temper. Please come inside and let's talk," he tried to smile but Big-Bosom's glare quelled his heart. She walked further away from him, pointing at him with fury.

"I'll not come near you, you horrid roach. Listen to me carefully and let me tell you a truth that even an ant knows. You'll never, ever, be the man that Diké is, do you hear me? Open your drunken ears and listen to me. Even if Igwulube divides himself into ten equal parts for each part to train you ten times as an Ogwumii warrior, he'll never make you a tenth of the warrior that your brother is. Ha! You, an Ogwumii warrior-leader! That'll be the day that a man's belly swells with pregnancy!"

Her eyes flashed with scorn. "Listen, you; go immediately and find Diké and tell him I didn't do anything bad to him, do you hear me? Otherwise, I'll tell Emeka that your friendship with him is as false as his own with you, then you'll really know how deadly he can be. You think you know my brother; that you're a match for him? Just pray he never thinks about you when he wakes up every morning, otherwise your ancestors will regret the day they sent you into this world to represent them," Big-Bosom hissed, her arms akimbo, glaring at him with enough fury to annihilate an entire clan.

Ife glanced around, praying no one had heard Big-Bosom's words—*Ancestors have mercy! The last thing he needs is the blasted girl blabbing his shame to everyone, especially the King.*

He'd heard about her temper, had laughed when people said it would take a hundred Ogwumii warrior husbands to tame her, such was the lightning that fed her temper. But with him, Big-Bosom had only ever shown her soft side. Now, he was witnessing the notorious fury that quelled the brashest male lips and fed the belief in the village that no sane man would ever risk giving

Big-Bosom to his mother as a daughter-in-law, unless he truly hated his mother and wanted to punish her.

"Big-Bosom, please I beg you, come inside." Ife raised his arms high in the air as he walked towards her, to show he meant her no harm. And to his surprise, he found that he truly harboured no more ill-will towards her anymore. Her rage had killed his own and now, it was vital that he regained her good thoughts, that she viewed him in the same positive light as before. "Everything you said is the truth, but you misunderstand me. Please, let's talk as the friends we used to be. Hear my side of the story, the entire truth and if you still feel you want to end our friendship, I'll understand."

"Throw me a knife first and I'll come into your hut," Big-Bosom said, wiping her tears with a furious flick of her hand.

"Very well." Ife reached into his loin and withdrew a knife, throwing it to the ground not too far from her.

Big-Bosom's mouth was as wide as her eyes as she stared first at him and then the knife.

"Oh my ancestors! You planned to kill my brother today, didn't you?" her voice was a stunned whisper.

"Do you blame me after all he's done to me?" Ife snarled. "As I said, you've no idea of the truth. Just come inside and for once, shut your mouth and listen, ok? You have the knife. If I do anything to you, just stab me. I won't even stop you. I just need someone I trust that I can unburden myself to before this burden sends me to the grave-soil."

Ife turned and went into his hut—*He's so tired. If Big-Bosom wants to follow him inside his hut, then fine. If she doesn't want to hear his words, that will be fine too. The sun will still rise in the sky tomorrow and his life will likely follow the same doomed trajectory now set by his fate.*

He heard soft footsteps behind him. His shoulders sagged as the tension left his body.

"Take a seat, Big-Bosom," he said with a smile. She didn't return his smile, but she also didn't look at him with hate. She took the only wood-stool in his hut and pulled it as far from him as she could, close to the open door. When she sat down, it was more a perch, like a bird ready to take flight.

Ife took a deep breath and sighed. He prayed that by the time he was done talking, her buttocks would occupy the entire stool and not a part of it; that she would look at him once more with the old look of affection, the eyes of a friend.

Ife cleared his throat and began to speak.

Eighteen

— · —

THE WITCH DOCTOR

DIBIA OKPOKO'S STUNNED face was the greatest joy Diké had experienced since he became a hostage inside the forbidden shrine of Ọgu n'Udo. The habitual glee in his squinty eyes had vanished, replaced with the look one usually found in the eyes of women caught in adulterous affairs. The witch doctor's mouth was opened so wide a full moon would have fitted into it. His fists clenched and unclenched, his breathing loud and fast.

"There is no need to ask me who my informant is," Diké said, squaring his broad shoulders and leaning into the witch doctor, his stance menacing, just as he intended. Dibia Okpoko was a man rarely intimidated despite his puny size. "All you need to know is that even as we speak, my informant is waiting for a signal from me and within minutes, the King and the elders will know of your crime and no ancestor or god can prevent your head from being separated from your body in a public execution. How you had the gall to trifle with the King's honour and believe you could get away with it is beyond comprehension." Diké jabbed a hard finger into the man's chest and saw him wince. "I know all about your meeting with the slave-girl by the stream-path and your evil threat which you finally executed. I know that you have committed a worse abomination by bringing in women into the sacred shrine-grove in your vile lust."

He saw the witch doctor's eyes darken with horror. He reached out a trembling hand towards Diké.

"*Agu-eji-ejemba*, I beg you, please have pity on an old man's grey hairs," Dibia Okpoko begged, clasping Diké's arm with fingers curved into steely claws. "I bow my head to you for the mighty man that you are, a warrior and a secret wizard whose powers eclipse my own."

The flattery dripped from his lips with the oleaginous ease of poisoned honey. Diké marvelled at the man's mendacity and conceit—*The fool actually believes he can buy his silence with his grovelling, no doubt expecting him to lap up every crumb of goodwill in his lowly slave status.*

"Stop insulting both my intelligence and yours, even though I seriously doubt you still have an ant's brain inside your wicked head," Diké snarled, pulling his arm from Dibia Okpoko's grasp. "I am neither a wizard nor a sage and do not wish to be one. I will leave all that to you. However, what I have are spies and powerful friends whose reach defy all your powers and the restrictions of this shrine. There is nothing about you that they don't know including your deal with that snake peer, Ọzọ Agwọ."

Diké threw that last bit in, gambling on a strong intuitive feeling following his conversation with Big-Bosom. His gut instincts told him the fat peer wouldn't have dared demand his son be made the Ogwumii cult leader without the support of Dibia Okpoko, whose duty it was to carry out the ritual of ratification inside the shrine-grove, just as he had done when Diké was chosen as the cult leader.

The look of dismay in the witch doctor's eyes confirmed Diké's hunch.

"Ha! So, you're not satisfied with dishonouring your King with his wife, you have also betrayed him with his enemy. You think with my fall you can now gather the vultures to devour my bloodline and lay waste to our hamlet?" Diké's voice was like thunder. "You vile snake! I've been looking for an excuse to return you to your ancestors and you have now given it to me. I have nothing to lose anymore and your death will be the one pleasure I would derive from my curse."

"Our warrior, please, I am begging you to hear me out," Dibia Okpoko grabbed hold of his arm once again, "Ọzo Agwọ made me do it. He said that since everyone knew your brother was unfit to carry the bronze machetes you left behind, then his son must protect the ten villages in your stead. He assured me that he didn't plan to wrestle power from the King and that he would no longer demand a rotational kingship once his son becomes the Ogwumii leader. I did what I did for the good of the King and your clan. I was only working for the peace of our land. How could I—."

"Stop! Shut your dirty, lying mouth," Diké shouted. "Do you think that being an Osu has also deprived me of my intelligence? Do you think that I don't know every evil plot you have hatched? The only thing keeping you standing and breathing, is the fact that you had no hand in my affliction despite your stupid curse of The Shadow Crows."

"I can tell you who did it to you, our warrior," Dibia Okpoko rushed his words, the familiar glee returning briefly in his dark pupils. "It was the traitor's son, Emeka, together with his brothers. He approached Ọzo Agwọ a couple of days ago to inform him that he was responsible for placing you in the forbidden shrine and that he would act as a spy for the peer, since his friendship with your brother is still intact. He wanted the peer to elevate him with a title once he took over the kingship from the King."

"Ha! I knew the truth would come out eventually. I thought you said Ọzo Agwọ had no desire to wrestle power from my father? And yet, you've just confirmed that very plot with your own lips." Diké grabbed the witch doctor's thin arms and shook him violently. "Listen carefully, vile demon; I already know about Emeka. He's no different from his father. The same treacherous blood flows in their veins. Believe me, I have already made plans for him which will ensure he never reaps the fruits of his treachery."

"But, what about your brother, Feather-Feet?" Dibia Okpoko's voice was soft, his eyes, watchful, glinting with secret malice. For a brief second, Diké felt the strength drain from his limbs. The old anguish stabbed his body with countless, sharp cuts. *Ifekandu!* He didn't want to think of his brother, didn't want to be reminded of the greatest betrayal of his existence. Chicken-Legs said that she would swear on his innocence. Yet, here was the witch doctor confirming everything.

"Ifekandu is not your business and you shouldn't believe everything you hear from your useless friends," Diké said, watching the shocked look on the witch doctor's face with satisfaction.

"You... you knew?" Dibia Okpoko stuttered. "You knew that your brother worked with the traitor's son to ruin your life and you don't mind?"

"As I said, a snake can only spew lies and you should be more concerned about *your* life than my brother's. What my brother did or didn't do causes me no worries, since I know the truth," Diké said. "We have talked enough. Say your last prayers to your ancestors before you join them. I am eager to be done with you so I can focus on my other enemies."

He pulled the witch doctor, and dragged him towards the exit of the cave. Dibia Okpoko dropped to his knees, terror turning his eyes a teary black.

"Mercy, our warrior; mercy," his voice shook as violently as his body. "I swear on all the gods and ancestors that I'll never, ever again touch another woman in the ten villages and beyond. I'll even refrain from touching my wives as well. Tell me what to do and I'll do it, but please spare the life of this foolish old man who was misled by the evil spirits. If you want, I can prepare a special poison to end the life of Ọzọ Agwọ this very day. Yes! I will even end the life of his son and ensure your brother is initiated as the leader of the Ogwumii cult without delay. Great warrior, I beg you, spare my life and you'll own my loyalty till my dying day. I swear this to you by everything I hold sacred."

"Shut your filthy mouth. Your words have no truth and your honour is non-existent," Diké snarled.

He leaned low and yanked the dirty raffia bag from the witch doctor's shoulder. He didn't want the demon working some bad Juju on him while he thought through his options. Killing the man was out of the question, but Dibia Okpoko didn't know that, otherwise, he wouldn't be grovelling on the ground. Diké pulled Dibia Okpoko's loincloth from his waist, ignoring the man's loud protests. He tore it into strips and bound the witch doctor's limbs.

"You can't do this to me!" shrieked Dibia Okpoko. "I am the priest to the gods, Ọgu n'Udo's representative and the people's witch doctor. Untie me now, do you hear me? Have you no respect for your elders? Have you forgotten that you're now an Osu slave? Let me go and we'll forget about everything we talked about today and I'll say no more about it."

Diké laughed. He shocked himself with the sound of his own laughter, an alien sound to his ears since the day of his ghosting. Looking at the humongous organ jutting between the puny thighs of the furious witch doctor, the mirth shook his body as nothing had ever done in a long time—*No wonder the demon-man has become the terror of virgins and women in the village, with him labouring under the burden of such a fearsome cock!*

Diké was sure that Dibia Okpoko's organ was superior to his own in both length and width, despite the man's advanced years. His mind told him that this phenomenon had to be the work of supernatural Juju. Maybe, he might ask the witch doctor for the penis-growth potion afterwards, when he had him sufficiently cowered.

"Ha! You need to hear yourself to realise how foolish you sound," he mocked the witch doctor. "Clearly, your nakedness and the insult to your body matters more to you than your life. Now, I see the powerful burden you carry between your legs, I can well understand why you have become the sex-pest you are, although I can't for the life of my ancestors figure out why an old hag such as yourself should want to inflict such a massive cock on yourself. You are using *Juju* to grow your penis, aren't you?"

Dibia Okpoko's scowl was both thunderous and haughty.

"I have never used any charms on my cock. This fearsome rod is the core of my powers. It should prove to you that I am indeed touched by the sacred hands of our deities and that you should think twice before trifling with me and the might of my pride," he warned.

"Ha! You still think that you can brag your way out of my vengeance, you rogue?" Diké cursed. "Who was it that was just begging for their life, pledging eternal loyalty if I spared them and kept the truth from Ezeala? Yet, the breeze cools your naked arse and you start threatening me and reminding me of my slave status. I thought I was your warrior, eh? Yet, you just reminded me that I am an Osu. I was right in my original plan to dispatch you to your ancestors' realm and free our villages from the curse of your wretched existence. Thank your ancestors that I am not a woman otherwise, I would castrate you and feed that foul organ to the dogs."

"I spoke in haste, our warrior," the terror was back again in the witch doctor's goggled eyes. "Of course, you're our warrior; who else can dare wear your loincloth or weld your machetes? Phew! All flies! That's what they are; cattle flies who will be swiped aside by your mighty tail."

"Shut up and don't speak a word till I tell you to," Diké snarled. He exited the forbidden shrine and stalked towards the entrance of the shrine-grove. He shut his eyes and inhaled the cool dawn air—*Phew! He really didn't realise how much his breathing and his sanity are slowly being devoured by the forbidden shrine.*

The familiar clangs of the hanging skulls filled the air with their sad orchestra and Diké wanted to get away from them, march into his father's compound, drag out Ife and thrash him like a wayward dog. He had lied to himself and to Dibia Okpoko when he said he didn't care. His rage was still raw, and thinking of Ife brought a whirlpool of emotions. One minute, he groaned with despair and the next, cursed with fury. Other times, memories brought tears to his eyes and he wondered how it could have all gone so bad, how his life could've been so utterly ruined by the brother he'd loved beyond his own life.

Dibia Okpoko's knowledge of Ife's treachery was the worst of his humiliations—*What did he do, say, or failed to do, that can possibly explain how he's managed to lose his brother's love, and instigated his own doom?* Several sleepless nights had yielded no answers and

Chicken-Legs' advise to speak to Ife was fast becoming his only option—*But, how to get to the boy? How to see him, listen to him, talk to him without killing him?*

A sudden clap of thunder broke his ruminations. He glanced up and smiled. *Finally!* He had prayed for the rain for so long that he had started to doubt the soil would ever feel the wetness of a drizzle, much less a thunderstorm. But the skies were a darker shade of dawn, the blackness of a storm.

Diké flung the witch doctor's raffia bag against an Ngwu tree and pulled off his loincloth just as the first drop hit his skin. In seconds, the heavens opened wide to drench the earth with pelting rain. Diké rushed to the small clearing in the shrine-grove which wasn't shielded by the wide branches of the trees, the part where the rain poured through like a gushing waterfall. He raised his face to the sky, drinking the clean water even as he washed off the matted filth of a complete moon-cycle from his skin.

The rain was cool on his skin and his head. It seemed to wash out both the filth in his body and the sick in his mind. He washed his loincloth with gusto, squeezing, wringing and shaking until he could once again see the secret abstract symbols of the ancient Nsibidi writing of the Igbo community clear on the loincloth. And for the first time in a very long time, he felt clean again, almost like a normal, uncursed man.

Nineteen

—·—

THE REUNION

JUST AS DIKÉ finished securing the loincloth around his waist following his rain-shower, he heard his name called out in a soft voice, a female voice. *Chicken-Legs!* He glanced around the shrine-grove, searching for the ghost of the slave girl—*Why is she visiting him at this unusual hour? And why does she sound frightened, as if she's afraid of the shrine-grove that is after all, her abode?*

"Diké! Can you hear me?" The voice was louder this time and it wasn't Chicken-Legs' voice. It sounded strangely familiar, but was muffled by the downpour.

"Who is this? Why do you seek me here? Don't you know that women cannot enter the sacred shrine?" *Unless they're women brought in by the wretched witch doctor for wicked purposes.*

"It's me, Iruka. I need to speak with you."

"Big-Bosom!" Diké exclaimed, feeling the sudden racing of his heart—*What does the girl want? He should have known that only a girl such as Big-Bosom, reckless and fearless, would venture into the forbidden shrine to see him.*

Diké's heart warmed to her. Regardless of everything, she was the only person that had reached out to him

162

and treated him kindly since his ghosting. There was a saying amongst their people, that it takes a great wind to reveal the chicken's filthy anus hidden underneath its pretty feathers. His ruin had revealed to him his true friends and his enemies, thrown up surprises he would have never imagined possible. He had always thought Big-Bosom was only good for her amazing body, and would have never believed her capable of the sensitivity and loyalty she had shown him since his ruin—*But then, who would have ever thought that his own brother would weave his downfall?*

"Are you coming out or do I come in?" her voice was back to its usual impertinence.

"I am coming out," Diké said, rushing towards the entrance. "Keep your voice down or do you want the whole village to discover you speaking to an Osu?"

"Stuff the villagers and stop calling yourself an Osu."

He stepped through the thatched gate of the shrine-grove and raised a hand to wipe the rainwater from his face. He froze. His body started to tremble and his heart pounded so hard he thought it would explode.

"Ifekandu?" he wasn't sure if he spoke out the name. "Ifekandu! You!" his voice was a roar as he rushed towards his brother.

Big-Bosom pushed herself between them, holding him back, her grip unnaturally strong. He could have swiped her aside with one arm had his heart been in it, but he couldn't get himself to handle her with violence; he couldn't trust himself not to kill the brother he suddenly discovered he still loved despite everything.

"Our warrior, please hold your anger, you hear?" Big-Bosom urged Diké back into the shrine-grove and followed him in. Ife trudged in behind her, his head hung low, as if shielding his face from the pelting rain. Somehow, it didn't matter anymore that Big-Bosom was a woman entering the sacred grounds or that he was breaking the laws of the shrine. Staring at the petrified face of his brother amidst the early morning downpour, everything else paled into insignificance.

"You need to listen to Feather-Feet and hear his side of the story," Big-Bosom said loudly over the roar of the thunderstorm. "I know what I told you and I know you think we're both guilty of betraying you; but if you'll just listen to us, you'll learn the full truth of what happened to you that dreadful day. Afterwards, feel free to beat us up if you still want to," Big-Bosom reached behind her to grip Ife's hand in hers, holding him like a mother leading her son to the circumcision ritual.

In a blink, his anger dissipated just as quickly as it had risen. Seeing Ife's familiar helpless face and the terror in his eyes made him ashamed of his earlier fury. How many times had he seen that look in the boy's face when confronted by their father's rage? It always brought out every protective and loving emotion in his heart—*Amadioha! How he rues this day that now sees him bring that same terror to his little brother's eyes.*

"Ifekandu," Diké said wearily. He opened his arms wide. "Come and give your brother a hug."

"Womb-Brother!" Ife's voice was almost a sob as he rushed into Diké's arms and held him in a tight embrace, his body trembling. They were almost the same height, despite their different builds. The familiar feel of his brother's tall lankiness was a joy Diké never expected to experience again. A tight knot formed in his chest, rising to his throat till he thought he would cry out with the pain.

"Forgive me; please forgive me," Ife sobbed against his neck, his tears warm to the cool wetness of the rain. Diké smelled the strong reek of Palm-wine on his breath. "I didn't know what they planned. Emeka promised me... swore to me that he would treat you well and we would only keep you for a few days until our father forgot about my marriage to Nightingale Voice and I believed..."

"Nightingale Voice?" Diké cut in, his voice loud with incredulity. "What's she got to do with this?"

"Everything! It was all because of her," Ife said, pulling away from Diké's arms. He turned to Big-Bosom as if seeking her instructions. She nodded at him encouragingly. Ife turned back to Diké, his eyes shame-painted. "I overheard you and *Nna-anyi* discussing my abduction by the Ogwumii to forcefully marry me off to Nightingale Voice and I panicked."

"Oh my ancestors and our gods!" Diké groaned softly, reaching out to pull Ife close once again—*So, all his misfortunes have been because of the rice-brained beauty, Ada of the Nightingale Voice!*

Diké wanted to laugh, yet, he also wanted to cry. "Little brother; how angry and betrayed you must have felt. Surely, you must have known that I would never harm you, that regardless of anything our father said, your best interest would have always been my priority."

Ife shrugged. "I kept waiting for you to confide in me that night so that we'd talk it through, but you didn't say anything, and I didn't want you to know I overheard your conversation," Ife mumbled. "Emeka said that if we hid you in his hut for a few days, our father would be so busy looking for you that my marriage to Nightingale Voice would be the last thing on his mind. I just wanted to buy myself time to dance for a little while longer before tying myself to marriage and the farms. I would never have done it if I thought for an eye-blink that you would be in any danger. When I found out what Emeka and his brothers did, I just wanted to die. I swear to you Womb-Brother, shame and pain have been my constant shadows ever since that terrible day. *Amadioha* knows I will gratefully take your place here in a heartbeat if there's a way to exchange places."

Ife fell to his knees sobbing loudly, his arms wrapped around Diké's legs, resisting his brother's attempts to pull him up. "Womb-brother, my knees are on the floor begging your forgiveness and pledging my life to you."

"Please forgive him, our warrior," Big-Bosom said. "I was equally deceived by my brother. I too hated Feather-Feet, thinking he was to blame till I heard his story and knew that we'd all been victims of my brother's evil. I won't blame you if you hate me for what my brothers did to you. I deserve it, coming from the same womb as them; but, please, don't blame Feather-Feet. If there's one person that is blameless in all this, it's him. You know how much he adores you. It's just the Palm-wine working its evil in his head most of the time. He would never do anything to harm you. I can swear that."

"You and Chicken-Legs both," Diké said with a soft laugh, finally succeeding in pulling Ife from the muddy ground. "Rise, little brother. I bear you no malice or anger, not anymore. Are you not my brother, my Feather-Feet? Come; we must thank Big-Bosom for her wisdom and kindness. Without her, we would have both lived under this dark cloud of suspicion and hate while our enemies thrived."

He reached out an arm to Big-Bosom and pulled her close. Her body was tense against the unfamiliar closeness to him. Her magnificent breasts felt soft against his chest, and suddenly, Diké felt the long-forgotten stirring of his loins. He laughed, long and loud, holding tight to Big-Bosom, savouring her female softness and the reawakening of his manhood. The rain weakened into a drizzle once again as the skies began to shed their night clothes for the approaching dawn.

"You have to go now before anyone discovers you," Diké finally said, releasing them, his heart heavy with pain and regret.

"Surely there must be something we can do to undo this?" Ife said desperately, his eyes still swollen from his tears. "I'll tell our father everything now that I've spoken with you. Nothing matters except your freedom. Tell me what to do and I'll do it."

"Me too," Big-Bosom echoed. "Tell me what to do. We will do whatever you want to secure your freedom."

"I thank you two for your loyalty, but there is nothing anyone can do. My fate is doomed unless I can—" Diké paused. Images flashed in his head; nine powerful warriors inside a room with walls dripping blood. *Blood.* "I lie! Big-Bosom, there is something you can do for me. Yes indeed, you can do me a great favour that will keep me in your debt for the rest of my life."

"What is it, our warrior? Tell me quick,"

"I will, but first, you must leave at once and return again at dawn tomorrow so that I can tell you two a story, a vision I had here might yet be my salvation from this curse. Before I forget, can you both bring me some food as well? At least, enough to feed a three-wives household. I can do with something better than the muck that Dibia Okpoko serves me." Diké laughed. "Also, I would be grateful if you can bring me a lot of honey, enough to last me for a whole day at the very least. I can't stress how important it is that I have the honey, okay?" He turned to Big-Bosom. "Can I have a private talk with my brother before you leave?"

Big-Bosom nodded and walked towards the entrance of the shrine.

"Tell me, brother, how is our father? How is he coping with everything?" Diké asked, his voice low, urgent.

"He doesn't rage as bad as before," Ife said with a shrug. 'He was angry the first few days following your..." he broke off with another embarrassed shrug. "Anyway, these days, he just sits inside his house, refusing to speak to anyone except the clansmen he's instructed to investigate and discover the people responsible for your misfortune." Ife paused, shame flicking in his eyes. "They say that Ọzọ Agwọ's compound is now busier than the King's as everyone now goes to him for advice and assistance since his son became the leader of the Ogwumii. Our father is hoping that I'll be trained up to take on the role, but you know me; my feet are made for dancing rather than marching in battle. The King won't listen to reason and I fear Igwulube is fast despairing of ever making a warrior of me. How I wish you could speak sense into *Nna-anyi's* head!"

Diké swore angrily. "Listen, I heard about everything and I want you to tell our father to watch his back with that snake, Ọzọ Agwọ. I am sure he already knows who his enemies are, but I've found that Dibia Okpoko is working with that wretched peer against our father and I am taking care of the man here." Diké paused, wiping off the remnants of the rain from his face. When next he spoke, his voice was casual, a contrived disinterest that hid the turmoil in his heart. "By the way, how is Mgboye?"

Ife gave him a startled look which didn't hide the guilt in his eyes. "Your wife is well," Ife mumbled. Diké waited for him to continue but Ife was looking at the trees, the sky, the empty space above Diké's head and everything that wasn't Diké's eyes.

"But? Come; tell me all, little brother," Diké encouraged.

Ife shrugged, the familiar stress-frown furrowing his brows. "The king wants me to marry her now that you're, you know... anyway, I told Nna-anyi that I'll never touch your wife as a wife since you're alive despite what they say. I'm so sorry, Womb-Brother, for all the dishonour I've brought you. But for me and my shameful actions, you'd be with your wife right now,"

"And Mgboye, how does she feel about it all?"

Again, Diké saw the flicker of guilt in Ife's eyes. "She's not happy with me for refusing to marry her. She says that the ancestors might open her womb with me now that they've taken you away from her. She complains about me to everyone and accuses me of being selfish and irresponsible by refusing to do my duty by her, so she can provide sons for the clan. I know what our custom demands, Womb-Brother. I know I must honour you by protecting and providing for the people that are precious to you when you're dead. But you're not dead, heaven forbid. Despite all this vile Osu thing, you're not dead and I just can't... I just can't bring myself to touch Mgboye as a husband. I can't..." Ife wrung his hands so violently that Diké pulled them apart and held them tight.

"It is okay, little brother; you've done nothing wrong, nor have you dishonoured me by refusing to care for my wife. I understand your feelings. I would feel the same if our positions were reversed."

"Except you'd never betray me as I betrayed you," Ife mumbled. "You're too strong and fearless to resort to such cowardly acts as I did,"

"I told you not to talk about that again. Everyone can make mistakes, and in your case, you were manipulated by a devious snake whose venom can wipe out an entire clan. In the meantime, I must ask you to desist from the Palm-wine. Can you do that for me, please?" Ife nodded, his face wreathed with shame. "I know it's tough for you and that the burden of now being the first son of the King is heavy on your shoulders; but trust me when I say that very soon, you will be free of that burden. I believe I might have a way out of this curse."

"Womb-Brother, did I hear you right?" Ife cut in, his voice high with excitement. "Did you say that there's hope after all, that this evil might yet be undone?"

169

Diké nodded. "Yes, there's hope, although slim. As I said, I will tell you all tomorrow. But listen carefully, I have several things to ask of you and I need your head to be as clear as water for the next couple of days, understood?"

Ife nodded again and Diké was glad to see a spark of resolution in his eyes.

"I have another question for you." Ife raised startled eyes and Diké gave his hands a reassuring squeeze. "It's okay, it is nothing serious. I just wondered about our father's last wife. Is she with child yet?'"

"Our father's last wife?" Ife said slowly with a puzzled frown.

Diké nodded. He had never shown any interest in their father's wives or half-siblings and knew his question must seem strange to Ife.

"I guess she's okay. I know she's definitely not pregnant because she was sitting in the ash all yesterday, which means she must be having her monthly curse."

Diké's heart leapt. "Did you say she is sitting in the ash?" Ife nodded. "Then we have no time to lose. You must go to her and give her a message from me. Do not ask her any questions or ask me the meaning of my message. Tell her that she needs no longer fear the witch doctor, that her secret is safe with me. Then, tell her that I said she is to collect her menstrual blood for me in a jar and give it to you. She must never discuss anything with anybody or risk incurring my wrath. She will understand. You must bring the jar along with my two bronze machetes when next you visit and some salt as well, okay?"

Ife nodded, his eyes still clouded with confusion.

"There is another final task I need from you, more like your opinion about something. I think you are better at this kind of thing."

Diké paused, his eyes staring into the pale, silvery moon fading away from the grey dawn skies. "Okay, my question is this; if our great-ancestors were to show up today, what kind of present would you give them? What would be the most unusual and greatest gift that you would offer them? Think about it and give me your answer when we speak tomorrow."

"That is a very strange question; but I'll definitely give it a great deal of thought," Ife smiled.

"Thank you; now go and remember your promise to stay clear of the Palm-wine, all right? I don't think I need tell you to stay clear of Emeka this time?" Ife shook his head. "From what I gather, he's been boasting to Ọzọ Agwọ that your friendship is so tight he could spy against the king through you."

"The vile, bastard snake!" Ife's fury was one Diké had never witnessed. "I should've killed him and damned the consequences. I went to his house yesterday to kill him, but Big-Bosom was at home and I just couldn't kill her brother in her presence," Ife said. Diké was shocked to see the rage in his brother's normally mild face.

"Ifekandu, promise me you will never attempt such folly again," he said, gripping Ife's arms with claw-like strength. "That snake is mine to annihilate, not yours,"

"But it was me that was betrayed by him. I want to cut him into small pieces and feed him to the dogs," Ife protested.

"I understand your rage, but I am the one paying with my life for his treachery. Let me be the one to give him the death he deserves. Be patient, okay? Have faith that I will leave this place soon and bloody vengeance will be fed in a great bowl to that snake, okay?"

Ife nodded, slowly, reluctantly. "It'll be as you wish, Womb-Brother. Had I listened to your warnings all those years back, none of this would've happened. I have the brain-cell of an ant. Even ants are smarter than I am."

"Silly boy! Stop beating up yourself and start making your way home now. The sky is rapidly lightening. Go now and may your dreams always be free of the bad dreams, little brother," Diké mouthed the normal greeting despite knowing the futility of the blessing. The raging spirits of the shrine would never allow any citizen of the ten villages a peaceful night's sleep free of nightmares.

He hugged Ife once again before leading him back to Big-Bosom, where she stood looking around the shrine-grove and the hanging skulls with goggled eyes. Again, his eyes took in her magnificent body with appreciation. It was a pity her heart still hankered after his brother's own, otherwise he would have married her the minute he became a free man again. He took her hands in his own.

"Big-Bosom, I thank you once again from the depth of my heart for everything you've done. I will never forget your kindness, not till the day I join my ancestors in the final sleep," Diké said. He saw the shyness in Big-Bosom's eyes before the habitual attitude chased it away.

She gave a nervous laugh. and pulled her hands from his before grabbing Ife by the arm and dragging him away as if he were her troublesome son.

"Come, let's go," she said to Ife. "We'll see you tomorrow, our warrior, and I won't forget your food. Feather-Feet can bring the honey. It's too expensive for me to afford."

Diké watched them go, feeling lighter than he'd felt since the day he woke up a slave inside the forbidden shrine. Suddenly, there was hope. He knew his stepmother would provide the required menstrual blood and that Big-Bosom would bath him in it as instructed by Ikolobia in his vision. All he now needed to worry about was how to get Dibia Okpoko to work with him. The witch doctor loathed him with a passion that matched his own, but without his aid, his mission to the realm of the ancestors would be impossible.

TWENTY

— · —

THE SECRET BURIAL GROUND

"So, you're back," Dibia Okpoko said when Diké returned to the cave, his eyes red with anger. "I heard voices in the shrine-grove. Who dares visit you in this forbidden shrine?"

Diké smiled. "The voices you heard were the voices of my ancestors. They spoke to me in the thunder and left me a message in the rain. So, listen well; you have two choices. The first is that I obey my strong instinct to squeeze the life from your neck this instant and avenge my father's dishonour. The second is that I obey my ancestors and spare your life provided you give me the eyes and the heart of the slave girl, Chicken-Legs, without delay."

The witch doctor stared at Diké as if he had gone completely insane.

"You want the eyes and the heart of the slave girl? Did I just hear you right? Are you saying that someone wants the eyes and heart of the slave girl? And don't tell me it's your ancestors I heard. I wasn't born yesterday."

Diké shrugged. "Believe whatever you like. All I know is that I want the eyes and heart of the slave girl without delay. You can either give them to me and live, or refuse and die. The choice is yours. Personally, I hope you will refuse so that I can do what I've been itching to do to you for all the insults you've given me since my ghosting."

Diké saw the terror return to the witch doctor's eyes as his body began to tremble on the floor.

"I'll give you what you ask," Dibia Okpoko said. "You can have them for your ancestors or whoever wants it. They're inside my raffia bag you took."

Diké cursed, sprinting back to the shrine-grove. The raffia bag was still by the tree trunk, wet from the rain. He took it into the cave, shaking it gently to drain the muddy water that ran mixed with blood. Revulsion crawled over his body—*Chicken-Legs' bleeding eyes and heart! He's done it, found them as he promised!* Now Dibia Okpoko's hold on the girl would finally be broken and her restless ghost would be free to exact her vengeance on him and return to her ancestors' realm for a better reincarnation.

Upon his return, he found the witch doctor still on the ground, but he was facing the statue of Ọgu n'Udo, as if seeking the god's assistance.

"Here it is. Do you swear that Chicken-Legs' heart and eyes are inside this bag?" Diké asked, squatting low by the witch doctor.

"Yes, they're there, wrapped inside the Ede leaf. Look inside and you'll find the package."

Diké opened the bag wide and looked in. He immediately saw the brown package nestled amongst other fetish items of Dibia Okpoko's trade. His hands were unsteady as he reached inside the bag to retrieve it.

He touched the bundle and quickly withdrew his hand as if stung by a scorpion. He dropped the bag and stepped away, staring at it with stunned revulsion. The package was alive. It was also very hot, searing his fingers like open flames. He felt the package move against his palm, throbbing harder than any heart, animal's or human's. Diké looked at his fingers and they were red. The pain was excruciating, and he bit his lips to hold in the groan.

Dibia Okpoko laughed. His voice rang with the familiar mocking glee Diké had come to detest. In a blink, he grabbed the man's throat and squeezed so tight that the witch doctor started to choke. His bound legs jerked frantically and his hands beat desperately against his naked thighs. Diké increased the pressure, wanting nothing more than to rid the world of the vile worm struggling beneath him.

Dibia Okpoko eyes popped and the bulging red orbs suddenly cleared the red mist from Diké's eyes, returning sanity to his mind. With a loud curse, Diké let go and stood up, walking away from the witch doctor to take several deep, loud breaths. He didn't trust himself around the man.

"I'm warning you, don't push your luck, do you hear me? Otherwise, ancestors or no ancestors, your life will end in this shrine today," Diké snarled, his face like thunderclouds. The witch doctor nodded hurriedly, coughing in spasms. "Listen carefully and do exactly as I tell you. Since you have sealed the package to ensure no ordinary hands can touch them, I am going to untie you and you will lead me to where you disposed of Chicken-Legs' body. Then, you will bury her heart and her eyes with her and our business will be done. Be sure you go to the right grave and don't try any stupid tricks."

"No! No! That wasn't part of the deal. You only said to give *you* the heart and eyes of the slave girl and you would let me go. Nobody said anything about burying them with her body. I won't do it. I'm telling you now, I won't do it."

"That's fine by me then; our deal is off. You can die right now. I have the heart and eyes and have all the time in the world to find her corpse and bury them with her. Choose your death, demon; the blade or my hands?"

Dibia Okpoko began to howl, his face, tear-drenched. The sight filled Diké with deep satisfaction. He felt like a man that had bested his love rival for the village beauty's affections. It was just retribution for all the insults the wretched man had heaped on him since his incarceration.

"Either way, I'm a dead man," Dibia Okpoko sobbed. "If I do what you demand, then the slave girl's spirit will kill me. If I refuse, you'll kill me. I must decide which death is better— man's or ghost's. Still, ghost or no ghost, she's just a woman, a mere girl. I have never feared any woman in my life, and I'm not about to start now," Dibia Okpoko looked at Diké, his eyes icy orbs of flint. "Untie me and I'll lead you to her grave."

Diké stared at the man. He wasn't sure if he should admire the man's supreme arrogance or pity his monumental stupidity. Suddenly, he couldn't wait to release the wrath of Chicken-Legs' ghost on Dibia Okpoko's head.

Diké untied the witch doctor's legs. He didn't trust him with his hands unbound, not until he had dug up Chicken-Legs' corpse. Thankfully, she had mentioned where it was during one of their nightly conversations—the secret burial ground.

"Come, let's go," he said, glaring at the kneeling witch doctor.

"Cover my nakedness before I leave this place, I beg you," Dibia Okpoko said, avoiding Diké's eyes. Diké scowled at him before picking the various pieces of the torn loincloth from the floor. He wrapped them around the witch doctor's narrow hips, all the while glaring angrily at the man's humongous organ—*He doesn't care what Dibia Okpoko says. There's no way the man wasn't using Juju to grow his penis, the wretched cheat.*

"I need some items from inside my bag to prepare my body for the job," Dibia Okpoko said, nodding towards the raffia bag on the floor.

Diké glared at the bag, loath to touch it. He didn't trust it either in the witch doctor's possession. With a frown, he lifted it with his fingertips and tipped it over, emptying its contents on the floor.

"Tell me what you need, and I will give it to you," he said.

Dibia Okpoko mentioned some items—a jar of *Mmanu-Igbo* oil, *Nzu* sacred chalk, *Uli* ink and *Aku* nuts. Diké eyed the items scattered on the floor with distaste—*No way is he touching them and getting himself hexed by the man's witchery.*

Diké picked the sharp blade used for the shrine chickens and pressed the blade to Dibia Okpoko's neck.

"I'm going to free your hands so you can do what you have to do," he growled. "Try no tricks, do you hear? One false move and you are dead. Just remember that I've watched you enough times preparing yourself before each ritual. So, I know what to expect."

Dibia Okpoko nodded and sat on the floor, folding his legs underneath him. He mumbled some unintelligible words as he prepared his body with the charms. When he was done, he chewed some of the black *Aku* nuts and gave Diké a couple.

Diké shook his head and waved the nuts away. "Do you take me for a fool? I will not eat any poison you offer me."

"It's for your protection, you fool. You enter that accursed burial ground without protection and you'll be the one joining the ghosts there, not I. Eat." Dibia Okpoko tossed the nuts at Diké's feet before resuming his chants.

Diké stooped and picked them up. He would have to trust that the witch doctor wasn't lying. Diké slowly ate the nuts. He waited for something to happen, but he didn't feel any different.

Dibia Okpoko rose with tired movements. Dots of moisture dotted his forehead and his breathing was laborious. "You'd better collect the digging shovel by the chicken line."

Diké nodded and ushered him out. Once outside, the witch doctor led the way towards the rear of the forbidden shrine, a narrow path that meandered past wastelands and thickets till they finally arrived at the desolate and ravaged grounds.

Diké had heard about this terrible burial ground at the rear of the forbidden shrine. Dibia Okpoko and his forebearers were the only ones that could enter the burial place —such was the malevolence of the spirits that haunted the graveyard. No one could tell for certain the kind of corpses buried there, except that they weren't the normal evil dead discarded at Ajọ-ọfia. It was said that the bodies dumped at the burial ground were powerful corpses with the ability to wreak great supernatural harm on the living. Diké could only recall one such burial in his entire lifetime, the twin 'born-to-die' babies of the mad woman known as Cursed Mother—*and now, poor Chicken-Legs.* Diké shuddered.

A cold chill hung in the secret grounds despite the bright morning sun warming Diké's skin. The ground was muddy on his bare feet from the recent thunderstorm and his wet loincloth felt like icy bands around his hips. The silence was solid, like a black void. Nothing grew on the damp, red soil except raised mounds. He noticed that each of the mounds bore a formation of heavy rocks arranged in a uniform *Nsibidi* symbol he couldn't recognise. He guessed they were the supernatural chains binding the vengeful ghosts to their graves.

Two small mounds sprouted on the soil to his left. Diké shivered again, quickly averting his gaze. He suspected the graves belonged to the evil twins of the poor soul known as Cursed Mother. It was said that the tormented woman gave birth to the same set of doomed twins over and over, only for them to die in childhood and return again in a new pregnancy. The witch doctor had finally sterilised Cursed Mother's womb to ensure there would be no further rebirths of the evil twins now buried in the secret burial ground.

Diké returned his eyes to the narrow mound which Dibia Okpoko was staring at.

"This is the grave you seek," the witch doctor said, his voice revealing a slight tremor.

"You dig," Diké ordered, nodding towards the shovel that was on the ground.

"I'm too old to dig. You're a young warrior with the strength of ten men."

"Not on your miserable life, you old rogue," Diké cursed. "When you were squashing the village girls in lust, I bet you had the strength of ten warriors. When you murdered and buried Chicken-Legs here, I bet you had the strength of ten warriors. I will not do your filthy work for you, you demon. Now, dig!" He brought the menace back to his voice and his stance. "And make sure to put back her heart and eyes into her corpse or you can be sure your body will be joining hers inside the grave."

Dibia Okpoko hissed and picked the shovel, and with a loud groan began to dig. Diké plonked himself on the ground, ignoring the muddy landscape. He watched Dibia Okpoko digging, heaving and swearing in-between chanting some unknown liturgy.

Diké smiled. Somehow, the graveyard now seemed quite peaceful and calming, with the tortured moans of Dibia Okpoko ringing sweet music in his ears. Even the habitual chilly air seemed to have thawed a little under the blazing sun, enough to banish the goosepimples from his skin and the icy terror in his heart.

The fury broke the serenity in the grounds without warning, bringing shrieking winds and hard, wet dust from the rain-soaked soil. Damp missiles smashed into Diké's body, stinging painfully. The air howled with rage and discarnate voices shrieked terror from the whirlwind.

Diké stumbled to his feet and rushed towards Dibia Okpoko where he was sprawled by the shallow grave that barely sank the depth of a human arm.

"Dibia Okpoko, what's happening?" He pulled the witch doctor up, shouting into his ears as the shrieking winds stole his words.

"Get me away from this place. She's awake... sh-she walks," the witch doctor shrieked in the voice of a woman who wakes to find a snake in her bed.

Diké looked into the open grave and his blood curdled. For several heartbeats, he was frozen by mind-stealing terror, his eyes glued at the exhumed corpse of the slave girl. Yes, he had expected something to happen when the witch doctor returned the eyes and heart to their rightful places. But of all the fantastical thoughts his mind had conjured, nothing would have prepared him for the horror he now witnessed in the shallow grave.

The slave girl's decomposed corpse glared up at him with animated white eyeballs lolling inside their deep sockets. Nestled in the gaping hole between her shrivelled breasts was the pulsating red heart, throbbing with the strong vibrations of a massive leather drum. Bloated worms crawled all over the body, and the funk of putrid flesh brought the sudden heaves to his stomach.

Chicken Legs' body wasn't still like a corpse should be. It shook as if pulled by invisible hands, heaving and straining to rise from the soil that nursed its naked, worm-infested carcass.

Diké shouted and stumbled away, tripping on one of the heavy rocks that had formed the *Nsibidi* protective symbol on Chicken-Legs' grave. His heart pounding, he scrambled to his feet and saw Dibia Okpoko fleeing, his feet as nimble as a little boy's flight.

Diké cursed and gave chase, shouting the man's name. The witch doctor looked back and increased his speed. It was as if some powerful *Juju* had added supernatural wings to the witch doctor's feet. Just when it seemed that Dibia Okpoko might escape, Diké saw a hail of rock missiles rise from several grave-mounds and hurtle towards the medicine-man. He heard his screams as the rocks slammed into his back, sending him crashing to the ground.

Diké quickly caught up with him where he lay groaning on the ground, blood dripping from several cuts on his body and head. As he stooped to grab the witchdoctor, he heard a sound behind him, the shuffling and heavy footsteps of an injured warrior. Except he wasn't in a battleground and the only warrior in the place was himself.

Diké glanced back and wished he hadn't.

She walked! *Oh Amadioha save his soul!*

Clad in her naked rottenness, putrid flesh dripping damp earth and decayed skin, Chicken-Legs shuffled her determined path towards the fallen witch doctor. Her white eyes glowed with hate. Behind her, several more mounds heaved and exploded in a hail of red soil, spewing the bodies and skeletons of the five witch-sisters freed from their chained graves. They shuffled towards the Dibia Okpoko, their eyes blazing with the same hatred in Chicken Legs'.

Diké thought he had witnessed every horror there was to see in the shrine grove, but what was happening before his eyes was beyond human imagination. Dibia Okpoko's petrified screech drew his attention. The man's terror-filled eyes revealed what Diké already knew—Dibia Okpoko was a dead man savouring his last seconds of breath above the grave-soil. The risen bodies of the murdered women had no other purpose but to deliver torturous death to him. The corpses staggered towards them, menace oozing from every piece of rotten flesh. Diké averted his eyes from them, terror racing his heart and stealing his breath.

He reached out his hands in a beseeching motion to the slave girl.

"Chicken-Legs, my kind and caring friend, I beg you to listen to me," Diké said forcing himself to hold the freezing glare of the fearsome corpse despite his terror.

She looked through him without recognition as she bore down on them, the reek of decomposition strong in the air, almost gagging him.

Diké's heart sank—*He's failed to get through to her. All is lost.* Dibia Okpoko whimpered and Diké wanted to shout at him— *'look now at the mere woman, the mere girl you were prepared to confront, and tell me again you've never feared a woman in your life, you worm!'* Instead, he dropped to his knees, bowing his head low.

"Chicken-Legs, your warrior kneels before you. Save for the King, these knees have never touched the ground for any other mortal. But for you, wronged spirit, I humble myself and plead for your ears. Have I not kept my promise to you and brought you back your eyes and heart? I beg you good friend, and plead with your sisters for mercy; just for a little while. Let us chat as we have chatted all these nights and listen to the favour your warrior asks of you."

He heard Dibia Okpoko gasp.

"You have spoken to the slave girl inside the forbidden shrine all this while and never said?" his voice was as stunned as his eyes.

"Shut up if you want to live," Diké snarled. He didn't take his eyes off Chicken-Legs' corpse.

She stood two arms-length away, her head cocked as if listening to some distant call. Behind her, the advancing ghouls also paused, as if awaiting orders from their leader. Diké noticed the fury-winds had died out and the air was once again chilly, almost bringing the rattle to his teeth.

"Our warrior, I thank you for keeping your promise to me," Chicken-Legs finally spoke. "I now have my heart and my eyes and can finally see my killer in the light of day. My murdered sisters are also free and it is time for us to pay our dues to the wicked liar, so our souls may finally rest. Allow us to touch him, my warrior. Don't deny us this final peace, that we may return to our ancestors and earn a glorious reincarnation back into our clans."

Dibia Okpoko moaned, terror glazing his eyes.

"The spirits of the air, sky, and earth have heard your words and so it shall be. May your soul be reincarnated back as a great queen, blessed with all the sons you never had in this brief lifetime," Diké said, bowing his head low again to the corpse. "But, kind friend, you recall my dream? The one you said was a vision from my ancestors?" Diké paused, waiting for Chicken-Legs' reaction. She said nothing but didn't advance further. She just stared down at him, waiting. "I too have suffered a great injustice and my freedom lies in the realm of the dead."

"What is this you speak about?" the witch doctor hissed, but Diké ignored him.

"Chicken-Legs, you know that the only way I can embark on that fearsome journey is through Dibia

Okpoko's guidance. But we know him to be a liar, full of malice and pride. He will not help me unless you make him. So, I ask that you give me three days so that I can gather everything I need for the journey and make myself ready as instructed by my great-ancestors. You and your sisters will be his guard as he guides my soul to the realm of my ancestors and brings it back. Afterwards, he is yours to touch."

"Forgive!" Dibia Okpoko shouted, scrambling on all fours towards the corpse with tears streaming down his face. "I am a worm too vile for birds to eat; I am a bat, neither bird nor animal; I am a snake to be trampled underfoot; I am so unworthy that my life is of no consequence to a great spirit as you. Spare me your touch, mighty spirit; spare me your rage and I'll never smile at another woman in my life or even breathe in their presence. I beg you all, mercy, mercy."

Chicken-Leg's eyes flashed and the other ghouls hissed. Diké stood to his feet and began to back away slowly. He feared their anger might override his pleas and he might end up being a casualty of their vengeance. One never knew how soured the souls of the returned could be. Chicken-Leg's body had spent a full moon cycle underneath the grave-soil, which might have soured her soul, poisoning it with dangerous malevolence.

"Your request is big, and I'm in a hurry to join my ancestors," Chicken-Legs finally said, and Diké's heart fell. "But I owe you a debt, so that I don't carry it into my next reincarnation. I will do as you have requested. My sisters will wait for him in their graves till it is time. Three days it is, not a day longer."

"Thank you," Diké said, his heart soaring, but she was no longer looking at him. Instead, she stared down at Dibia Okpoko, observing him silently for several tense seconds as if he were no better than a bug. Diké observed the violent tremors that wracked the witch doctor's puny body with cold detachment, remembering the man's earlier brags.

Finally, Chicken-Legs addressed Dibia Okpoko, her voice, merciless, cold.

"Vile worm, you also have three days to put your house in order and prepare yourself to meet your ancestors," Chicken-Legs said. "You did not give me half a day to prepare myself, but you can thank our warrior for your luck. Henceforth, I shall be your shadow, day and night. I will be the first thing you see when you wake up and the last thing you see before you sleep—*if* you can sleep," her voice suddenly hardened. "You will do everything our warrior demands of you and do it with truth and efficiency, do you understand?"

Dibia Okpoko nodded as he whimpered.

"Should I see any falsehood in you, even the slightest hint of deceit, I shall clean the floor of your hut with the blood of your sons, till the last bloodline of your house ceases to exist. Then, I will touch you; and you will wish that your accursed foetus was aborted by your mother."

Dibia Okpoko was a quaking, bundle of piss-coated insanity. Diké smelled the stench of his terror-piss as strongly as the slave girl's putrid corpse. His heart throbbed with relief and exhilaration—*Amadioha be praised! It is as he thought! Everything is linked by destiny. Finally, his day is about to come!*

Behind Chicken Legs' corpse, Diké saw the five ghouls turn and shamble back towards their open graves, accompanied by the fury-winds which rose again like a curse sent from the deepest realm of the grudge-hag herself, *Ikuku-Muọ.*

TWENTY-ONE

— • —

THE PREPARATION

IFE WAITED FOR Big-Bosom under the Bat-Tree before the rooster crowed in the dawn. Above him, the colony of bats that claimed the tree as their home roosted, squirming and fluttering as they jostled for sleeping space on the thick branches of the giant Iroko tree. His heart raced with excitement just as it had done since his meeting with Diké the previous evening. He hadn't stopped smiling since, and had even executed several dance steps inside his hut. The heavy darkness that had clouded his mind was now a distant memory and the new day filled him with hope and happiness.

Diké's bronze machetes weighed heavy in his grip while the small, sealed jar his stepmother had left outside his hut felt warm to the touch. Knowing the contents brought a wrinkle of distaste to his nose—*He'll make Big-Bosom carry it for him when she arrives.*

Ife recalled the stunned look on his stepmother's face when he relayed Diké's message to her. Initially, she had been angry with him for invading the intimate privacy of her ash pile where the menstrual blood flowed into the ash in an odourless and clean process. Custom dictated that women sat on the ash pile for the duration of their monthly curse. No man was allowed into the ash

187

room, and Ife had felt like a child catching his parents in a love tangle when he'd snuck into the room to see his stepmother. By the time he finished speaking, his stepmother's anger had turned into gut-wrenching sobs that seemed to go on forever till Ife started to panic. He almost didn't ask her for the blood as Diké had instructed, but in the end, it had been the easiest part of his mission.

His stepmother had looked at him strangely, and nodded.

"The jar will be outside your hut before dawn," she had said, not meeting his eyes. "Thank our warrior for me when you see him. Tell him I'm making daily sacrifices to our ancestors and the deities to bring him back to us. We await the glorious day of his return with impatience and faith."

Now he couldn't wait to give the jar to Diké and receive his smile of approval. It felt wonderful to be in his brother's good thoughts again.

"Feather-Feet," Big-Bosom's hushed whisper followed the soft touch of her fingers on his shoulder. He turned and smiled at her, though he doubted she read his face in the darkness.

"You're early," he said. "I couldn't sleep either. Do you have everything?" He saw her nod, the dark dawn making visibility almost impossible.

"Yes, I got lots of honey. I told you that you gave me too much money. I have some change for you."

"Keep it. You deserve more after everything you've done for me."

"Don't be silly. I just wanted to do right by Diké after what my brothers did to him."

"You're not to blame for your brothers' actions. You're nothing like them even though you share the same bloodline." Ife gently squeezed her arm.

188

"It was me that took your message, remember? If I hadn't told Emeka that the Palmwine was ready as you told me, then none of this would've happened," Big-Bosom lifted the large clay pot from her head and placed it on the ground. "Anyway, the important thing is that we get Diké everything he needs so he can get out from that horrid place. You did say he told you there might be a chance of that happening?"

Ife nodded. "Yes; he said he'll tell me everything today. Come, let's start while the village still sleeps. We don't want anyone seeing us and finding out our business,"

"Tell that to my wretched brother. You know he banned me from leaving the house for several days after the first time I spoke with Diké. So, I've been carrying this empty water pot each time I leave our hamlet, so I can go straight to the stream afterwards and cover my track."

"Big-Bosom, you're a very brave and kind girl," Ife said, his voice soft. "You've taken so many risks for my brother and I, and I just want you to know that I think you're wonderful,"

"Huh! Finally, he notices," Big-Bosom mocked with a small laugh.

Ife didn't join in her laughter. He was silent for several seconds. He felt his heart thudding as he prepared the words in his head. When he spoke, his voice was low, hesitant.

"Big-Bosom, you and I have been friends for a long time, haven't we?"

"I guess—why?"

Ife shrugged. "Just that I'm wondering if you still like me as before?"

"Why do you ask?"

"Well, you know my father wants me to marry a wife? I was wondering if you would like to marry me?"

189

There; he's said it. Ife had thought about it all night and he felt this was the only way he could reward Big-Bosom for her incredible kindness. He would've never reconciled with his brother if it wasn't for her.

"No, I don't want to marry you."

Ife shook his head, not sure he heard right. "Sorry, my mind was far away. I was asking if you'd like to be my wife so I can place a bowl of assorted meats and Palmwine outside your brother's hut, so he knows my intentions are honourable?"

"I said no; didn't you hear me?" Big-Bosom sounded impatient. "I don't like you that way anymore."

Ife wasn't sure if the sudden thudding in his heart was from shock or relief—*She didn't want to marry him! She doesn't want to marry him?* "Big-Bosom, when did you stop liking me? Is it because of what I did to my brother? I thought I explained everything to you and you understood. What have I done to earn your dislike?"

"You haven't done anything, and I don't dislike you. How can anyone dislike Feather-Feet?" she laughed, shoving him playfully. "Listen, I know I used to like you and wanted to marry you more than anything, but I don't feel like that anymore."

"Big-Bosom, we're talking of a time-frame of days, not moons," Ife said. Her words stung him despite the fact he didn't really want to marry her or any other woman. "Up to the time Diké became ghosted, you still liked me. I think I'm right, that you still blame me in your heart despite everything you say."

"Feather-Feet, let's not stay here arguing, okay? Let's just get to the shrine before the sun wakes up. Later, we can talk about it if you like, but I'm warning you now, my answer will be the same. I'll not marry you," she stooped and picked up the water pot containing the honey and placed it on her head.

Ife scowled and thrust the small jar in his hand at her. "Here, put that inside your pot."

"Why? Why can't you carry it?" she asked. "It's not as if it's heavy. I'm already carrying several jars of honey inside this pot, not to mention Diké's food which I stayed up last night to cook. Carry the jar yourself,"

"I can't," Ife's voice sounded pained. Big-Bosom paused and peered into his eyes.

"Why? What's in it?" suspicion coated her voice.

"Menstrual blood," he was almost inaudible.

"What?" Big-Bosom shouted. "I swear, this man will kill me one day!" She lowered her voice, looking around nervously in case she'd been heard. "What in the ancestors' names are you doing with menstrual blood? What shameless woman gave you her blood? Tell me, whose blood is it?" Big-Bosom shuddered. "Actually, I don't want to know." She snatched the jar from his hand, chucking it into the water pot balanced precariously on her head. "*Chei!* I swear, there's nothing my ears haven't heard from this crazy man! Huh!"

"Shush, Big-Bosom; shut your big mouth, you hear?" Ife cursed angrily. "You always think the worst of me these days. I got it for Diké. I told you he's found a way to free himself from the curse. This blood is one of the items he requires for the ritual. My stepmother was kind enough to give me her blood. In fact, now I think about it, I should have asked you for yours."

"You can forget it. I won't give you my menstrual blood, not for all the meat in the world. Come; let's go before I lose my courage. That walk-path of human bones really gives me the creeps. I swear, if not for Diké, nothing in this world would make me walk that path."

Ife glanced at Big-Bosom and quickly looked away. He thought he heard a possessive tone in her voice when she mentioned his brother's name—*Amadioha! Could it be that Big-Bosom likes Diké?* He didn't know why the thought surprised him. She wouldn't be the first woman to fall for his brother's virile good looks and deep, calm voice. Still, he felt somewhat peeved by the idea, as if someone had taken his favourite loincloth without his permission—*Women! Why do they have to be so complicated? One second, they want to marry you and the next, they want to marry your brother or an obese peer old enough to be their father. Huh!*

Ife scowled at Big-Bosom. She didn't seem to notice his frown. He doubted if she'd even care if she noticed—*Fickle girl! Maybe he should rile her, say something derogatory about her breasts, something to get her notorious temper going. That'll teach her to go trifling with a man's heart, the tease.*

Ife smiled. The dance was back in his steps he followed Big-Bosom towards the shrine-grove.

From the corner of his eyes, Ife saw Big-Bosom loitering by the entrance to the shrine as Diké raged. He knew that she was terrified of the hanging skulls on the trees, despite the indifference on her face. Sudden admiration sparked in his heart—*If only he has just a tiny bit of Big-Bosom's fearless spirit!*

"Absolutely not! Put that idea out of your head." Diké's face was as thunderous as his voice and Ife forced himself to hold his glare with steady eyes, despite the quake in his heart.

"Womb-Brother, I've thought this through, believe me. I don't make this decision easily or in jest. My head is clear of Palmwine and my thoughts are as steady as a king's," Ife held Diké's hands tightly. "I've listened to everything you've said, and I agree with Chicken-Legs that this is no dream but a vision. What you saw was real. If a ghost tells you that you've been visited by ghosts, then you must believe it to be true. Think about this; everyone says that I'm the reincarnate of Mgbada, the greatest dancer in the history of the ten villages. His legend has lived through endless generations and the elders say that until they saw me dance as a boy, and consulted with the oracles, they never believed they would live to see the reincarnation of Mgbada. Do I lie?"

Diké shook his head. "That doesn't mean that I'm going to let you offer yourself as my gift to The Old Ones. You are my little brother and our father has already lost one son. I cannot risk costing him the heir he has left. More importantly, the journey to the realm of the ancestors is an arduous one. I quake at the prospect of it and I'm a warrior. I will have to die the death-sleep of the black herb, go through the three deaths of earth, water, and fire before The Old Ones will grant me entry into their realm," Diké paused and looked at Ife, his gaze gentle, weary. "Little brother, how can I put you through that ordeal when I'm not sure that I'll come out of it alive?" Diké shook his head. "No; I thank you for your love and generosity, but this is one time that I will refuse your gift."

"And this is one time that your will can't suppress my own!" Ife argued. "You've always faced life like the warrior you were born to be. You fight everyone's battle, yet nobody fights for you. For once in your life, brother, I need you to accept that you can't face the Death-Lord alone. You weren't born to die alone when you have a brother that can hold your hand when death comes for you. In this your hour of need, let me be the lamp you'll hold to guide you through the darkness of peril."

"No Ifekandu; I'm sorry good brother, but I can't accept your offer."

"And my mind is just as resolute as yours," Ife said. "The Old Ones won't refuse the thrill of the Igede drums or the famed River-dance of Feather-Feet, the reincarnate of Mgbada. It's a treat they haven't experienced in their dead realm for eternity. I'll dance the greatest dance of my life for the dead, brother. My feet shall fly beyond the flight of the eagle, and my body will bend with the flexibility of a snake. It will be a dance to end all dances, one that will live in the memories of The Old Ones and the ancestors for all eternity. I don't say this in boast. I know what my feet can do; I know what the drums can do to my body. I will be your gift to the dead. Come; let's end this argument now and begin our preparations for our journey."

Ife waited, watching Diké fight his words.

Coward! He mocked himself silently. *See how tough you're sounding when you're quaking inside, ready to piss on your loincloths.* He didn't want to die the three deaths of the black herb, whatever that meant. He didn't want to die any death for that matter, but something strong in his heart told him that the choice he made was the right one, that his hand was the one his brother needed to hold when he entered the realm of the dead.

According to Diké, the witch doctor had confirmed that the process would last less than a full day in human timeframe, even though it would seem a full moon-cycle in the realm of the ancestors. Ife doubted if their father would miss his absence, not with the matter of Diké's enslavement and Ọzọ Agwọ's encroaching influence eating into the king's peace—*Not that he gives an ant's fart anyway.*

"I have no words to thank you, little brother." Diké hugged him in a tight embrace and when he released him, Ife saw tears in his eyes. He could count the times he had seen Diké cry in less than one hand. It was proof he had made the right choice after all.

"Don't thank me," he said, clearing the sudden hoarseness in his voice. "I made this mess, so let me help clean it up. Come, Big-Bosom grows impatient with us and you'll need her to bathe you now, you lucky man." He forced a laugh.

Ife didn't know what was wrong with him. Ever since Big-Bosom told him she no longer wanted to marry him, his heart had a burning desire to win her back. But he'd seen the way her eyes lit up when she saw Diké as soon as they entered the shrine, the way her breasts rose and fell as she spoke to him, the unfamiliar coyness in her smile and softness in her voice. He had also noticed the special care she had taken with her appearance, adding dark eye-ink to emphasis her large eyes and wearing a flamboyant rainbow-coloured raffia skirt he'd never seen before. Even worse, she'd happily agreed to bathe Diké in the menstrual water despite all the fuss she had made about having to carry another woman's blood; *the little hypocrite.*

Ife sighed. It was his fault. He'd dallied too long and ruined his chances with her.

Big-Bosom waved an impatient hand and Ife turned to Diké.

"Just a thought; do you think I'll also need Big-Bosom to wash me in the water for the journey?" he asked.

"I do not think so, since you're not an Osu who requires cleansing," Diké said.

"Sounds good to me," Ife said. "I don't fancy bathing in stepmother's menstrual blood, yuk!"

Diké laughed. "Not even for the thrill of having Big-Bosom wash your body?"

Ife shook his head. "She's all yours. Something tells me that she prefers running her hands over your muscled body than on my bony carcass, anyway."

"Idiot," Diké laughed again. The sound of his laughter was like nectar to Ife's ears. The difference between the Diké he'd seen yesterday and the one who now laughed with carefree joy was unbelievable. Suddenly, he found that he didn't quite mind about Big-Bosom washing Diké as much as he'd done before, and his laugher was soon as joyful as Diké's own

TWENTY-TWO

–·–

A MAN'S PRIDE

THE SUN WAS starting to give way to the moon when Ife and Big-Bosom finally allowed themselves to be chased away from the shrine-grove by Diké. As they walked towards the village, each lost in their own thoughts, Ife found his mind reminiscing over everything that had happened on what he considered the happiest day of his life.

From the instant Big-Bosom laid her hands on Diké's body as she bathed him in the cool water mixed with salt and menstrual blood, Ife had known that his days of fleeing her unwanted attentions were truly over. They were like two lovers discovering each other after a protracted separation. At one point, Diké had given Ife a quizzical look, silently seeking his permission. Ife had smiled and winked his approval, reassuring Diké with a thumbs-up that he was free to follow up on the amorous signals Big-Bosom had been giving him all day.

"After all, I should've known the girl will end up in our clan one way or another, what with your fixation on her impressive breasts," Ife teased, dodging Diké's playful fist.

The three of them chatted and laughed throughout the day, oblivious to the dire realities of their lives, determined to grab every morsel of happiness with greedy desperation. At a point, Ife even danced while Big-Bosom sang. Her voice was surprisingly melodious and almost rivalled Ada of the Nightingale's Voice in range and purity. Diké was thrilled by the discovery and urged Big-Bosom to sing more songs for him. The look in his eyes as he watched her sing convinced Ife that he was looking at his future sister-in-law should they make it through their terrible journey the next day and return with their lives and sanity intact.

"I'm guessing you won't bother filling your pot with water tonight since no one goes to the stream at night?" Ife said, his voice tinged with amusement. They were now halfway to the Bat-Tree, their rendezvous spot. Big-Bosom hissed. A full water pot was supposed to be her alibi.

"What's the use? By noon when I didn't return to feed my brothers, Emeka would have been planning my murder. I decided if I was going to get thrashed, I might as well make it worth the pain and know I've earned it. I would have spent the night at the shrine-grove if Diké had agreed."

Ife felt hot rage rise once more inside him, both against himself and Emeka. He had known the bastard hit his sister, but never realised the abuse was this extreme. Seeing Big-Bosom's reaction, her reluctance to return alone, filled his heart with sudden resolve—*This time, he'll be damned if he stands aside and feigns blindness; not anymore.*

"Do you want me to follow you home so Emeka doesn't beat you in my presence?"

"Would you?" she asked desperately.

Ife nodded and held her hand. It trembled, just like the body of a terrified puppy.

"With pleasure. Let's go through our compound first," he said, veering towards the left, the path that led to the

King's compound. "I need to get something that belongs to Emeka. I might as well hand it over to him when I get to your house since I'm not sure how things will go tomorrow."

Big-Bosom gripped his arm tightly. "Feather-Feet, are you sure you want to go through with it?" her voice was low, hushed. "I'm worried about you. You're a dancer. Let's leave it to the warriors and witch doctors. We can still come up with a different gift for Diké if we put our heads together. Honestly, it'll kill me if anything happens to you. It's not too late yet. What d'you say?"

"I say you allow us men to do men's work while you focus on women's chores," he pulled her long braids playfully. "Don't worry, okay? I'll be all right and will return to see you and Diké fill our hamlet with your children,"

"Idiot," she thumped his shoulder hard and laughed when he groaned. When next she spoke, her voice was small. "Do you mind, you know, about me and Diké?"

Ife laughed. "Of course, I mind," he said, feigning dejection. "After all, I've been the sun of your days and the moon of your nights for as long as I can remember. To see you making the eyes at my brother is a knife in my chest," he put his hands on his chest and staggered. It took her a moment to cotton on and she aimed a kick at him, which he dodged with a merry laugh.

"Just you wait till I become your sister," she warned. "I'll make you dance the women's dance for your punishment." She paused. "Feather-Feet, do you think Mgboye will be kind to me as her sister-wife?" Her eyes wore anxiety, but there was also a steely resolve in their brown depths. Ife didn't think Mgboye's good or bad thoughts would affect anything or prevent Big-Bosom from becoming Diké's second wife.

"Mgboye will be fine," Ife lied, not wanting to spoil her joy. His brother's wife was a shrew who had perfected the art of crying while killing a man. Any other woman in her shoes would've since married a second wife for her husband to ensure the bloodline didn't die out. That's what a good and caring wife did.

But not Mgboye. If she couldn't have a child for Diké, she was determined no other woman would. Each time Ezeala suggested Diké take a second wife, Mgboye would wail and moan for days till Diké gave in and abandoned the idea—*Yet, see how eagerly she'd pursued a marriage between them following Diké's enslavement.* Ife shook his head. He didn't doubt the woman would make Big-Bosom's life miserable if she was allowed, but something told him Mgboye had finally met her match in Big-Bosom.

Ife kept Big-Bosom waiting outside his hut while he dashed in and retrieved his knife. As before, he tucked it into his loincloth before leaving the hut. His heart was beating and his hands shaking. He prayed Emeka wouldn't give him cause to use the knife. After everything that had happened between them, he couldn't trust himself in the man's company without some form of protection.

He craved for some Palm-wine, just a mug to calm his nerves. All day, he'd felt the intermittent trembling of his body as he struggled against the headache and confusion that plagued his mind. Thankfully, Diké had been too engrossed with Big-Bosom to notice his state, otherwise, he would've insisted they abandon the plan.

Ife groaned and leaned his head briefly against his wall—*He must stay focused. After tomorrow, he intended to drink nonstop for four market days in a row.*

"I'm done; come, let's get you home in one piece," he said, taking Big-Bosom's hand as he led her out of the compound.

The full moon lit up their path as they walked in tense silence towards Big-Bosom's compound. It wasn't

199

a silence of peace, more an exercise in fear on her part and panicked adrenalin on his. As they drew closer to her hamlet, Big-Bosom's legs dragged the more, while Ife's heart raced faster than an antelope fleeing a lion's claws.

They spied Emeka standing arms akimbo at the entrance to his hamlet. He saw them the same time that they saw him. He started to run towards them, his voice raised in fury. In the light of the full moon, Ife saw the madness in his eyes. Emeka's fists were already raised in menace even before he got to them. Big-Bosom made a small whimper and ran behind Ife, shielding from her brother's fists.

"*Mbarama! Whore!*" Emeka shrieked, lunging at Ife in a bid to drag Big-Bosom away from him.

Ife pushed him hard and watched with satisfaction as Emeka stumbled. He fell to the ground and grazed an elbow. Emeka roared and scrambled to his feet, his eyes burning a red rage now directed at Ife.

"You drunken, useless weakling! How dare you defile my sister with impunity? You think because your father is the King it gives you the right to insult my honour? Let me tell you, your father's days as King are like dwarves. In a very short while, Ozo Agwo will become the King and I'll be a member of his closest cabinet. Then we'll see who has more power in the ten villages."

Emeka rushed at him again and they clashed. Ife was the taller by several fingers but Emeka's bones were stronger, honed by years of brawling and grueling farm work. Emeka's words filled Ife with rage, a reminder of the treacherous heart of the man he'd once called his brother-friend.

Ife fought Emeka like the enemy he had become, throwing his weight behind every punch. Big-Bosom cried as she tried to separate them, her voice loud in the still night.

"Emeka, please stop! Ife didn't defile me. We haven't done anything wrong, I swear in our late father's name," she tugged frantically at her brother's arm, trying to break up the fight.

Ife saw two figures run out of the hamlet, Emeka's two brothers. He knew he was outnumbered, that they would inflict great damage on his person before the rest of the villagers came to his assistance. He hit Emeka with a flurry of punches, hoping to knock him out and contend with two adversaries instead of three. But, Emeka clasped his legs as he fell, sending Ife crashing on top of him.

In a blink, Ife felt the weight of Emeka's brothers on his back. He heard Big-Bosom howl as one of her brothers punched her face when she tried to pull him off. She started screaming to the villagers to come and assist Feather-Feet, that he was being attacked unjustly. Ife's heart warmed towards her, even as he fought to escape her brothers' brutal fists.

Suddenly, he screamed as a hand reached into his loincloth and grabbed his organ, yanking it with fury, intent on separating him from his pride. The pain was a fire in his groin, an agony beyond anything Ife had ever experienced. A wave of dizziness almost sent him into unconsciousness. He reached down to separate the hand, but his own hand encountered metal, the bronze hilt of his knife lodged inside his loincloth. Relief washed over him—*He'd forgotten he had it!*

Ife pulled the blade out and stabbed the hand that was holding him, the treacherous male hand that would ruin the pride of a fellow man. He heard a scream and stabbed again, over and over till his hand was wet with blood and the screaming underneath him died. The fists pounding his body were now frantic hands trying to pull him off the person underneath him. He allowed them

201

to drag him away. He collapsed on the hard ground, clutching his groin and howling with pain.

Under the lights of several lanterns, he saw Big-Bosom amongst the gathered villagers attempting to break up the melee. Her face was wet with tears as she ran to Ife and raised his head with her arm, wiping the sweat from his face. He raised his hand to hers and smeared her with blood.

She screamed when she saw the blood and let go and his head hit the ground hard. Ife groaned and her brothers shrieked on seeing Emeka's bloodied body. The crowd gasped, then howled. Pandemonium ensued. Trampling feet and jostling bodies merged with screaming voices and wailing keens. Ife's head was exploding, his heart pushing hard against his chest. Their screams filled his ears with words that sealed his doom.

"Emeka is dead! Feather-Feet has murdered our brother! Murderer! Our ancestors come to our aid! Murder! Murderer!"

Ife heard the howls of Emeka's brothers with horror. He struggled to his feet, shoving his way through the crowd with blind panic. He dropped the bloodied knife and started running, fleeing from the scene of his crime. In the moon-lit night, his feet took him to a direction he recognised, the bone-littered path that led to the shrine-grove.

Ife stumbled into the shrine-grove and screamed, "Dike!" before collapsing on the dusty ground sobbing, his body trembling violently—*He's a murderer, ancestors have mercy! He has spilled human blood! He's now surely as cursed as Diké, destined for a grave in Ajo-Ofia once he's tried and convicted!* His chest heaved so hard every part of his body hurt. By the time both Diké and Dibia Okpoko ran into the shrine-grove, accompanied by the shambling corpse of

Theresa Chicken-Legs, Ife had given in to the dark void of unconsciousness.

TWENTY-THREE

—·—

THE DEPARTURE

DIBIA OKPOKO OFFERED Diké the bowl of crushed black herb, his hands trembling. By his side, the loose eyeballs of Chicken-Legs' corpse-ghoul followed his every movement with chilling intensity. They were outside the forbidden shrine, as the witch doctor had explained that Ife would become an Osu as well should he enter that terrible cave.

Diké took a handful of the dry herbs, his hand shaking as badly as the witch doctor's. He had never seen black-coloured leaves and had no idea what to expect once he ate the strange-coloured herb that smelled like burnt fruits and rotten flesh—*or perhaps, it's the decomposed corpse of Chicken-Legs that he smells.* The slave-girl had been true to her promise and had shadowed the witch doctor with malevolent grit, keeping just enough distance between them to ensure they never touched. Diké didn't know what would happen when their bodies finally made contact except that it was something bad, something so ghastly that it'd kept Dibia Okpoko in a permanent state of quaking terror. Her presence gave Diké the confidence to embark on his unknown journey, knowing a fearsome sentinel guarded his vulnerable body from the witch doctor's malice.

By his side, Ife sat trembling, still in the catatonic shock that had followed him into the shrine-grove the previous night. The boy had killed Emeka. Diké was still stunned by the news that his arch enemy was dead, and that the killer was none other than his harmless little brother, who had never killed a chicken in his life. But then, anyone that tampered with a man's pride should be ready to face the consequences—*Surely only a desperate woman or a despicable and cowardly man would dishonour the bonds of brotherhood and strike a man at the crest of his pride —his manhood. Emeka deserves the violent death he suffered and more. In Ife's shoes, he would have gone further and separated Emeka's treacherous hands and head from his puny body.*

Diké had tried to tell Ife that he did the right thing, that he didn't need to worry about being cursed by the ancestors for the crime, or being punished by the village elders either.

"But what about Big-Bosom?" Ife wailed. "She'll never forgive me; never! Why am I so useless? I always make a mess of everything. Oh, my ancestors! Womb-Brother, I've ruined things for you once again. Forgive me, please. I promise I'll make up for this when we get to the land of the ancestors. How soon can we go? I need to get out of this place without delay."

"Don't be silly; you haven't ruined anything for anyone," Diké held his hands tightly. "Listen; Big-Bosom does not hate you; I promise. She's not as air-headed as people think, despite her stubbornness. If she's the woman I know her to be, she'll stand with us through drought and battle. As for our journey, we will travel once Dibia Okpoko completes the ritual. Don't be in a hurry to get away from our world, brother, not when we have no idea what awaits us in the other realm," Diké worried that Ife now saw the impending journey to the realm of the ancestors as an escape from his troubles and feared that the burden may prove too great for his frail mind.

Dibia Okpoko looked ready to send them on their way, wiping his hands on his tattered loincloths. He glanced fearfully once again at Chicken Legs' hovering corpse before addressing Diké directly.

"When you eat the sacred black herb, you'll become drowsy and fall into a death-sleep," Dibia Okpoko's quivering voice broke into Diké's thoughts. He returned his attention to the handful of dry herbs he clutched. "Your blood will freeze inside your body and you will become still like a true corpse. Even your heartbeat will still."

Diké nodded and Ife looked petrified. He clutched the leather-bound drum he had borrowed from Dibia Okpoko like a lifeline, his breathing shallow and fast. Diké knew the sight of Chicken-Legs' corpse was still a terror the boy struggled to conquer. Despite everything he'd told Ife about the ghost girl, seeing her in the rotten flesh had proved too much for Ife. He had collapsed at the shrine-grove and lost consciousness for a brief period before Dibia Okpoko finally resuscitated him. It was only when Chicken-Legs called him by name, Feather-Feet, and spoke to him in the familiar gentle tones he remembered, that Ife finally calmed. Still, Diké noticed that he avoided looking directly at the fearsome corpse that hovered over the witch doctor like a giant bird of prey, poisoning the air with the stench of death.

"What happens next after we fall into the death-sleep?" Diké asked.

"Feather-Feet will go straight into the realm of the ancestors to embrace his destiny. It will be a painless and easy journey for him. As for you, the journey is different, tougher. You are now an *Osu* and will need cleansing to be granted entry into the realm of The Old Ones. You will need to prove your worthiness by enduring the three deaths of earth, water and fire."

Dibia Okpoko paused, his small eyes calculating, watching Diké's face for his reaction. Diké waited with terse attention, shrouding his face in cool neutrality. He was glad Ife's experience would be an easy one. It was one less worry for him.

"You will enter The Empty Realm and meet enemies from your past, people you have killed in the battle front. Some of them are good men with strong *Chi* and great ancestors," Dibia Okpoko continued, a sulky tone in his voice. "You will become their destiny, their redemption and reward for the good lives they led before your machete felled them in the battleground. You'll also meet some bad ones, people whose evils have followed them into their dead world. All these men will fight you in The Empty Realm. You have your two bronze Machetes with you to defend yourself against them. Some of them will fall to you for a second time. Those ones are not yet ready for a reincarnation. However, you will meet the ones who are worthy and ready, and they will kill you. You will die, our warrior; you will die. From my end, I cannot tell if or when you've earned the right to enter the realm of the ancestors. If by dawn tomorrow you do not awaken, then I'll know that your souls did not survive the journey and I'll tell the King that his house is dead and to prepare the village for Feather-Feet's burial. Having seen the state of his organ when he arrived at the shrine last night, I can testify to the village elders that he murdered Emeka in self defence against a cowardly attack on his man-pride. That will ensure that he'll get a deserving burial as a free and innocent man rather than be thrown into *Ajọ-ọfịa* as a murderer." ·

207

Dibia Okpoko's voice rose with indignation, his fury and contempt for Emeka's actions evident in his words.

"As for you, our warrior, your body will be offered to Ogu n'Udo as sacrifice, since you're still an *Osu*. That is all. The choice is now yours. The black herb is in your hand. I await your will," the witch doctor said.

Diké turned and looked at Ife. The boy looked ready to collapse once again. His face was an ashy hue, and his eyes had the wild look of madness.

"Womb-Brother, must you do this?" Ife whispered. "This is too dangerous for you. He said you'll die. What's the use of me having a safe journey without you? Ask him if he can send me with you to this Empty Realm that he's talking about. That way at least, you'll have someone to fight by your side and tend to your wounds if you're injured. I may not be a warrior, but I'll use everything in me to keep you safe."

Diké reached out an arm and pulled Ife close. He held him tightly, shutting his eyes to ward off the tears that threatened to disgrace his courage. Around them, the gentle clacks of the hanging skulls on the Ngwu trees rang a mournful dirge into the cool dawn air. Diké was glad that the ritual was being performed outside the stifling gloom of the forbidden shrine.

"Ifekandu, don't you have any faith in your brother's strength?" Diké leaned over and whispered into Ife's ears, his voice harsh, hard. He didn't dare let the boy see how frightened he was. "Trust I'll meet you at the realm of our ancestors and we shall return together safely. Hold my hand, little brother, and we will enter into the death-sleep together." Diké looked at the hovering corpse of Chicken-Legs. "Chicken-Legs, good friend, I thank you for all your kindness to me. I commit our bodies into your care and pray that we return tomorrow to repeat our thanks to you again."

Chicken-Legs nodded, or tried to. Her movement was heavy and clumsy and her head lolled to the side. "Our warrior, may your ancestors grant you a safe journey to their realm. I will guard your bodies like my own. No harm will come to you from this viper here while you sleep," she fixed her cold gaze on the witch doctor as she spoke. An icy air seeped from her body like a dense fog, shrouding Dibia Okpoko in cold mist. Diké saw the witch doctor's body quake, heard the loud chatter of his teeth. The bowl of black herb in his hands shook violently and man looked ready to pass out.

"We are ready," Diké looked into Dibia Okpoko's glazed eyes, his gaze resolute. He gripped Ife's hand tightly as they simultaneously raised their hands into their mouths.

The black herb tasted dry and sour, like rotten lemon peels and bitter *Onugbu* leaves. He heard Ife gag and heave. Diké thumped him on the back, even as he too fought to keep down the herb. The boy's eyes were wide, glazed with fear. Diké smiled at him and squeezed his hand. Ife tried to return his smile, but his face resembled a ghastly mask. Dibia Okpoko was chanting and weaving his hands over their heads, intoning invocations to chase away the evil spirits and clear the path for their journey.

Diké started to feel drowsy. His head felt as if he'd drank ten jars of strong Palmwine at a sitting. He glanced at Ife again, struggling to see through the sudden fog that clouded his gaze. This time, Ife was smiling, a foolish smile, the smile of a happy drunk. He fell to the ground without a word. Diké felt his body weakening. He fought it, his action instinctive, shaking his head to dispel the fuzz while his legs kicked against the ague.

"Don't fight it, our warrior," Dibia Okpoko's voice was surprisingly kind. "Let the black herb take you to your destiny. Your brother has already gone. He now laughs

209

with the great ancestors. Face your destiny like the warrior you were."

Diké heard his words from a distance. His pride stung—*Damn the man! He's an Ogwumii cult warrior despite everything. He'll not be accused of cowardice by the wretched witch doctor*. He took a deep breath, stopped his limbs from resisting, felt the overwhelming rush of the dark and surrendered himself to oblivion.

TWENTY-FOUR

— · —

THE EMPTY REALM

(THE ABANI CLAN)

He is drowning inside a deep, silent river. The water feels like sludge, sticky to his skin—and icy. It fills his lungs, choking him and sending searing fire to his head. He thinks his head will explode from the pain. His mouth tastes something metallic, something vile and gluey. He tries to spit it out and swallows even more. He thrashes blindly in the icy water, fighting its gooey pull with frantic flaps of his arms. The two bronze machetes on his shoulders hang heavy on their leather straps, dragging him deeper into the cold river. Somehow, he breaks to the surface, inhales deeply, coughing and gasping as he treads water to stay afloat.

He wipes the water off his face, opens his eyes and screams. His voice echoes back to him in delayed reverberation, hollow and lonely. Everywhere he looks is red, an endless expanse of blood water, devoid of land or plant life. Even the sky is a red hue, glowing a dusky haze that is neither day nor night. It hangs low, almost touching the sea. He thinks he can touch the red sky if he stretches his arm. It looks like a giant red slab above him and fills him with intense claustrophobia. A burning urge to break through the low, red sky for a sun-kissed human landscape engulfs him.

He cups the water and lets it fall back to the sea, seeking to confirm the evidence of his eyes. The water drips off his hand with the slow trickle of blood. He raises his hand to his nose and sniffs. He doesn't know why he does so since the odour of blood pervades the air. Force of habit, he guesses.

The silence is oppressive, hanging heavy in the air. He thinks he can hear the heavy pounding of his heart, but he can't be sure. When he places his hand to his chest, he feels nothing, not the rise and fall of his chest or the thudding of his heart. He tries to remember who he is, and why he's trapped in such a desolate place of cold misery. But it's as if he's just emerged from the womb, devoid of memory or knowledge. And like a new-born, his body shivers so violently he fears he'll wail in protest at his terrible rebirth.

Something pulls his legs from underneath the river. It feels like hands, cold, hard claws. In a blink, he's dragged under the blood-river, thrashing his arms wildly and kicking out at the hands clawing his legs. More hands find him, grabbing him around the waist and pushing hard on his shoulders. He tries to hold his breath, to open his eyes underneath the blood-water.

For a brief instance, he sees them; a clan of men with the mien of hunters, their eyes burning with vengeance and hate. Memories rush back with terrifying clarity. Suddenly, he remembers his name and why he's in the blood-water nightmare. Diké! His name is Diké and he's a prince and a warrior on a dangerous journey to the land of the ancestors! The Empty Realm! This must be The Empty Realm that Dibia Okpoko spoke about!

He shudders, terror gripping his heart. He thinks he recognises the men underneath the river from their zebra loincloth and zebra body art, the hallmark of the Abani

212

clan, the fearsome cannibal clan his Ogwumii warriors decimated in one of their bloodiest wars. The Abani clan had terrorised their neighbours for a long time with their trademark kidnapping of pregnant women, ensuring the head of their clan got to eat his special delicacy of human foetuses, while the rest of the clan feasted on the butchered mothers. Their downfall came when they kidnapped a citizen of one of the ten Okoro villages.

Ezeala had sent the Ogwumii to avenge the murder. His instructions were ruthless. No member of the fearsome clan, man, woman or child, was to be left breathing. It was the first and last time he'd ever received such a terrible command from the king. He had almost sobbed as he slaughtered the children, the crying children raised on the flesh of humans. But he had steeled his heart against their pitiful voices and the king's orders had been executed in their brutal totality.

Now, they've come for him, their angry hands dragging him under the blood river. He knows he'll get no mercy from them. The water washes over his head, steals his gaze and chokes his breath.

He fights their hands with blind desperation, swiping his machetes at them. Somehow, miraculously, he disperses them like leaves, hacking into them like soft dough. They dissolve into the water like blood-flavoured mash. His body is suddenly free of their cold claws.

He's stunned by the ease of their defeat and his unexpected victory. Clutching his machetes, he pushes once again for the water surface. His lungs are busting, and his chest is in agony. He breaches the blood river for the second time and inhales large gulps of air. Is this the water death prophesied for him, *he wonders? If so, he's glad it's over and he's survived it with his life. He wonders what will come next.*

He doesn't have long to wait.

This time, when the hands come for him, they come in their multitudes, tiny hands that sear his freezing skin with fire. They don't attack him from underneath the blood-river. There's nothing surreptitious or hidden in their attack, unlike the men's. They come with the power of righteousness and justice, innocent victims of his brutal warfare on their cannibal clan. They surround him, the murdered children of the Abani clan.

He's unprepared for them, the ferocity of their attack and the strength in their tiny hands. They fall on him like locusts and drag him under the thick sludge of the blood-river. He knows his struggles are useless this time, that these little warriors will not dissolve into the river like the men of their clan. He thinks he deserves their vengeance and his machetes remain still in his hands.

Their teeth are sharp and greedy on his flesh and his blood mixes freely with the blood-river of his doom. As the water fills his lungs and the agony steals his sanity, he begs for their forgiveness. When the roar fills his ears and his head implodes, he surrenders to the cold river and the darkness of death with a grateful sigh.

(THE PALE SISTERS)

He wakes up in a thick forest of giant trees, perched atop the highest tree. From his position on the swaying branch, his eyes take in the vast expanse of forestry, spread like a green carpet beneath a dazzling white sky that defies the whitest teeth and shiniest bones. It's a sky devoid of the golden rays of the sun and the silvery glitter of the moon, as if a child has coated it with a thick paste of chalk.

There is nothing between the sky and the endless forest, no eagles, vultures or hawks. His skin breaks out in goosebumps as he realises the air is as chilly as the secret burial place behind the forbidden shrine. He feels the cold bronze of his two machetes and grimaces. They hadn't done him much good the last time, when he was paying his karmic debt to Ofor n'Ogu. *He wonders who his next adversaries will be, if they'll hold a moral lien on his life like the Abani children. The memory of his recent water death still fills his heart with dread. At least he's still alive. The deaths must be temporary—he hopes so, but it still doesn't make it any easier to die.*

He feels the tree shudder. His branch sways, almost toppling him to the distant ground he's yet to spy from his great height. He holds tight to the thick branch. His heart is thudding like drums in his ears except it isn't the sound of his heart that he's hearing. The heavy beats of the drums rise to the treetop, muted, yet audible. His throat goes dry and his heart begins an endless race as he listens to the drumbeats.

Amadioha save his soul! *His head starts to contract and expand, icy claws trailing the back of his neck. He recognises the sounds. It's the distinctive rhythm of the Umase village drums. They're the exact sounds he heard on the day he invaded the village with his Ogwumii warriors and sent a great number of their women to their ancestors' hell.*

With lightning speed, his mind recalls that fateful day with grim distaste. It was said the women of Umase never married outside their village, that most of them were infected with the witch virus carried by the women of Uchichi clan, the master coven. People said the Umase women never aged and the grandmothers looked as young as their young marriage-age granddaughters. But worse than everything else, was the colour of their skin which wasn't the normal dark hue of humans, but an unnatural hue that resembled the skin of pigs and the peel of ripe bananas, skin the colour of the sun and kinky hair of golden corn-straws. They also had strange, pale witch-eyes that danced in the sun and saw into the souls of men, stealing their thoughts and their deepest secrets. People called them The Pale Sisters.

He had not believed it possible for such strange folks to exist and his father had been reluctant to act on the rumours, even when the stories of spontaneous abortions and deformed births started to surface, supposedly caused by the witchery of The Pale Sisters.

Eventually the King sent some spies from the village to investigate, but they brought even more harrowing stories. They had seen The Pale Sisters of Umase village. They were indeed witches, but worse than that, the women had developed the power to mutate into men. The spies also noticed another strange peculiarity with the women. They said the Umase witches feared the sun and only ventured out with their heads covered with wide straw hats.

After that, the King was convinced. He ordered the Ogwumii to invade the village and annihilate every female with the unnatural colour, together with the faux-men wearing the same pale skin. The date was set for the Eke market day, when the men would be at their farms, according to the information received from the spies.

Except the Umase men weren't at their farms when the Ogwumii arrived. They had been warned of the attack by the traitor, the treacherous father of the snake, Emeka, who had formed an unnatural liaison with one of the witches. Unwilling to have his witch lover killed, he had warned the Umase villagers of the impending attack. His Ogwumii warriors had been ambushed and had met one of the fiercest resistance of their career. Several of his men fell on the accursed soil of the witches' stronghold on that fateful day of great treachery.

Throughout the bloody encounter, the Umase village war-drums kept beating, pounding madness into the heads of several of his warriors. He had never known *the drums to be beaten by women, had never heard such ghastly drumbeats that poisoned the bloodstream and sanity with their insidious, terrifying rhythm that seemed to imbue their men with strength and weaken the will of his Ogwumii warriors.*

In the end, his men had broken through their ranks and dispatched the pale-coloured witches with merciless brutality, until the drumbeats finally stilled. After that, it had been easy to subdue the rest of their men. He had extracted the truth from one of their wounded men, who confessed that they'd been pre-warned about the attack by the vile snake that lived amongst them as a villager and friend.

The king's justice had been swift and brutal. The great loss of his Ogwumii warriors brought the rage to his heart for several days. By the time he was done raging, all the grown men in Emeka's bloodline, including his grandfather, three uncles and two cousins, were all hacked to death in the village square and their corpses disposed inside Ajọ-ọfia.

The young sons and daughter of the traitor were spared, together with the main snake himself. Ezeala decreed that a quick death was too merciful for the man. Instead, his chest was engraved with the diagram of a snake with its forked tongue exposed, the symbol of the Ọgba-Ama curse, the mark of the traitor. He was proclaimed an outcast and paraded around the ten villages over a ten-day period, for everyone to know the face of the snake. People spat at him, pelted him with stones and cursed his household with venom. He was reviled and vilified till he finally took his own life in the enforced prison of his hut, damning his soul for eternity, since no suicide was allowed into the realm of the ancestors or given the chance of a reincarnation into their family.

Now, from atop his tall tree, he listens to the accursed drumming of The Pale Sisters. with the quaking heart of a woman. Of all the adversaries he must confront, he thinks this is the worst. He recalls the hate in their dancing pale eyes on that fateful day he hacked them down with his machetes and saved the Okoro villages from their evil hex. He knows they will come for him with a vengeance beyond the imagination of man.

He feels his tree shudder once again; it sways, bending to its side. A loud crack fills the air as the tree surrenders its trunk and starts to fall. The drums' manic pounding drowns his screams as he falls, still clinging to the hard branch of the tall tree. Another tree breaks his fall, sending him toppling to the ground. He lands on his back, knocking the wind from his lungs. Suddenly, their drumming ceases and all he hears are his loud pants and soft groans.

Then, they come for him, just as he expects. They're led by their priestess, the tall cold-eyed head-witch from the Uchichi clan. Her hair is the longest hair he's ever seen on a woman and the braids hang almost to her buttocks in their thickness. Even in death, she's still a stunning specimen of supreme womanhood in her shapely and majestic physique. She had been the first casualty of his bronze machetes on that fateful day, together with her tall sisters. He later discovered she was the one that had held Emeka's father in her thrall. The Uchichi sisters had been a family of tall women in their lifetime and now, he sees that death has not stolen their height.

He stumbles to his feet, pulls his machetes and swings. His blade cuts into several of the witches, but they refuse to bleed, and their skins quickly rebind their cuts.

Ancestors have mercy! *His eyes almost pop out of their sockets. What he's seeing is an impossibility, made only possible by witchery. He grinds his teeth and grips his machetes tighter. He will fight to the end whatever that end bodes.*

With a roaring cry of rage, he strikes out at them, hacking and stabbing, swinging and slashing until his arms weary and his breath is stolen from his lungs. His feet collapse underneath him like wet mud and tears of frustration pool in his eyes.

They laugh at him as he lies panting on the ground, surrounded by tall trees and tall, smooth-skinned women whose injury-free bodies mock the power of his arms and the sharpness of his machetes. In the clear brightness of the white skies, he suddenly gains a frightening illumination—He can never kill them because, like the cannibal children of the Abani clan, they hold the *Ofor n'Ogu* moral lien on his life! *This Igbo doctrine of clean hands, allows them to invoke righteousness and justice before the ancestor and deities, and stake their claim on his life.*

A deep groan escapes his lips as the truth dawns on him. It means one thing—The Pale Sisters were not witches in their lifetime! *Their only crime had been their strange skin colour of albinism, and now, their brutal massacre is another debt he owes to karma. A violent shudder quakes his body. He knows with a feeling of dread that it is now time to pay up.*

They come at him with cold smiles, bearing large clay-pots of earth in their hands. They surround him and strip him of his loincloth. He's as naked as the day his mother pushed him into the world and their dancing eyes mock his nudity with icy contempt. He does not resist or fight them.

The one he views as their priestess speaks to him, she of the majestic build and long hair.

"Dike, proud prince and heartless warrior, we welcome you with a gift," she says, nodding at the clay-pots held by the women. "We have decided to gift

you with our skin, this pale skin you so loathed that you wiped out almost every member of our clan. Prepare yourself for a nice body scrub as we scrub off your proud black skin with our special soap," her voice is neutral, devoid of hate or spite.

Before he can speak, they hold him down and tie up his limbs. He's trussed like a shrine-chicken and the shame is great in his heart. Soon, the shame is the last thing he thinks about as the pain drowns his sanity. They scrub his skin with their pots of grainy earth, bearing hard and deep into his body till his skin starts to peel. He sees the earth in their hands turn the colour of red as it mixes up with his peeled skin and blood. The sand bites into his exposed flesh as he's methodically scalped. When his screaming becomes too much for them, they stuff his mouth with handfuls of wet earth till he chokes on his own screams. Now, he's fighting for his breath, for freedom from the agony searing his chest and his body.

All is earth; wet sand clogs his eyes, his nostrils, his mouth, and his throat. The last thing he sees as the darkness creeps closer, is the brown drums carried by the laughing women. Their joyful rhythm is a macabre lullaby that sends him into a nightmare world of agonised death. Soon, his eyes gaze into the endless white skies with sightless horror.

(THE IKO CLAN)

When next he regains awareness, he finds himself stumbling along a narrow path in a dark world devoid of light, flanked by thatched huts that are squeezed so close the neighbours can shake hands without leaving their doorway. He's never seen a village such as this, with huts built only from dried straw and palm-fronds. It's a place devoid of space, light and sound.

He cocks his head and waits for the sounds of barking dogs, laughing or crying children, grumpy elders and nagging wives, but all is as still as the secret burial ground and he feels the skin behind his neck start to twitch. The air is cold, freezing like all the worlds he's visited in The Empty Realm. He feels his teeth chatter and his body shiver.

He smells something unsavoury, a pongy reek, something unpleasantly familiar, that he can't put a name to. His instincts tell him that badness lives in this night village and his instincts have been his most trusted companions for as long as he can remember.

Something scuttles across his path and dashes into one of the straw huts. It looks like someone walking in four legs, a female creature, going by her rounded rump and long hair. Diké shakes his head—his imagination is clearly playing havoc with him. *He follows her to the hut and knocks.*

"Greetings sister," he calls out in a loud voice. "I'm a stranger to your lands and wonder if you can tell me the name of your village?"

He waits for her answer, but there's no response from the hut. He considers pushing the doors open and seeking warmth away from the biting chill, despite the unfriendliness of the people. Rudeness and inhospitality are not in the nature of most Igbo villagers and he wonders whether this village is one of the foreign-tongued people of the Yoruba race he's heard about, the ones they say worship a deity of thunder, Shango, said to be even more powerful than Ogu n'Udo. It's well known that people protected by powerful gods tend to be haughty and unfriendly.

But, once again, the strange odour assaults his nostrils. He takes a step away from the hut and knocks on the next door, a rickety affair of twigs and straw, entwined in a thin wooden frame. He waits for an

221

answer, but something tells him none of the huts will open their doors to him.

He pushes the door and it opens. The ice hits him, a chill that is worse than the cold outside. He hugs his chest and tries to still the rattle of his teeth. The darkness is denser within and he sees nothing at first. Gradually, his sight adjusts to the gloom and he picks out two figures on the ground, two people engaged in silent copulation, their bodies humping and thrusting with violent intensity. The room reeks of sex and finally he identifies the unsavoury odour that has assailed his nostrils since he entered the night village of freezing misery.

He feels like a thief and quickly exits the hut. He strokes his icy bronze machetes, wondering what to do next. An uncomfortable feeling spreads over his flesh, the sensation of waking up to a bloated cockroach crawling on your exposed body—Oh please ancestors, let this not be what he thinks it is...who he thinks they are!

He shudders; a terrible anger begins to build inside his heart. Even as he reaches out a hand to push the next door, he knows it will swing open, and that there'll be a naked couple engaged in frenzied copulation. Even so, he goes ahead and pushes the door open.

Just as he expects, the room is freezing and pitched in blackness. His now acclimatised eyes see the humping couple on the floor. Except this time, there are two humping couples instead of one.

He stares at the abomination with stunned eyes. From somewhere deep in his mind, a thought takes hold and refuses to leave. With a loud shout, he rushes to the third hut, then the fourth and fifth, till he's puffing with breathless adrenaline—It's them, all right. He's not mistaken. It's the accursed Iko Clan! *Once again, his mind travels to his first encounter with the vile citizens of that cursed clan.*

The King had ordered that no adult of that accursed village was to be spared after the story of their abomination reached his ears. Outraged villagers had swung their arms over their shoulders, casting off the evil, after the story broke. Only a demon-possessed clan would have intercourse with their womb-siblings, daughters and sons! If not for an escaped slave from that community, no one would have discovered the abomination behind the unusual number of deformed births in their village.

It had been thought that the Iko villagers had offended their ancestors and were cursed with bad reincarnations as punishment. Even Dibia Okpoko had visited them to carry out a ritual of purification and atonement, which the King hoped would end the cycle of deformity and misery; but it had been in vain. Their women continued to birth multiple children with strange deformities, resulting in a high rate of spinsters and bachelors as no one wanted to be tainted with the cursed reincarnation by marrying into their community.

His mind's-eye flashes back to the day his Ogwumii warriors invaded the village on the King's orders. They had arrived at mid-day and even at that strange hour, they discovered several copulating couples who were so closely related that such an act should have never happened. He had obeyed Ezeala's command with joy, dispatching the adults with brutal efficiency until only the children were left. Many of the children—the ones who didn't escape—were placed in normal homes on their route back to the Okoro villages. He had thought he'd put an end to that vile evil -- until now.

Diké pulls his machetes and re-enters the first hut.

"Are you related?" he snarls. "Answer me now, and watch that you speak the truth as there can be no lies in the spirit world."

The humping couple pause, and the man slowly nods,

"We are brother and sister," he says, his speech deformed, just like everything about them, from their elongated limbs to overblown skulls. Diké decapitates them on the floor where they've been engaged in their abomination and turns to leave.

He hears a grating sound and freezes, staring in stunned disbelief. The severed heads are quickly reattaching their necks to the corpses and once again, the siblings are reaching out to each other in humping, frenzied fornication. His body quakes in a powerful shudder—Amadioha! What evil is this he has stumbled into?

Diké quickly shuts the door, breathing hard. After several minutes, he forces himself to walk into the next hut. This time, they are a man and his son-in-law, both also nursing unsightly deformities. His loathing is great, and again, his bronze machetes are soon stained with the blood of the vile ones. By the time he visits the fifth hut and dispatches his fourteenth soul, he realises that he could spend a lifetime in the night village without achieving his goal of annihilating the cursed community.

For, each time he enters the next hut to kill the inhabitants, the ones he's already slain are once again alive and humping away with silent determination. An icy shiver slivers over his body as horrible clarity hits him—Ancestors help him! He has stumbled into their cursed karma! *Diké realises he's witnessing their endless misery of joyless copulation, doomed to their freezing village of eternal night. Their obsessive humping is the only way they can generate body warmth in their icy hell.*

That's when the solution hits him – Fire! Burn the evil to the ground! *He runs over to the nearest hut and collects some straw. He places the dry hay underneath his bronze machetes and starts to rub them together. Very quickly, the sparks kindle the straw and he scoops the flame and tosses it at the hut. In a blink, the hut is on fire, blazing a heat that is intense and satisfying.* Burning them might be the best way to end their evil for good, *he thinks. He listens out for the cries of the people trapped within.*

What he hears instead is their laughter. His mouth drops open, his mind stunned by the happy sounds. Even as he stares goggled-eyed, other doors finally open and he sees a crowd of naked monstrosities emerge, drawn to the lively flames. They stumble into the burning hut with blissful faces, welcoming the heat denied them in their night village of icy damnation.

The fire consumes them, melting their flesh like animal fat and ending their accursed afterlives for good. Still, they troop to it in their dazed multitude till the fire is almost smothered by their stampede. He curses as he rushes to ignite the next hut, praying for the tiniest breeze to spread the blaze and speed up their annihilation.

The crowd suddenly turns on him.

"Heat...heat...fire," they moan, crowding around him with grasping, greedy hands. Their actions are mindless, their movements catatonic, as they beg him for more of the blissful heat their bodies crave. Soon, he's drowning in their swamp, as they hold him down inside the hut that is now raging with lively flames. He's shoving at them, but they've already abandoned him, trampling over his body in their desperation to get to the second blazing hut.

His loincloth catches fire and he screams. He tries to beat off the flames, but the smoke is in his lungs and he cannot breathe. His body feels as if a herd of elephants have danced on it and he knows his bones are crushed. The pain is like no other as he finds himself trapped inside the fiery hut with the cursed souls of the night village.

The flame licks his toes and he howls. He continues to shriek as the fire travels over his body, charring his flesh even as the monsters above him moan in ecstasy as they're burnt to ashy cinders. By the time the flames flick the taut contours of his face, shrivelling the skin and scorching his thick hair, he has ceased to feel the pain.

Twenty-Five

THE ARRIVAL

THE NEXT TIME he awoke, Diké was lying on the ground, looking into a dazzling sky that blinded him temporarily. He quickly shielded his eyes, turning his face away. Before he could calm his racing heartbeats, he felt himself being pulled up by lean, strong arms.

"Womb-Brother, you made it! You finally made it to us!" Ife cried, holding him so tight he thought his ribs would crack. "I was starting to get worried. We've been coming to this portal for the twenty-three days I've been here to receive you and everyone was starting to despair. I should've known my brother is a warrior beyond par, and no death can keep you down in the grave-soil of the spirit world."

Warm tears filled Diké's eyes and crawled down his cheeks—*He's made it! Amadioha be praised; he's finally in the realm of the ancestors!*

At one stage during the three deaths, he had started to doubt his own strength, his ability to endure pain and fear. He doubted if even the witch doctor had any idea of what truly took place in The Empty Realm. Dibia Okpoko had an inkling but that was all—just an inkling. Only a person that had visited and survived that terrible place could really know what went on there. He was one such and his gratitude to his personal Chi and his ancestors was great.

Ife said it had taken him twenty-three days to make the journey to the land of the ancestors. It felt more like twenty-three moons to him, twenty-three long and terrible moons of indescribable horror. His terrible reckoning with his past mistakes made him fear he might never make it into the realm—and they were mistakes. He now knew with a drowning sense of guilt that, with the exception of the Iko clan, he had committed terrible crimes as a warrior.

"Brother, have you seen the sky? Can you believe the wonder of our ancestors' realm? Isn't this place truly wonderful?" Ife's voice was excited and Diké glanced up instinctively.

His mouth dropped as he stared at a wonder beyond anything he had ever seen. Three golden suns and three silvery moons spun in a mesmerising dance across the bluest of skies. "Can you believe it? Isn't this place truly wonderful?" Ife's voice broke into his thoughts. "I found our mother! She lives here and looks just like a young girl, not at all like the mother of two grown men like us. Why didn't you tell me how much I look like her? Come, she's waiting for you with everyone else. Wait till you meet the rest of our ancestors! You're very famous here. The whole realm is buzzing with excitement at your arrival. Just wait till you try the Palmwine here. There's nothing as sweet as it in all the villages in our realm. I tell you brother, you'll never want to leave this place again."

Ife's voice was pitched with so much excitement that Diké felt like he was once again listening to the little five-year-old brother he had raised. Ife's face glowed with joy, his skin healthier than Diké could remember in a long time. His eyes were bright and clear, free of the sadness and misery that had weighed him down in their realm. It was as if Emeka's murder had never taken place and the whole *Osu* tragedy had been a bad dream. He wished he could trap Ife's joy inside a sealed jar, so that he would never again shed a tear of sadness.

"Ifekandu! Little brother! I thank our ancestors that I've lived to see you again. How was your journey to the realm of the ancestors? Was it a smooth one?" He could barely contain the indescribable sense of relief he felt at his escape from The Empty Realm, and its desolate, icy horror.

Ife nodded. "It was like a dream. I slept and when I woke up, I saw the nine ancestors warriors. They were expecting you, you see. So, when they felt movement of spirit in The Soul-Path, they came to guide you. You should've seen their faces when they saw me!" Ife giggled, his face full of mischief. "But, when I told them that I was your gift, ha! I think I'm now more popular than you in our ancestors' realm. They took my hands and happily led me into their realm once they realised who I was. And guess who else I've met? Guess?"

Diké shook his head.

"Go on, try; take three guesses; you'll never believe it in your wildest imagination," Diké shook his head again. He could see Ife was burning to tell and didn't want to spoil the boy's fun.

"I've seen the great traitor, Emeka's father himself!"

"What?" Diké shouted, taking a step back. "Did you say Emeka's father is here? Impossible! He's a suicide; he can't enter the realm of the ancestors for a rebirth if he takes his own life. Surely, you must be mistaken, little brother. Perhaps, you saw someone that looks like him,"

Ife shook his head, his eyes twinkling. "I told you you'd never believe it, didn't I? But it was him all right, and I spoke with him too," Ife looked at the ground "I told him everything that happened between Emeka and I and begged his forgiveness for killing his son. He didn't know about it because Emeka never entered the ancestors' realm after his death and now, I think I know why."

Ife paused, his eyes lost in a far place. Then, he lifted his shoulders in the familiar shrug Diké recognised when things got too complicated for his mind to tackle. "You know, Emeka's father is a good man. I think we might have misjudged him in our realm. He never took his own life. Emeka killed him in his bed, stabbed him with a knife. That's why he's here, welcomed and loved by the rest of the ancestors. There's no evil in this realm, brother. Look at the three suns and the three moons and tell me how evil can thrive in such a glorious place!"

Ife flung his arms wide, smiling up at the incredible sky. He did a little dance jig and let out a happy whoop.

Diké's mind was a whirlpool. Ife didn't realise the significance of the information he just gave with his typical casual indifference. Diké was already entertaining doubts about the whole treachery business after his experience in The Empty Realm with The Pale Sisters. Ife's words were like a crushing rock on his conscience. A great injustice had been done, not just to Emeka's father, but also to the Umase community of The Pale Sisters. Should he make it back to their realm with his life and sanity, he intended to right those wrongs.

Suddenly, he heard the clamour of a crowd, the joyful voices of women raised in song and the deeper rumble of the men. He looked up and saw amongst them, the familiar faces he last encountered in his vision inside the forbidden shrine, the nine ancestor warriors, leading a crowd of—what could only be—his ancestors to him.

"I found him, great ancestors," Ife called out, running towards them, falling happily into the ready arms of the singing women. "My womb-brother, the people's warrior, has arrived in your realm!"

Ife led a slender, young woman towards him, pulling her along with impatient hands. She was a woman of incredible beauty and Diké recognised her even before she spoke. His heart constricted, and tears filled his eyes.

"Mama?" he whispered.

But she heard him, and her tears flowed down her face. She held him tightly with gentle arms he remembered from his youth. Their mother had been a famed beauty in her lifetime and her untimely death while giving birth to Ife was a wound that had never healed. The King had never recovered from her loss despite his three subsequent marriages.

"Diké-di-o̩ha-mma!" She called him by his full name, tears trailing the beautiful curves of her face. *Diké-di-o̩ha-mma, the strong man loved by all.* No one else had ever called him that name since her death. His tears were like a hot river as he held her, sobbing and laughing—*Maybe Ife is right. He might never want to leave the realm of the ancestors again.* Already, his soul was starting to remember his past life in the realm, the scent, the sounds, the indescribable bliss of the ancestral bonds he'd given up for his latest incarnation.

Someone tapped his shoulder from behind and Diké pulled away from his mother and turned to see. It was Ikolobia, one of his nine ancestor warrior-leaders. Diké stared at him with awe, remembering every feature of Ikolobia's face from his vision inside the forbidden shrine. He marvelled at the impossibility of what he was witnessing.

"*Agu-eji-ejemba!* You have returned to us again, great son!" Ikolobia said. "Today is a day of immense joy and pride for us. Now, we look upon the faces of two of our best sons and we know we have not lived and died in vain,' Ikolobia hugged Diké tightly.

Diké stared at him with awe, remembering every feature of Ikolobia's face from his vision. He marvelled at the impossibility of what he was experiencing, the

wonderous interaction with his ancestors. He pinched
his right thigh surreptitiously, just to convince himself it
was all real and that he was truly gazing into the faces
of the warrior leaders from his vision. Without their
intervention, he would have never escaped the prison of
the forbidden shrine. Their love had guided him to this
special world of magic and suddenly, he felt his heart
swell up with a love that was almost too intense to bear.

The remaining ancestor warrior-leaders welcomed
him with happy hugs, their faces wreathed in the
same wide smiles Diké saw on the faces of the
cheering crowd. Amongst them, he saw many others he
recognised—fallen warriors, several relatives, and many
whose funerals he had attended in the village, all looking
young, strong and joyful.

As they rushed over to embrace him, it dawned
on Diké that there was no old age in the realm of
the ancestors. Each ancestor coaxed him for news of
their family, friends and even their enemies in the
human realm. He understood their desperation. The
bad dreams clouded their access to their loved ones,
for it was mainly through dreams that the ancestors
could commune with the living. But for the fact that the
forbidden shrine shielded him from the dream-attack
of the hanging skulls, his ancestors would have never
known of his plight until someone died in the village and
brought them the news.

As he looked at them, Diké felt his body shiver like
one struck with a fever. A cold carpet of goosebumps
layered his skin in tiny dots—*He's in the midst of his
great ancestors, in the same space as his beloved mother!
He's looking at the faces of the ones who existed before
the birth of his great, great-grandfather, the men and
women whose blood flowed through his veins, whose
traits and mannerisms he mimicked. These are the ones
he and every other man in their village fed Palm-wine*

whenever they poured wine into the ground in libation. These are the names he called upon for protection. These are the beginning of his existence!

This time, Diké's tears were tears of gratitude and humility. He fell on his knees before them and bowed his head to the ground, the dusty earth that smelled just like his village and hamlet. Everywhere he looked, he saw Ukari, from the village square to the great Bat-Tree, the cassava farms to the hamlets. Even the very air smelt of Ukari, just sweeter, fresher.

"Great ancestors, my creators and guardians, your son pays homage to you," Diké said, his voice choked. He felt arms around him, lift him to his feet, wipe his tears and place his bronze machetes into his hands. The ancestor warrior-leaders surrounded him, raising his arms high into the air, his machetes glittering in the intense suns and moons of the realm. They raised their own double machetes in a show of solidarity and marched him through the crowd, chanting his warrior name, *Agu-eji-ejemba*. Just like in Ukari village, in the days when he walked a free man, the crowd broke out in impromptu songs, praising his great exploits in the battlegrounds, his strength and his valour.

But their songs touched a place of shame that came with the new knowledge he had gained in his journey through The Empty Realm. There was no pride in killing innocent children who had no control over the cannibal ways of their parents, or killing vulnerable women just because of the colour of their skin. He wondered if there were more mistakes he'd made all in the name of war, if there were more innocent lives he had destroyed under a false belief.

He heard the familiar laughter of his brother behind him. He smiled and looked over his shoulder. Ife was back in his element, surrounded by their female ancestors, his hand clasped tightly in their mother's own. Like the women in their village, old and young, Ife's graceful beauty and harmless smile drew them in. They sang songs to him and offered him endless cups of Palm-wine. Diké was yet to have a drink, but knew his quest was more serious than Ife's. As long as the boy was happy, enjoying the attention of his admirers and fresh Palm-wine, Diké was content.

A sudden hush descended on the crowd just as they drew close to a wide clearing. They paused, cocking their ears, their eyes raised to the great mountain that jutted out of the landscape like a deity's fist.

As Diké stared, a plume of smoke rose from the pinnacle, swirling into a thick cloud that briefly dimmed the brightness of the sky. The smoke rapidly spread outwards and downwards, hurtling towards the crowd like a tornado of clouds.

Diké turned around and found Ife staring with wide-eyed awe at the plunging clouds.

"Ife." Diké motioned him over. Ife rushed to him, standing close behind him with his eyes still glued to the mountain. Diké felt better having Ife close. Even though he knew they were in the safest place they could ever be, amongst those who loved them the best, nonetheless, they were from the world of the living, and it was best they stayed together.

"The Old Ones are walking," Ikolobia said, his voice hushed, filled with reverence. Then he raised his voice and shouted into the crowd. "The Old Ones are walking! Bow your heads to them that hold the wisdom of the universe and our existence!"

There were scuffles as people dropped flat to the ground with their arms outstretched. Only the nine warrior-leaders remained upright, each resting on one knee in their lined formation, their bronze machetes held high in the air. Diké followed their lead, feeling his heart quicken with anticipation and awe—*The Old*

Ones! He's finally about to meet the greatest of the ancestors, the ones that hold the power of his destiny in their hands! His limbs shook so much he feared he might not keep his arms raised for much longer. It would kill his soul to disgrace himself before his ancestors.

When they emerged from the cloud, Diké gasped. From the great distance, he could only make out their dark colour and the fact that they were moving, walking at a pace that defied reality. They strode down the mountain, their steps long and wide in a gliding motion. A distance that would have taken a mere man several days to cover, was traversed in seconds by The Old Ones. Diké felt as if he had barely taken a deep breath between his first sighting of them at the top of the mountain and their arrival. In an instant, they were upon the crowd, ten mighty giants in flowing cloaks of shimmering black fur.

Behind him, he heard Ife's scream, quickly hushed by their mother. The nine warrior-leaders bowed their heads low. Diké wondered how they could restrain themselves from prostrating before the raw power radiating from the ten greats, as he yearned to do. But he guessed he wasn't an ancestor with eons of moon-cycles to get used to the sight of such magnificence. He forced himself to steal another glance at The Old Ones and felt his body quake with terror and awe.

What is this impossibility? Amadioha have mercy! He was looking at a vision that defied belief, ten living giants with the faces of Ọgu n'Udo, the two-faced deity of war and peace.

Except they were all women.

Diké shook his head, rubbing his eyes violently—*How can it be? How can Ọgu n'Udo, the all-powerful deity of war and peace be female?* He was seeing the impossible become terrifyingly real, like seeing his own face on the body of a cow. When The Old Ones pulled off

235

their hoods, their long dreadlocks flowed almost to the ground in thick ropes, while their full breasts pushed against the glimmering fur coat cloaking their powerful bodies. A thick cloud of white smoke shrouded the spot where they stood, and Diké marvelled once again at their splendour.

Five of the giants wore the frontal face of the deity, the fearsome war face, complete with pointed horns and blazing red eyes that seemed to burn into his soul. The other five wore the benevolent rear face of the deity, the peaceful face with the kind smile and gentle eyes that filled him with warmth. Their thick robes flowed to the ground, and it was hard to tell where their long, black dreadlocks ended and where the rich black fur of their robes started. In his entire existence, he had never seen such a spectacular attire.

Diké felt goosebumps layer his skin as he stared at the vision before him—*Amadioha in His great heavens! How pathetically ignorant the humans of the Okoro villages have been!* In their arrogance, they had foolishly believed that the deities of war could only be male, that the powerful ancestors were equally men. He was now witnessing the stupefying secret—*These are the spirit-women that have touched the hands of gods and gained their divine powers and wisdom. These are the ancestors of the ancestors, the ageless ones whose lineage are unknown to all except themselves. These are the incarnations of a deity!*

"Step forward, Diké, first son of King Ezeala of Oma clan, unlucky son of man and favoured son of his ancestors. Step into the sight of your old ancestors," the five benevolent ones spoke in one synchronised voice that was highly pitched, like a woman's voice magnified over and again.

He looked at Ikolobia for directions.

The ancestor warrior nodded. "First lay down your machetes, and then go to them."

Diké did as he was bade, and rose from the ground. When he got within several yards of The Old Ones, he dropped to his knees, bowed his head, and awaited their instructions.

"Speak now, son and tell us your story. Your warrior ancestors have already spoken for you. But what you know is greater than the meagre knowledge they hold. We shall decide your fate when you're done," the five benevolent ones said.

"His fate shall be decided after we have seen his gift," the five fierce ones spoke for the first time. Their collective voice was the rumble of thunder and the shriek of a hurricane. It sent the terror thuds to Diké's heart.

He heard Ife's soft gasp and turned to look. Ife's pale face mirrored the same fear he felt, but no one else in the gathered assembly seemed afraid or bothered. All of them were sitting on the ground in a relaxed pose, legs stretched out and wide smiles on their faces, as if waiting for an exciting tale under the moonlight in the human realm. He caught his mother's eyes. She smiled at him and gave him a nod of encouragement.

"Yes, the gift of course," said the five benevolent ones. "Have you brought a suitable gift for your ancestors, good son?"

Diké nodded, striving to still the trembling of his body.

"Yes, great ones," he answered, his voice hoarse, as if layered with sand.

"Good. We shall listen first to your story and then we shall receive your gift. Let us hear what has brought you through your perilous journey to the realm of your ancestors."

Diké took a deep breath and began to speak.

He spoke till the three suns turned into six moons in the sky, dazzling the realm in a clear silvery blaze. The ancestors listened in silence while he spoke, the fierce ones coldly neutral, and the benevolent ones, gently encouraging. He spoke till he was hoarse, and his head was empty.

When he was done, The Old Ones asked for his gift.

Twenty-Six

A DANCE FOR THE DEAD

IFE LISTENED TO the beating of the drum, the intoxicating rhythm of the Igede dance. The three moons lit up the realm with a dazzling brilliance that left no shadows, since the dead were the shadows themselves. Behind him, one of his ancestors beat Dibia Okpoko's leather-clad *Igba* drum with the same skill he had displayed in his earthly days as an Igede drummer. Ife was glad the man hadn't lost his skills in his unearthly abode. Softly, with tentative taps, the man built the tempo, enticing Ife into the rhythm with the throbbing, seductive beat of the *Igba*.

Ife's feet flew with the joy of the Igede dance. The dust was a brown cloud underneath his hopping legs. His body gyrated and twisted as he allowed the magic of the Igede to transport him to breathless ecstasy. He stooped and rocked his waist, executed a perfect twirl and jump, in sync with the thunderous drumming of the drum.

The ancestors gasped, roared their approval with loud claps and hoots, cheering him on. The air was charged, fevered with excitement. Ife paused, held his body still, allowing their adulation to wash over him and infuse his limbs with renewed energy as he prepared for the next sequence.

"Feather-Feet! Dance for your ancestors! Magical son! Thrill your ancestors!"

The ancestors' wild cheers filled the air. Their praise infused Ife's heart with joy and pride—*Yes! Yes! This is what he was born to do, the culmination of a lifetime of dancing. To dance for his ancestors and gain their approval is the greatest achievement of his life!*

He glanced quickly at The Old Ones shrouded in their cloudy mist, especially the five fierce ones with the blazing eyes and fearsome faces. Their lips were curved in a small smile. It wasn't much, but it was a start. The five benevolent ancestors were beaming, their smiles wide and joyous. The only person without a smile was Diké. He sat amongst the nine warriors-leaders, his face taut, his hands tucked between his knees as he followed Ife's movements and the faces of The Old Ones with eyes cloaked with anxiety and fear.

Ife smiled. Diké had no idea what was coming, the secret moves he had planned for this very day. He lifted a hand to wave his gratitude, calm their excitement and ready them for his next dance, The River Dance.

A hushed silence descended as they waited for the magic to restart. Ife raised his right arm to invite the drummer back into the dance. The ancestor drummer beamed and raised a fist of approval to Ife before resuming his drumming. Ife bowed to him and straightened, his lithe body glistening with oiled sweat. The ancestors glued their eyes at his ebony-skinned beauty with pride, waiting for the dance to resume.

With a loud shriek, Ife yielded his body to the magic of the *Igede*. He stooped, stretched, and with a nimble twist, freed his body for the spectacular River Dance. It was a dance that demonstrated the flexibility of his body, the fluidity that turned his bones to elastic as he executed the moves, mimicking the undulating flow of the Asata River, meandering and twisting along the dusty ground.

The ancestors gasped, their eyes wide, breaths hushed in awe at the wonders of the human body revealed to them by their young descendant. Tears flowed down their cheeks as they were overcome by memories, coupled with the beauty and grace of the dancing youth.

Ife completed the final loops of the River Dance, raised his arms over his head and swung them down with the final crash of the manic drumming.

The ground heaved as the ancestors jumped to their feet, roaring their approval with loud clapping and cheers. Again, Ife stole a surreptitious glance at The Old Ones. This time, all ten wore wide smiles. The five benevolent ones were clapping, while the five fierce ones watched him with folded arms and smiling faces. He turned his gaze to Diké. His brother was still sitting on the ground, but his face was now relaxed, his eyes smiling.

His mother was waving to him, her face filled with pride. Ife felt his eyes fill with tears. He waved back to his mother and bowed again to the crowd of ancestors before turning his attention once again to the drummer. The man was bowing to Ife, again and again, respect and admiration glowing in his eyes. Ife returned his bows and called out his gratitude for the flawless accompaniment.

Then, once again, he raised his hands for silence.

This time, the air sizzled with anticipation as the ancestors remained standing, unwilling to return to their sitting positions on the ground. Ife raised his arm to motion his mother over to his side. She looked surprised, then pleased, as she joined him on the dance floor, her face creased in a wide smile. Diké looked perplexed, just like the rest of the ancestors. Still, they all watched, their interest piqued the more by the unexpected twist. Ife hugged his mother gently, then motioned her to the ground. As she sat down, he nodded to the drummer and the man began to beat the drum.

This time, it was a beat without rhythm, a steady tap that sounded like a dirge drum. Ife knelt before his mother, and began his dance, a story and poetry dance, the first of its kind in the history of the ten Okoro villages. None of the ancestors had ever seen such a dance and they watched with intense concentration, mesmerised by the tragic story Ife acted out in a mixture of dance, song and acting.

He told them their story, his and Diké's story; the tale of two brothers deprived of a mother's love by the cruel hands of death. With swinging arms and fierce shouts, he danced Diké's great exploits in the battlegrounds. With songs, he told Diké's sadness at his childless state and with poems, he recited his brother's lonely burden of leadership.

Ife's feet flew wildly in the air as he demonstrated his carefree life of dancing and drinking. His laughter was wild, and the crowd laughed with him even as they cheered him on. Then with a gentle sway of his hips, he fell before his mother and laid his head on her lap and howled. With his song, he begged their mother's forgiveness for the evil he had wrought on her firstborn.

Her tears were still hot on his skin as he crawled a slow dance towards the gathered ancestors, begging their forgiveness for the shame he had brought to their honour. He heard the soft wails of the women as their tears joined his own. He avoided their outstretched hands and leapt into the air in a stunning acrobatic display that landed him right before Diké.

With a dusty face drenched with tears and a manic smile, he bowed before Diké and shouted his name.

"*Agu eji-ejemba*! The people's warrior! Your womb-brother bows before you!" Ife hailed.

The crowd cheered loudly, also calling out Diké's name. Ife bent his waist, raised his arms and executed a sequence of mesmerising dance moves for Diké, his feet hopping in a frenzied rhythm, body twisting, head shaking, and arms contorting in impossible angles. With nimble alacrity, he dragged Diké to his feet and danced his way towards The Old Ones. Diké fought his hands, resisting his pull, but Ife's tug was insistent, and he soon had them both before the ten great ancestors standing in their swirling cloud.

Again, Ife twisted his body in loops, gyrated magic into his bones and kicked his legs with acrobatic brilliance. Then, with his hands gripping Diké's shoulders from behind, he pushed his brother closer to The Old Ones.

"Our great mothers, our makers, please grant the wishes of your worthless son," Ife sang, his voice a sorrowful dirge. "I've brought shame to my brother and my family, to my clan and my ancestors. But please, great ones, free my innocent brother from the *Osu* curse. I pledge my feet and my drum to you for eternity; I yoke my soul and my dance to your whim. I beg you, restore pride and dignity to your great son, Diké, that his name shall once more be spoken by his people, and his feet roam free again with pride in our village."

Even before he finished his speech, Ife heard Diké's shout as he tried to stop Ife's song. But he danced away, crying and laughing as he executed a manic flurry of intricate dance steps before collapsing on the floor before the ancestors in a dead faint.

Twenty-Seven

DESTINY

THE CROWD RUSHED at Ife before Diké could get to him, their wails filling the air. Diké saw his mother by her knees beside Ife.

"Ifekandu! Ife! My good son, please wake up, open your eyes now. Please Old Ones save him," their mother cried, casting desperate eyes at the ten great ancestors.

There was pandemonium everywhere as Diké finally pushed his way to Ife's side.

"Ifekandu! Ifekandu! Come; open your eyes now; do you hear me? Wake up now!" He shook Ife, his hands violent, fuelled by desperation and terror—*He'll die if anything happens to Ife; his heart will not cope with the guilt and pain. Amadioha have pity!*

Ife opened his eyes and smiled when he saw Diké, a weary, yet, blissful smile. Their mother wept with relief, and crowd cheered, singing joyfully as they celebrated his return to health and the magic of his dance. Diké felt his tears join their mother's own as they hugged Ife and raised him to his feet, assisted by some ancestors.

Just then, a loud sound filled the air like the sigh of a thousand giants and a sudden stillness descended on the crowd, an unnatural stillness that was swift and total. All eyes were once again fixed on The Old Ones.

"Good people of our true realm, former citizens of the ten Okoro villages, peace and joy be with you," the synchronised voices of the five benevolent ones rang out in the air.

"Ise! Ise!" The ancestors returned their blessings with loud enthusiasm.

"Diké, son of King Ezeala of Oma clan, please present yourself before your ancestors," The Old Ones ordered.

The crowd parted for him as Diké started walking. As he passed, they patted his shoulders in encouragement, their faces wreathed with love and compassion. Ife's dance-tale had affected them deeply and their tears still stained their cheeks.

"Take heart, brother-son," Ikolobia whispered into his ears when he walked past. "Your brother has done you proud today. The Old Ones must surely grant your request. Fear not, brave warrior. Our time has finally come."

Ikolobia clasped his arm and pushed him towards The Old Ones where they waited in the splendour of their smoky shroud. Diké fell again to his knees and bowed his head. "Today, you demonstrated why you are the greatest warrior of the ten Okoro villages," the rumbling voices of the five fierce ones rang loud in the air. "Today, you brought your ancestors a gift beyond price, beyond imagination, and beyond beauty. Today, the magical feet of your gift brought tears to the eyes of every ancestor in our realm, including our old eyes that have witnessed great wonders in our long existence. We remembered and mourned the great loss of our magical *Igede* dance, and we wept for the blessing of experiencing it again through your wonderous gift."

They paused and turned to the five benevolent ones, who nodded benignly before turning their attention to the crowd.

"Ukari Ancestors gathered here today, we ask for your thoughts before we make our decision," the five benevolent ones said. "You have met our two sons who both fill our hearts with immense pride. Some of you might remember Diké, son of King Ezeala of Oma clan when he was last in our realm, before his latest reincarnation. Others might not. Regardless, we have all experienced the wonder of his gift today, a gift like none other we have ever seen. He wishes to be freed of his curse and a return to his former glory. What is your wish?"

"Freedom! Freedom! Freedom!" the air thundered with the ancestors' cheer.

Diké's heart constricted, almost exploding with the intensity of the love and gratitude he felt for his ancestors—*This is it, the end of his long and terrible journey! He's now on the cusp of breaking his curse!*

"It will be as you have said," the benevolent ones continued. "Arise and greet your destiny, Diké, first-born of King Ezeala of Oma clan."

Diké stumbled to his feet, his heart thudding.

"We call on the nine blood machetes to join their brother-warrior and complete the magical ten of the feline spirits, in preparation of their transmogrification and rebirth."

Diké heard the sudden gasp of the ancestors as The Old Ones spoke. In an instant, he was surrounded by the ancestor-warriors. Ikolobia had tears in his eyes, same as the rest of the rest.

"Finally, the prophecy is fulfilled. The ten lion spirits will ride as one again in the realm of man. On his return to his father's compound, the warrior will call upon your services for the first and final time. The next time he shall meet you all again will be when he welcomes you as his sons, the nine sons out of the ten that his wife will bear for him."

The nine warriors wept aloud. Finally! They were going back. Cheers filled the air and the women chanted praises to the ten great lions. The Old Ones motioned Diké closer and spoke directly to him. Sizzling sparks emitted dangerously from their bodies and he struggled to hold their fiery gaze.

"Diké, son of King Ezeala of Oma clan, listen well to our words," The Old Ones said in a unified voice that was all female, a matriarch's command issued in a mother's voice. "Today, you have seen the faces of your great-ancestors. You have seen us, the ancestors of ancestors. From our wombs rose the first spark of life, and to us must all souls return. Know this wisdom. We do not thrive on the blood of men, be they slaves or free-born. A sacrifice of goats and chickens is enough to show us that you still cherish and honour us," they paused as a great cheer rendered the air. Diké bowed low, his heart racing with joy—*Finally! An end to the old practice that had stolen the life of Chicken-Legs!*

"For the first time in our long history, a living person breached the realms and our message can finally be delivered without the confused and corrupt interpretations of the Seers that can only meet us in the dream-state," The Old Ones were speaking again. "Now prepare yourself to receive the secret word of your freedom. On the day you speak that word, the ten lion spirits shall once again walk the realm of mankind with great devastation. Your enemies shall fall, and your name will be immortalised in the memory of men. Are you ready, Diké, son of Ezeala of Oma clan?"

Diké's body trembled—*Amadioha save his soul! He isn't ready, not by a long chalk!*

"I am ready, great ones," Diké nodded as he spoke. Instantly, he was engulfed in a thick cloud that smelt of burnt wood and Harmattan dust. He closed his eyes and felt a wave of dizziness as his head opened to receive the unspoken word of power into his brain. He thought he would faint from the dazzling light that showered him in glory, power and knowledge. When he opened his eyes, everything looked clearer, brighter, as if a mist had been cleared from his eyes.

"You have walked The Empty Realm and have seen the injustice suffered by one of our own, the wronged one marked with the sign of the snake," The Old Ones spoke again in unity, their voices reverberating in the realm. "His daughter shall bear you ten sons. Nine of your sons will be your nine warrior ancestors. The tenth son is the wronged one, the father of your wife. He will become the tenth lion-warrior in his next reincarnation. That is his reward and your penance. Go, great son; go and live your destiny."

Diké gasped as he heard their words—*Big-Bosom is to be his wife!* Intense joy washed over him. He had hoped and even dreamt that she would one day share his name. The Old Ones' prophecy dazed his mind, and when his sight cleared again, they had vanished, carried away by their tornado of clouds. When Diké looked up, all he saw was the distant smoke atop the high mountain.

The crowd was chanting praises, dancing and celebrating the great wonders of the day with Palm-wine flowing like a swollen river. Laughter and songs filling the air, and Diké was hugged and feted by all.

"Diké!" Ife rushed towards him with their mother by his side. Their faces wore an anxious look and Ife struggled to meet his eyes.

"Ifekandu, it seems... I think it is now time for us to say our goodbyes to our mother," Diké held their mother's hands, wishing he didn't have to let go. "Mama, I wish there was a way I could take you back home with us. It kills my soul to have to part from you for a second time." The band in Diké's heart grew tighter as he saw his mother's face dampen with tears, even as she tried to smile through her pain.

"Diké-di-ọha-mma!" Once again, their mother called him by his full name, her voice fiercer than he could ever remember during her lifetime. "My son, seeing you and your brother has been the most wonderful gift any mother could ever wish for. I must have done something to please the deities for them to reward me in this big way. No mother could be prouder than her sons as I am, and my blessings will follow you till you return to us again, long may it be," she paused and held his gaze for several seconds, and he could not stop the tears escaping. "Go home in glory, great son and proud warrior. Stay well till we meet again."

She stepped away from him and took hold of Ife's hand. Her face wore a sad smile.

"Womb-brother, I have a confession to make," Ife said, looking at their mother for help. She smiled her encouragement at him. Ife cleared his throat. "I will not be going home with you."

"What?" Diké shouted, grabbing Ife's arms and shaking him. Ife winced, and tried to extricate his arms. "Ifekandu, what do you mean by this? Of course, you will be coming back with me. Have you forgotten where this place is? As much as it is the realm of our ancestors, it is also the realm of the dead. We took this journey together and by Amadioha, we will return together. I intend to deliver you back to our father in one piece."

Ife shook his head, his face wearing the familiar look Diké joking referred to as the mule look. Despite his easy ways, once that particular look entered Ife's eyes, Diké knew it would be impossible to shake his will.

"Womb-Brother, please understand. I love it here. Everything I want and need is here. Our mother, aunties, grandparents, and cousins are here, as well as the best Palm-wine in the world. Best of all, I can dance forever

249

without seeing the disapproving eyes of our father. Instead, I'll be encouraged to dance here, my skill appreciated by all our ancestors. I'll never have to farm or tie myself down in marriage either. Already, I'm loved and cherished by my ancestors, and my happiness here is beyond anything I can describe," Ife explained, his voice urgent.

He gently unclasped Diké's hands from his arms, and when next he spoke, his voice was gentle, as if he were the older sibling.

"What do I have to go home to? Nothing but sadness and stress. Emeka's murder hangs over my heart even though I know it was self-defence. Regardless of what you said, how can I ever again look Big-Bosom in the eyes knowing her brother's blood stains my hands?" he shook his head. "Father is still determined to marry me off and force me into the farm. He's already banned me from dancing and drinking Palm-wine. The person I thought was my best friend turned out my worst enemy. People view me with contempt because of my drinking, even as they praise my dancing. Here, I don't need to watch myself or my words,"

Ife paused and took Diké's hands in his.

"Please brother, let me stay. I am happy here. I don't need to be on my guard or worry about people's thoughts because all the thoughts here are loving ones. Go back and bury my body without tears, knowing that I'm finally happy and free for the first time in my life. I know we'll meet again in this realm; not too soon I hope."

Ife laughed, a hoarse sound. Diké didn't join his laughter. He couldn't find a way to stop the tears that clouded his vision, nor the pain that cut his heart with countless stabs.

"Think about it, brother; I'll be just as I am now when you eventually return to this realm. As you can see, this is a realm of eternal youth where people never age."

Ife cleared his throat and squeezed Diké's hands even harder.

"Our warrior, I've never thanked you enough for all the love and protection you gave me," Ife said gently. "Without you my life would've been the life of a donkey. So, thank you, Womb-Brother. Travel well and tell Big-Bosom that I'm truly sorry, and that her father is well and happy with the ancestors. That'll make her happy I think, knowing her father made it here. Tell her that I said she must make you a good wife and watch that horrible temper of hers, otherwise, I'll haunt her dreams!"

Ife hugged Diké tight. It took a second for Diké to hug him back but when he did, he squeezed so tight that Ife thought he might break in half. "Farewell, Womb-Brother, till we meet again."

Ife walked away abruptly, without a backward glance. By the time Diké said his goodbyes to his ancestors and was taken to the same bright portal where Ife had met him on his arrival, Ife was nowhere to be seen anymore.

The nine ancestor warriors bid him an emotional farewell.

"Brother-warrior, how can we ever thank you for this great gift you have given us today?" Ikolobia clasped arms with him, followed by the rest of the ancestor-warriors. We cannot wait to join you again in our true form. Nna-Ọra, go in peace and long may your name live!"

They called him by his new name, *Nna-Ora*, meaning, father of a nation. It was a name that left a sour feeling in his heart. He didn't want to be the father of a nation. He only wanted to be the brother of a hero, the big brother of the sweetest and most wonderful little brother that ever walked the soil of man.

Diké wept.

Twenty-Eight

–·–

BLOOD DUES

DIKÉ'S TEARS WERE with him when he opened his eyes and found himself back inside the dark gloom of the forbidden shrine, his mouth bitter with the vile liquid that Dibia Okpoko was forcing down his throat.

He coughed and pushed the mug away, stumbling to a sitting position. His head throbbed, and strong waves of dizziness threatened to topple him to the ground again.

"I am sorry, our warrior," the witch doctor had tears in his eyes. "I did my best for your brother, but I could not bring his spirit back. I fed him double the potion of the reviving juice that I fed you, but even now, his body remains still and his chest no longer rises. Feather-Feet is no more! The killer of sorrows is dead! The house of King Ezeala of Oma clan has lost another great son!"

Diké glared at him. "The house of King Ezeala of Oma clan has gained back *another* great son." His voice was croaked, as if he nursed a cough-throat.

He heard Dibia Okpoko gasp as he looked into his eyes, saw the awed look on the man's face, as if he were seeing a ghost—*Idiot fool!* He turned to look at Ife's body slumped beside him. Ife looked peaceful and serene, as if he had just slept after enjoying the sweetest cups of Palm-wine.

253

Diké felt tears prick his lids and forced them back. This wasn't the time to cry for the loss of his brother. That will come later. For now, it was time to put his house in order and give Ife the greatest burial ever witnessed in the ten villages and beyond.

The tight knot in his throat hurt so much he groaned—*Ifekandu! You foolish, sweet boy!* For all he knew, the little wretch could well be guzzling Palm-wine now, dancing to his Igba drum and celebrating his own funeral with the ancestors—*Lucky boy!* Ezeala was right. He had spoilt the boy rotten, otherwise, he should have insisted he returned with him and shared some of the burdens of their house with him.

He had no idea how their father would handle his return from the forbidden shrine, Ife's death, and his future marriage to Big-Bosom, the daughter of the man that he had branded with the snake symbol of treachery. He didn't fancy the troubles from his first wife, Mgboye, when he brought in a second wife. But no power on earth could stop him marrying Big-Bosom, not after all she had done for him, coupled with the prophecy of The Old Ones.

Diké ground his teeth as thoughts ran a manic race inside his head. He was uncertain how the vultures in the realm would handle his return, though he knew it wouldn't be with joy. But one thing was sure; he was back to reclaim his Ogwumii leadership mantle. As far as he was concerned, Ozo Agwo's house was over—*The flight of the eagle may be a source of envy to the hawk, but the eagle has no obligation to tolerate the hawk's envy.*

He stood up and turned to Chicken-Legs' corpse. The slave girl looked ghastly, a horror beyond horrors. He wondered how Dibia Okpoko had survived the entire day in her shadow. The rapid decomposition of her reeking corpse was terrible, with bits of decayed flesh and grave-soil dropping in clumps from her body. The maggots feasting on her corpse seemed to have multiplied in the brief period he was away, and they now heaved her flesh, crawling from every orifice. He doubted her ghost would hold up her fast-decaying body for long. Her face was almost gone, leaving behind a grinning jawline beneath a hollow cheek. One of her eyeballs had sunk deep into its hollow, while the other rolled inside its own hole. But he saw the joy radiated briefly in them when he smiled at her.

"Chicken-Legs, true friend, I thank you for all you did for me," he said, forcing himself to hold her rotten hand with the near-skeletal fingers. "My journey was successful, and Feather-Feet is happy where he is. You are free to return to your ancestors, brave spirit. I make you this promise, that never again shall anyone be taken as a slave by my warriors, not while I live. The ritual of The Soul-Eaters will be stopped once I reclaim my status. No one shall ever again suffer the fate you and so many others suffered. I have seen the true face of Ọgu n'Udo, and The Old Ones do not demand the blood or hearts of slaves. I am done with this accursed place, and will now take my brother and bury him like the hero he is. May your spirit finally find the peace it craves. Sleep deep, restless soul; and may your reincarnation be blissful."

Diké placed his machetes into their holster and hung it over his shoulders. Then he lifted Ife's corpse and stumbled towards the exit of the shrine grove. Dibia Okpoko's desperate wail followed him.

"Our warrior, have mercy! I beg you, spare my life! Don't abandon me to these pitiless ghouls, I beg you. Have mercy on my children, my wives. Our people need me to speak to the ancestors and our deity. Save me, please!"

He heard the hollow voice of the slave girl issue a command. It was icy, oozing hate. He turned to look and shivered. The shambling corpses of the witch-sisters were dragging Dibia Okpoko towards the forbidden shrine, led by Chicken-Leg's cackling corpse. He was still kicking and screeching, his eyes wide with horror.

"Come," Chicken-Legs said. "Let's visit your secret burial ground together. We have a tight embrace to share. That's what you wanted, wasn't it? Now you finally get to touch me and share my soil-bed for eternity, as well as my sisters. Aren't you the lucky man who gets to feel the touch of six young women? You're truly blessed amongst men."

Chicken-Legs' hollow laughter was gleeful, as loud as Dibia Okpoko's ear-killing screams.

Just as Diké got to the entrance of the shrine, the hanging skulls began rattling in a deafening din. He heard something crash to the ground and turned to look. The skulls were dropping from the Ngwu trees like over-ripe fruits, roiling like a bony river towards the secret burial ground.

Diké shivered, goosebumps layering his skin as he walked away without a backward glance. Ife's cold corpse lay heavy in his arms—*Everyone has their destiny to live and their own karma to serve,* he thought. *Dibia Okpoko has killed his last slave.*

The long walk back to the King's compound was the longest and most agonising experience in Diké's memory, with Ife's corpse in his arms heavier than a river. The myriad of stunned eyes that followed their progress along the village route to the King's house intensified his distress.

Diké knew he had changed. He had seen his image in the water bowl Dibia Okpoko offered him and seen the great change the journey to the underworld had wrought

256

on his features—*no wonder the witch doctor had looked stunned*.

His once black hair was now the grey shade of an old man, and his eyes had glazed in a stare that had ceased to blink. Their previous black colour was a new hue that was neither gold nor silver, just an unnatural pair of glassy orbs that could now see through the gloomy dawn with the clarity of a cat's eyes.

As the dawn brightened, the crowd grew in great numbers as news of Ife's death and Diké's emergence from the shrine spread. By the time he arrived at the King's compound, a greater crowd of kinsmen and clanswomen awaited him there, together with the King. As he stumbled through the entrance to the compound, his legs collapsed beneath him.

Diké fell to his knees, still holding tight to his brother's corpse. People staggered back, fear widening their eyes at his terrible visage. Then the King moved; he took several staggering steps, before his mouth opened with a terrible scream. He dropped his staff and started running towards Diké, quickly followed by his kinsmen who now took their cue from their King.

"My son! My sons! Oh Ancestors have pity!" The King fell to his knees in front of Diké, tears streaming down his eyes, his arms reaching for both him and Ife's corpse.

"*Nna-anyi*, Ifekandu is gone! Forgive me our father, for bringing you this grief. Though I bring you back Ifekandu's body, his soul dances at our ancestor's realm. I have been there, our father. I have seen our ancestors and The Old Ones. Ifekandu rests with our mother and your son is now a free-born again. I am freed by The Old Ones of the *Osu* curse, and I return to you a free-born today. You have regained a son, our father, even as I bring you back pain beyond endurance."

Diké gently placed Ife's body on the ground and bowed his head low. He felt arms enfold him, his father's loving and accepting arms and finally, he allowed his tears to flow freely—*He has been welcomed back into the fold of his family and humanity!*

Until he felt his father's arms around him, he never realised how terrified he had been of rejection, how much he had feared the people's disbelief. But with the King's acceptance and the great changes the people saw in his altered appearance, the wonder in their gazes as they stared at him and howled their grief over Ife's death, Diké finally knew that his terrible ordeal inside the forbidden shrine was finally over.

Big-Bosom came into his hut later that night after most of the crowd had dispersed, save the kinsmen who were making preparations for Ife's burial. He had seen her briefly in the crowd, but she had avoided him, quickly disappearing after their gaze briefly caught. Even though she had given him a smile, but he had seen the shock in her eyes and the sight had filled him with dread—*What if she now finds his altered appearance too repulsive and decides to kill her affections for him?* All he had to give him hope was the prophecy of The Old Ones that she would bear him ten sons. *But still...*

"Our warrior, may I come in? It's me, Iruka," her soft voice startled him to his feet as he rushed to let her inside.

"Big-Bosom!" he held his arms wide and she fell into them, a soft sob escaping her lips. He held her as if his life depended on her—which it did—and she pressed herself tight against him, her tears warm on his chest.

"I wanted to come earlier but you were very busy," she whispered, leaning away to stare into his face. In her eyes, he saw the same stunned wonder on the faces of the villagers, except hers were filled with a love that brought intense bliss to his heart. "Oh our warrior, what did they do to you? See what the ancestors have done to you," her voice broke and tears filled her eyes again.

"Do you mind?" his voice was quiet, his body taut. His eyes held hers, searching, waiting.

"How can you ask such a mad question? Don't you yet realise that I will follow you to the end of the world even if you crawled on the floor like a snake?" she held his face with her hands. "I have waited and prayed ever since Ife killed Emeka and escaped into the shrine. I've been staying in the King's compound because my brothers disowned me. I couldn't tell anyone about your journey to the ancestor's realm, and the waiting has been hell. And then you return with Feather-Feet's body, oh ancestors have mercy!" she shut her eyes briefly, shaking her head.

"Don't weep for him, my love," Diké stroked her damp cheek with his thumb. "He made the choice to remain behind at the realm. It's a wonderful place, identical to our village, right down to the great Bat-Tree, just better. I'll tell you about it one day. But right now, just know that Ifekandu dances happy in the company of our mother and ancestors, including your father, with whom I spoke."

Big-Bosom's eyes widened to saucers. "My f-father? You saw my father?" her voice was hushed, awed. Diké nodded, smiling.

"Yes, my love; I saw and spoke to your father, who is happy with our ancestors. Your father did not kill himself as was thought."

"I know; Emeka killed him. I saw him do it with my own eyes, but he threatened to kill me if I ever spoke."

Diké stared at her with horror-filled eyes.

"Oh my poor, poor girl!" He held her tighter. "It's a good thing Emeka is dead or I would be seeking his neck with my machete right now," his voice was hard. "Listen, don't worry about anything, all right? The King's compound is your home now, and I promise you nothing and nobody will ever again harm or insult you, not while

259

I live and my machetes hang over my shoulders. Come; sit with me. We have a lot to talk about."

TWENTY-NINE

—·—

THE DAY OF THE TEN LIONS

ỌZỌ AGWỌ STRUCK on the day that Ife was buried.
It was a sun-dazzled day that belied the sadness of the
occasion. The obese peer arrived at the King's hamlet
with a delegation fit for three kings, including other
chieftains, dancers, praise singers, and an intimidating
number of fully-armed warriors. He conducted himself
with the pomp of a king, waving benevolently to the
crowd, receiving their obeisance with haughtiness and
shouting orders as if he owned the King's home. At his
side were several Ọzọ chieftains and Ogwumii warriors,
men who had once pledged loyalty to the King, but were
now openly aligned to the man they considered their
true king.

From his position beside his father, Diké observed
the intrigues carried out with brazen disregard for their
loss and the solemnity of the day. Ọzọ Agwọ and
his entourage went around, smiling and waving to the
people, their voices loud and hearty, as if they were
attending a wedding rather than the funeral of a young
man who was the son of a King. And more ominously,
was the five eagle feathers on the peer's head, a clear
message to the King that a new King walked the land.

"Just look at the fat idiot and his useless son walking as if they own the ten villages," Big-Bosom snapped. "How dare he wear more feathers than the king? I don't know what you're waiting for before putting him in his place inside the shit-pit."

Diké almost laughed. He squeezed her hand. It was amazing how important she had become to him in such a brief period.

"Hush, my heart," he said. "Don't let your enemies hear your thoughts. Everything has a time. For now, we bury Ifekandu and then take things from there."

Big-Bosom made a hiss of disgust as she glared at Ọzo Agwọ and his rowdy supporters. Diké observed the flagrant disrespect displayed by the peer and his followers. None of them had acknowledged his presence, ghosting him just as if he were still confined within the forbidden shrine.

Despite the King's announcement that his first son was no longer an *Osu*, none of the peers accepted the proclamation. The sudden cessation of the collective nightmares since Diké's return had been a thing of wonder and great relief amongst the villagers. Yet, the peers would not accept it as a sign of the ancestors' intervention.

Ọzo Agwọ was loudly vocal about his stance—the King's bloodline was dead and his son, Ikenna, was now the permanent Ogwumii leader. Diké had heard that the peer, in open rebellion to the king, had employed a witch doctor from a distant village to officiate the ritual confirming his son's status, following the mysterious disappearance of Dibia Okpoko. Now, he watched with repressed fury as Ikenna swaggered around with an elite group of warriors, hugging a pair of gold machetes and exuding a menacing air that intimidated all present at the funeral.

Feather-Feet's fame had spread beyond the ten Okoro villages and his sudden death saw a great outpouring of grief. Diké had been stunned by the King's reaction, recalling how harsh their father had been with Ife while he lived. In the three days since Diké stumbled into the king's house with Ife's lifeless body, the king had neither eaten nor slept, holding a permanent vigil beside Ife's cold body, laid out underneath the Ngwu tree for all to view and pay their final respects.

The funeral crowd flowed beyond the king's compound and into the village square. All day, people had stared at him with goggled eyes, though none dared greet him for fear of incurring Ọzọ Agwo's wrath and the violence of his henchmen. Diké nursed no bitterness towards the villagers. They were the powerless masses, led like mindless sheep by the will of the powerful. They would go wherever the wind of power blew and right now, it was a hurricane in the direction of the wealthy peer. Even his first wife, Mgboye, had packed her bags and returned to her people, stating she would rather lose her life than remain the wife of an escaped *Osu* masquerading as a freeborn. He was happy to see her go. If nothing else, Big-Bosom would get some respite from her endless spite, while he might finally be spared the sight of her sour face.

Diké looked at the small group of supporters in the King's circle, a few yards from where Ife's grave-mound rose from the ground. It was a pitiful number, comprising of his former warrior-leader, Igwulube, his clansmen, and Big-Bosom. This was not an army that could challenge the powerful peer and his military might.

Diké looked at his father and felt a tight band constrict his heart. The king was a husk of the man he used to be. Diké had hoped his return might restore the spirit to the King's heart and imbue him with the passion that fueled his famed rages. But it was as if the fighter's soul had fled the towering body that used to house it.

A sudden commotion in the crowd drew Diké's attention. The crowd parted, making way for a group of men led by a great force of Ogwumii warriors. This time, there was no doubting the threat in their pose. Their machetes were raised high and their voices loud in a war chant. Diké heard Big-Bosom gasp, followed by a loud curse. Igwulube moved immediately to Diké's side. The King watched the approaching peers with the new air of distraction that had clung to him since Ife's death.

"This isn't good," Igwulube said, his voice hard. "This has been a long time coming and I fear they plan a show-down today. I think we may have to fight. I can still count on some of my warriors to obey my command. Give me your command, my prince, and it shall be done."

Diké smiled his gratitude. "Fear not, good friend. I have awaited this day with great sadness and strong preparation. Show me your loyalty today by obeying my command to the last word. No matter what you see today, I want you to stay by your King and protect him with your life." He turned and took Big-Bosom's hands and placed them in Igwulube's callused ones. "I place the hands of my future wife into your capable hands too. Guard her life as you would guard the King's own."

He saw the stunned look in both Big-Bosom's and Igwulube's eyes and smiled. "Yes, this headstrong girl is indeed my future bride. Surely, you know that if there's any man in the ten villages that can handle her temper, it's me, eh?" Igwulube laughed and Big-Bosom rolled her eyes, but Diké saw sudden joy light up her eyes.

Diké stepped to the King's side taking his rightful place as heir. He heard the loud gasp of the crowd and the angry hiss from the warriors flanking the group of elders and peers. A small-statured peer wearing a congenital tragic expression, stepped forward and walked towards the King, bowing low before him. Diké recognised him immediately. It was Ezugo of Okoh clan, the father of Ada of the Nightingale Voice and Ọzọ Agwọ's father-in-law.

"Our great king, I bow to you and wish your house long life and prosperity," Ezugo said. His eyes avoided Diké's own. "Today, I have lived to see things I never knew could be possible in our lands. My heart wails at the end of the way of life we grew up with, the laws we followed, and the paths we walked. Your house and mine have a long history, Ezeala. You and I also have a long history as boyhood friends, with countless lizards hunted between us and numerous trees conquered by our nimble, young limbs. Although the marriage between our children did not cement our long friendship as we'd hoped, you still hold my first loyalty in your realm. Kingship is divine, not by force,"

Ezugo paused as he pulled out his Ostrich feather of peerage from his head and laid it at the King's feet. "Today, I pledge my loyalty to you, my king." He straightened up and with his head held high, he walked over to the King's left side. A loud rumble issued from Ọzọ Agwọ's supporters. Diké heard several voices brand Ezugo a traitor and a coward, but the peer absorbed their insults with a stoic expression, his stance unwavering by the king's side.

The King reached out a shaky hand and shook Ezugo's hand, long and hard.

"Good friend, your bravery and loyalty today will never be forgotten," Ezeala said, his voice uncharacteristically tremulous. He turned to Diké and leaned in to whispered into his ear, his voice hushed, urgent. "Good son, don't forget this day should you live to survive the treachery staring us in the face. Remember your true friends, those who stood by our side in our greatest need. Don't forget your enemies either, even in your death."

The king paused, his face breaking into a sad smile. "I remember all you told me after your return from the forbidden shrine. It was a beautiful fantasy which I chose to believe because I wanted to have my son back with me again. But we both know that the legend of The Ten Lions is nothing more than a folktale told to lift the hearts of our children and our people,"

The King held up his hand as Diké made to interrupt him. "Listen to your father, my good son, and don't do anything rash now. We are outnumbered. As our people say, the bat recognises that it is ugly, so it only flies at night. The wise man like the bat, recognises his limitations. You are the last of my bloodline, the only son that will ensure my name never dies. I need you to live and avenge my death and the treachery heaped on our house today. I will distract them so you can find a way to make your escape. You must survive. What lies in your future is greater than my past and what's about to unfold. May our ancestors be with you till we meet again, my son."

Diké wanted to tell his father that a warrior, even one that is a king's only son and heir, does not abandon the battlefield; that they would fight this war to its bitter end. But the King quickly turned to face the gathered peers. He saw his father smile, and when Ezeala spoke this time, his voice was the same old voice Diké recalled from the days of his glory—strong and mighty.

"Ozo Agwọ! Finally, you show your filthy hands. Ogwumii warriors, you dare gather before your King with threatening machetes? And follow the orders of another while your true king lives?" The King jumped to his feet, striding towards them with his own machete drawn. In his days as a young prince, he had also been an Ogwumii warrior, an elite soldier trained in the art

266

of human annihilation. Now, his soul thirsted for the traitorous blood of his enemies.

Igwulube rushed over and placed himself before the King, stopping his stride. "Great king, let your warrior fight your battle," Igwulube pleaded. Turning to the crowd he shouted, "Ogwumii warriors, those of you who belong to my squad and are still loyal to my voice, I call on you now to lay your machetes at the feet of your King."

With a loud roar, the loyal warriors raised their machetes and pushed their way to their leader's side, instantly surrounding the King. Even so, they were heavily outnumbered, but Diké saw their readiness to die in the King's defence.

"The house of King Ezeala of Oma clan is dead, and the King has lost his authority," Ọzọ Agwọ said, stepping to the front of his warriors. He pointed an accusing finger at Diké, his eyes blazing. "That *thing* that stands there before you is no longer human! Look at its eyes. It has no business walking in the company of humans. Yet, the one that we call our King welcomes it into his house and tells us that it is now human, that the ancestors have freed it from bondage. He offers us no proof save the grey hairs on its head and the unblinking eyes of a demon. The king insults the intelligence and honour of the peers with his arrogance. Even now, the abomination stands by the throne, defiling the bronze machetes of the *Ogwumii* warrior-leader, my son's rightful machetes. So, hear this, Ezeala of Oma clan; we the peers have spoken, and you have ceased to be the King of the Okoro territories. Moreover, for your crime of defiling your people with the accursed thing that was once your son, you have been condemned to immediate death by beheading."

"You fat demon-pig! You'll die in a pit of vipers like the snake that you are!" Big-Bosom screamed, breaking past Igwulube to spit into Ọzo Agwọ's face. Before Diké could reach her, he saw the peer's fist smash into her face, sending her toppling to the ground. Something snapped inside him, a rage unlike any other he'd ever known.

Diké bellowed at the peer, fury trembling his body. He shrieked a secret word whispered into his head by ten terrifying, dreadlocked giants, garbed in flowing robes of the blackest fur. His voice was one that started out sounding human, but finished as the thunderous roar of a lion.

The crowd froze. The silence in the compound was total. Diké's roars were the only sound filling the air. Fury burnt his skin, his head, his thoughts, and his blood. He pulled at his loincloth, seeking to free himself from the sudden heat devouring his body. His hands scratched his chest as the fire within threatened to engulf him. They left a bloody trail on his skin, like the claw-marks of a beast. Thunderous voices were suddenly inside his head, drowning his thoughts—*His nine brothers-warriors! The nine ancestor lions! They've returned, back in their true feline form.* They spoke into his head, informing him they were riding the bone-path of the shrine, bounding towards the King's compound.

Diké saw someone charge at him and he pulled his bronze machetes. It was Ọzo Agwọ's son, Ikenna, with his gold machetes raised. Diké swung and decapitated Ikenna. His head fell to the floor and rolled to Diké's feet. The squirting blood from his neck sprayed into the nearest section of the crowd, dousing them in red.

Ọzo Agwọ's blood-coated face was a nightmare of shocked horror, as he reached out to grab the stumbling body of his headless son. Gone was his habitual arrogant mien, his blood-shot eyes bulged to the size of overripe *Udala* fruits, ready to drop into his gaping mouth.

As the rich peer's warriors rushed at him, Igwulube's men sprung to his defence, thwarting the machetes aimed at the King. The roar of this battle was like none Diké had ever heard; it was the hatred of brothers, an odium more powerful than the hatred of strangers. Diké heard a stampede of terror as the crowd screamed and fled in all directions. He heard their roar before he saw them, his nine ancestor warrior leaders, prowling in a semi-circle formation, a magnificent pride with the largest mane of a rich golden colour.

His attackers fled, abandoning their machetes and Ọzo Agwọ who was cradling the bloody corpse of his first son, keening with choking sobs.

"Our warrior, stay back," Igwulube shouted, as he saw Diké run towards the prowling pride of lions. But Diké was deaf to his warning and was instantly swallowed up in a warm, suffocating blanket of thick fur and mane. The lions rubbed their heads on his body with loud purrs and growls, their pungent smell filling his nostrils with heady bliss. Diké heard their voices inside his head.

"Agu-eji-ejemba! Brother-warrior! You did it! You brought us back in our true form!" Ikolobia's voice was like thunder inside his head. "Once again, our feet walk the soil of our land and our hearts explode with joy. We thank you; you are truly great. Now your ancestors are here to fight your battle, lead us to our enemies that we may quench our thirst with their blood." Diké's head was ready to explode from joy, and his shout was long and loud.

The reunion didn't last for long. Diké led the ancestor-lions to the King. They entered the compound, a magnificent pride of awe and terror. And at the sight of the nine lions led by the striding prince, madness descended on the villagers, the unique madness of terror. The warriors lost their strength and the men, their pride, at the sight of the prowling lions. Each scrambled to save their own lives, the women forgotten and abandoned, left to fend for themselves and their children by their fleeing men.

The King stumbled forward, a dazed look on his face. The lions shook their manes, barred their fangs and growled. The King fell to his knees before them and bowed low, crying praises and prayers to them. They fixed their fierce golden gazes at him, then roared once again before making their way to Ife's grave-mound.

They formed a circle around the grave, a ring of honour; nine magnificent lions with the longest manes and fiercest eyes. At the sight, a sudden silence descended in the compound as the returning crowd, enslaved by killing curiosity, halted their flight and gaped with wonder. Everyone knew about the lore of The Ten Lions of the Oma clan, but that was all it was, a story told to children under the moonlight. Nobody believed it— till now.

Then the lions began to roar, one after the other, their heads raised to the skies, until it was Diké's turn. His keening was the longest and the strongest, the sounds coming from his lips, the identical rumbling of the lions. He heard the King and all gathered in the compound sobbing loudly as he bid Ife goodbye. And when his tears stole his voice, the nine lions roared together for him in a terrifying sound that shook the grounds, the trees, and the souls of the quaking villagers across the nearest villages.

When they were done, the leader of the golden pride, Ikolobia, lowered its great mane before Dike.

"Lead us, Brother-warrior," his voice rumbled inside Diké's head, filled with menace. "Ride on my back and lead us to glory. Take us to our enemies, that we may be avenged and reclaim our honour."

Diké jumped on Ikolobia's back, leading his feline warriors to his enemies. His voice roared like a lion's, and his head was filled with a bloodlust that rivalled the great felines' own. Even his limbs were imbued with a strength unnatural to man, and people cowered behind the false safety of their huts, shrieking for mercy and forgiveness.

Some were granted their wishes, while others paid for their treachery with their blood, to the last bloodline. Even his love for Big-Bosom couldn't restrain his thirst for vengeance when his lion-ancestors entered Emeka's hamlet. He rode Ikolobia into the small hut where her two brothers hid, crashing through the feeble wooden door and tearing the flesh from their necks. As their screams died out, so too did his fury over their treachery finally perish.

Together, they rode through the ten villages and into hamlets, tearing envious flesh and treacherous hearts, drenching the soil with the blood of the human vultures and human snakes. He didn't need to guide the lions to the right hamlets; they already knew the names and crimes of the enemies of the Ọma clan. Even when they came across the old woman in her feeble pathetic flight, the one that had keened Diké's tragedy with such anguish on his way to the stream, the lions merely sniffed her feet and left her unharmed, to the awe of all watching from their huts and atop tall trees.

Ozo Agwo's kinsmen did not receive the same mercy, nor did the clansmen of the other treacherous Ọzo chieftains and Ogwumii warriors. The lions broke down doors, and climbed the tallest trees. Wherever the enemies of the Ọma clan hid themselves and their accomplices, they were all found and devoured. Their triumphant roars sent shivers down the spines of the villagers, and the sight of Diké riding on the back of the leading lion was one that would remain in their memories for life, growing into legend even in his lifetime.

And by the time Diké's rage was done on that fateful day, a day that would go down in the chronicles of the village lore as "The Day of The Ten Lions", the house of Ọzo Agwọ of Uba clan had ceased to exist.

THIRTY

— • —

ATONEMENT

THE KING DECLARED a day of atonement thirty days after The Day of The Ten Lions. Invitations were sent out to all the ten Okoro villages to attend the momentous event at the great Ukari village square and participate in a ritual of atonement for ancestral wrongs. A different village outside the Okoro community was also invited, the Umase village, home to the unfortunate Pale Sisters. By noon, the vast square was heaving with an unprecedented number of villagers. News of the Umase guests had spread through the ten villages and interest was great amongst the people.

Seated on his high stool beside the King's ceremonial chair, Diké observed the small group of albino villagers huddled together at the left exit of the square, separated both by space and soul from the rest of the other villagers. It was clear they did not want to be there and were only enduring the wide-eyed stares of the villagers out of fear of the King's retribution should they fail to honour his invitation. They did not trust the King and the memory of the last attack was still fresh in their minds. Diké observed their stiff shoulders and tense faces with deep shame and regret.

In the centre of the square, a solitary wooden coffin lay on the ground, surrounded by white chickens, gourds of Palm-wine and red Kolanuts. The newly ordained medicine-man, Dibia Okafor, was carrying out the Rites of Appeasement to the wronged spirit of the deceased, whose skeletal remains had been exhumed earlier that morning from *Ajo-ofia*—Emeka's father, the man who had been wrongly declared a traitor for trying to save The Pale Sisters.

By Diké's side, Big-Bosom sobbed softly, her head lowered and her shoulders quivering. Diké reached out and took hold of her hand, giving it a gentle squeeze. It was an unusual demonstration of affection in a public place, since no real man worth his hamlet would exhibit such weak and undignified behaviour in a public space. But he doubted anyone would notice, not while all eyes were on the pale citizens of Umase in their wide straw hats that kept the blistering sun away from their skin. Big-Bosom was the breath that fed his life, the keeper of his soul and the protector of his bloodline. He would give his pride, his life and his reincarnated soul for her happiness. Even now, their son, the first of the ten ancestor warriors, nestled inside her stomach. She had missed her monthly flow and as she said, she had never missed it from the first day it stained her thighs.

There was a sudden hush as the King raised his staff in the air and rose from his ceremonial chair. He began to speak, once again the great and strong king of old, save for the new humility that now guided his words and a gentling of his once-fierce features.

"Today, we are gathered here to carry out an important ceremony demanded by our ancestors, The Rites of Appeasement and Atonement. It is no news to you that my son, Diké, Agu-eji-ejemba, the people's warrior, is back amongst us, having been cleansed of his curse by our great ancestors. You have all experienced the end of the accursed nightmares that have long plagued our sleep and witnessed the return of the ten lions that came to the defence of our people from the treacherous pretenders to the throne."

The King paused as the crowd erupted in wilder cheers, chanting Diké's name with unrestrained adulation. Diké smiled, a tight smile. Once, he would have been pleased with the praise of his people. But that was before he realised the fickleness of man and the transiency of life. Instead, his eyes remained glued on the tense faces of the Umase villagers. Theirs were the only faces without a smile in the square, the only lips that did not cheer.

"I need not go into details about our warrior's journey to the realm of our ancestors. Suffice it to say that he brought back messages, instructions and secrets that we are now honour-bound to reveal and implement," the King continued. "Widen your ears and hear your King's declaration! Today, we return the good names of the young girls accused of witchcraft by the false witchdoctor, Dibia Okpoko. We declare them innocent of witchcraft, and will have a week of mourning to give them the honour and respect they were denied."

The King's staff rose and crashed deep into the soil sealing his edict. Loud wails broke out in the square as the families of the witch-sisters, the young girls abused and impregnated by Dibia Okpoko, burst into tears of relief and renewed anguish. Diké felt goosebumps layer his skin as the terrifying image of the five fire-ghosts flashed across his mind. He prayed the poor witch-sisters were now at peace, and all the shrine ghosts were now sleeping deep, just like the rest of the villagers who were no longer plagued by the bad dreams.

The King's voice reclaimed his attention. "I have spoken with our new medicine-man, Dibia Okafor, and he has spoken to the oracle to confirm the message our warrior brought back from the realm of our ancestors. Widen your ears and hear your King's declaration! From today, there will be no more human sacrifices to Ogu-n'Udo. Our ancestors and gods demand no human blood from us, just our veneration and gratitude. From this day, there will no longer be two classes of people in our communities. Everybody will be considered equal, each citizen of Ukari, a freeborn. The *Osu* caste system is hereby abolished. Tomorrow, Dibia Okafor will lead all the *Osu* in the ten villages to the free-born river for a cleansing rite, after which they will become full citizens of the Okoro territories."

The crowd gasped as the King brought down his staff. Their faces reflected their confusion. There was even dismay on the faces of several of the elders who had been born into the *Osu* culture, and feared the ramifications of the king's edict, both on their pride and their privileged status.

"Yes, I know it will be difficult for some of you to accept that you are not superior to your fellow humans who share the same red blood and stinky fart as you," the King paused as the square erupted in laughter. "Seriously though, I want you all to bear in mind that this is not my will, but rather, the will of our ancestors. And their will, will be done, with or without your will,"

The King kept the pleasant smile on his face, a smile that failed to cloak the steely look in his eyes.

"Finally, today, we shall return the remains of the wronged one, the man who had worn the treacherous snake mark of Ogba-Ama on his body for an act of goodness and bravery, a man who recognised evil and sacrificed his life to prevent it, and who would have been my in-law had he lived." Ezeala smiled at Big-Bosom, whose marriage to Dike had taken place just seven market days prior to the day's event. "Today, his body will be buried inside his own compound with all the honour and dignity he deserved and the stain on his name removed for eternity. Your King has spoken, and his words can never return to his mouth."

Diké saw the startled look on the stiff faces of the pale Umase villagers, a sudden animation, as it finally dawned on them that they were in no peril, that the King meant them no harm. The other villagers were also staring at them, uncertain of what to do, if to smile, wave or cheer.

They opted for the last.

The villagers' rowdy enthusiasm soon relaxed the stiff bodies of the Umase visitors, whose faces finally broke out in tentative smiles, before joyful cheers erupted in their midst.

"Today, we celebrate our new friends, the good people of Umase, who in the past had wrongly suffered the pain of our prejudice," the King continued. "On behalf of all the citizens of the Okoro villages, I, King Ezeala of Oma clan, apologise and give them our hand in friendship and protection. Umase people, we embrace you and we welcome you into our fold. We give you the truth of our hearts, and share with you the blessings of our ancestors and our gods. May today be the beginning of a new era for us, and lasting friendship between your people and ours."

The King gestured for the Umase people to come forwards and they did, their steps tentative, as if still unsure about their sudden reversal of fortune. The crowd parted for them, patting them on their shoulders, no longer afraid of their rumoured witchery. They came before the King and fell to their knees, bowing their heads low in respect.

As they rose to their feet, Diké walked over to them and took their leader's hand, a tall elderly woman who bore a striking resemblance to the cold-eyed head-witch from *The Empty Realm*. A flicker in her eyes, a sudden coldness, told him that she recognised him, knew him from that fateful battlefield that decimated her clan. She wanted to free her hand from his, and tugged hard to break his hold. But he would not let her go.

"Forgive me," Diké's voice was low, hoarse. "My heart bleeds regret every day the sun rises and every night it sleeps. I walked the realm of the ancestors. I saw your sisters that I harmed, and I confronted my monumental ignorance, my great regret, and my eternal shame. I stand before you today as your servant, who will dedicate his life to ensuring your protection from all harm. But please, free my heart from this poison that is slowly tearing it to shreds. Tell me what to do, what you want, and your wish will be obeyed."

Diké held her gaze as she read his soul and saw the anguish that had stolen the sleep from his unblinking eyes since his return from Ogu-n'Udo's shrine. Finally, the leader's lips curved into a smile, softening her weathered features. Her hand in his ceased tugging.

"It is well, son of Ezeala of Oma clan," her voice was husky. "All is well between us now. Go, good prince; there is now peace between our clans. May the gods and ancestors guide your actions and bless our paths."

She gave his hand a final squeeze before letting go. Her people surrounded her as she left to join the festivities with the rest of the villagers.

Diké heaved a deep sigh. His body trembled and he felt a sudden lightness in his soul— *Free! He's finally free! Praise and glory to the ancestors and Amadioha!* He knew his work was not finished. There were other reparations to be made, slaves to be freed, wounds to be healed, and life-debts to be paid. But for now, he was sure that Ife and their mother were smiling at him from that wondrous realm, and the great ancestors were rooting for him.

Diké turned back to Big-Bosom, and for the first time since his return from the forbidden shrine, she saw on his face a smile that finally touched his eyes.

Acknowledgments

To my two beautiful daughters, Candice and Jija, whose existence continues to be the anchor that keeps me rooted to life.

———◦⊱✦⊰◦———

To my editor, Jennie Rigg, who did a brilliant first edit and suggested a second final chapter.

———◦⊱✦⊰◦———

To my dearest friend, Ted Dunphy, whose encouragement and support kept me writing even in the direst of times.

———◦⊱✦⊰◦———

To Paul Tremblay, a true horror icon, whose amazing support and encouragement showed me I should always be true to my literary convictions.

———◦⊱✦⊰◦———

To Jeremy Bates, one of my all-time favourite authors, who instantly offered his support when I reached out to him out of the blue.

To my wonderful friend, Stuart (Asap) Hale, whose support and wonderful hand-made cards and joyful hand-written letters kept my spirits up throughout the dire lockdown.

To Jarod Barbee, Jeremy Wagner, and the amazing team at Stygian Sky Media, the undisputed coolest publishers in the horror arena, who made me fall in love all over again with this story and the amazing cover they created.

Love, light, blessings and gratitude to you all!

About the Author

Nuzo Onoh is a Nigerian-British writer of Igbo descent. She is a pioneer of the African horror literary subgenre. Hailed as the "Queen of African Horror", Nuzo's writing showcases both the beautiful and horrific in the African culture within fictitious narratives. Her books, *The Reluctant Dead* (2014) and *Unhallowed Graves* (2015) are both collections of ghost stories depicting core Igbo traditions, beliefs and superstitions. She's also the author of the novels, *The Sleepless* (2016), *Dead Corpse* (2017), *The Unclean* (2020) and the non-fiction work, *Call on Your Ancestors for Happiness and Success* (2017).

Nuzo's works have featured in numerous magazines, podcasts, and anthologies, and she is listed in the reference book, *"80 Black Women in Horror".* She has given talks and lectures about African Horror, including at the prestigious *Miskatonic Institute of Horror Studies, London.* Her works have also appeared in academic and feminist studies such as *"Routledge Handbook of African Literature"*, *"Horror Fiction in the Global South: Cultures, Narratives and Representations"*, and *Women Write About Comics.* Her novellas have been longlisted twice by *The British Science Fiction Association* and recommended by *The Locus Magazine Reading List.* Nuzo is the first African horror writer to have featured in *Starburst Magazine*, the world's longest-running magazine of Cult Entertainment.

Nuzo holds a Law degree and a Masters degree in Writing, both from Warwick University, United Kingdom. She is also a trained Civil Funeral Celebrant, licensed to conduct non-religious burial services. An avid musician with an addiction to *JungYup* and K-indie pop music, Nuzo plays both the guitar and piano, and holds an NVQ in Digital Music Production from City College, Coventry. She currently resides in The West Midlands, UK, with her cat, Tinkerbell.

To my daughter Ruby, for her love,
patience and optimistic spirit.

First published in 2012 by New Holland Publishers (NZ) Ltd
Auckland · Sydney · London · Cape Town

www.newhollandpublishers.co.nz

218 Lake Road, Northcote, Auckland 0627, New Zealand
Unit 1, 66 Gibbes Street, Chatswood, NSW 2067, Australia
86–88 Edgware Road, London W2 2EA, United Kingdom
Wembley Square, First Floor, Solan Road, Gardens, Cape Town 8001, South Africa

Copyright © 2012 in text: Joelle Thomson
Copyright © 2012 in photography: individuals featured, except where otherwise credited
Copyright © 2012 New Holland Publishers (NZ) Ltd
Joelle Thomson has asserted her right to be identified as the author of this work.

Publishing manager: Christine Thomson
Editor: Brian O'Flaherty
Cover and interior design: Nick Turzynski, redinc. book design, Auckland

National Library of New Zealand Cataloguing-in-Publication Data
Thomson, Joëlle.
The wild bunch : movers, shakers and groundbreakers of the
New Zealand Wine Industry / Joëlle Thomson.
Includes bibliographical references.
ISBN 978-1-86966-300-1
1. Vintners—New Zealand. 2. Wineries—New Zealand.
3. Wine industry—New Zealand. I. Title.
641.220993—dc 23

10 9 8 7 6 5 4 3 2 1

Colour reproduction by Pica Digital Pte Ltd, Singapore
Printed in China at Everbest Printing Co, on paper sourced from sustainable forests.

THE
WILD BUNCH

Movers, shakers and
groundbreakers of the
New Zealand wine industry

JOËLLE THOMSON

❧ CONTENTS

꧁ FOREWORD BY TIM ATKIN MW

WHAT IS RISK? THERE'S A STORY, QUITE POSSIBLY AN APOCRYPHAL ONE, ABOUT A CANDIDATE FOR THE OXBRIDGE ENTRANCE EXAMINATION BEING FACED WITH THIS VERY QUESTION. HIS ONE-WORD ANSWER WAS – 'THIS.' OR, MORE DRAMATICALLY, THERE'S THE TALE OF WHAT HERNÁN CORTÉS DID WHEN HE LANDED IN THE YUCATÁN PENINSULA IN 1519 TO CONQUER MEXICO – HE BURNT HIS BOATS, ENSURING THAT HIS CONQUISTADORS WOULD TRIUMPH OR DIE.

Setting up a winery lies somewhere between these two extremes of jeopardy. It doesn't involve mortal danger, provided you stay away from carbon dioxide, but it's a lot more dangerous than spurning a valuable place at an elite university, especially if it involves your life savings. Multimillionaires can afford to dabble in wine production; for the rest of us, it's a high wire act with no safety net.

As someone who's been writing about wine since the 1980s, I never cease to be in awe of people who choose to get their hands dirty; growing grapes, driving tractors, pulling hoses, punching down caps and (the bit that everyone forgets) pounding pavements in search of importers and, finally, customers. It's a lot easier if you come from an established wine region, particularly if you inherit a business. For the pioneers who do it from scratch, it's much more of a struggle.

That's what makes the story of the modern New Zealand wine industry so remarkable. As recently as 1965, the two most planted grapes in the country were Baco 22A and Albany Surprise. Today, New Zealand is recognised as the home of some of the best wines in the world, a leader in Sauvignon Blanc, Pinot Noir, Chardonnay and increasingly Syrah, red blends and white aromatics, too.

There have been other well-written overviews of the Kiwi wine industry, but

no one has sought to tell this extraordinary tale through the eyes of the people at the sharp, or rather sticky, end — Joëlle Thomson's magnificent wild bunch. And what a group they are; passionate, committed, talented, determined, stubborn, creative and (as I can confirm) great fun to interview and share a cold beer with. As a nation, Kiwis tend to be quieter and more contemplative than their neighbours across the Tasman Sea, but they are no less engaging.

I've been lucky enough to get to know all but one of the people in this book. Several of them are individuals I count among my friends. More to the point, I've watched them and their wines develop over a period of 20 years. Looking back at the New Zealand wine scene of the early 1990s (when I first visited) and comparing it with today, I can't quite believe the transformation. Has any wine-producing country achieved so much in only two decades?

Joëlle's talents as a wine writer and journalist are apparent on every page of this wonderful book. She has the skills that are essential to good reporters: the ability to listen, the charm to encourage people to talk and the talent to portray their lives on the page. Some of these stories will be familiar to lovers of New Zealand wine, but many won't. So sit back and enjoy them.

If Joëlle brings empathy, intuition and perception to her interviews, she also brings a good palate, linking winemakers to their wines and terroirs. I like her approach, not only in print, but also as a valued colleague who has been a taster and critic of her country's wines for 20 years. As you will discover, the modern New Zealand wine industry has benefited from the talents of some brilliant, risk-taking individuals. In Joëlle, it has found the perfect advocate.

www.timatkin.com

⸙ INTRODUCING . . . THE WILD BUNCH

NEW ZEALAND WINE IS HOT. AND OBVIOUSLY I'M NOT TALKING ABOUT THE NON-EVENT THAT WAS LAST SUMMER — THE 2012 VINTAGE WAS SAVED IN THE NICK OF TIME BY A WARM APRIL — NOR ABOUT THE HIGH ALCOHOL LEVELS OF SOME NEW ZEALAND WINES OR EVEN ABOUT ITS BEST-LOOKING LABELS.

'People have said to me it was like dodging a bullet in 2012, but it was more like dodging 12-inch shells because the warm weather came so late. Everybody in the New Zealand wine industry was on a knife edge until April's warmth finally arrived,' says Philip Gregan, CEO of New Zealand Winegrowers. New Zealand wine is hot thanks to the passion and energy of its makers. Their willingness to embrace change has been swift. Their rise from a stab-in-the-dark attempt to make classic wines to creating some of the world's most highly regarded whites has been meteoric. In less than 30 years this country's wine industry has gone from mostly small and mostly family-oriented to being part of the global wine industry. And it is an industry but, just as importantly, it is one built largely on the passion of those involved.

That's what this book is about.

My goal in these pages is to expand on the lives and contributions of key people in New Zealand wine, whose tales of tenacity reveal what makes them and their wines tick. Here you will find philosophers, scientists, entrepreneurs, modernists, perfectionists and hedonists — not to mention a couple of party animals, too — who define New Zealand wine.

This group of quietly powerful individuals got New Zealand wine out of its 2-gallon minimum sales size into 750 ml bottles and then into the glasses of wine lovers around the world. They helped to introduce screwcaps to the world of wine. They pioneered (and still continue to develop) biodynamic and organic winemaking. They planted Sauvignon Blanc in New Zealand then defined its taste before introducing the world to an inimitable white wine. They spearheaded Pinot Noir in the southernmost wine region in the world, and they

continue to define the style, quality and value of New Zealand wine today.

Villa Maria was the first large New Zealand winery to move 100 per cent to screwcaps, and on that basis the story of Sir George Fistonich deserves to be told here. But there is so much more to say about Sir George than a mere few thousand words allow. As his lifelong friend and fellow winemaker, Ross Spence, says, 'George is a very unusual man. He knows how to get the best out of people and how to get the best people.'

Convincing the Villa Maria board that screwcaps were the right way forward was no easy task for Fistonich, a former winemaker who began selling wine at his parents' gate in Mangere, and was convinced that wine quality is more consistent under screwcaps.

'Drinkability is what wine is all about and we have to keep that in the front of our minds,' he says, adding that, 'We make a product people like, and we have to do the best we can to make it an enjoyable drink.'

The stories of the Babich, Brajkovich, Fistonich and other Dalmatian wine families have been told many times; this book recalls them but also aims to delve deeper and shed fresh light on the experiences of these families whose wineries are now run by second- and third-generation family members.

Then there are those whose wines are known but whose names remain, for the most part, unsung. Ivan Sutherland and Alan Brady top this list, for me. Sutherland, a former Olympic rower (winning bronze in the eight for New Zealand in 1976), was one of the first to plant decent grapes in Marlborough. He was one of the keystones in the early days of Cloudy Bay. By teaming up with fellow ex-Cloudy Bay-er, James Healy, he is now making some of Marlborough's most outstanding white wines. Their wines speak for them. As does Alan Brady's pioneering work in Central Otago. Not that you would ever hear of him attributed with getting Central's wine industry on its feet, at least not in mainstream New Zealand circles.

The trio of Ivan and Mat Donaldson and Lynnette Hudson — and their partners and family — at Pegasus Bay winery in Waipara, North Canterbury have, in my opinion, done more for this still relatively unknown wine region than anyone else in the country.

I hope this book goes some way to addressing the powerful pioneering impact people like this have had, so that everyday New Zealanders who enjoy wine — and even those who may not yet drink it — will recognise their contributions.

This is not a definitive list of movers, shakers and groundbreakers. No list I could come up with would do justice to the many winemakers who have spearheaded innovation in introducing new grape varieties, winemaking methods, bottling techniques, labelling styles and, most importantly of all, in putting New Zealand wine on the world wine map.

Even with 18 outstanding individuals and their partners, a line had to be drawn in the figurative sand. Forgive me, if your name was on the other side of it. Anyone wondering how I decided who to include can rest assured that I had a great many sleepless nights pondering the same question myself. Originally a bunch of 12 people — a 'case' of wine — it swiftly became 13, then 14 . . . If a baker's dozen is actually 13 — strong yeast, one presumes — the winemaker's yeast is even more potent. And yet this book still covers a mere smidgeon of those

whose determination to create quality wine makes their stories worth telling.

Just as this book was going to print, Martinborough winemaker Clive Paton of Ata Rangi was made an Officer of the New Zealand Order of Merit in the Queen's Birthday Honours for his contribution to conservation in Wellington and the Wairarapa. At the same time, industry elder statesman Terry Dunleavy was awarded honorary membership of the British-based Circle of Wine Writers. And Gisborne winemaker James Millton was overseas at a biodynamic wine seminar when he was awarded a New Zealand Order of Merit. He is still the pioneering forager he was as a young teenager when out harvesting wild berries to ferment, which eventually saw him expelled from high school on the West Coast of the South Island. I can relate to his story, perhaps because I've lived there; perhaps because I like walking in New Zealand's hills where I, too, picked wild berries as a teenager. But of those who can relate to his story, how many had parents open-minded and trusting enough to encourage a child's passion? James's father handed him his first book on fermentation when he was a teen.

Or take Tim Finn in Nelson — the quiet perfectionist. He was born in India and grew up in Lower Hutt as the son of displaced parents who missed the Raj lifestyle when they moved to New Zealand in the 1940s to escape upheaval in India. When Finn graduated from Massey University and, later, with a masters degree from the University of Waikato, he moved to his own 'luxury' lifestyle block of land in Nelson, where he and his wife Judy Finn split five jobs between them to plant their vineyard, build their winery and create a home in the Moutere hills. Such was life in the early days of New Zealand wine.

It's a mystery how the Babich boys survived when they first moved to Auckland in the 1920s, planted grapes and eked out a living off the land with no discernible income for the first five years. They were boys, just teenagers, when they left their parents and home in Croatia in search of food. There was none on the table at home. They had to emigrate to survive, which meant they never saw their parents again.

West Auckland winemaker Michael Brajkovich's earliest wine memory is draining a small glass of it as a toddler when he was being photographed. He was the first New Zealander to become a Master of Wine and, later, the first spokesperson for the New Zealand Screwcap Initiative when it launched in August 2001; achievements he downplays with characteristic humility. At the screwcap launch, I remember thinking how lucky I would have been to have had a science teacher with Brajkovich's gift for imparting complex ideas with clarity, calmness and ease.

Like all those who are profiled in this book, Michael understates the role he has played. If there is any PR machine propelling these people into the limelight, I suggest it comes from elsewhere. These 18 inspiring individuals are focused on making the best wine possible. The exception here to this occupation is the incredibly driven, determined Terry Dunleavy, who has — I consider — done more to get New Zealand wine's message to the world than any other individual.

For nearly three decades, Martinborough has been home to South Australian Larry McKenna, who followed his heart to New Zealand to make wine after he had grown up drinking broad-shouldered Shiraz and Cabernet Sauvignon. He now shares the crown of New Zealand Pinot Noir maestro with

others such as Clive Paton. Both their stories are inspiring.

As are many others who did not make it into this book, who have also ascended the crest of the new wave of wine and managed to ride it through a sea of troubles from wine gluts and oversupply to underpricing and competition from low-quality 'wine' lookalikes. Their stories of survival and success are just as inspirational, just as perspirational and just as worthy of telling.

There are the likes of born-and-bred North American Mike Weersing of Pyramid Valley Vineyards, who developed a fascination with New Zealand that has seen him move here and begin what is undoubtedly one of our most boundary-pushing wineries. Also, second-generation winemaker Nick Mills of Rippon Vineyard; Gerry Gregg who now works for Pernod Ricard New Zealand in Marlborough and who was there when the first vines were stuck the wrong way up into the ground; Master of Wine Steve Smith of Craggy Range winery in Hawke's Bay; wine pioneers John Buck and Peter Cowley of Te Mata; Allan Scott in Marlborough; the Dicey family in Central Otago; Jose Hernandez (who drove sales of European and local wines in New Zealand for decades); and, if wishes could be granted, I would bring back the most gentlemanly of them all, the late wine writer Stanley Harris. There are still more names, stories and wines worth investigating, and no doubt they will occur to you as much as to me.

New Zealand's biggest white wine strengths are its fresh, full-bodied Chardonnays, crisp Sauvignon Blancs, Rieslings, Gewürztraminers, the occasional Verdelho and Viognier and, even more occasionally, a few well-made Pinot Gris. In red wines the picture has never looked or tasted as good as it does today. Pinot Noir is a delicious work in stylistic progress and Hawke's Bay's reds — Malbec, Merlot, Syrah and, in smaller quantities, Cabernet Sauvignon — are a revelation compared with 20 years ago.

But if the wine genie ever appears in front me, I will ask her to show all wine drinkers the great treasure that is Riesling. If there is one white grape and wine style in this country that has the power, the structure, the nobility to do what Sauvignon Blanc and, to a lesser but growing extent, Chardonnay are already doing, it is Riesling.

Try as I might, I can't possibly put it better than the late Mark Twain's late, great rival, Ambrose Bierce, who once said:

'Wine, madam, is God's next best gift to man.'
— Ambrose Bierce, *The Devil's Dictionary*, 1907

It sure is.

www.joellethomson.com

Note: This introduction and many of those interviewed in this book refer specifically to the 2012 vintage; what sets wine apart from all other alcoholic beverages is that it's a unique product each year, dependent for its colour, aroma and flavours on the weather conditions. Unlike other drinks, which can be produced many times over in an annual calendar, wine can be made only once every 12 months. It is this challenge which winemakers, wine drinkers and wine lovers all look to each year as the seasons favour— or not — the grapes at the end of their crucial ripening period.

MAT DONALDSON AND LYNNETTE HUDSON

WINEMAKERS, PEGASUS BAY, WAIPARA, NORTH CANTERBURY

'I was getting into Riesling when a sip of Pegasus Bay Riesling changed my life — it convinced me to quit the law and pursue wine as a career.'

— Hattie Thodey, wine student, New Zealand School of Food & Wine, Auckland

'Not only have they almost singlehandedly put a new region on New Zealand's vinous map, they are always working seemingly close to the edge compared to the safe norm; using all that makes life interesting in the winery (wild ferments, solids, lees work, to begin with). Their Rieslings always stand out as being world class, and they skilfully incorporate botrytis influence into the myriad styles that they make, sweet and dry.'

— Andrew Hedley, winemaker, Framingham Wines, Marlborough

'Mat and Lynnette lure you into their world with the descant of Riesling, a place of both passion and intellect.'

— Angela Clifford, friend and Waipara Valley wine ambassador

'Lynnette Hudson and husband Mat Donaldson have shown over many years that Waipara Valley can consistently offer a range of fine aromatic whites and Pinot Noir.'

— Guy Porter, Bellbird Spring winery

13

GREATEST ACHIEVEMENTS

Mat Donaldson: 'Making my parents proud and being an integral part of our family business that keeps four families in a reasonable lifestyle.'

Lynnette Hudson: 'Finding Pegasus Bay, making wine here and marrying Mat.'

KEY ACHIEVEMENTS: LYNNETTE

- Living in Burgundy for a year and working with producers such as Christophe Roumier, Nicolas Potel and Pascal Marchand.
- Receiving recognition as a quality producer of Pinot Noir by international critics such as Robert Parker, Stephen Tanzer, *Wine Spectator* and Jancis Robinson.

KEY ACHIEVEMENTS: MAT

- Working with Patrice Rion in Burgundy.
- Pegasus Bay achieving a five-star producer rating from Robert Parker.
- Winning the Waipara Riesling Challenge.
- Having Riesling become our number-one-selling wine variety.

LYNNETTE: TAKE TO A DESERT ISLAND . . .

'Christophe Roumier's Les Amoureuses, and I'd take Mat because he has the most interesting ideas and conversations; there's no one I'd rather talk to. He also has a great selection of music, so we'd always have something to listen to.'

MAT: TAKE TO A DESERT ISLAND . . .

'I would take a 2009 FX Pichler Riesling Smaragd Loibner Berg and a 1999 Domaine Joseph Matrot Meursault-Blagny, and for a red wine it would be 2002 Christophe Roumier Chambolle Musigny. I would take Lynnette, and the music would be *Converting Vegetarians* by Infected Mushroom — my all-time favourite album.'

THE STORY

Driving down the long straight road that leads to the gates of Pegasus Bay's winery, restaurant and winemakers' home on Stockgrove Road in Waipara, it's hard to imagine none of this existed three decades ago.

There were no grapevines, no groomed garden spilling down the slopes from the winery, no constantly awarded restaurant serving delicious dishes with such stylish ease that it feels almost resort-like, no tower in which to stand with a cool Riesling gazing at a hot Cantabrian sun setting gradually over the nearby hills. There were no Mat and Lynnette in residence, pumping out great music, and even better Riesling, to a market where most wine drinkers never reach for Riesling but, thanks to the dedication and realism of this duo, often buy theirs.

The seeds of this winery's early success were planted by the now retired

---

Ivan Donaldson, a professor of neurology, wine lover and one of Canterbury's first winemakers. He and a group of like-minded medical professionals and friends experimented with grape growing on the relatively cool Canterbury Plains back in the late 1970s and early 1980s, making wine in their double garage after hours — as the French would say, 'garagiste' winemakers.

The garage was in Christchurch city, nearly an hour's drive south of where Pegasus Bay is today.

How this winery came to be here is as much the story of the region as of the extended family and partners who run it; but if it weren't for them, Waipara and North Canterbury would still be a fledgling wine region — rather than the up-and-coming Riesling and Pinot Noir area it is now. Not that the Pegasus Bay team claims the glory for putting North Canterbury and Waipara on the wine map. It is just that, until about a decade ago, every other winery and winemaker to ever set up shop here has either been tiny and entirely hobbyist, corporate-owned and then disappeared, or so small and perfectionist that their wines have been tried by only a lucky few.

What makes Pegasus Bay different is that it was planned, then it was capitalised properly, and that it had a trained winemaker from the start. These three key ingredients are now, finally, becoming commonplace in this region.

The first vintage was 1991. The winemaking at Pegasus Bay is run by a husband and wife team who are as well known for their love of great French and German wines as they are for their own winemaking talent.

He's the party animal of New Zealand wine: a Riesling, red burgundy and music lover in equal measure. She is a winemaker who thrives on experimentation in a quest to make the best Pinot Noir she can from the grapes they grow at Pegasus Bay. They met over two decades ago at a wine tasting in Christchurch and have lived together almost ever since. And yet, when Mat Donaldson and Lynnette Hudson met, the winery we know today as Pegasus Bay was a virtually unknown, fledgling new venture in Waipara.

MAT DONALDSON'S EARLY WINE DAYS

Mat's earliest wine memory is of helping himself to his dad's early experimental drop and drinking it behind the bike sheds at school when he was about 11 or 12. He didn't enjoy the taste.

Then in 1982 his parents took Mat and his three younger brothers — Edward, Paul and Mike — to Europe where they all tasted and consumed more wine before returning home to New Zealand, where Ivan continued making experimental wine in the garage.

'Dad would ask us to rack off a barrel of wine in the garage when we were

teenagers and if we didn't do it, we didn't get our pocket money,' recalls Mat.

'One of Dad's first wines must have been a Cabernet Sauvignon because it was really tannic and really bitter, and I remember thinking it tasted like blotting paper. Really green Cabernet Sauvignon from Canterbury does taste like that. They had very few grapes in those days, and they would break up the marc [grape skins and pulp] in their little basket press quite a few times and squeeze as hard as possible to get the maximum amount of wine, which accounted for the bitterness.

'The first time I really liked a wine was from Dad's vineyard at Halswell; they nicknamed it 'Pleurisy Point' because it was so cold there. It was actually the first vineyard planted outside of Lincoln University in Canterbury, and up the top of the vineyard the Riesling was on stakes, the way it's planted in the Mosel, in Germany.'

The wine was a glass of red: a 1985 Pinot Noir from 'Pleurisy Point Vineyard'. Says Mat: 'That vintage must have been a good one because it was such a cold site. Last time I tried that wine was about 10 or 15 years ago, and I thought it was like the 1982 St Helena Pinot Noir, which was inspirational at the time because it showed the region had the capability of producing grapes good enough to make good-tasting wine.'

It was after their trip to Europe in 1982 that Ivan and Christine Donaldson started looking for land in Waipara on which to plant their own vineyard, but it was another two or three years before they found the property they liked.

'It became clear by about 1983 that it was really too cold to ripen the types of grapes we wanted to at Halswell or anywhere on the Canterbury Plains, to our knowledge, so we started looking for land further north and it took a while to find it,' says Ivan Donaldson, who attributes his late friend, Professor Don Beavan, with having been the main impetus behind starting winemaking in Canterbury.

Beavan was the first professor of medicine at the Christchurch School of Medicine, a wine lover, author, TV wine presenter in the 1970s and also Donaldson's friend — and boss.

'But he never really behaved like a boss. He was such a good friend and we became very close because he had such a strong interest in wine. He was the driving force behind getting the first modern vineyard going in Canterbury, where I made the first wines,' says Ivan, who made the first two vintages in the garage from grapes grown on the new Waipara vineyard. He made about 20 barrels of red and a few old beer tanks of a Sauvignon Blanc/Sémillon blend. They were the only registered winery in the middle of Christchurch city at the time.

'I remember driving the posts into the ground in my school holidays in 1986,' says Mat Donaldson, who finished high school in 1988 and went straight to Roseworthy Agricultural College (the pre-eminent wine training facility) in South Australia in 1989, finishing four years later with a degree in oenology and a graduate diploma in viticulture.

This wasn't quite the plan his father had foreseen.

'When Chris and I first bought the land and started the vineyard, we had no expectation the children would join us. I hoped they would all go into the medical profession, but none did. Mat had no real interest in the vineyard until he went to work at Danny Schuster's winery and vineyard as a school holiday

job. He came back convinced he'd be a winemaker. I thought it would be far too narrow and tried to talk him out of it, but he was absolutely determined and so by the time he went to Roseworthy College to do his university degree in Australia, we had every expectation he would come back and be the winemaker.'

And so it was. Mat returned home to Canterbury in 1992 to make the vintage in the half-erected first stage of the winery, which had been planned jointly with his parents as part of a six-stage building project.

The family had about 50 acres (20 hectares) of grapes planted in Waipara in the mid-1980s, compared to the 100 acres (40 hectares) they now have. Skip forward a few decades and today three of the four Donaldson sons now work full-time at the winery. Mat is the winemaker (with Lynnette), Edward is in marketing and sales while Paul is the business manager. The fourth, Mike, works in Ireland.

LYNNETTE HUDSON'S WINE STORY

'Mat invited me to stay for a vintage and I never left,' laughs Lynnette Hudson, remembering the early days of their relationship at the young winery.

The first vintage Hudson worked in North Canterbury was about 20 minutes' drive north of Pegasus Bay winery in Omihi, on Danny Schuster's vineyard, which he no longer owns.

Her interest in wine began shortly after her elder brother started taking an in-depth shine to the subject. She was studying at the University of Auckland; he had started drinking wine and making notes about the wines he tried.

'I thought, "Jesus, that's pretty over the top, why would you want to do that?" Then I did a basic wine understanding course and got really interested. I wanted to be able to select a good-quality wine relative to the money I wanted to spend. My passion grew from there.'

When she left university, Hudson moved to Christchurch with her partner, who was studying for a masters in entymology. She intended to use her science degree to work in marine biology but instead accepted a job as a sales representative.

'I hated it and had to do something else.'

So, she moved to Australia in 1991 and worked for a fine wine shop, which is where she started developing her palate. 'The owner taught me lots about winemaking, so I decided to come back in 1992 and do the one-year postgraduate winemaking course at Lincoln University in Christchurch.'

It was after a wine tasting one night at the end of 1992 that she met Mat. They stayed in touch and, just as she was about to start working the vintage at Omihi a couple of months later, he invited her to stay at the cottage. She has been there ever since. She never thought Canterbury would be her home when she first moved from Auckland in the late 1980s.

In one sense at least, she has left Christchurch.

Her home with Donaldson in Waipara is always warmer, always drier, always sunnier — with rare exceptions to this better weather rule — than it is in Christchurch. And while Christchurch has been rocked by two major

'AS WE HAVE LEARNT HOW TO GROW BETTER GRAPES AND MAKE BETTER WINE . . . IT HAS HELPED US TO BUILD A STRONG FOLLOWING. . . . THEY FEEL A CONNECTION TO US, HAVING BEEN ON THE JOURNEY WITH US.'

earthquakes and a never-ending stream of aftershocks in the past three years, Waipara and North Canterbury have remained largely unscathed. It is this warmer, drier and sunnier weather that attracted the region's winemakers from their early starts on the chilly Canterbury Plains in the first place. Yet North Canterbury and Waipara remain relatively youthful wine regions, even by New Zealand's young winemaking standards.

WAIPARA AND NORTH CANTERBURY CHALLENGES

'In the past we felt we were doing it all alone here. Even 10 years ago, there was a lack of serious wine producers in the region; most people didn't treat it as anything more than a hobby and didn't have much cash flow to put into what they what were doing,' says Hudson.

'It takes more than just one or two wineries to make a region stand out; it has to be a cohesive group of people doing really good things with wine.'

Things have changed in the past decade. Today there is a growing number of larger wineries, which are earning the greater North Canterbury region its mantle as a top spot for Riesling. It is also home to a growing number of promising Pinot Noirs, with Chardonnay, the occasional bubbly, Sauvignon Blanc, Sémillon and even a little Pinot Gris also occupying local vineyards. One of the most promising local wineries — Muddy Water Fine Wines — has now been sold, and Danny Schuster, a Waipara pioneer, has also now, sadly, gone. In their place a bunch of winemakers with vast experience, in some cases gained further afield than New Zealand, have stepped in. These new winemakers are proving the region is home to quality rather than quantity. Names such as Black Estate, Bellbird Spring, Bell Hill, George's Road, Greystone and Pyramid Valley, among others, are all producing consistently top-shelf wines each year.

The flip-side, for Pegasus Bay, of previously being the sole large, well-known and non-hobbyist winery is that the winery had the nearby Christchurch market pretty much all to itself.

Asked how they established strong sales of their Rieslings early on, Hudson says it was about working on quality and being in the right place at the right time.

'In many ways it worked in our favour being the only big winery here making Riesling as one of our main wines early on. Because we were one of the few wineries who were serious and committed to quality, we were able to establish a strong local market in Christchurch, and we were very lucky in that respect. As we have learnt how to grow better grapes and make better wine, year on year, people who drank our wines in Christchurch have tasted the changes along the way. It has helped us to build a strong following. I think they feel a connection to us, having been on the journey with us,' she says.

WAIPARA'S GREAT WHITE: RIESLING

'You can definitely pick Waipara Rieslings in a line-up. It's a spicy orange zest character. It's pretty unique. You don't get it in any other region anywhere else in the world,' Mat Donaldson says.

The regional orange zest character intensifies the longer the fruit is left on the vines. 'A well-hung Riesling is a great Riesling,' Donaldson laughs, adding that 'We do like to leave our grapes hanging on the vine for as long as possible and because it's a pretty dry region here, we don't mind having botrytis (aka noble rot) characters in the wine.'

While all winemakers and many wine lovers know that a little botrytis goes a long way, Hudson says that rather than fear it, they look forward to using it to their advantage.

'We actually want a bit of botrytis because, if handled properly, it adds concentration and character to our Rieslings. We're not scared of it. You often hear winemakers worried about the risk of botrytis because it can prematurely age a wine or create undesired flavours, but we want a bit. Between 5 and 20 per cent is about perfect for our Rieslings; the variation depends only on the type of season we've had, which dictates to an extent what type of wines we make.'

The style of Pegasus Bay Riesling has changed along with Donaldson and Hudson's own wine experiences.

'About five years ago we tasted some 2006 Mosel Rieslings which had really high levels of botrytis but had been fermented to complete dryness, rather than making sweet wines, which is the usual thing to do. Those wines had high alcohol, but they tasted so good because they were so well balanced and really succulent. They just blew us away. We were out at a tasting, so I rang the restaurant at the winery since they were the only ones I knew I could contact there — it was about eight o'clock at night — and I asked the staff to turn the switches off to let the wines finish fermenting. The result was a very different style than our previous Pegasus Bay Rieslings.

'I met a few people out and about who said, "I just really don't like your 2008 Riesling." The family wasn't that happy and made us promise not to make a wine in that style again, and we came to a compromise. We have agreed not to go to that extreme again. We have also changed to not fining our Rieslings (fining is a process to remove particles left in wine after fermentation), which makes a massive positive difference to them.'

Over the past half decade, they have experimented with earlier harvest times as well as later than usual harvest times; it has been part of their journey of discovering what works best for making top-tasting Rieslings.

And then there is Main Divide: the apparent second label of the winery but a range of wines on which Donaldson says he spends proportionately more time with each passing year.

'It's much bigger volume than Pegasus Bay, and you know a lot of people are going to be drinking it, so it's really important to make a good basic wine. We have ended up putting a lot more resources and time into it than we originally planned to and it's paying off because people love it, especially the Riesling.'

CHALLENGES FOR NEW ZEALAND AND WAIPARA

Of the international surplus of wine that exists in 2012, Ivan Donaldson says it's not all doom and gloom. Although there is a surplus, there is not an international surplus of New Zealand wine, he says.

'Even the biggest players in New Zealand are small by world standards. There is a problem at the moment, but that will pass. When we first bought the land and started the vineyard, we only bought it because it was dirt cheap, and it was only dirt cheap then because farming wasn't doing well and because there was a surplus of New Zealand wine at that time, too. It was just before the big national grape pull. Wines were a dime a dozen back then, too, and everything was on special offer, as it is today. Since that time the New Zealand wine industry has had a bit of a cruisy run.

'I think this brings it back to a bit of a dose of reality, and that will be a positive because those who invested in the wine industry only to make money will hopefully disappear,' says Ivan.

One of the major challenges for Waipara and North Canterbury is achieving cohesiveness.

'There are people who still don't want to partake of the joint marketing body; in the wine industry you have to spend a lot of money to keep people interested and occupied because there are so many wines that will woo them, if yours don't,' says Lynnette Hudson. The larger problem of the national wine surplus will also rectify itself, she says.

'As a wine industry, we're relying on Mother Nature to bring us back into balance because man knows no form of regulation because there are dollar signs in his — in our — eyes.

'We know we're in an oversupply and surplus situation, but due to greed for profit, some producers are reluctant to reduce their crop levels.

'The long-term answer is trickier. If the government said, "Let's regulate crop levels", where would it stop? As soon as we go down that path, we're heading for what hampers Europe with its convoluted rules and regulations in winemaking.

'What's good as a result of this year's low crops is that the surplus will start to sell out, wine will go up in price again and a lot of really cheap third labels — created to get rid of the oversupply — will just fall by the wayside.'

On a more local front, the physical challenges in Waipara tend to come early in the grape-growing season: spring frost. The end of the growing season, however, is generally benign.

'We always have amazing autumns, 2012 being a case in point. Every year the

most settled period is over autumn. From late March the weather settles and there's not that much wind, but there are beautiful warm days and cool nights,' says Lynette.

WHERE TO NEXT?

Hudson and Donaldson sit on slightly different fence posts when it comes to natural grape-growing methodologies.

'Matthew's not a star, moon, hippy sort at all. I could swing both ways. For me, the environment in which you live is everything, and making it a better place to live is important. So no chemicals is a very good way forward for me, and Mat thinks the same way, but you have to be completely dedicated to go down the biodynamic path. Since we take different positions on this, it's not something we can do wholeheartedly,' says Hudson.

'It's more important to me to try to understand the growing season and how that's going to reflect in the grapes, in terms of what we do with them.'

LEARNING PINOT NOIR SECRETS

Four years ago the Hudson–Donaldson winemaking duo began a Pinot Noir experiment. They processed the same grapes in three different ways, playing around with varying quantities of whole berries (which tends to produce wines with lifted aromas) to no whole berries.

The results have been analysed by winemaking students at Lincoln University for varying levels of anthocyanins (also known as flavonoids, they are responsible for the level and type of colour in grapes and other fruits and vegetables). There have been other differences, too, enabling Hudson and Donaldson to evolve their Pinot Noir production, depending on what type of weather they encounter each year.

'Whole berries gives a very perfumed but light wine . . . We find 30 per cent of whole berries gives us a beautiful harmony with perfumed aromatics but still colour and richness. This type of approach tends to make my favourite wine. The majority of the time this method is preferable, but it does depend on other factors; what the vintage has been like determines what type of tannins we'll encounter and we need to respond to those in the Pinot Noirs we make.'

The sales figures might agree, too, but for Hudson and Donaldson there is something more to wine than just business.

'Wine is the most exciting subject in the world. Why wouldn't you want to read more, taste more and drink more widely?' asks Hudson.

'It's just like this massive plate of candy out there waiting to be enjoyed. It totally rocks my world. There's nothing more exciting in my life.'

'WINE IS THE MOST EXCITING SUBJECT IN THE WORLD. WHY WOULDN'T YOU WANT TO READ MORE, TASTE MORE AND DRINK MORE WIDELY?'

LYNNETTE'S GO-TO WINES
'White and red burgundy are my ultimate always. I lived in the region for 14 months, and there are so many things about Burgundy that make it my second home. Nothing makes me happier than a great white burgundy followed by a great red burgundy. I'm open to any wine in the world and also love aromatics; German and Austrian Rieslings are amazing. My next ultimate would be Syrah from the Rhône and Barolo and Barbaresco from Piemonte in northern Italy.'

MAT'S GO-TO WINES
'White burgundy used to be my favourite, but these days it's definitely Riesling. It's pretty crazy having a favourite; it's like saying what's your favourite type of person, but as a single variety Riesling is so versatile and capable of more different styles than anything else. There's something about Riesling that makes it tight and structured, even when it has low acids. At home we drink only Riesling and burgundy. It sounds pretty pretentious, but it's true.'

IVAN'S GO-TO WINES
'My everyday wines are made from Riesling — surprise, surprise; in particular German Rieslings and especially from the Mosel. Riesling for me is number one. It's so versatile and you can get wonderful Rieslings in all sorts of styles and at all prices. It's not something great that you have to dream about; it's affordable so it's something everyone can experience and get the quality from.'

TOP WINES FROM MAT HUDSON AND LYNNETTE DONALDSON AT PEGASUS BAY
- Bel Canto Dry Riesling
- Prima Donna Pinot Noir

NICK NOBILO

WINE INDUSTRY PIONEER;
OWNER, VINOPTIMA, GISBORNE

'Nick emerged as a crusader for classic red wines, first with Pinotage, then Cabernet Sauvignon and, a little later, Pinot Noir, a forerunner from the warmer Auckland climate of what was later to emerge in Martinborough and further south. Of equal importance were his other brothers: Mark, one of the country's most skilled and dedicated viticulturists; and Steve, a shoe-leather salesman on first-name terms with every wine retailer in the land.'

— Terry Dunleavy MBE, New Zealand wine elder statesman

GREATEST ACHIEVEMENT

'Being an integral part of creating the Müller-Thurgau style of the mid-1970s because that wine converted the drinking habits of New Zealanders from beer to wine. There's a bottle of my 1975 Nobilo Müller-Thurgau at Te Papa.'

KEY ACHIEVEMENTS

- Being instrumental in changing New Zealand wine from fortified wines and hybrids to classical *Vitis vinifera* varietal wines.
- First New Zealand winemaker to produce Pinotage in 1970, aged in new French oak for 22 months, which won champion wine at the National Wine Competition in 1973.
- Pioneer of varietal Cabernet Sauvignon using Bordeaux methods and new French oak in 1970, along with Tom McDonald, who approached my father in 1970 asking for me to become his assistant winemaker.

- First New Zealand winemaker to commercially produce Gewürztraminer in 1972 and Pinot Noir in 1973, and the first in New Zealand to use French oak barrel fermentation for Chardonnay in 1973.
- First winemaker to export New Zealand wine to the UK when a pallet of 1976 Nobilo Cabernet Sauvignon was shipped to Avery's in 1979 after the wine was judged Champion Wine at the National Wine Competition.
- Receiving an export award from Rt Hon. Jim Bolger for New Zealand's most successful export wine in the 1980s with White Cloud, a blend of Müller-Thurgau and Sauvignon Blanc.
- Winning a contract to have a Nobilo Chardonnay selected by British Airways for all its European flights against stiff international competition in 1991. The contract continued for 15 years and resulted in millions of 187-ml New Zealand Chardonnay being consumed, while helping to establish the quality and status of New Zealand wines across Europe during the 1990s.
- Achieving the highest Robert Parker score ever for a New Zealand wine: 97 points for 2004 Vinoptima Noble.

TAKE TO A DESERT ISLAND . . .

'My desert island is somewhere with a warm climate, southern Mediterranean, preferably, so I would take the 2010 Vinoptima Noble, a corkscrew, backpack with utensils and a pair of sturdy walking shoes as there are bound to be rocks around while I explore the island for natural food, hopefully tropical sweet foods — dates and figs. Then I would look to the sea for food. Once I've discovered what's available, like Heston Blumenthal I would create the perfect dish to go with this wine. The passion and effort I put into making the Noble would need to be within the food, too, so it wouldn't just be a survival dish.

'Once I had made the food and enjoyed the wine, I would lie back and look at the stars. It would be an escape because life is so full of intrusions, so I would go by myself.'

THE STORY

'I was a born winemaker. It's all I ever wanted to be,' says Nick Nobilo, sipping an Alsatian Pinot Gris and talking about fast cars and travelling to the great wine regions of the world in his early twenties.

His first fast car was a Bathurst Holden Monaro, which he inadvertently wrapped around a power pole on Great North Road in Grey Lynn, Auckland, in the 1960s.

'I was lucky to survive, but I was young and single, and I like to push things to the edge, which comes through in my winemaking, too.'

While there were more fast cars to come — a Valiant Charger was next — Nobilo became better known for creating radical new wine styles than for losing cars to inconveniently placed power poles.

He left Henderson High School aged 17 in 1960 and began work at the family winery 'immediately', happy to be doing what he had wanted to do all his life.

VINOPTIMA GEWÜRZTRAMINER

The Latin word Vinoptima means 'best wines' and Nick Nobilo has done everything he can imagine to ensure his wines live up to their name.

It starts in the vineyard. Nobilo created his own Gewürztraminer clone as well as designing and patenting rain covers for his vines, for use in tricky vintages. His 9.7-hectare Vinoptima vineyard was planted in 2000 but first dreamt of in 1975, the year he persuaded a Gisborne grape-grower, David Thomas (now retired), to plant Gewürztraminer in a nearby vineyard.

Thomas was a meticulous grape-grower, whose Müller-Thurgau was among the best supplied to Nobilo Wines, back when that winery was still in family hands and Müller was still in the ground in New Zealand. Having long loved the taste of Gewürztraminer and never being able to coax it into submission in Auckland, Nobilo asked Thomas to give it a go at his Bond Road vineyard in Ormond.

For the next three years Nobilo walked around the vineyard at harvest time, tasting grapes from each vine and marking with spray-paint those which tasted best. Once he had narrowed it down to 50 vines, Nobilo took cuttings off each and commissioned Corbans Viticulture in West Auckland to build up supplies of Gewürztraminer 'budwood' (young, grafted grapevines), which he now grows.

In 2000 the Nobilo wine company left family hands when it was acquired by BRL Hardy (now owned by the North American-based wine company, Constellation). Nobilo used some of the proceeds to pursue his passion for Gewürztraminer and created Vinoptima at Ormond, 26 kilometres inland from Gisborne. The vineyard is an almost equal mix of the vines he now calls 'Nick's clone' and another clone of Gewürztraminer from Colmar in Alsace, France, and Geisenheim, Germany.

The first vintage was 2003. Since then Nobilo has released only another three Vinoptima Gewürztraminers because 'I want them to taste exceptional when they reach people, not just taste like any other wine, released too young to drink.' Each bottle is sealed with the dense fibre of a solid Sardinian cork, Nobilo's pick after testing sackfuls of cork from around the world. The Sardinian corks won the day in both sensory and visual evaluations. They are 55 millimetres long and graded 'royale' — the top level. Cork taint has been minimal, although he confesses to using cork predominantly because his favoured bottle — a taller than average Alsatian bottle in deep green — is manufactured only for a cork seal.

About 85 per cent of Vinoptima wine sells overseas in countries ranging from Australia, the UK, USA and northern Europe to Singapore, Japan and China.

When released, the 2011 Vinoptima will mark Nobilo's fiftieth anniversary in winemaking and, he says, a new height in the taste of New Zealand Gewürztraminer.

'I love the flavour of the Gewürztraminer grape; it's beautifully grapefruit and ginger-like. I love the complex layers of flavour in the wine it produces, and I love its food-matching ability. Gewürztraminer will change its character with the phenolics in the food, according to what you're drinking it with. I call this the chameleon effect and have experimented with this.'

He had made his first wine at the age of four in a bucket filled with leftover grapes at his parent's West Auckland winery. His late father was the founding winemaker: Croatian-born Nikola Nobilo, OBE, who emigrated to New Zealand in 1937 from the island of Korcula to work at his uncle's farm in Wellsford. His wife-to-be — and childhood sweetheart — Zuva came a

> '**I WAS LUCKY DAD LET ME EXPERIMENT WITH PLANTING NEW GRAPES AND MAKING WINE FROM THEM. IT WAS A BIG CALL IN THOSE DAYS; YOU KNEW THE TRIED AND TRUE, BUT TO VENTURE OUT INTO NEW TERRITORY AS I WANTED TO WAS A REAL RISK.**'

couple of years later. They planted their first grapes and began making wine in West Auckland in 1943, so their three sons grew up with it. And from as early as he can recall, Nick Nobilo (Jr) wanted to follow in his dad's footsteps.

It was his father's open-mindedness that allowed and encouraged young Nick to spearhead major change in his own maverick fashion, moving the New Zealand wine industry away from fortified wines made with hybrid grapes, sugar and water to classic wines made from *Vitis vinifera* grapes at a time when most people laughed at such lofty goals.

'I was lucky Dad let me experiment with planting new grapes and making wine from them. It was a big call in those days; you knew the tried and true, but to venture out into new territory as I wanted to was a real risk.'

His first new territory was trialling classic European grapes, which he discovered through his relationship with the late Frank Berrysmith, one-time government viticulturist.

'Most people in New Zealand wine back then thought he was just an idiot, maybe because he smoked a curved pipe and had a hand missing, but he knew what he was talking about. Dad and I used to drive to Te Kauwhata to see him, and that's how he offered me cuttings of the grapes he was trying to get going in New Zealand.'

But that was only the beginning of Nick Nobilo's deepening relationship with real wine as opposed to the fortified lookalikes which characterised New Zealand's 'wine' back then.

TRAVELLING WITH WINE

In 1965 the Nobilo family joined forces with the UK spirits firm, Gilbey's — producers of Gilbey's Gin — which gave both companies something they didn't have before. Gilbey's acquired a New Zealand winery to add to its large global portfolio and Nobilo's gained cash to expand its winery and vineyards.

As soon as that cash hit the bank account, the family bought 12 acres (5 hectares) of land adjacent to their West Auckland winery, and Nobilo convinced his father they should plant an experimental mix of grapes on the new land. Nikola agreed. So into the ground went a fruit salad of vines ranging from the sublime — Cabernet Sauvignon, Pinot Noir, Pinotage, Merlot, Riesling, Gewürztraminer, Pinot Gris, Chardonnay, even Sauvignon Blanc and Müller-Thurgau — to the ridiculous: Grüner Veltliner, Pedro Ximénes, Aligote and Tannat. Several rows of each grape went in, with extras thrown in for good

measure. Few of these grapes were known of at the time, and plenty of people sniggered at the trial plot.

'Looking back at that era, no one was forward thinking. I was probably the only one, and I say that without apology because we used to have viticultural field-days, attended by members of the wine industry, who would all go to the Government Viticultural Research Station at Te Kauwhata where viticulturist Frank Berrysmith was planting classic *Vitis vinifera* grapes instead of the awful things we had at the time. Frank was our source of the grapes we planted on that experimental block. He brought them here through the government from Geisenheim in Germany and the University of California at Davis,' Nobilo says.

'I often heard that someone had said, "Stupid old Nick Nobilo trying to get Pinotage going out west," but I wasn't deterred because I wasn't just going to follow the rest of the industry and plant a continuation of Seibel 5455 or Baco No 1, horrible hybrids from which it was impossible to make great wine.'

It is ironical that when Frank Yukich from Montana embarked on his ambitious planting programme in Marlborough in 1973 following advice from Professor Berg as to the suitability of that region, Frank asked Nick Nobilo for permission to come to the Huapai vineyard and take cuttings from these experimental vines. Therefore it can be legitimately claimed that the origins of the initial plantings by Montana in Marlborough came from vines originally planted by Nick Nobilo at Huapai.

His determination was cemented during an almost year-long trip to the world's great wine regions. Immediately after vintage had finished in 1971, Nobilo visited wineries owned by Gilbey's in all the major wine-producing countries.

'Gilbey's owned a *cru bourgeois* Château Loudenne in the Médoc, where I stayed, then I went to Bouchard Père & Fils in Burgundy, to Quinta D'Roaja in the Upper Douro, Croft's Sherry in Jerez, and also to Stellenbosch in South Africa, to Italy, Spain, Croatia, Austria, Germany and Hungary. I visited all the greats in Bordeaux and was fascinated by the old world, but I got the greatest inspiration from the Napa Valley in California because what was happening there at the time was similar to what I wanted to see happen in New Zealand. I remember sitting on the lawn with Robert Mondavi with his sons, Tim and Michael, tasting his wines and realising what I wanted to see achieved in New Zealand.'

He came back pretty fired up. André Tchelistcheff — the most influential winemaker in the United States during Prohibition — became a mentor, as did others, inspiring and encouraging him to bring classic winemaking back to New Zealand.

'I was able to implement the changes I did to New Zealand wine in the early 70s not only because I knew we had the grapes here, thanks to Frank Berrysmith, but because I knew there were better wines we could make from them. I had tasted them.'

When he arrived back in the early 1970s the fruits of the trial vineyard were starting to show, and Nobilo realised swiftly that reds did far better in the Auckland climate than the whites he had planted at the time, although his favourite was one of the latter, Gewürztraminer. He made his first commercial Gewürztraminer in 1972. It tasted good but was a financial disaster. Compared

with the other new grapes he was harvesting, Gewürztraminer yielded just half a measly tonne of grapes to the acre, as opposed to the usual 4 tonnes to the acre the others tended to yield.

'I told Dad the next year would be better and it was. We had a 50 per cent increase to three-quarters of a tonne to the acre, so we decided we'd give it another go, and in its third year we got half a tonne again. Dad said, "Son, we have to pull this out or we'll go bankrupt."'

About 85 per cent of the trial grapes suffered from one complication or another. Some didn't flower properly and bore very few grapes; others wouldn't ripen fully and tasted green. Even so, Nobilo's passion for making classic wines had been sparked.

MÜLLER SAVES THE DAY

Fortunately, the day was saved when the late wine critic Frank Thorpy paid Nobilo a visit in 1971, bearing a bottle of German Müller-Thurgau and saying, 'Nick, if you can make a wine like this, it'll be a winner.'

'I seized on that because I had great respect for Frank. I analysed the wine, saw what the alcohol, pH, sweetness and acidity were and discovered why it tasted that way. It was only 9.5 per cent alcohol, which meant it had been back-blended. This meant it had unfermented grape juice put into the finished wine to add weight, flavour and to reduce the alcohol content.'

So he followed suit, and in 1975 Nobilo made the first commercially available and varietally labelled Müller-Thurgau in New Zealand, modelled on that wine, with the words 'German style' added to the label. It was an overnight success. The first Nobilo Müller-Thurgau set a new trend, bringing beer and 'sherry' drinkers to its fold and spawning so many copies that, by 1979, Müller-Thurgau was the most widely produced wine in New Zealand. Nobilo still believes New Zealand winemakers were too hasty in obliterating Müller-Thurgau in later years.

'It is a delicious wine when well made and reflects freshness and floral tones. We used to drink it by the bucketload because it was only 9.5 to 10 per cent alcohol.'

It also spurred the major growth of the New Zealand wine industry outside of Auckland because land was not available to expand within the region. The Nobilo family employed contract grape-growers in Gisborne; their first was Martin Tombleson, chairman of the Grape Growers Council in the early 1970s and 'very dedicated to quality grape growing'.

From the mid-1970s Gisborne became the bread basket of the New Zealand wine industry, right through until the late 1980s when Marlborough took over with its Sauvignon Blanc.

THE BIGGEST CHALLENGES

It wasn't enough to just make Müller-Thurgau; the market to drink it had to be created. And the right climate in which to grow it — and other classic grape varieties — had to be discovered.

'Aside from having a beer-drinking culture in this country, our other big challenge was dealing with the vagaries of nature. West Auckland was not conducive to growing certain classical *Vinifera* grapes.

'We soon discovered that Cabernet Sauvignon was not going to work in Auckland, apart from on rare occasions, like 1976. We probably lost 10 years of time by having it planted in the wrong place, Nobilo says.

'We discovered Gisborne was good for growing aromatic grapes, Müller-Thurgau and Chardonnay, and then we moved to Hawke's Bay, Marlborough and the Wairarapa. We gradually discovered which areas of New Zealand are more suited to certain grape varieties than others. It was frustrating in those early years knowing we could produce wines of great character, but not from the right area. There was a lot of discovery we needed to make.'

In terms of shifting the cultural perspective towards wine, Nobilo says writers and critics played a key role then — and now.

'In my mind, the characters of the late Jock Graham and Stanley Harris and others like Michael Brett, Frank Thorpy, Vic Williams, Peter Saunders, Keith Stewart, Bob Campbell, Michael Cooper, Joëlle Thomson and others more recently, have played an integral role in bringing the wine-drinking public forward to try new wines.'

YOUNG WINEMAKERS IN THE 1970S

There was one more key to unlocking the door to quality winemaking — sharing and comparing.

'We were sitting around on beer crates, comparing notes, going into each other's wineries with a "barrel thief" (also known as a glass pipette) to extract a little of our neighbours' wines and see what they were doing. We were exchanging ideas, and we knew by then the way to self-improve was to meet, taste and share,' says Nobilo, talking about the early days of the infamous Young Winemakers group in West Auckland. Its members included Joe Babich, Ross Spence, George Fistonich, the late Joe Corban, Paul Erceg, Tony Soljan, Jim Delegat and John Hancock.

'We were determined to elevate the industry to a new level of quality and so far as I was concerned that started in the mid-1960s, with the move away from hybrid grapes,' Nobilo says.

New Zealand wine elder statesman Terry Dunleavy recalls the Young Winemakers not as a formal club but as one of the most important tools in the arsenal of these early winemakers, which they were able to use to improve the quality of their wines.

'Beyond their own brothers, winemakers such as Nick Nobilo and Ross Spence also had the support of the small group of Auckland-based wine producers who gathered under the name of the Young Winemakers, along with notables such as George Fistonich, Joe Babich and Joe Corban, who gathered once a month at one or other's winery to taste and critically analyse each other's table wines, and compare them with leading overseas wines,' says Dunleavy.

'Their dedication to quality, their preparedness to take criticism and learn from it, their willingness to share what in other industries would be regarded

as trade secrets, was one of the key factors in making the 1970s the decade in which unfortified New Zealand varietal wines came of age.'

WINE IN ONE BASKET

Over-reliance on and oversupply of one variety are the challenges for New Zealand wineries today. Locally owned or not, wineries looking for profit as opposed to mere turnover have to move away from bulk supplies, says Nobilo.

'I would never have wished for or imagined it but deep down I know that history does repeat itself, so you always get boom–bust in any industry. Wine is no exception, but we have to take heed of our lessons. The bottling of bulk wines offshore is risky as it demeans the quality perception of New Zealand wine. My biggest fear is of this happening in China, which is a fast-growing export market for our wines.'

It is figures like the 30 per cent of overall wine exports leaving New Zealand in tankers — in bulk — during 2011 that give rise to such concerns for Nobilo. Just as worrying is the dominance of Sauvignon Blanc in New Zealand's vineyards and wineries.

'We've done very well with Marlborough Sauvignon Blanc, but our heavy reliance on one single variety gives us the appearance in many international markets of being the only thing we can do. We must look towards newer varieties, as an industry. A little bit like I was doing in the 60s and early 70s. We need trials of more new varieties to meet changing trends in the market in the future.'

If bulk sales continue, Nobilo says, New Zealand winemakers will find themselves in the same quandary as its beer producers are at present: trying to climb out of bulk production by growing the perception of their craft beers.

'Unfortunately, this may be driven from outside New Zealand through offshore control of our wine sales that tends to turn wine into a commodity. Because supermarkets now are the biggest sellers of wine in many Western countries, it has become part of the food-purchasing mentality of consumers; people slip a bottle into their trundler with the bread and milk. I'm not against that, but once wine begins to lose its personality and identity, it loses something which is hard to regain.'

CRYSTAL BALL GAZING

'It's my belief there will be a shift away from Sauvignon Blanc over the next 10–15 years and that we will still stay focused on aromatic whites because that's what we do best. Part of that shift will be to Gewürztraminer, which will be very significant in my view with the burgeoning Asian market. In my book, it's the most noble of all whites.'

New Zealand winemakers have yet to come to terms with Arneis, Grüner Veltliner and Viognier, which are all currently in the experimental phase in New Zealand, says Nobilo.

'It's good we have Arneis and Grüner Veltliner now, but these grapes are not going to be market changing. We don't know enough about them in New Zealand and how they will do. Other grapes we could trial include Teroldego from

'ONCE WINE BEGINS TO LOSE ITS PERSONALITY AND IDENTITY, IT LOSES SOMETHING WHICH IS HARD TO REGAIN.'

northern Italy and several varieties out of Croatia and Eastern Europe.

'We need a lot more time before we can say with any accuracy at all how well these grapes and the wines they make will work for New Zealand.'

WHITE CLOUD — SILVER LINING

It would be impossible to tell the story of Nick Nobilo without talking about the silver lining to the dark cloud over New Zealand wine when Roger Douglas introduced excise tax in 1984.

Within 18 months, excise tax cut 40 per cent of the sales of Nobilo Müller-Thurgau in New Zealand. Nick Nobilo called a meeting of the company's board of directors.

'There's only one way we're going to survive this and that is to get out into the world and establish a market there, so let's create "the son of Müller-Thurgau" — White Cloud.'

In 1988 he launched White Cloud. It was created for the Swedish monopoly-governed wine market and was made from Müller-Thurgau, with one very notable difference; it contained 25 per cent Sauvignon Blanc. Within three years it grew to become a 150,000-case export wine brand, the biggest wine export in New Zealand and all sent offshore in bulk. Which worked, says Nobilo, because Swedish bottling laws are stricter than New Zealand's so quality standards were not an issue. In 1991 it was launched into New Zealand where it remained a strong brand, declining only into the early and mid-1990s as Chardonnay, then Sauvignon Blanc and Pinot Noir, moved in to be the most widely planted grapes in the country.

NICK'S GO-TO WINES

'I love champagne so it's my first choice. Complex, full-bodied Chardonnays are also high on my list. I like the elegance and finesse of Montrachet and at the other end, I also enjoy the 2010 Selaks Favourite Chardonnay. I'm a big fan of Pinot Noir, so I drink them selectively as well as Cabernet Sauvignon — but it has to be good. I don't like vegetal Cabernets. I tend to drink Cabernet from Australia or better French ones, as well as one or two blends from Hawke's Bay, which I really enjoy.'

TOP WINES FROM NICK NOBILO

- 1976 Nobilo Huapai Cabernet Sauvignon
- 2011 Vinoptima Reserve Gewürztraminer — yet to be released as a *vendange tardive* (late-harvest) style: 'Not a noble.'

GORDON RUSSELL

ESK VALLEY ESTATE, HAWKE'S BAY

'Gordon is an intensely passionate winemaker and his commitment to the Terraces reds have helped put Hawke's Bay reds modelled on Bordeaux varietals on the map — especially Merlot, Malbec and Cabernet Franc. These wines have helped shift popular opinion of our red wines away from the thin, green examples of the 70s and early 80s, to the classically elegant and structured wines of the last 20 years.'

— Grant Edmonds, Sileni Estates

'Gordon is always ready for a laugh but also very passionate about wine.'

— Ian Isaacs, general manager, Scenic Cellars, Taupo

GREATEST ACHIEVEMENTS

- 'Having an open mind and willingness to push the boundaries — making the first Malbec-based red wine in New Zealand is one example; making Verdelho is another. Malbec-based wines or blends with Malbec are common practice now, but someone had to have the gumption to do it in the first place.'
- 'To strive for the best without being constrained by convention.'
- 'A lot of people over the years have come and worked vintages at Esk Valley and have left more enthusiastic than when they arrived. Many have ended up in great winemaking jobs around the world. That's what Stephan Jelicich did for me, and I feel a lot of satisfaction doing that for others.'

KEY ACHIEVEMENTS

- Being named Winemaker of the Year at the Royal Easter Show 2007.
- Esk Valley being named Winery of the Year at the Hawke's Bay Wine Awards 2011.

TAKE TO A DESERT ISLAND . . .

'One of mine; 1998 The Terraces. I chose that wine because it's the most thought-provoking wine, for me. It's from the hottest, driest year we ever had, and yet we made great wine at just 13.5 per cent alcohol. I still wonder how we did it and whether we would ever do it again. The wine speaks of its place and it's obviously a great place because 15 years on, it still tastes amazing. It gives me loads of satisfaction and poses lots of questions . . . every time I try it. I would take my wife, Pia, and my ideal dinner party guests, if I could choose them: Lucinda Williams, Danger Mouse (aka Brian Joseph Burton), Jamie Oliver because he would talk and talk; Ferran Adrià from el Bulli restaurant in Spain; the late writer William Burroughs — a bit twisted but I like that — and the late French oenologist, Émile Peynaud, who would be someone to theorise about wine with. I would also take the late Italian viticulturist Romeo Bragato, who came to New Zealand at the turn of last century. He seemed to have an eye for landscape and predicted Central Otago would be a great place to grow Pinot Noir. I think I like the laconic and the weird.'

THE STORY

How times change. The winery once described as a bomb site by the now-defunct *Auckland Star* has become home to the Merlot and the little known Malbec, the barely heard of Verdelho and one of New Zealand's top reds — The Terraces. Its maker is a former punk rock lover, a self-confessed fashion victim and, by his own admission, a man who can understand why he didn't get the first wine job he applied for; he was wearing a beat-up leather jacket and riding an old Suzuki.

Meet Gordon Russell.

In 2012 he celebrated 20 years of winemaking at Esk Valley on the coast north of Napier, where he has pioneered the use of overlooked grape varieties and made maverick wines.

It's no surprise to those who know Russell that he approaches wine as a renegade. It echoes his passion for fashion, music, food and popular culture — 'I think anyone who knows me understands that my love of music, fashion and clothes extends to all spheres of life. I like changing with the changes in society. I find that exciting. It's one of the great things about life: that it never stands still.'

'I LIKE CHANGING WITH THE CHANGES IN SOCIETY. I FIND THAT EXCITING. IT'S ONE OF THE GREAT THINGS ABOUT LIFE: THAT IT NEVER STANDS STILL.'

Asked to name his most satisfying achievement, Russell says Malbec springs to mind, but not because he first planted it at Esk Valley. He didn't. It was Master of Wine and highly experienced viticulturist Steve Smith who first planted Malbec on the precipitously terraced slopes at Esk Valley. And it's not because Russell thought of Malbec as the great red grape to propel Esk Valley The Terraces red wine into the limelight.

'I think Esk Valley has been at the forefront in some respects, when it comes to innovation; being among the first in New Zealand to make rosé and the first to make Merlot Rosé with some Malbec in it, a signature which is now widely emulated. We were the first in Hawke's Bay to make Merlot-based blends, to make a straight Malbec and then to use it as the key ingredient in high-quality red blends. Then we were the first to make Verdelho when others were making Pinot Gris. I'd like to think that even though Esk might be seen as a traditional old winery, we have actually shown new ways of doing things,' says Russell.

'It staggers me that the "New World" is called the New World when some parts of it have been around longer than many of the "Old World" regions, Hawke's Bay being a classic example. We have actually revived grapes, which might originally have come from France, but which the French don't have sole preserve on — Malbec is a classic example of that.'

In the same vein, Verdelho has a dryness and mineral nature which is so 'un-French' in style that it's clearly from Spain, says Russell, who also adores many Austrian wines.

'It's more that Austria is making the wine rather than the grape variety. I feel every time I taste great Austrian wine that I'm tasting the place rather than the grape variety the wine is made from. There's a linearity, a steeliness married to fruit flavours, which is so unique — I find that really inspiring.'

WINES THAT TASTE OF PLACE

Wines that taste of where they come from is a concept that is innate to Russell's own ambition when it comes to winemaking.

The terraced hillside vineyards at Esk Valley have more in common with many European wine regions than most New Zealand ones, in the sense of their altitude. This type of vineyard — planted on slopes — is a defining feature of high-quality winemaking in most countries. One glance at the cottages sparsely dotting the hillside in three directions and the dramatic ocean view in the other, and there is no doubt this is New Zealand. It just happens to be at geographical odds with most of this country's vineyards, planted as they are on large flat plains and gently undulating, rolling slopes.

Esk Valley breaks the usual mould and so does its winemaker.

If the name Esk Valley rings only faint bells rather than clanging gongs, that's because the focus here has always been on the quality rather than the quantity, although the winery's second-tier wines may yet change that.

'I would certainly like the name Esk Valley to become more prominent internationally,' Russell says.

The semicircular, amphitheatre-like vineyard named The Terraces at Esk Valley is the jewel in the crown of the much larger Villa Maria Estate.

Esk Valley also makes wines from grapes grown further afield in Hawke's Bay, most notably on the Gimblett Gravels, and also from Marlborough.

The Terraces wines, though, remain the *raison d'être* for all the others. They are made in tiny quantities from the 1.36 hectares of Malbec, Merlot and Cabernet Franc vines grown on the immaculately groomed, steeply sloping terraces that hug the land around the historic old winery. While Merlot and Cabernet Franc are important, neither leads the blend — that starring role goes to Malbec, unlikely as that was once thought to be.

'It's one of the things I have loved about my job, proving that Malbec has surprises up its sleeve. It's historically been regarded as a traditional blending grape, never in the starring role. As soon as we put it in the lead role, The Terraces was a better wine,' says Russell.

Originally, the land at Esk Valley was going to be part of a market garden when an Englishman named Robert Bird bought land nearby in 1933 and planned to expand with a vast fruit orchard. Wine writer and historian Michael Cooper writes that 'during the Depression the return for grapes of under twopence per pound soon encouraged the 51 year old Bird to enter the wine industry'. By the time of his death in 1961, Cooper writes that 'Bird owned a 28-hectare vineyard and a large modern winery'.

It was called Glenvale Winery and it remained in family hands till the mid-1980s; it was run by Bird's sons until it was bought by George Fistonich in 1987.

Today the vineyards around the winery include 1.3 hectares of Chardonnay and a newly planted, experimental patch at the top of the hill of just 0.8 of a hectare of Syrah, which will make a standalone wine rather than being included as part of The Terraces red blend.

EARLY DAYS AT ESK

Russell has been at the winemaking helm of Esk Valley since 1993, having started out with winemaker Grant Edmonds, to whom he was the assistant winemaker for two years.

The first time this duo made The Terraces red was in 1991. They picked all the grapes on the hillside at the same time and fermented them together because there was so little fruit growing there. They sold it as The Terraces for the 'ridiculous price at the time of $29.95, as much as the highly revered Te Mata Coleraine. No one could believe we were audacious enough to charge that much.'

But they were and the wine sold.

'We knew we had captured something entirely different for New Zealand,' says Russell, who was appointed winemaker two years later.

'The wine tasted dark and spicy like the Malbec that was in it, even though it was a smaller component of the wine than today.'

THE TERRACES HISTORY

Cabernet Sauvignon played a role in The Terraces when it was first made, but this late-ripening French grape didn't ripen fully every year . . . so it was

removed from the vineyard after the 1994 vintage.

'Full credit to George Fistonich and Steve Smith, whose idea it was to plant Malbec, Merlot, Cabernet Franc and Cabernet Sauvignon on the hillside. It showed a lot of foresight, especially incorporating Malbec, which was virtually unknown back then. We've since removed the Cabernet Sauvignon because its particular site on the hill was too cold. It ripened some years but not others, but of course nobody knew which parts of the vineyard were the warmest back then and which were clipped by the sea breeze,' Russell says.

Every year the three grape varieties in The Terraces — respectively, in order of importance, Malbec, Merlot and Cabernet Franc — are all harvested on a single day and fermented together in one of the winery's old concrete fermenters: 'Which is pushing the boundaries in anyone's language,' says Russell.

'We spend the growing giving the three varieties what they each need, so that we can find a date that works to pick all three together. They normally don't ripen together at the same time,' says Russell, who takes some inspiration from the French winemaker, Marcel Deiss, one of the most respected winemakers in Alsace, France's driest wine region and home to the country's finest Rieslings, Gewürztraminers, Pinot Gris and Muscats. Deiss has carved his name by making wines which are more about place than the grapes growing in that place. Mambourg is a classic example. A blend of Pinot Noir, Pinot Blanc, Pinot Gris, Pinot Meunier and Pinot Beurot, it is a wine about the taste of the vineyard rather than the grapes.

'I like that he ferments all those grapes together, which is so unconventional, so that the wine becomes an expression of the site instead of an expression of the vine. When you taste the wine, it's about nature. That's our aim with The Terraces: a bit of romance, a bit of practicality. We've taken the winery out of the wine. It's all about the vineyard. It's unreproducible. When you're tasting The Terraces, you're tasting as close as we can get it to a taste of the place rather than of our winemaking. It's all about this particular part of the world.'

FIRST GREAT WINE

Rather than a eureka moment with wine, Russell says his love of and passion for wine came from an accumulation of experiences.

'I was lucky enough to begin drinking New Zealand wine when it was just getting going in the modern era: Chardonnays, Sauvignon Blancs and many more. Passé now, but new and exciting back then, it was those early days when you'd try a wine and every time it was a whole new world. In the early days at Esk, a group of us from the cellar would drive to Wellington to Regional

'WE NEED TO ADD SOME SEX TO OUR MARKETING. I DON'T MEAN THAT LITERALLY, IN TERMS OF SHORT SKIRTS, BUT WE NEED TO SHOW THAT HAWKE'S BAY WINES EQUATE WITH COOL RATHER THAN QUAINT.'

Wines for tastings such as Domaine Zind-Humbrecht, Guigal, Loosen, and we'd be back at two in the morning. I've been like that my whole life in the wine world; I seek out those opportunities. Once you lose that, it's time to find something else.'

The stars aligned for Russell in 1987 when he was living in Auckland around the corner from Glengarry's wine store in Jervois Road.

'I was a university drop-out at the time and didn't really know what I wanted to do, but I saw a job in the paper for a cellar hand at Collards winery on Lincoln Road in Henderson and thought, "That's me," because my favourite jobs ever had been working in pubs in London, working in the cellars, conditioning the beers and looking after the lines. I rode out to Collards on my trusty 125 Suzuki, wearing a leather jacket, where I was interviewed by Lionel Collard. It wasn't a great interview; I wouldn't have given myself a job either, in hindsight, and sure enough I didn't get it. But it piqued an interest in me, so I begged a job in every winery in West Auckland and got a break at Bellamour (no longer in existence) where Stephan Jelicich was the winemaker and I became his apprentice.'

Russell's next step was a job at Villa Maria in mid-1988 where winemaker (and now Master of Wine) Kym Milne became his role model.

'Villa was quite small at the time and Ian Isaacs, now at Scenic Cellars, was working there with me. We did everything in the cellar together; it was a juggling act and quite mad but made us learn everything there was to know and do in a winery to keep it operating.'

THE BAY'S BIG CHALLENGE

'We need to add some sex to our marketing. I don't mean that literally, in terms of short skirts, but we need to show that Hawke's Bay wines equate with cool rather than quaint.'

Hawke's Bay may be New Zealand's second-largest wine region, but it is also, arguably, the country's most geographically fragmented one. There's an upside in that the region has great diversity; and a downside in that it is so sparsely spread.

'It stretches from Te Awanga to Gimblett Gravels to Dartmoor Valley to where we are, and then there is southern Hawke's Bay and central Hawke's Bay — which has enough soil and climate diversity in itself to support a whole wine industry,' says Russell.

'Hawke's Bay doesn't do things dramatically. It does things consistently and

comfortingly. It's more Chanel than Donna Karan New York, and Chanel's been there a long time. That's how I look at Hawke's Bay.'

'One of the problems for Hawke's Bay is that its stories have been quiet, compared with places like Marlborough and Central Otago. Craggy Range and others have obviously done a really good job, but we generally seem to have been a quiet region rather than trumpeting our strengths. We need to market them more.'

The most outstanding of those strengths are clearly Chardonnay and reds modelled on the best from Bordeaux, France.

'We've been unlucky in that the Bay has been making fine wine for a long time — we make some interesting Sauvignon Blanc — but the Marlborough style is what has captivated the world. Pinot Noir has come along and dominated the red wine market in New Zealand and internationally as well, so it can seem as if Hawke's Bay is out of step, but there is always a market for the classics — for elegance rather than power.'

FUTURE HAWKE'S BAY

While its diversity can work against Hawke's Bay, the area's wide range of sub-regional climates, soils and grape varieties gives it many strings to its bow, even if some of them go without due recognition. Russell has been one of the region's most open-minded winemakers, producing Verdelho. He has also been a champion of Chenin Blanc and would also like to try Tempranillo, Albariño and co-fermented white wines, such as a Pinot Gris, Gewürztraminer and Sauvignon Blanc.

'It's not about making a blend. It's making something in which all the elements combine together to become something else. I think the unexplored things for Hawke's Bay are generally new varieties and styles of wine, rather than new sites. I think we know where the right vineyard sites are now, but it's a matter of matching the right grapes to them.'

For all the different, unusual grapes he champions, Russell is a pragmatist: 'Hawke's Bay's biggest strengths are obviously our Chardonnays, which have a purity, great natural acidity and ripe-fruit flavours as well. And then there are the outstanding Merlots, Malbecs and Cabernet Sauvignons.

'Hawke's Bay seems to have been a more conservative region than some others in New Zealand, but there's no doubt these classic grapes will be highly valued in a wider sense again, even if they are not at the height of fashion right now. For some people, these are their go-to wines all the time,' says Russell, speaking like the Mr Esk Valley that Sir George Fistonich once hoped for.

'George has been a great mentor. He once said to me, "I want you to be Mr

Esk Valley." I laughed nervously at the time because I honestly didn't have a clue what that comment meant, and yet 20 years later it seems so obvious: to take such pride in what you do that you turn your work into your life. It feels great to sense that's now true, especially because it just happened naturally.'

GORDON'S GO-TO WINES

'I often drink our wines because I like to see how they taste with food; it helps me understand them and improve them. I love things like Côtes-du-Rhône or dusty Spanish reds; a $20 bottle of Côtes-du-Rhône is often better for me, in some respects, than a more expensive Châteauneuf-du-Pape, which often tends to be an oaky, show-off wine; whereas Côtes-du-Rhônes are humble, warm, earthy and unpretentious. I like their wildness.

'I've reacquainted myself in the past three years with my love of Chardonnay, in all its different guises, and it's difficult to find a more satisfying winter wine than a bottle of red from the Gimblett Gravels, whether Syrah or made from the Bordeaux varietals.'

TOP WINES FROM GORDON RUSSELL
- Esk Valley The Terraces
- Esk Valley Hawke's Bay Verdelho

PETER BABICH MBE

BABICH WINES, WEST AUCKLAND

'Peter was legendary when it came to financial matters on the Board of the Wine Institute. As was once said at a meeting, you could give Peter Babich your complete worldly fortune and you could be absolutely certain that you would receive the lot back, with interest, when you needed it.'

— Ross Spence, QSO

'In my eyes, the Babich brothers are both pretty amazing — they have come a very long way from quite humble beginnings and could not have achieved what they have achieved without each other. They have strengths in different areas, which is a huge part of their success, and their personalities are such that everything always worked out and still always works out.'

— Maureen Radford (née Babich, sister of Peter and Joe), Babich Wines

'Peter's greatest skills have been as a businessman and wine industry politician. He was extremely influential during the 1970s and 1980s, when the government pressured winegrowers to form a single, representative body, the Wine Institute, in 1975, and then a decade later forced them, by removing import protection, to abandon their traditional focus on the domestic market and plunge into export.

— Michael Cooper ONZM, wine writer and historian

GREATEST ACHIEVEMENT

'Being part of the change of New Zealand wine from a fortified beverage to real table wine. When I began, everything was wrong. We woke up knowing every day the whole New Zealand wine industry needed to be turned over — so my greatest achievement is being part of that.'

KEY ACHIEVEMENTS

- Member of the British Empire (MBE), June 1989.
- Fellow (Life Member) of the Wine Institute of New Zealand, 1995.
- Deputy chair of the Wine Institute of New Zealand, 1985–91.
- Inaugural member of the Waitakere City Business Hall of Fame, 1997.
- Life member of the Waitemata Rugby Club.
- Living with wine all my life — and working with it for 63 years.
- Being part of the family-owned company when it was named one of the World's Most Admired Wine Brands in Drinks International's Top 50 list for 2012.
- Retaining family ownership of a relatively large New Zealand wine company.
- Continuing to be part of a pioneering winemaking family now into its third generation of winemakers.

TAKE TO A DESERT ISLAND . . .

'I would take Chardonnay with my wife, Lise. Having said that, I wouldn't like it to be narrowed down to one wine. If it was red, it would be Pinot Noir.'

THE STORY

Peter Babich grew up with wine on tap whenever he wanted it. There were no messages on the wall saying 'Watch what you drink', but everyone in the family knew the unspoken rule — don't get drunk — and they stuck to it.

'They say you should have a day a week when you don't drink wine, but we've never tried it,' says Babich, aged 80, in 2012, pouring himself a small glass of Babich Pinot Noir to enjoy with the light lunch his wife, Lise, has prepared.

The couple live right next door to the winery, have active gym memberships — and use them several times a week — and he goes to work every day, despite a brief and unsuccessful retirement about 17 years ago. He works because he wants to.

Despite trips up and down the country becoming less frequent — he would rather someone else spent their time monitoring the vineyards the family owns in Marlborough and Hawke's Bay — he is as active in other aspects of

---

'THEY SAY YOU SHOULD HAVE A DAY A WEEK WHEN YOU DON'T DRINK WINE, BUT WE'VE NEVER TRIED IT.'

this relatively large family-owned winery as he has always been.

Babich Wines was begun by his teenage immigrant father in 1916 in Kaikino, Northland, before shifting in 1919 to Henderson Valley, West Auckland, on the same site it is today, in Babich Road.

Peter Babich was one of the most politically influential members of the New Zealand wine fraternity in the mid-twentieth century, when 90 per cent of New Zealand's wines were made from hybrid grape varieties, the minimum wine purchase was a 2-gallon flask and adding sugar and water to wine was commonplace — born of necessity rather than ignorance. His role in bringing about radical cultural and legislative change to the wine industry is mostly unsung — aside from within Auckland wine circles — and Babich himself downplays it; but he was without doubt one of New Zealand wine's most effective movers and shakers at a time when 'wine' in this country was 'confected most of the time', he says.

By the age of five, he knew he wanted to spend his life among the vines, vineyard and winery in which he had grown up.

Sitting in his sun-drenched, computer-less office in Babich Road in 2012, he is surrounded by the romantic reds, burnished browns and golden yellow hues of vines tumbling down the hillside of the vineyard as he describes how he began at the winery as general dogsbody at 16 years old. He spent just two years at Avondale College before beginning work, and the transition felt natural, like stepping into the world in which he had lived all his life, knowing what the work was about and loving the tactile nature of it.

'We worked hard, but because I knew most things about how Dad made wine and grew grapes it was an easy transition into beginning my working life. It just felt right.'

His earliest memory of drinking wine is aged five. He and his father, Josip, visited their many Dalmatian neighbours who made wine for family consumption. Peter, the eldest son of Josip and Mara Babich's five children, tagged along, hoping for — and expecting — a taste of all the wines the adults tried. If he didn't get one, he was offended.

'I remembered those who didn't give me a taste, and in my young mind I really didn't take too well to not being included,' he says with a wry smile, 'even if it was only about a teaspoonful I was poured.

'I was lucky growing up in the winery because from a very early age Dad gave us a lot of responsibility for helping, and he never criticised us if what we did wasn't perfect. He seemed to take the approach that if we were doing it, if we were helping, then we were doing our best. He was good that way.'

'HE ... HAD A MASSIVE INFLUENCE ON THE WAY WE DRINK WINE IN THIS COUNTRY AND THE TYPE OF WINE MADE IN THE MIDDLE OF LAST CENTURY, BUT HE WOULD NEVER CLAIM THE GLORY.'

The same is true of Babich's son, David, the sole third-generation family member working at the winery today and in the role of general manager. Of his formative years growing up at Babich Wines, David echoes his father: 'I always thought I would work at the winery, right from when I could first remember. I used to go with Dad around the vineyard, and he would show me things I should know about the vines and the vineyard. I have always enjoyed and appreciated wine as a product. It is very pure in a sense — a product of the land, reflecting the soil and climate of the specific vineyard preserved in a bottle — like capturing nature.'

His father, Peter, has captured nature as part of the wave of transformational change last century which saw New Zealand wine grow slowly away from being sweet, fortified and unfriendly, when it came to trying to drink it with food, to being real table wine. Not that Babich talks about himself with such high regard.

Babich is unassuming, humble and self-deprecating when he speaks of having had an impact. He is proud of being part of the change which saw table wine propelled into the spotlight, but it is only at a push that he acknowledges having had a strong role in the meetings, the sessions with Cabinet ministers in Wellington and at the many heated debates which saw wine sales legislation, consumption of wine and the type of wine made completely overhauled for the better in this country.

Why the humility?

'It's just how Peter Babich is. He is a very calm and caring man who had a massive influence on the way we drink wine in this country and the type of wine made in the middle of last century, but he would never claim the glory. He's not that type of person,' says Rachael Carter, founder and owner of Soho Wines, whose family grew up with the Babichs in West Auckland.

TURNING WRONGS INTO RIGHTS

'When I began working with New Zealand wine in 1948, it was all wrong. You woke up to this every day, knowing that the whole industry needed to be turned over,' Babich says.

'The law around selling wine in a minimum of 2 gallons was wrong, the food and drug regulations were wrong, the area we grew grapes in being "dry" [local prohibition] was wrong. How on earth could you have an area where grapes grown for wine were allowed to be grown, but the wines made weren't allowed to be consumed? It was just all part of the madness of the age. The grape

varieties themselves were wrong, the style of wine we were making was all wrong. We knew we needed to be making dry table wines, but we were making sweet wines. It just wasn't right in any way.'

It took 25 years, in Babich's words, to get it 'right'.

'Not that it is ever perfectly right but it is at least on the right track now,' he says, calmly, in the understated, low-key style that typifies him and brother Joe. (Joe was for many years the winemaker and a key figure in wine-judging circles in New Zealand. He is now managing director of the company. Their sister Maureen also works at the winery and is the friendly, knowledgeable and characteristically quiet face behind the scenes at Babich Wines.)

CHANGING OUR WINE WORLD

So how did the change begin?

'We had about 2 million people in New Zealand when I first began in the wine industry and everybody was drinking beer and spirits. The style of wine we made was not the style of wine that you would want developed. It would be the last sort of wine you'd want developed, but that's what was wanted here because Kiwis were pretty strongly into spirits, that was their perception of alcohol, so that was where we — the collective wine industry — wooed our customers.'

The strongest impetus for cultural change was the return of troops after the end of the Second World War. Soldiers who had been stationed in places such as Greece and Italy returned to New Zealand after years in Europe, looking for wine to drink rather than other types of alcohol.

'There were a hell of a lot of them drinking wine then because they had tried a casual way of drinking in Europe; they knew how to enjoy it in a different way.'

There were also immigrants to New Zealand after the war who knew what sort of wine they wanted and had no choice but to drink what was available, which meant 'dry port'. Their desire for wine rather than fortified wine enabled producers such as the Babich family to start innovating to meet market demand. The first thing the family did was lower the alcohol in their previously fortified wines into a naturally fermented level of alcohol; Vintara Red was one of the first of these. It was still made from hybrid red grapes, but it was not fortified and had a drier taste than previously, not least because fortification adds a flavour of sweetness — alcohol itself tastes sweet.

The trouble was, says Babich, even when it was labelled as 'dry', wine made from hybrid grapes had sugar and alcohol added; dry port was anything but.

There were exceptions, but they were few and far between. The late Tom McDonald from Hawke's Bay was the most notable. His personal love for Bordeaux reds saw him plant some of the country's first bona fide wine grapes, *Vitis vinifera*, which were extremely rare in New Zealand in the middle of last century. McDonald was quite possibly the only exception to the hybrid-winemaking rule that characterised wine in this country for many years. Corbans were also forerunners in growing Müller-Thurgau and Pinotage.

HOW DO YOU CHANGE EVERYTHING?

Where do you begin when everything in an industry is wrong? The raw material had to change before anything else could.

'Because it lends itself to food we knew table wine was the way ahead, but when we thought about that we found everything was wrong. The grape varieties we had in the ground needed to be replaced with *vinifera* varieties. It had to start in the vineyard. You can't make good wine from the wrong types of grapes, so we had to change the type of grapes we were growing,' he says.

'Moving from hybrid grapes to Müller-Thurgau and Pinotage was a bigger step in the 1960s than going from these grapes to Chardonnay and Riesling later on, because when we first moved to Müller-Thurgau it was a member of the classical winemaking grape family, *Vitis vinifera*. This enabled us to totally change the style of wine we made. All of a sudden we were able to ditch the use of added sugar because the grapes had enough of their own.

'It sounds terrible now. People hear this and think we just added sugar because we didn't know any better, but we added it because hybrid grapes had so much acid that wine made from them tasted like battery acid, unless we added sugar. It was a necessity for the sake of making drinkable wine.'

Asked to explain sugar and water additions to wine made from hybrid grapes, Babich says without them the wines would have about as much appeal as a lemon drink without sugar or honey added.

'They needed major adjustment to make them palatable. That's what was so disheartening when I got into the industry because we all knew this, and it was hard to change it due to lack of wide availability of better grapes.'

Once it was acknowledged that sugar was no longer to be added, it was a matter of amending the legislation so that wine was made with integrity.

The use of water in grape juice could be eliminated at this point, too.

'We got it down to about 3 per cent just so that it allowed us to dissolve finings used in winemaking to create clear wine. Once we had better vines to grow, we didn't have to put any water or sugar or anything in those because they got what they needed on the vine. So the next step was to eliminate the hybrids. That was a big step up on the quality ladder.

'By the mid-1970s the hybrids would have just about disappeared off the radar. And even if they hadn't, nearly everything that was planted in vineyards by then was good material so they were losing ground anyway,' he says.

Once those better grapes became available and were planted in New Zealand, change began to snowball. Better genetic variations of the traditional wine grapes became available. The availability of these new improved, different and unusual variations — also known as 'clones' — kick-started more innovation. By the late 1970s, Babich was employed predominantly as viticulturist for the family company and working with new types of Chardonnay available to the winery.

'Having decent grapes helped us achieve better results. Then we started entering wine shows overseas, which did a tremendous amount of good for the industry here. It took European judges to open the eyes of local judges to how good our wines were beginning to get.'

It also took a major change in the way wine was sold in New Zealand and a cultural shift in Kiwis' attitude to alcohol.

'EVEN THOUGH THE TAXES ON OUR WINES WERE HIGHER THAN THEY HAD EVER BEEN, THEY WERE FAR MORE AFFORDABLE THAN IMPORTED WINES. IT WAS A STRANGELY POSITIVE OUTCOME AT THE SAME TIME AS WE WERE CHANGING THE WAY WE MADE OUR WINES. WE NEVER LOOKED BACK.'

THE EFFECT OF THE BLACK BUDGET

At the same time as the vines in the ground were changing, the way wine was sold changed, too. The biggest change was inadvertent, or so it seemed.

New Zealand winemakers got a major shot in their vinous arms, so to speak, in June 1958 when the infamous 'black budget' was introduced by the Labour Government of the day.

The budget descended like a massive cloud over wine importers in New Zealand, who suddenly found their businesses extremely difficult to make money from. Finance Minister Arnold Nordmeyer's budget slapped tax increases on imported beer, tobacco, cars and petrol; it is generally attributed with having cost the Labour Government the next election, and saw Nordmeyer labelled a wowser, although he later became leader of the Labour Party, in 1963. For the New Zealand wine industry, the black budget heralded a positive change. New Zealanders turned to domestic wine because they couldn't afford to buy imported wine any longer.

'All of a sudden the taxes on imports just became prohibitive. Prior to that, we couldn't get our foot in the door to sell our wines, but then we were off. Even though the taxes on our wines were higher than they had ever been, they were far more affordable than imported wines. It was a strangely positive outcome at the same time as we were changing the way we made our wines. We never looked back.'

Prior to the black budget there was also the 2-gallon rule, which Babich looks back on with loathing.

'We were trying to get people to drink wine, not binge-drink it. If they could only buy it in 2-gallon minimum sales, there was nothing good about selling it and we really struggled with that for a long time. I was active in long negotiations with those in the New Zealand Viticultural Association [of which Babich was secretary] and constantly in talks with Cabinet ministers to break down that minimum sales transaction rule. First of all we got it down to half a gallon, and then to a 750-ml bottle sale.'

WINEMAKERS JOINING FORCES

Formalising the production of quality table wine was another challenge. It was one thing to form the Wine Institute of New Zealand but quite another to make it a legal requirement that everyone who made wine had to belong.

'BECAUSE THE WINE-DRINKING AUDIENCE WAS FAR SMALLER BACK THEN WE HAD A MUCH BIGGER BATTLE AND IMAGE PROBLEM TO OVERCOME THAN WE DO TODAY.'

It took 18 months, a lot of conversations — many heated — and a couple of Acts of Parliament to make it compulsory for all people making wine in New Zealand to belong to the Wine Institute of New Zealand, formally established in 1975. Once it became a legal requirement to belong, from 1976 all winemakers began to be levied — as they are today — by the institute. The amount of the annual levy each winemaker pays is based on the amount of wine produced and sold.

'The change was quite big. The wineries are divided into size, based on literage of production, so there are small, medium and large-sized wineries. Each of the groups — small, medium and large — has an elected representative. There are three votes for large growers and two each for the middle-sized and the smaller wineries; that breakdown has stood the test of time. It has never emerged as a problem that the small and the medium could outvote the large. Basically, it worked on consensus rather than voting power. There have been suggestions to make membership voluntary, but the minute you do that, there will be guys who sit on the fence and enjoy the achievements of others.

'The whole power of that body, which was especially noticeable when it was first created, is that for once we were all pushing in the same direction rather than having the New Zealand Viticultural Association pushing this way, trying to guess what the New Zealand Wine Council members were doing and what the Hawke's Bay winemakers were doing. In the past we were all arguing in different directions and that meant we had winemakers all over the country going to Cabinet ministers with different ideas. Now we're going to them with the same joint approach.'

(In 2002, the Wine Institute and the New Zealand Grape Growers Council formed the industry body New Zealand Winegrowers.)

TODAY'S ISSUES

Nothing is plain sailing, but making and selling wine is a hell of a lot easier now than it was in the 1950s, says Babich.

'Because the wine-drinking audience was far smaller back then we had a much bigger battle and image problem to overcome than we do today.

'The biggest problem for the New Zealand wine industry now is overproduction, even with the smaller 2012 harvest looming. The world is experiencing a global wine glut.

'That will find its own level sooner or later because the guys growing grapes will go out of business if they can't make money. That's the most important problem. The other problem is that we don't become a tax-revenue stream for some minister of finance who targets us. You can see the likes of this offshore

where wineries get taxed virtually out of existence. If you've got overproduction of cheap wine filling the shelves in the marketplace that's a major issue, which pulls everybody down to that point.'

BULK MISTAKES

'We don't want to become a commodity seller as we've run the risk of becoming; an industry selling wine overseas in bulk. It might be a short-term fix, but it's hard to come back from that once we go too far down that route.

'This year [2012] our manager in Blenheim tells us the industry crop is down quite a lot, and I think that some bulk stuff will disappear from shop shelves. We need to add value for New Zealand's sake — we can't fight the world on price. We can fight other wine-producing countries on quality, presentation and anything else that counts, but not on price. We're a small country, land's expensive, it's not an easy climate for grape growing and all the best wine in the world is made where the climate is difficult for grapes, so we've got that in our favour.'

And, last but not least, Babich says, we need a positive attitude by government towards the wine industry so that we don't become a revenue stream only.

'I think the industry can look after itself these days. We've got to the point where we can do that now. Capital for the industry is now not a major issue either. Banks look on the industry as being a pretty good bet. It has ups and downs, but for most of my life it was not like that, and also we've got corporate money invested in the wine industry.'

WHAT WILL WE DRINK IN THE FUTURE?

'We need to discover new grape varieties for New Zealand, which suit this climate, our soils and the conditions here, then we need to work on them at a research level.'

The past decade has been a busy one in New Zealand's vine nurseries, vineyards and wineries. Aside from double the number of vineyards planted nationally — from 15,800 producing hectares in 2003 to 33,600 in 2012 — there is a trickle of new grape varieties finding their way into vineyards from Northland to Central Otago.

First, there was Viognier in its varying array of dry, sweet, peachy and neutral wine styles. Then the Piedmontese Italian white, Arneis, joined the alternative wine movement; in theory north-west Italy's climate has more in common with New Zealand than most places further south on the Italian boot.

Now, Austria's native Grüner Veltliner grape is making its presence felt in vineyards nationwide, albeit in tiny quantities and mostly in the South Island. Thanks to North Island-based wineries and wine brands, such as Babich Wines,

'IT'S NOT JUST HAVING A SUCCESSFUL NEW WINE; IT'S [LEARNING] HOW TO MAKE THE WINE.'

Grüner Veltliner is seen on labels created from Auckland to Central Otago.

Then there is the north-western Spanish white grape, Albariño. Originally from Galicia in Spain, Albariño is, apparently, named in homage to the white grape ('alba') of the Rhine ('rino') in Germany. In other words, it may be a type of Riesling, although this seems unlikely to many wine tasters (including this author). Origins aside, the verdant maritime and coastal countryside it comes from may just suit New Zealand's relatively cool climatic conditions, too.

'If we have a success with any of these varieties — a major success — it will be a good thing. I find it a little dangerous today in that all our eggs are in one basket: Sauvignon Blanc. That's never a good position to be in. We have to try to have two or three wines which are internationally successful,' Babich says.

Such as?

'Chardonnay is the great white calling card for New Zealand,' says Babich, who also believes innovating with new and different, untried grape varieties is important for a small wine-producing country such as New Zealand because it spreads the risk in terms of marketability of wine styles and market demand. Not only that but it gives winemakers options in seasons when weather may favour one type of grape over another, especially when vintage variability is relatively high in New Zealand. There are vastly different climatic risks from north to south; rain and frost affect different wine regions at different times, potentially devastating a large percentage of a year's total crop.

Important as it is to find other trump cards for the New Zealand wine industry overseas, it takes another commodity, which is harder to define: time.

'It's not just having a successful new wine; it's how to make the wine. You've got to give the winemakers at least four to five years to try making it and then more time to compete at show level so they can demonstrate what style they can make. The shows do a hell of a good job at highlighting what will work best. Forget about winning, it's about showing the grapes to an audience and the wines they can make.'

PREDICTIONS

'It would be nice to strike another grape as distinctively "New Zealand" as Sauvignon Blanc has proven to be,' says Babich.

'I don't think anybody is certain about why Sauvignon Blanc is doing so well here, and if we could get another one like that, I think we would be sitting a lot more comfortably in the international marketplace than we are currently. It's encouraging to see that China's in the swim now as a marketplace, so the demands on red will probably continue to rise, with their consumption of wine.'

NORTHERN EXPOSURE

Peter Babich's father, Josip Babich, arrived in New Zealand aged 14 with his 17-year-old brother, Stipan, in 1910, from Croatia. They were the fourth and fifth of a family of five sons to emigrate to New Zealand.

'They had to go away from home because where they lived there was no future for young men. Dad and his brothers knew they had to go somewhere far away to find work and provide for themselves. They had heard there was money to be made in New Zealand from gum digging in the Far North. Josip never saw his parents again, although he did return to Croatia in 1951, by which stage his parents had passed away.

'He went home to Croatia for six months when I was only 21. At the time he gave me power of attorney, which he never ever cancelled till the day he died. He had total faith in you, which made you perform. This sort of trust had a bearing on how we worked; we did the hard yards physically outdoors but also by being alone in doing it, with very few people to talk to about our mistakes, our challenges and how to move forward. I'm sure some of the drive we had to succeed came from being so isolated.'

Josip first planted grapes when he was 16 in Kaikino in the Far North. He made wine there in 1916, before moving south to Auckland in 1919, where the brothers had originally bought scrub-covered land in the Henderson Valley, the site the family still owns today on Babich Road. Josip bought 72 acres (30 hectares), of which the family still owns about 70 (28 hectares).

While all the brothers moved to Auckland together, they did not all remain in business together. The oldest brother went back to Europe where he was wounded in the First World War, later dying of his wounds. Ivan, the middle brother, died aged 32. Of the remaining three, Mate and Josip were both leaders and clashed, so Steve and Josip bought Mate out, leaving two of them to pioneer the vineyard and winery in West Auckland. As families developed, Steve branched out on his own into dairy farming and fruit orchards.

There are three mystery years when nobody in the family knows how the brothers survived.

'When they first moved here they had very little, and I don't know how they survived for the first three years, which none of them spoke of while we were growing up. To our knowledge, they had no income during that time and they also had no house, no electricity, no running water and no obvious source of food for either themselves or for their horses to feed on. We didn't ask that question when they were still alive, so we don't know. Everybody that knew was dead by the time we wondered.

'Dad said to me several times that life was pretty harsh when they got here. They had no money, didn't speak the language, most of them hadn't been to school and they had no parents to turn to. Their father had been in the Austrian army and he taught his children how to read and write. My father had a lot of common sense and was clever, although he was honest to the point of being naive. I don't know whether people twigged to that or not, but it seemed to work in his favour.

'The 70 or so wineries I remember in West Auckland were all making wine to sustain the family. There was no thought to make wine to be commercially viable. They may as well have been growing tomatoes to sell at the door. They knew how to grow grapes and they were hamstrung with the quality of the fruit, so it was not commercially driven, but with the next generation of young fellows coming through — and I was the oldest one in this generation — we started growing the industry.'

BABICH'S BOARD DAYS

Ross Spence, founder of Matua Valley Wines:

'It was 1976 when I first joined the board of the Wine Institute of New Zealand ('WINZ) and I was blessed in having Peter Babich as a mentor. He assisted me, being a very young 33-year-old on the board of a group of very well-known industry people such as himself, Alex Corban, Tom McDonald, Peter Fredatovich, Mate Brajkovich, Mate Selak, George Mazuran, Russell Gibbons and of course all rounded up by Terry Dunleavy — the ultra-heavies of the industry. It was all a bit daunting to begin with, and Peter was a tremendous help to me, especially in getting through the fiery industry politics of the time along with the most amazing demonstration of eye-opening political lobbying.

'Pete had many approaches to stand for the WINZ Chairmanship as he would have made a great chairman. His answer was always, "I am uncomfortable in the limelight and do my best work in the backroom." You could always rely on his effectiveness when it came to resolving a tricky problem with politicians or other influential business people and Peter would always say, "I'll give him a buzz and point him in the right direction." Then he'd get on the phone and sort it out.

'Peter and I for many years purchased grapes for our respective wineries as a consortium. This usually meant an early morning trip to Gisborne, Napier or Marlborough. Pete would usually arrive at the airport with a small carry bag and we would be seated together so we could have a chat on the way down.

'Once on board the plane, usually a Fokker Friendship in those days and rather noisy, Pete would take out of the bag a large pair of bright red ear muffs and put them on. You could feel the eyes on the plane looking at this bloke with the largest pair of ear muffs I had seen. He would be asleep before take-off and would wake, completely refreshed, when the plane was landed at the destination.

'When grower or WINZ meetings would get a little heated Pete would use a phrase he is legendary for, "Now, just a mo' you guys", and he would bring some order to the matter by calming things down and reasoning with his summing up.'

THE PINOT NOIR WOW FACTOR

'Pinot Noir is an excellent variety, but to make it well it's also an expensive one, and you don't sell as much that way. You can't go and sell Pinot Noir successfully at $12 or $13 a bottle. To get it right you're going to be selling it in excess of $20. There are no short cuts with Pinot Noir. You've got to put everything into it, and the vineyard site is probably more important to Pinot Noir than any other variety, which is something all the wines made from this grape are teaching us.

'With Sauvignon Blanc we can grow it in a range of soils and it'll grow well, but with Pinot Noir, the first thing you have to do is get off the heavier soils, and of course it then depends on which region it's growing in as to which soil types it's going to do best in.'

So, which New Zealand region is most likely to have a long-term X-factor with Pinot Noir?

Babich predicts it will be Central Otago.

'Basically, Central has got it right, I think, except that, as a wine-producing country we're going to have failures, and that's expensive in this industry. In

Marlborough, there won't be too many failures and you can get it pretty good, but I think we'll have to bow still to Central, in terms of the X-factor that people look for in the bright fruit-driven styles of Pinot Noir we see from that region.'

LOOKING BACK

'Joe and I are very fortunate that our third generation, which is so far David, is coming into the industry. We could have been a family without a natural-born leader so we're very fortunate in that, and hopefully others will join us because if you don't have a succession plan, you have to start wondering what you're doing this for.

'I think if Dad was up there looking down, he'd be pretty pleased with his efforts and the start he gave us, to see the direction we've taken. I think that's the biggest reward for anybody: to be able to sit back and say, "Well, you've done well with the business I began",' Babich says.

'My part in all the political issues was aided by the fact that Joe was often left running the business on his own. For this, I am very grateful.'

PETER'S GO-TO WINES

'We freelance a bit with both imported and domestic wines so that we get away from having a cellar palate. Champagne is the one that really gets the sparks flying. For everyday drinking, though, I take a bottle of wine home every night, but I can't say it's Chardonnay every day of the week. Our cheapest Chardonnay is a favourite; stainless steel-made, no wood age, and it's uncomplicated and very enjoyable. Another one I've taken a bit of a liking to is Viognier and it has a screwtop, which suits me better than pulling corks. Pinot Noir suits me as a style, and I like Merlot.

TOP WINES FROM PETER BABICH
- Irongate Chardonnay
- Babich Winemaker's Reserve Pinot Noir

ROSS SPENCE QSO
WINE PIONEER, SAUVIGNON BLANC

I remember listening to an interview Ross gave on Radio 1ZB with Marina (she took over from Aunt Daisy) soon after he came back from California. I was impressed. He had fresh thinking about winemaking, far away from the ports and sherries of that time. I knew then Ross had a great future in wine. Always an innovator, Ross's winemaking claim to fame was in producing the first commercial Sauvignon Blanc wine in 1974 long before its time had come. Today Sauvignon Blanc is New Zealand's most successful varietal.'

— Nick Nobilo, Vinoptima

'Behind the fame of Ross Spence as winemaker was a brother of lesser fame but of equal importance in their success. In the case of Ross, there was Bill, not only ensuring that the right grapes were grown in the right way, but also handling the marketing and sales.'

— Terry Dunleavy MBE, New Zealand wine elder statesman

Although his name may not sound Eastern European, Ross Spence is of Dalmatian descent, and grew up with wine on the table that his family had made from some of New Zealand's earliest vineyards. He introduced Sauvignon Blanc to New Zealand from a forgotten, lone vine he discovered languishing in a trial vineyard in West Auckland, and went on to chair the board of the Wine Institute of New Zealand (WINZ) and found Matua Valley Wines.

Now retired, Spence's round the clock passion for wine has not slowed. He is still trailblazing new grape varieties on his small West Auckland vineyard, eternally optimistic in the hope of finding the next big thing. Arneis,

Montepulciano and Tannat all jostle for space in his Kumeu vineyard. His clear thinking about, love for and knowledge of wine are qualities he prefers to have inherited from his successful artist mother rather than his winemaking father, who was aptly described by Dick Scott as 'a prisoner of his own product'.

GREATEST ACHIEVEMENT

'Staying married for 45 years. That's a pretty good achievement, especially nowadays. Family is of paramount importance to me.'

Adrienne Spence, Ross's wife, adds: 'Your Sauvignon Blanc days,' to which he replies, 'I don't know if that's an achievement, especially right now with the glut.'

KEY ACHIEVEMENTS

- Board of West Auckland Liquor Trust.
- Appointed an independent director of Auckland Trust Services, 2008.
- Director, Sileni Estates Limited, 2007.
- Matua Valley Wines, 1973–2007: responsible for the establishment and development of the company in 1973 with continuing responsibilities in development, production, winemaking and administration areas. Also Chairman of the Matua Valley Board of Directors for 10 years.
- Rapaura Vintners Board Chairman 1996–2001. Director 2001–2007.
- Villa Maria Wines, 1966–1972: winemaker for six years prior to starting Matua Valley Wines; Chairman of the Wine Institute Board 1997–1999, deputy chairman 1990–1996; committee member and chairman of Wine Institute subcommittees of Viticulture, Oenology, Industry Supplies and Wine Competition; Wine Institute representative on Winegrowers Industry Research Board 1986–1996.
- Foundation member of the New Zealand Grape Growers Council.
- Senior wine judge at the Royal Easter Show and Air New Zealand Wine Competition for eight years.
- Responsible for the introduction and establishment of Sauvignon Blanc in New Zealand in the 1970s.
- Awarded Queen's Service Order (QSO) for services to the New Zealand wine industry, June 2000.
- Awarded Fellow of New Zealand Winegrowers for wine industry services, 2006.

TAKE TO A DESERT ISLAND . . .

'I'd go with Adrienne and we'd take a bottle of Krug or Dom Pérignon, or something like that. You'd want something refreshing. And preferably a tanker load of the wine, if you could get it in bulk.'

SECRET TO MAKING WINE IN NEW ZEALAND

'To be a good winemaker in New Zealand you need to have a very strong back and a good sense of humour. It's bloody hard work.'

THE STORY

Some people might say Ross Spence's biggest achievement is giving Sauvignon Blanc to New Zealanders, but Spence says some people might want to kill him right now for 'the Sauvignon thing'.

He's referring to the tidal wave of Sauvignon Blanc that has flooded wine stores around the world in the past three years. 'Sauvignon Blanc's rarity value has gone,' says Spence, in early 2012. In its place lies a sea of low-priced bottles and bargain bins. Both are an indicator of the worst thing to have happened to New Zealand wine since he became involved in making it, in the 1960s.

Who would have thought New Zealand's initial white wine success would come to this, bulked up and turned into a common cheap commodity?

The quality has never been higher, the prices never lower. It's not quite what Spence had in mind when he rescued a lone Sauvignon Blanc vine on a forgotten trial vineyard in West Auckland, then propagated it in the hope of giving New Zealand its new modern white wine success.

Is he a visionary?

Absolutely. But he's the first to admit thoughts of mortality are on his mind today. It is unseasonally rainy for any mid-February in New Zealand. And as the rain continues to pound down during the non-summer that has wreaked havoc on his small vineyard and the vines around the country, he surveys the 10-acre plot of land that he bought in 1961, wondering what the next step will be.

His working life has been punctuated with family — rather than the other way round — and now, with his seventieth birthday approaching in 2013, there are things he wants to do, things that don't necessarily revolve around wine.

'Life is short. We haven't done all that we want to yet. Don't ask me where we're going or what we're doing, but it'll be in the countryside with a smaller house, less work and a door we can shut and disappear for a month or two every now and again.'

Pausing briefly to sip his tea, Spence glances at Adrienne, who adds: 'I can't see you doing that at all, Ross. I'm going to have trouble getting you away any time.'

There's no trace of humour in her face either, nor is there a hint of resignation in her voice; rather, an acceptance of her husband's passion and preoccupation with wine.

It has defined his working life and their family life and neither Ross nor Adrienne seems unhappy with that fact. He has known wine ever since he can remember.

Like many in this book, Spence grew up with wine on the dinner table at a time in New Zealand history when alcohol generally meant binge beer drinking, sips of sherry or fortified lookalikes for maiden aunts and port for the older blokes.

The son of a troubled heavy-drinking Irish father and a part-Dalmatian

mother whose father began the Henderson winery Santa Rosa, Spence remembers clearly his early life with 'wine' always around, but it was not quite what we know as 'wine' today. Sherry and port lookalikes and blackberry 'nip' were in hot demand and were made year-round at his family's winery during the 1940s when North Americans stationed in New Zealand during the Second World War wanted a drink.

'They just wanted some alcohol and didn't care what it was, as long as it gave them a buzz,' he remembers the winemakers of the day recounting.

His parents met during the Second World War while his father was in the air force. They married in 1942 and in their spare time started a vineyard and made wine.

'God knows how they got together as they were such different people, apart from the fact they were both very strong-willed.'

When the war was over the vineyard was expanded and for many years operated pretty successfully, but the family eventually split up, due to his father's ongoing problems with mental illness and his excessive consumption of his own product. In those days there was no such thing as a women's refuge or any assistance for families that had such problems; in fact it was something that was not spoken about so therefore didn't exist.

'Mum left and eked out a living as an artist. She was bloody good, actually, and, as unlikely as it sounds, she began to make a good living from it once she got going.'

The time she spent doing an art degree in her earlier days at the Elam School of Art was to eventually provide her with a liveable income.

'My grandfather Ivan Luketina came from a little village called Tucepi in Croatia; he sailed to New Zealand from the city of Split when he was about 13 as a boy working on the sailing ship. Children of this age were often sent off to work as there was not enough food for the family. I have heard stories of my grandfather and his five brothers when they were young, being so hungry during the night their mother would bring them dried bread to suck on to soothe their hunger pangs.

'The sailing ship he was on took passengers to New Zealand and Australia to work the goldfields. I think they were going to Australia and they stopped in New Zealand on the way to Australia — or vice versa. He came and then he returned to Croatia, and on his second trip he jumped ship to also work in the Waihi goldfields. Unfortunately, he found that the gold had dried up for the prospectors and he, along with many other Croatians, went north to dig kauri gum and make a living from selling this new gold that had a ready market.'

At that time Ivan and Joe Babich were very good friends. Later he was involved in a partnership with a couple of other Dalmatian friends, and they bought gum from the diggers in the north and onsold it to traders who marketed it around the world.

'When he had got enough money together, he married my grandmother, whom he met when she was living in Kaiwaka. They came down to Auckland and set up a boarding house, and he also worked as a chef in one of the hotels in Auckland. He was quite a good chef. I remember he used to make the most delicious brawn from pig's heads, among other especially well-made food.

Olives, for instance, were just part of our life. In those days the first olives I remember seeing were the olive trees that the Corban family brought over and planted at the winery, and Joe Corban gave me a couple of plants that he took as cuttings. Two of them are still out the back here.

'Eventually, my grandfather planted a small vineyard and orchard in Henderson and as a small child I was quite fascinated when he would have his friends come around for a chat, as they would speak Croatian. I also remember the visits he would occasionally have from old Joe Babich, who started the Babich winery in Henderson.'

KEEPING IT IN THE FAMILY

When Ross left high school, he assumed he would work for his dad, 'but the old man had other plans and bought me a ticket to California and told me I was booked to go to the University of Fresno to study wine there. That was the last I heard of him for two and a half years.'

Well, almost the last.

His mother's extended family in California provided Spence with a ready source of accommodation and holiday work, the latter as a deckhand on his uncles' tow boats. The income put him through university. Less than a year from his graduation, he received a note from home saying his father was ill and suffering a nervous breakdown.

'Sadly, he was a paranoid schizophrenic and had a terrible life, with lengthy periods of treatment. I knew that, but I came back to see him and to help the family, then, once I arrived home in Auckland, he made a recovery and I was tossed out. I had no money to go back to the States to finish my degree in viticulture and oenology, so I applied for a few wine industry positions. At each one I had it explained to me that I was a Spence and so would end up working at home.

'As a last resort I started driving heavy earthmoving machinery to make money; it made very good money in those days beause halfway through the week you'd be on double time. There were terrible long hours but great money. The money was saved so that I could get a vineyard of my own going.'

REDISCOVERING HIS WINE PASSION

'One day George [Fistonich — owner and founder of Villa Maria Estate] said to me, "What the bloody hell are you doing driving those for? Come and work for me."'

So, he did. Starting in the brick cellar at Villa Maria's old home in Mangere, he worked there for about seven or eight years, doing everything from hoeing the vineyard to making the wine to labelling it.

'ONE DAY GEORGE SAID TO ME, "WHAT THE BLOODY HELL ARE YOU DOING DRIVING THOSE FOR? COME AND WORK FOR ME."'

If it hadn't been for Fistonich, Spence says he would still be driving earthmoving machinery till he retired, and would never have gotten back into wine, despite his strong passion for it. 'He rescued me. He was very good to me and we had a great time in those early years.'

Those early years were the late 1960s. Spence had met and married Adrienne and bought the 10-acre block of land they still live on at the time of writing; it's a block of land they now plan to sell in order to downgrade, but it has served them well as both a home and a trial vineyard from which he still makes small amounts of wine — purely for family consumption.

Like many of New Zealand's most successful winemakers, Spence started off with George Fistonich, whom he describes as 'a very unusual person. He has this ability to get the best out of people and he is constantly thinking ahead — a great visionary. He still is and he's always been that way.'

SPENCE AND THE SAUVIGNON BLANC STORY

Nobody is exactly certain who brought the first Sauvignon Blanc vines to New Zealand or when.

There are records pre-1960 of a Sauvignon Blanc clone called TK00204 (named after the Te Kauwhata Viticultural Research Centre, now a small winery). A grape clone is a genetic variation rather than a genetically modified plant; vineyards around the world are full of different variations — 'clones' — of most of the grapes we know today, from Cabernet Sauvignon to Syrah to Pinot Noir. Spence's first brush with Sauvignon Blanc was at university in California.

'This wildly aromatic variety which ripened mid-season caught my attention. I remember thinking, an early to mid-ripening grape like this one was just the thing for a cool climate like New Zealand's and, once I was home in the late 1960s, I came across a Sauvignon Blanc clone at the Te Kauwhata Viticultural Research Centre. There wasn't enough to plant an entire vineyard, so I grafted the vines I could get onto 1202 rootstock until I had sufficient to plant 250 vines.' (Rootstocks are what most grapevines are grafted onto.)

That was 1969. The vines grew well, if a little on the vigorous side, but they were susceptible to phytophthora, a fungus root infection, and they were severely infected with leaf-roll virus. Like all winemakers of that time, Spence expected large crops from these vigorous vines, so he was disappointed to find poor fruiting vines, despite promisingly large embryonic flowers on the vines. The leaf-roll virus infection made matters worse. Although the small crop of

---

'THE FIRST WINE I DRANK THAT REALLY HIT ME WAS WHEN I WAS ONLY A VERY YOUNG BOY AT AVERILL BROTHERS' WINERY IN HENDERSON. MY FATHER TOOK ME THERE AND WE HAD A PINOT NOIR OBERLIN, WHICH THEY CALLED BURGUNDY.'

grapes he did manage to pick were strongly aromatic and the wine he first made from them, in 1974, received accolades from the Wine and Food Society of Auckland, the crops from his Sauvignon Blanc vineyard were so small they sent him searching for a healthier clone from which to make Sauvignon Blanc.

Scouring around for healthy Sauvignon Blanc vines seemed like looking for a needle in the proverbial haystack, till he heard that a vine had been imported by the Ministry of Agriculture and Fisheries (MAF). All he could find out was that it had been planted in a trial block at what was then a Corbans vineyard in Kumeu.

'After much searching with an ampelography [grapevine identification] book in one hand and notebook in the other, I found one Sauvignon Blanc vine and a Sémillon vine alongside it. It was later confirmed that this clone had been imported by Frank Berrysmith, the government viticulturist at the time, from the University of California at Davis (UCD), and was released to the trial block in 1970, numbered TK05196. To the best of my knowledge nobody knew about this new import prior to me finding it.'

That trial block was destroyed just weeks after he took the cuttings from the vines.

SPREAD LIKE WILDFIRE

As well as taking cuttings from the Sauvignon Blanc vine growing at the Corbans trial vineyard to plant in his own, Spence was persuaded to part with some by Wayne Thomas, at the time chief viticulturist for Montana (which had a very large propagation unit in Avondale). Thomas had the task of finding new varieties to plant in the Marlborough vineyard Montana had just purchased.

'Thomas managed to convince me to part with a couple of cuttings which he was going to use for bulking up and growing in Marlborough.'

During the winter of 1974, Wayne Thomas turned those few cuttings into thousands of plants, which were trucked to Marlborough and planted at Montana Wines' first vineyard in the South Island.

At the same time, Spence and his brother Bill, who by that time was working with him, also bulked up the vines they had, propagating enough of them to plant the first commercial Sauvignon Blanc vineyard block at the Matua Waimauku vineyard in 1978.

THE NEW SAUVIGNON BLANC

This new Sauvignon Blanc vine was a UCD clone and it grew well; instead of just *looking* promising, its flowers set well, growing into a healthy crop of grapes and the small 7-acre block at Waimauku flourished. The wine these grapes made was distinctive, powerful and unlike any other that most New Zealanders had encountered at that time. Given that Müller-Thurgau was the most popular wine of the day in the late 1970s, Sauvignon Blanc was a big step up in quality and style. Dry instead of off-dry, more intense in taste and, best of all, a wine made from *Vitis vinifera*.

The Sauvignon Blanc wine heralded the start of a new wave for New Zealand winemakers. Before long, demand had spread and Montana, Corbans and

'THE 1974 MATUA VALLEY SAUVIGNON BLANC WAS THE FIRST WINE TO SET SAUVIGNON BLANC ALIGHT IN NEW ZEALAND . . .'

Hunter's Wines were all using the Waimauku Sauvignon vineyard as a source of scion wood from which to create new plants of Sauvignon Blanc for their fledgling vineyards in Marlborough. All of the vine wood for the original Marlborough plantings came from the Matua Valley Waimauku vineyard block.

'The 1974 Matua Valley Sauvignon Blanc was the first wine to set Sauvignon Blanc alight in New Zealand, or should I say in Auckland, as there were no vineyards planted in Marlborough at the time. The late Jock and Susan Graham and the late Stanley Harris used the wine at an International Food and Wine Society tasting, and it was quite a stunning wine for the time, given that Baco 22A and Palomino were the leading white wine styles of the day with Müller-Thurgau styles beginning to shine through.

'We never had enough to make a wine show entry, but the small amount we produced in 1974 did make considerable impact and I think was the wine that convinced Montana's viticulturist Wayne Thomas and winemaker Peter Hubscher to obtain some propagation wood from us, to bulk up for planting in their first Marlborough vineyard. The wine we made was very European in style and quite distinctive for New Zealand to produce at the time, and although it attracted people used to French styles, there were plenty who disliked the lovely dry distinctive flavours and continued with their sweet preferences.'

Another wine which also helped set Matua Valley Wines on the road to success was made from a less respected grape, although it was named 'Burgundy'. It was the 1974 Matua Valley Burgundy, which won Champion Commercial Red Wine at the New Zealand Royal Easter Wine Show in 1975.

'This was the wine that put Matua Valley on the map as it was our first show entry and our first award ever won. It was made from a wonderful hybrid grape called Seibel 5455. At its best, it produced rich, darkly coloured, soft red wines that had distinctive blackberry nuances and was very precocious and able to be consumed very early in their life. At worst, this grape was a devil that could not take even a hint of rain before it would split, rot and drop berries on the vineyard floor. This 1974 Matua wine was a beauty and exhibited all the wonderful characters we would always look for but never regularly got.'

GAP FROM VINEYARD TO GLASS

As exciting as it was to winemakers, Sauvignon Blanc was not an easy sell to wine drinkers. It was dry at a time and place where medium-sweet Müller-Thurgau ruled the vineyard roost in New Zealand. It also had a foreign name, which, Spence says, made it tough to get past most Kiwis, the majority of whom had not grown up with wine.

'I had a meeting with the father of Californian Sauvignon Blanc, Robert

Mondavi, when he visited our Waimauku winery, and Bill and I discussed the problems we were having getting the public to accept Sauvignon Blanc. Mondavi told us about similar problems he'd had in California with Sauvignon Blanc he made and advised us to change the name, as he had, to Fumé Blanc to see if it lifted sales. We did and, to our delight, sales grew.

'When I asked why he chose the name Fumé Blanc, Mondavi said that it came to him when he was in the home of Sauvignon Blanc, the Loire Valley in France. When he was looking down the smoky valley he decided to use the French word for smoke to describe Sauvignon Blanc which that region was so famous for. It's hard to know if that's exactly where it came from, but it really helped our sales and made this new wine acceptable to most New Zealanders.'

Not to mention making New Zealand Sauvignon Blanc accessible to the world. By the mid-1980s, Marlborough Sauvignon Blanc was being poured into the glasses of the highly critical London wine trade, which began writing rave reviews of this bright, fresh white from Down Under. And all from one forgotten MAF trial vine grafted by the late Joe Corban, whose grandfather — like Spence's — had been one of the earliest wine pioneers in New Zealand, at the turn of the twentieth century.

THE SPICE OF LIFE

Variety has always been close to Ross Spence's heart, not to mention his vineyard.

At the vineyard where he and Adrienne have lived for the past 41 years, they grow a melting pot of experimental grapevines on a small trial plot, from which they make a few cases of wine each year 'for family and friends'. Among the vines growing there, he has planted Arneis (a north Italian white grape); Montepulciano (a central Italian red) and Tannat (a French red, which is most widely grown in Uruguay today and virtually forgotten elsewhere).

He is searching for new grapes to plant, to discover and to introduce to New Zealand winemakers, too many of whom, he feels, have become obsessed with Sauvignon Blanc.

'It's one of my disappointments that people say, "Oh, we've got Sauvignon Blanc; we don't need anything else but this." Fashion comes and goes. We've got to have something else and you can't tell me, for example, that Pinot Gris is something we can offer. The worst thing is all the Pinot Gris with lots of residual sugar made in this country. Why do people do that? It's just awful.'

'What New Zealand does well are white aromatic wines, and we need to look at the freshness we have here with our climate and white varieties. Arneis is one. I'd be surprised if you could get Vermentino [a northern Italian white] to ripen fully here, but there are lots of others. There are a lot of Spanish varieties that I'd like to see; Verdejo, for instance. There is quite a bit of Albariño [a

'I AM SURE WE WILL FIND OTHER STRINGS TO OUR WINE BOW. WE NEED TO.'

Spanish white] already being trialled and it looks like it's got potential. I am sure we will find other strings to our wine bow. We need to.'

THE WINE GLUT

It's not exactly a high priority for most working winemakers in New Zealand today to search for the next big thing when they're saddled with a difficult-to-dispose-of glut of wine. But, for Spence, it could partly help to answer the dilution in price of New Zealand's most widely produced wine, Sauvignon Blanc.

Evolution is a constant, he says, and now that the New Zealand wine industry has moved away from hybrids and crosses of wine grapes with wild grape varieties to the exclusive use of classical vines, it's time to find what else will work succesfully in this country.

'When we first began winemaking, we made a "Chablis" from Baco 22A [a cross between Folle Blanche and Noah; an American hybrid] and Palomino [a Portuguese variety] blended together,' he says.

'That Chablis sold around 18,000 to 20,000 cases a year. That was a lot of wine then. We labelled them all by hand. It was actually a dry white wine, but it was just a name and Baco 22A made quite nice wine because it had quite nice acidity and didn't have any of the real American hybrid grape characters. It was a clean style. It was used to make some of the brandy trials done at Delegat's; many were absolutely stunning.'

The big change to the New Zealand wine industry came when the government of the late 1970s precipitated a change from hybrids to proper wine grapes.

'The government told us we'd have to clean up our act and stop making wine from water and sugar additions, and start using grape juice. At that stage we started moving to things like Müller-Thurgau, Palomino and even Chardonnay. We knew we had no other option because at that stage the government had opened the highly tariff-protected New Zealand wine industry up to imports,' Spence recalls. 'We were forced to export to survive.'

RARITY VALUE?

Is a wine better because it's rarer? Or does the surprise of a totally new flavour fade?

While it might be a bit of both, it would be fair to say Spence has more belief in the former.

'It's just not viable to sell Sauvignon Blanc in big quantities in the UK. The bulk sales of New Zealand Sauvignon Blanc there in the past three years were a huge mistake and should never have been allowed to happen, but they did, so we have to get over that. I think with the crops this year [2012] being considerably less than the previous two years, it may come into balance, but winemakers are not going to recover quickly from the glut, the lack of profitability and the downturn that we're in.'

NEXT STEPS

'What a day! Just what grapes still hanging on the vine don't need,' says Ross Spence, on one of Auckland's wettest mid-March days he can recall in the past 40 years — the length of time he's been growing grapes.

So much for the Indian summer he had been hoping for. It's more like monsoon than balmy autumn weather but, as Spence says, this is probably Mother Nature offering a helping hand to winemakers by giving them far fewer grapes than they would otherwise have chosen to pick this year, had the choice been theirs to make.

Thanks to a relatively cool spring in 2011, followed by a relatively cold summer, a distinct lack of sunshine and an unseasonal amount of rain, the weather will go some way towards rebalancing New Zealand's part in the current global glut of wine. Spence wants to see an end put to sending cheap Sauvignon Blanc overseas. He remembers the first time New Zealand winemakers moved away from cheap and not particularly cheerful wines towards quality wine tables.

'The current bargain-bin wine prices must end for the country to remain a high-quality wine producer. The failure to quickly address cheap bulk exports of wine to overseas buyers has cost the New Zealand wine industry some hundreds of millions of dollars and a long and difficult recovery period.

'It's interesting to have played a role in Sauvignon Blanc's growth, but I think it should be one string to New Zealand's wine bow, not the entire orchestra.'

ROSS'S GO-TO WINES

'Sileni Estate Cellar Selection Merlot for everyday drinking and for more special occasions Sileni Triangle Merlot Estate Selection. In Matua days, we had a young French winemaker, Gilles Corsin, who came and worked for us for about six months and we were so impressed with him we gave him 20 tonnes of Chardonnay to make a tank of wine the way he would like. You may remember that he made a very nice Chardonnay we called Gilles Chardonnay. I regularly buy his wine from importer Paul Mitchell. The one I am currently drinking is Saint Veran Tirage Précoce, from Domaine Corsin 2010 — one of the best value-for-money French Chardonnays you will buy. I also like Millton Viognier for special occasions.'

TOP WINES FROM ROSS SPENCE

- 1974 Matua Valley Sauvignon Blanc
- 1974 Matua Valley Burgundy (which won Champion Commercial Red Wine at the New Zealand Easter Show 1975)

KIM AND JEANETTE GOLDWATER

WINE PIONEERS, WAIHEKE ISLAND

'Where else in the world can students live and learn on an "island of wine" and researchers engage so closely with winemakers and wine marketers? The gift of Goldwater Estate to the University of Auckland establishes a unique programme of wine education and research and is set to turn the deepening relationship between the university and the island's wine economy into a long-term commitment.'

— Nick Lewis, School of Environment, University of Auckland

'Kim and Jeanette Goldwater's philanthropic gift to the University of Auckland says more about their commitment to the New Zealand wine industry than any amount of awards ever could.

— Tessa Nicholson, editor, *New Zealand Winegrower*

GREATEST ACHIEVEMENT
Kim: 'We both feel incredibly proud of all our children and that in itself is at the top of our achievements.'

KEY ACHIEVEMENTS
- First winemakers on Waiheke Island.
- Founders of Goldwater Estate winery, Waiheke Island.
- Bequeathed Goldwater Estate to the University of Auckland's Wine Science Department, in the hope it will become the pre-eminent training facility in the southern hemisphere.

TAKE TO A DESERT ISLAND . . .

Kim: 'I'd have to take a boat so that I could get off when my wine supply ran out. I'd have to have good music, probably classical guitar and Mozart. To drink I'd take Goldie Chardonnay, some Waiheke Syrah, and if I could be really outrageous I would probably want to take a few bottles of Argentinian Tempranillo and some decent Burgundy wines such as Grands Echezeaux or Romanée-Conti. And, of course, I'd take my wife.'

THE STORY

'Coming back to New Zealand felt like landing in East Germany during the Cold War, after living in Spain. There was barely any wine, the food seemed incredibly plain, the culture was so conservative that there wasn't a day when I didn't want to just throw it all in and go back to Spain to work,' says Kim Goldwater.

But they did stay in Auckland — for a time at least.

The year was 1966 and New Zealand was home, in the sense that they were both raised here. It was just that, having spent several years overseas — two of them in Spain — they found Europe at the time to be refreshingly laid-back. And when they arrived back in New Zealand in the mid-1960s, they pined constantly for its exotic wines, its piquant food, its buzzing cultural life and its love of children.

To ease the dreariness of life without Spanish wine, late-night tapas and even later night socialising with other families, they tapped into the only reliable source of New Zealand red wine they could find: they had a standing weekly order of wine delivered to them by West Auckland winemaker Mate Brajkovich. He dropped off a couple of flagons of his San Marino Dry Red and collected the few dollars payment left under the doormat for him.

Kim and Jeanette weren't well off, by any stretch. And that wine was the best they could do, unless they splurged on Bakano, which was enormously more expensive at the time. It was just one of their many frustrations with the New Zealand culture of the time, with its binge drinking supported by six o'clock pub closing; a world of bangers and mash rather than gazpacho and olives; a country so far from the rest of the world that it made them wonder if they would not have been better off emotionally to have stayed in Spain.

Their spirits were lifted by their Samoan neighbours in St Mary's Bay, Auckland, who were every bit as family-oriented as the Spaniards they had lived alongside the previous couple of years.

'THERE WASN'T A DAY WHEN I DIDN'T WANT TO JUST THROW IT ALL IN AND GO BACK TO SPAIN'

GETTING TOGETHER

Kim and Jeanette met in the late 1950s at a Friday night dance at the University of Auckland. Kim was a student at the engineering school, at the time based at the Ardmore Air Field — a former US air base used during the Second World War from 1942 to 1946. In the 1950s and 1960s, the University of Auckland used the cold and draughty hangars as an overflow for courses it had no room to house at its city campus. The barracks were accommodation, the hangars lecture theatres and laboratories.

'Nobody lived together in those days, so we got married and, after graduation, we went overseas, as nearly everybody in those days did. About half the graduates went to Canada and the United States, while the other half went to the United Kingdom. Only a few graduates stayed behind,' remembers Kim.

He and Jeanette chose the UK but when they arrived 'it just didn't feel at all like the "home country" that people had talked about and we really couldn't relate to their "foreign" culture'. So, after three long years living and working in London they headed south to Madrid, where they instantly felt connected to the people, culture and place. Kim got a job as a civil engineer for two years. Returning to New Zealand after an absence of half a decade they found themselves slightly older, far more worldly and incredibly frustrated with the conservative New Zealand to which they returned.

'In essence we missed the freedom and the good-quality, everyday drinking Spanish wine. It led us into a way of living which was very social and also very family-oriented; our children were treated like royalty there. While they might have stayed up later than most children in New Zealand at the time, the social aspect of being around adults who were focused on them as well as each other made it a magical time for us all,' remembers Jeanette.

WORLDLY WISE

Jeanette had always known there was a big wide world outside New Zealand, having been born and lived in Malaysia until she was five years old.

'One day in 1941 my father came home and said the Japanese were 20 miles away. We were living north of Kuala Lumpur. I had a little brother and my mother had just got a new car of her own, so she put milk powder for the baby in the car and off the three of us drove to Singapore. My father was an engineer in tin mining. He was conscripted into the "volunteer" Malay forces and as an electrical engineer did some work as a radio operator. He was captured but we escaped. It's amazing he survived. He was put in Changi Prison and then forced to work on the Burma Railway where they said that every sleeper represented a dead prisoner. That was in 1941.

'We were evacuated to Australia. My mother never knew if my father was alive or dead or what the story was. Towards the end of 1945 when we were living in Goulburn, New South Wales, which was fairly rural, my father joined us. I remember thinking it was absolutely fantastic when this man came back because we lived across the road from the swimming pool and I thought I'd have someone to take me swimming every day.'

The reality was rather different. While the Red Cross had swung into

extremely efficient action after the war and, sans cellphones, email or internet, had rapidly reunited former prisoners of war with their families, there was a disconnectedness in all their lives.

'He was a stranger to us by then. I've never been able to imagine how it is for men trying to reintegrate who have lived like that and who have to suddenly get back into family life.'

But move on they did. As did Kim and Jeanette when they returned to New Zealand. One thing they knew for sure was that they wanted to live differently to the 9 to 5 working lives to which they were now accustomed.

But how?

The answer came swiftly one day when a friend of Kim's bet that he would never give up engineering, even though he was dissatisfied with the lack of significant projects to work on.

Kim handed in his notice there and then, told Jeanette he was going to turn his photographic hobby into a career and then created a photographic studio in the old Brown's Mill building in the city.

'There's no point continuing in a career which is not stimulating when you know what you want to do,' Kim recalls, when being interviewed for this book, aged 75 and embroiled in a house move as part of a radical downsizing, after gifting their vineyard and winery to the University of Auckland. But to get into the story of why they downsized — and why they gifted millions of dollars of family wealth they created to the university — would be to get ahead of ourselves.

SURVIVAL MODE

'As soon as Kim told me he was going to be a fashion photographer, I planted lots of vegetables,' says Jeanette, remembering the uncertainty of Kim's bold act of defiance when he threw in his lucrative civil engineering career.

Kim recalls being one of the few Auckland fashion and advertising photographers in the 1970s to make sufficient money to support a family.

'We survived very well when I took up photography. At that time a number of New Zealand photographers were often prepared to work for nothing, but I worked only for people who did pay. I just told people upfront that I like to be paid for my work,' Kim says.

'There was then no option. I had to earn money to support my family and because I'd had a keen interest in photography as a hobby, I knew how to deliver good results.'

This was the beginning of radical change. Both Kim and Jeanette say they had a burning ambition to own a yacht. So he built one. And in 1972 they launched their yacht and sailed around the Hauraki Gulf and Waiheke Island in particular, where they discovered a stunning piece of land at Putiki Bay, which they later bought with the help of a large mortgage.

'WE WANTED TO TRY DIFFERENT WINES BUT COULDN'T BUY THEM IN NEW ZEALAND BACK THEN, SO WE JUST THOUGHT, WE WILL GROW OUR OWN.'

'I remember going to a lecture that Mate Brajkovich gave in West Auckland where I asked him how much vineyard land a person could look after purely at weekends. He said 2 acres would be the maximum.'

So, in 1978, they planted 2 acres (under 1 hectare) of red grapes.

Fencing off those first Cabernet Sauvignon grapes from the animals they ran on the land was essential. The cattle and sheep were in collective ownership with five adjacent landholders, all of whom ran the farm together, which helped the Goldwaters earn extra to help with the expense of their hobby winemaking.

Given that they had no equipment, no experience and no idea how to make wine, the success of Goldwater Estate from day one was surprising, to say the least.

'We wanted to try different wines but couldn't buy them in New Zealand back then, so we just thought, "We will grow our own." It was a DIY philosophy, really. The idea was that nothing is impossible, and if you work hard enough at it and make the right decisions, it will happen.'

The biggest challenge in planting a vineyard in the early 1970s was in sourcing high-quality grapes. At the time there were very few classic wine grapes available in New Zealand.

The New Zealand wine industry was built on a firm foundation of hybrid grape varieties such as Müller-Thurgau, with the odd table grape, such as Albany Surprise, thrown in for variety's sake. The occasional *Vitis vinifera* variety also made its way into wine, such as the classic sherry grape, Palomino, from Jerez in Spain. Most of this motley crew of grapes found their way into spectacularly mediocre fortified 'sherry' and 'port' lookalikes and wannabes. In theory, these wines emulated the great European sherries and ports of the world. In practice, they were poor reflections. Today there are barely any Palomino, Albany Surprise, Müller-Thurgau or Chasselas grapes left in New Zealand. Once the mainstay of the country's wine industry, they have pretty much all been replaced, bar the odd bunch grown mostly for eating — table grapes — rather than winemaking.

THE BIG MOVE

'We followed the advice of the so-called wine experts of the day and didn't produce wine for three years because back then we were told that young vines don't make good wine. In 1981, just as we were about to produce the first wine, Jeanette's mother became terminally ill, and we had to up anchor and tear down to Christchurch and support her in her last hours. When we got back, the birds had eaten our entire crop. Our first wine was made the following year, 1982,' says Kim.

'IT SOUNDS AUDACIOUS, BUT YOU DON'T GET ANYWHERE BY BEING SHY ABOUT WHAT YOU'RE DOING. ONE SHOULD ALWAYS AIM FOR THE TOP AND WE DID.'

By this time, they had shifted themselves, their children and their family home from Auckland city to Waiheke Island. Convinced their hobby would work and with a small income from the adjoining farm, they took the plunge and in 1983 sold their Auckland house.

The first two vintages, 1982 and 1983, were released for sale together, in 1985. The 300-odd cases sold out in just two days.

'I have no idea how this happened. We initially only had a few people on our mailing list. We had not contacted or sent samples to any wine writers. Michael Brett (former *Sunday Star-Times* wine writer) had previously interviewed and written about us, but more oriented towards our Mediterranean lifestyle rather than our wine. Information about our wine just seemed to have travelled via the legendary grapevine, and suddenly we had people in the South Island, on the West Coast and in lots of little towns all over the country contacting us, wanting to buy our wines. Before we knew how or why, we had about 1000 people on the mailing list. People just heard about us somehow and said they wanted to be on our list. Computers were virtually non-existent at that stage, but I knew of one person at the university who had a computer and asked if she could print out our mailing labels, so she sat there for hours and did that. It was extraordinary,' says Kim.

'We never had any other thought in mind other than to produce the best.'

It's a philosophy the couple shared equally: 'It sounds audacious, but you don't get anywhere by being shy about what you're doing. One should always aim for the top and we did,' says Jeanette.

MOBBED BY TELEVISION

Even more extraordinary was the arrival of a dark blue van with blacked-out windows at the vineyard late one day.

'I thought it was the Mongrel Mob when I first saw the van, but out of this sinister-looking vehicle emerged Roger Price, a TV One news presenter for a current affairs programme called *Town and Around* that came on after the six o'clock news. He told us the crew were on the island for a couple of days and asked if we would mind if they did a film about us! He came back next day and made a 10-minute film on us, which aired on a Monday night during the network news with a maximum viewer audience; the same day we posted out our first mail-order brochure. It was absolutely incredible luck; the film finished up with a close-up shot of the bottle, which zoomed in on the label. Can you believe that?'

'One of my former colleagues from university rang me within minutes of it being screened, asking how I got 10 minutes on prime time news for the launch

of our wine when he only got three minutes for the collapse of a power supply dam he designed. The honest answer was: I don't know. We were in the right place at the right time — out in the vineyard pruning.'

Word spread. Within two days of the TV coverage, the first Goldwater vintages sold out. Kim kept 10 cases but ended up parting with most of those, too, due to an unexpectedly dramatic theft of wine.

'We decided to take our new little Daihatsu van to get its warrant of fitness check and we filled it with the first load of wine to take to the couriers. We got there, gave them all the documents and left the wine in the care of the manager of the courier company. About three weeks later we started getting letters from frustrated customers asking us where their wine was. I checked with the courier company and discovered that it had been the manager's last day with the company. He had a grievance with the company so had taken six cases of our wine to get even, which we had to replace.'

The former courier company employee eventually went to jail, but the stolen wine was not recovered. The Goldwaters ended up with only four cases of their first wines from 1982 and 1983, but with a reputation for fine wine from Waiheke.

GROWING PAINS

Now they needed to get a winemaker's licence in order to be able to legally sell their wine.

At the time it wasn't possible to get a winemaker's licence without being a member of WINZ, but nobody could become a member without first having a licence. It was a catch-22. The few wineries in the country that then existed had been automatically signed up for membership and given winemaker's licences when the institute was formed in 1975 by Act of Parliament.

'We were the first winery to apply to join the Wine Institute after its formation, but because we didn't have the essential winemaker's licence as required by the Act we were unable to become members. All the existing members — there were only about 60 of them — had been grandfathered into it,' says Kim.

'Eventually, after all the bureaucrats and the legal advisers said that it was impossible, their hands were tied, I said, "For Christ's sake, let's look at this logically and do something!" I suggested they sit around a table and on the word go, just pass the papers around the table simultaneously so that nobody could say that one condition had not been satisfied before the other. I am reliably informed that is what they did. It took more than six months to resolve.'

THE GIFT

Two and a half decades and millions of dollars of successful commercial winemaking down the track, a conversation at the family dinner table one night in 2009 led the Goldwaters in an entirely new direction: to gift $4 million dollars worth of their property to the University of Auckland.

It all began when their daughter, Gretchen, who now works at the university

in public relations, told her parents one day that the wine science department was going to construct a new building at the university's Tamaki campus in Glen Innes.

'It seemed inappropriate to me that the wine science programme (WSP) should be located in a virtual industrial estate, so I sent an email to Randy Weaver, the director of the WSP, offering him the use of our Waiheke property. Randy was excited by this suggestion and talked to his dean who talked to the vice-chancellor, Stuart McCutcheon, who rang me and asked exactly what we had in mind. I said, "Well, just use it. We have all the facillities you need."

'He told me the university would require a more formal arrangement, which after referral to the University Council it eventually evolved that they would like to buy the property if we could somehow assist them. Negotiations were finally brought to a satisfactory conclusion on 30 June 2011, when the university's WSP took possession of the property.'

Why did they give away millions of dollars of self-generated wealth that could have gone to their own family members? The Goldwaters say their family has benefited from a University of Auckland education and will continue to do so in the future.

'All our children are graduates of the University of Auckland, as are my father, my elder brother and myself; my younger brother taught there after graduating from university in London. And now the fourth generation — our grandson — is in his second year at the university's engineering school. The first three generations of our family who have benefited from attending the university never had to pay for their education, so this is our way of giving something back.'

SOUTHERN HEMISPHERE'S TOP WINE SCHOOL

'Southern hemisphere's pre-eminent school of winemaking and viticulture' has a distinct ring to it that Kim Goldwater likes the sound of and it's exactly what he wants his former winery to be.

'Randy Weaver, as head of the wine science department at the University of Auckland, decided right from the outset that is going to be the goal. Rather than just carrying on with the wine science programme which, up until now, has been a postgraduate course, they are going to introduce an undergraduate course soon. The winemaking facilities that were Goldwater Estate will provide the home for that.'

The arrangement is a commercial one. While the Goldwaters have donated a substantial portion of the purchase price — at least $4 million — to the

university, there is still an undisclosed sum which is being gradually paid out to them over the long term.

It's generous, even without knowing the exact amounts. Included within the entire gifted amount are two areas of land that formed their original vineyard and winery as well as another block, which used to be the Goldwaters' Zell Vineyard — home to some outstanding Chardonnay grapes, as well as Viognier and Syrah. Then there are two winery buildings and two houses. In total, the university gains approximately 14 hectares of land, all of which are planted in grapevines, aside from a small portion which the couple had been gradually converting from introduced gorse back into native forest.

The Goldwaters have retained two houses on adjoining residential land in their ownership.

WHAT NOW?

A new family home at Matiatia on Waiheke Island, a city bolt-hole 35 minutes' boat ride away at Auckland's Viaduct Harbour, and a strong interest in the winery they established — not to mention eight grandchildren, ranging from 13 to 23 — all keep the Goldwaters occupied these days.

On the face of it, their gift to the University of Auckland may look like they have forfeited a large amount of everything they built up from nothing, but, because four generations of their family have studied and still do at the university *and* because their winery is destined to be a wine training facility, they are certain it was the right choice.

Ask if they had any second thoughts and the answer is an emphatic 'No' from both of these pioneering wine lovers.

It sounds like a brave gift to make but it was, they both say, 'a pleasure — just like the past 30 years in the wine industry on Waiheke Island'.

'The timing and the continuity for the vineyard and the staff seemed to be such an optimistic future for the land and the staff, and we really needed to move into a less hands-on phase in our lives. We are both 75,' said Jeanette, in 2011.

Their old home will become student accommodation and they will enjoy their new house, which is more convenient; being five or six minutes' walk to the ferry — as long as it's low tide.

TODAY'S CHALLENGES

The biggest challenges in winemaking in New Zealand are the weather and the market — the supermarkets especially.

'The power of the supermarkets is what I call the race to the bottom. They have removed the profitability from all of their suppliers. They take the profit while nobody else does, and the sooner we can do something about that situation the better. They have too much power. Their presence in selling wine has made it more accessible to most drinkers, which is a good thing, but the power they have removed from businesses trying to make a small profit is not a good thing. It is crucifying the industry,' says Kim.

'It's the first thing that needs to change dramatically. The "how" of that is the hard part.'

KIM AND JEANETTE'S GO-TO WINES

'We've been drinking quite a bit of Riesling from Marlborough and further south. I quite like some of those drier styles of Riesling which are coming out now; the only trouble is, we never leave them long enough to get any bottle age. We also drink a fair bit of Chardonnay and I like the styles of the Goldie and also Man-O-War Valhalla, which we've been drinking a bit of lately (2011 and 2012). As far as red wine goes, I think just about any of the Waiheke Syrahs are pretty good.'

Asked if they still drink Spanish wine, Kim enthusiastically says: 'Yes. There's a winemaker called José Maria Fernandez, at Viña Tondonia, who runs a winery in Rioja which has no running water, has penicillin mould growing all over the place and produces some astonishing Rioja. If I could get my hands on it, I would drink more of it. I've been to this winery and they opened a 44-year-old Spanish white for us to taste, which was absolutely extraordinary and in great condition. It was stunning.'

TOP WINES FROM KIM AND JEANETTE GOLDWATER

- Goldie Cabernet Merlot Franc (the successor wine to the Goldwater Waiheke Island Cabernet Merlot Franc)
- Goldie Chardonnay (the successor wine to the Goldwater Waiheke Island Zell Chardonnay)

MICHAEL BRAJKOVICH MW
KUMEU RIVER WINES, WEST AUCKLAND

'Michael Brajkovich is one of the most intelligent, articulate and gifted winemakers I have come across. He commands immense respect and is a source of inspiration to those who know him and to those who drink his wines. His love of great wine knows no bounds and, combined with his quick wit, gentle nature and enquiring mind, makes for rare and engaging company.'

— Nick Stock, wine writer

'Michael has been brilliant to work with and learn from over the years. It was a fantastic learning experience and introduction to the international wine trade when I travelled with Michael to the London Wine Trade Fair in 1988. Michael had made his third vintage of Kumeu River Chardonnay (the 1988 vintage was not made due to Cyclone Bola) and had already begun to earn respect from the British wine trade and press. Being on a stand at the London Wine Trade Fair and getting such good reaction to the wines from the trade as well as press such as Oz Clarke and Jancis Robinson was very exciting. It was obvious that Michael was held in very high regard (and still is) so to be on the stand serving the Kumeu River wines made my job very easy and enjoyable. Michael has always been very open with his knowledge and has the ability to explain even the most complex things in wine in a very digestible way.'

— Paul Brajkovich

GREATEST ACHIEVEMENT
'The Master of Wine qualification.'

KEY ACHIEVEMENTS
- Dux of Roseworthy Agricultural College, Australia, 1981.
- Chief winemaker at Kumeu River Wines, West Auckland.
- Master of Wine.
- Chair of judges, Air New Zealand Wine Awards 2012.
- Deputy chair of judges, Adelaide Wine Show 2012.

TAKE TO A DESERT ISLAND . . .
'My wife Kate and, for my desert island wine, a magnum of Domaine de la Romanée-Conti Richebourg would be lovely.'

ON WINEMAKING IN AUCKLAND
'An unfashionable place to grow wine but still *very* good.'

BIGGEST RISK EVER TAKEN WITH WINE?
'Jumping into wild yeast fermentations with white wine in 1986. I was fairly confident with reds, which we began in 1984, but whites were a complete unknown. It wasn't really a risk in the end, but we needed to do it, and it worked really well.'

THE STORY
They say you shouldn't judge a book by its cover, but when it comes to the towering physical presence of six-foot-four Master of Wine Michael Brajkovich, the cover is a direct reflection of impressive academic achievements, career milestones and notable firsts in wine.

He was the first Master of Wine in New Zealand; among the first in New Zealand to make Chardonnay using traditional French winemaking methods; he was dux of his graduating year, 1981, at Roseworthy Agricultural College in South Australia; and he makes the only wines from West Auckland that shine on the global wine stage.

More importantly, for Brajkovich, he and his family have converted what was once a fortified wine company into one producing high-quality Chardonnay, whose wines and name are constantly on people's 'favourites' lists around the world. This, ahead of every other one of his formidable achievements, is the apex of his career and what gives him the most satisfaction.

He also belongs to a rare breed: an immigrant family which began the winery in 1944 and has retained it as a family business to this day.

In 1944 his late father, Mate, bought the land the family winery still sits on. Today it is run by Mate's widow, Melba, and their four children: Michael as

'EVERY SINGLE ASPECT OF OUR FOCUS IS BASED ON HIGH QUALITY AND IF WE WERE BIGGER THERE IS JUST NO WAY THAT WOULD BE POSSIBLE.'

chief winemaker, Paul as the marketing brains, Milan as the viticulturist and Marijana who works in administration.

And while this is Michael Brajkovich's story, he refers frequently to his family. It simply wouldn't occur to him — when asked about his achievements — to take more credit than any other member of the close-knit Brajkovich clan who run the winery today.

Speaking of which, Kumeu River Wines is one of New Zealand's most successful wineries, in quality terms, and significantly larger than many of the country's 'small' wineries — defined by New Zealand Winegrowers as having wine sales not exceeding 200,000 litres per annum — with 350 tonnes of grapes harvested each year. Brajkovich attributes success to assistant winemaker Nigel Tibbits, a pivotal person in the running and evolution of the winery, having begun there in 1979.

Is the tiny size related to the high quality?

'Yes, absolutely,' says Michael, without a millisecond of hesitation. 'Every single aspect of our focus is based on high quality and if we were bigger there is just no way that would be possible.'

HOW IT BEGAN

His first wine memory is of a well-told family story about him around the age of three. A photographer from the now-defunct *Auckland Star* came to take photos of him holding a glass of wine — 'Apparently, I kept draining the glass so Dad had to keep refilling it,' he smiles.

'Eventually, they got the picture. All I did that afternoon was sleep. My first memories are from about the age of four, of wine with water in it.'

Despite the early enthusiasm and growing up with wine on the dinner table every night throughout his childhood, he didn't particularly like the taste of it, although he and his three siblings were always allowed to take a sip and try it, if they wanted to.

'I didn't really. Because it was on the table all the time, you just got used to it. It wasn't a big deal.'

Later on wine did became a big deal. So big a deal that, by the age of 11, he had decided to become a winemaker. Not only was the taste growing on him but he liked the social rituals ingrained in his family: eating well; making a product people liked; meeting and serving a diverse range of people at the winery shop counter every weekend when poets, politicians and artists, among others, flocked to the cellar door to stock up on wine. He also enjoyed the sheer physical diversity of winemaking.

'It was all starting to make sense and following that I began to appreciate differences in wine styles during my teenage years. Dad always had a very

good collection of French wine. On special occasions you got to taste something very good.'

The real epiphany came when he was 16. A friend of his father's brought a bottle of 1962 Château d'Yquem to the house for dinner. 'It was mind-blowing. If I try hard, I can still taste it. I had never tried anything as amazing as that '62 d'Yquem and never knew wine could be like that.'

Given the time lag between his enthusiasm as a three-year-old and his actual appreciation of wine, it may be a surprise to know he wanted to be a winemaker by the age of 11, but there was absolute certainty in his mind because he had also decided which subjects to take at secondary school.

'I didn't go to high school wondering: "What should I do?" I had already chosen to focus on subjects that would enhance a winemaking career: science and French, both of which became incredibly important in tertiary studies, and later.'

Earlier, however, growing up at the winery meant helping out.

'I would come over from the house to the winery to help Dad by turning the pump on and off. I remember standing there for hours and hours and hours, watching the pump go around. That type of work ethic around the winery was instilled in me from a very early age.'

'Although some of that repetitive work could be a bit boring to a young child, it was interesting just to be involved and to meet the politicians, poets, artists and others who were regular customers on Saturdays at the winery, back in the day when cafés, shopping malls and even supermarkets either didn't exist or didn't open at the weekend.'

The family wine shop was so busy back then that every member of the family took turns to serve behind the same counter that forms the front face of the renovated winery today.

'Our first customer on Saturday mornings was always this guy with a roll-your-own who came in and bought two flagons of dry sherry. One day Dad asked if I knew who he was, but I had no idea, until he told me it was Colin McCahon, the artist. He had a bach at Muriwai and would pick up his wine for the weekend on the way out there to paint.'

Regular visitors to San Marino Vineyards, as it was back then, included politicians such as David Lange, Rob Muldoon, Roger Douglas, Michael Bassett, Jonathan Hunt, Bob Tizard, Warren Freer, Jack Scott and Walter Nash. The poets included Denis Glover and Rex Fairburn.

And, to Michael, winemaking seemed to be a natural extension of this interesting business, these interesting people and this good life.

'We ate and drank well, too — and still do. It's not a business you go into to

make a whole lot of money because you simply can't, but you can have a very nice life. That appealed to me.'

What didn't appeal by the time he left school were the limited educational opportunities for winemakers on offer in New Zealand. Biotechnology and food technology at Massey in Palmerston North were both too general, he decided. Instead, he marked time for a year before starting a Bachelor of Science degree at the University of Auckland.

A year later he discovered a more focused path and headed off to Australia's Roseworthy College to begin a three-year degree in oenology.

At the time there were no tertiary qualifications in New Zealand tailored specifically to the wine trade. He had heard about Roseworthy and, just as importantly, his father Mate was impressed both with the place and the people teaching there.

Roseworthy was terrific for Michael. Not only did he graduate as dux of the college, he made lifelong winemaking friends there who now work on both sides of the Tasman, and he has since become a firm regular on the wine-judging circuit in Australia. In 2012 he became Deputy Chair of Judges at the annual Adelaide Wine Show, where he has judged wine since 2000.

'Having opportunities to go and judge in Australia has been fantastic. From very early on I had the chance to be an associate judge in Canberra, and from that I have had other opportunities to judge at Hobart, Perth, Launceston and then the Adelaide one arose in 2000, when Master of Wine Michael Hill-Smith was on the wine show committee and James Halliday was Chair of Judges. It was terrific to be invited and regarded as a local judge. Most years I haven't been referred to as an "overseas" judge, more of an honorary Australian, which is very nice.'

In late 2011 he also became chair of judges beginning in 2012 at the annual Air New Zealand Wine Awards.

These new feathers in his wine-judging cap offer an opportunity for him to subtly influence the style of wines which are awarded medals.

He also wants more small wineries in New Zealand to enter wine shows, the great irony being that Kumeu River Wines hasn't entered a show since the 1990s.

While he admits that entry requirements can make this a challenging task — making enough wine to sell on a commercial scale is a tall order for many very small scale producers — it is still the best marketing tool for new and small winemakers to get their name and quality well known.

Today he benchmarks Kumeu River Wines in other ways, with magazine reviews 'and the like'. But in the early days of Kumeu River, the family entered shows to establish their wines as high quality and to set their profile in the marketplace.

'Entering wine shows is one of the most helpful ways to cement a winery in the minds of consumers. Coming from a winery and vineyard that used to specialise in fortified wine in the 1960s and 1970s to being a Chardonnay specialist today has been an amazing change and wine shows, along with magazine reviews, certainly played their part in that.'

If it was a surprise to wine drinkers that a West Auckland winery could make world-class Chardonnay, it also took the family aback.

'Originally, we thought it was going to be Merlot that would fly our flag for us; our 1983 Merlot was really on the map for New Zealand, but that was because there wasn't much around. There was a time when there was only 80 tonnes of Merlot harvested in New Zealand and Kumeu River Wines had 50 of them.'

And because Michael had worked a vintage in France, in 1983, for Jean-Pierre Moueix at Château Pétrus — home to what is widely regarded as the best Merlot in the world — he held the Merlot grape in higher regard than many.

Returning to New Zealand in 1984 he began experimenting with wild yeasts immediately to get fermentation going in his red wines, and then in 1986 he made his first Chardonnay using wild yeasts. Instead of the widely practised inoculation with commercial yeast strains, Michael waited for 'wild' or indigenous yeasts from the vineyard to kick-start the ferment. He has never looked back.

At the start of 2012 he gave a talk about the growing trend by winemakers to use wild yeasts — rather than purchasing commercial yeast strains — at the International Cool Climate Symposium, this time held in Tasmania.

'Today we use 100 per cent wild yeast fermentation rather than buying in any commercial yeast strains because, over the past 26 years, the vineyard environment here has built up its own yeast population which we can rely on to begin and finish the fermentation, without worry. This population of wild yeasts is so well known in the industry that the University of Auckland utilises the close proximity of Kumeu River Wines in yeast studies, which are part of its wine research programme.

'The kind of research that's being done now is first rate. Of course there's a lot of pressure from funding bodies who want practical research outcomes, not just esoteric stuff. However, there needs to be a balance between what is pure research and what is applied research, and I am very encouraged by the current New Zealand research that they are getting that balance right. We are leading the world in a lot of these areas, especially aroma-related research with Sauvignon Blanc, Pinot Noir and Syrah.'

This research is also focusing on how ultraviolet light — UVB in particular — impacts on the aromas of grapes and wine.

'In regions like Tasmania, New Zealand and Australia generally we have much higher UVB levels than the rest of the world, which may have a major bearing on why our wines are so varietally vibrant.'

Which is another way of saying that scientists are finally trying to prove the long-held theories that strong sunlight makes New Zealand and Australian wines taste incredibly intense.

'Viticulture ultimately determines the quality of wine and it should be an important part of what all winemakers learn. It's the way we improve our wines here,' he says, indicating the vineyards that surround Kumeu River winery today.

From its inception in 1883 as Roseworthy Agriculture College, the campus's strongest focus was on how things grew; hence, viticulture was as important as winemaking to those who went there to learn. In fact, winemaking students initially had to study agriculture first, but by the time Brajkovich got there, the diploma in oenology had become a degree in its own right.

'We were also very lucky having Dr Richard Smart on our course, a brilliant lecturer.'

Thanks to Smart, Brajkovich learnt hands-on viticulture in Coonawarra, South Australia.

'It's a pretty isolated sort of place. I still think it makes the very best red wines in Australia. This unique little hill of soil that is Coonawarra has some sites there that just produce outstanding wines.'

During his time at Roseworthy, Brajkovich wrote his third-year project on trellis design and canopy management in Coonawarra under Richard Smart's supervision.

Smart had contacts in Coonawarra and Brajkovich needed to work a vintage somewhere, so Smart arranged a vintage job at Mildara where Michael got to work with the late, legendary Jack Schultz, who was nearing retirement but who had helped lift the profile, perception and quality of Coonawarra wines.

'Jack was a crusty old guy but with a really good practical knowledge of wine,' Brajkovich remembers.

'I can also remember tasting the 1963 Mildara Coonawarra Cabernet Sauvignon, famously dubbed "Peppermint Patty" and was Mildara's first-ever Coonawarra wine from their new winery. We tasted it on Jack's birthday, 5 April 1981, and I still have my tasting notes: "Undoubtedly this is the best wine I have ever had the pleasure to try from Australia. It is tremendously complex, with a nose especially characterised by an intense peppermint aroma. On the palate it has everything expected from a mature claret. A superlative wine."'

THE MW — A BIGGIE

'It's a biggie,' admits Michael Brajkovich, who was one of just 299 Masters of Wine in the world at the time of writing, in early 2012.

The qualification is not aligned to any educational institution, but it has a long history with the wine and spirits trade in the United Kingdom. The Institute of Masters of Wine was established in 1953 by the Vintners' Company, which established its first charter in 1363; it is one of the Twelve Great Livery Companies of the City of London. In 1969, in conjunction with the Wine and Spirits Association (UK), the Institute of Masters of Wine set up the Wine and Spirits Education Trust.

Like most in the wine trade, Brajkovich says he held 'these guys — Masters of Wine — in awe', but he never expected to add the letters after his own name until, in 1986, Sarah Morphew Stephen, Master of Wine, who was the chair of the Institute of Masters of Wine at the time and visiting New Zealand as a guest wine judge, suggested he should attempt to gain the qualification.

Assuming there was no way he could move to London for the three years he thought it would take him to study it back then, he dimissed the idea. Then Australian winemaker Michael Hill-Smith passed the exam and Morphew Stephen phoned Brajkovich again, suggesting he attempt it.

'I thought it was pretty hard so I was pleasantly surprised when the results came through and the chairman of the Masters of Wine David Stevens rang me and said, "Welcome on board."'

MAT DONALDSON AND LYNNETTE HUDSON

Wearing angelic white — the *enfant terrible* of the New Zealand wine industry, Mat Donaldson, with fellow winemaker, wife and Pinot Noir perfectionist Lynnette Hudson; they are famed for their love of Burgundy, Rieslings from all over the world and some of the best parties in the southern hemisphere at Pegasus Bay winery in Waipara, North Canterbury. Pictured in their vineyard in autumn 2012. Photograph by Stephen Goodenough

Modern family — the Pegasus Bay winery family team includes three of the four sons of founders Chris and Ivan Donaldson (sitting in front), who began making wine from their chilly Halswell vineyard — nicknamed Pleurisy Point because it was so cold — before seeking warmth and moving north. The team (left to right) is: head of marketing, sales and details man Edward Donaldson and his wife, Belinda; general manager Paul Donaldson; wife-husband winemaking team Lynnette and Mat.

NICK NOBILO

Father and son — Nikolas Nobilo senior (left) with his winemaking son Nick, sampling their own early table wine in the 1970s; 'young' Nick was allowed almost free rein to pursue new grape varieties at a time when few were willing to experiment.

Five decades on, still strong — Nick Nobilo signing a bottle of Jubilee Red, a wine released in 2012 to celebrate his 50 years of winemaking in New Zealand; exactly which red grapes are included in this mystery red remains a secret.

A scientific approach — wearing his trademark white coat, Nick Nobilo at the family winery (when it was still family owned, prior to its sale in 2000) in West Auckland.

Pushing boundaries and perfecting the results — Nick Nobilo confesses to his love of taking things to the extreme, something he has done for the past 50 years in his winemaking.

GORDON RUSSELL

Taste test — drawing wine via pipette for tasting in Esk Valley's red barrel ageing room.

Punk turned winemaker — Gordon Russell has always been attracted to the edge in fashion, music and wine (think Ryan Adams, Grüner Veltliner and Verdelho rather than Bryan Adams, Pinot Gris or vast quantities of wine); pictured here with winemaking equipment which is not only rare this century but alternative in New Zealand wine circles, where modern stainless steel predominates: old concrete fermentation vats at Esk Valley, built in the first half of last century by the winery's former owners and founders, the Bird family.

Carved in hills — The Terraces vineyard overlooks the sea north of Napier city, enjoying a microclimate all of its own.

Attracted to curves — vines snake their way along the contours of the meticulously hand-tended hillside vineyard, The Terraces; the top wine takes its name from this site.

PETER BABICH MBE

Teen spirit — the late Josip Petrov Babich was born in Dalmatia (part of modern-day Croatia) and arrived in New Zealand, aged 14, with nothing but an empty stomach and four hard-working brothers.

The original Babich wine cellar at Kaikano in Northland, 1916.

Peter Babich (left) with Peter Fredatovich Snr among the vines at a Viticultural Association Field Day held at Lincoln Vineyards, Auckland, 1970.
Photograph by Marti Friedlander.

Change maker — Peter Babich, political mover and shaker and unsung hero for those who appreciate what he did to move New Zealand towards a table wine culture (instead of minimum 2-gallon sales of sugared-up wine made from non-classical varieties). Peter (left) always acknowledges the work of his winemaking brother, Joe (centre), who held the fort while he lobbied Parliament. Peter's son, David (right) is general manager of Babich Wines today.

ROSS SPENCE

Brothers in wine — arguably the most influential man in New Zealand wine in the 1980s and 1990s, Ross Spence (left) with his brother Bill Spence. Together they did everything from planting their own vineyard to making and marketing their wines, as well as pioneering Sauvignon Blanc in New Zealand. Not that Spence would ever describe himself in such hallowed terms. He rarely refers to the QSO he was awarded in 2000 for services to New Zealand wine.

Bill's (left) grape growing expertise and Ross's (right) winemaking skills saw the first ever Matua Valley Sauvignon Blanc made in 1974; the first of the many hundreds now made each year and the key to New Zealand's wine export success.

KIM AND JEANETTE GOLDWATER

Giving it away — Kim and Jeanette Goldwater with daughter and son-in-law Gretchen and Ken Christie, pictured on Waiheke Island prior to gifting their winery to the University of Auckland's Wine Science Department in 2011.

MICHAEL BRAJKOVICH MW

Mate's Vineyard — opposite the winery and below the home of eldest son, Michael Brajkovich.

Like father, like son — Master of Wine and winemaker Michael Brajkovich not only looks like his late father, Mate Brajkovich, but he has carried the pioneering torch to a new generation to be part of creating a new wave of wine in New Zealand.

Foundation stone — at Kumeu River Wines, at the entrance to Kumeu township, West Auckland.

Wine family — the four Brajkovich siblings with their mother, Melba, who brought them all up in the winery (left to right): viticulturist Milan, Melba, winemaker Michael, administrator Marijana and marketing man Paul.

SIR GEORGE FISTONICH

His best side — the young George Fistonich taste tests a barrel of red at Villa Maria Estate, the family-owned winery in Mangere, South Auckland. Ambitious from the start is how his colleagues in the New Zealand wine scene describe Sir George.

When young George Fistonich started making wine in the 1960s, many in New Zealand said grapes couldn't be grown in the South Island. While there are few large tracts of viable vineyard land waiting to be discovered today, Sir George says that promising pockets of land can still be found, especially in Hawke's Bay, and particularly for red grapes.

100 per cent screwcaps — swift adoption of screwcaps saw a complete ban on cork: Sir George (pictured here in 2001) said, 'It was a quest for quality; it's always our aim to make the best wine possible without compromise.'

CLIVE PATON

Man of many talents — Clive was a single dad in 1980 when he first planted vines at Ata Rangi with young daughter Ness.

Sister and brother team — Alison and Clive at Ata Rangi vineyard.

Enjoying the line-up — Clive samples some Ata Rangi wines; the distinctive label of Crimson (featuring pohutukawa flowers) sits on the far right next to Ata Rangi Pinot Noir (three times winner of the Bouchard Finlayson Trophy for Best Pinot Noir in the World at the International Wine and Spirit Challenge) and the third red, Célèbre.

'MY ABSOLUTE HIGHLIGHT IS KUMEU RIVER BEING
RECOGNISED AND LISTED IN PEOPLE'S FAVOURITE LISTS
OF CHARDONNAYS. WE ARE THIS LITTLE WINERY IN A VERY
UNFASHIONABLE PART OF NEW ZEALAND.'

MAKING WINNING CHARDONNAY

'My absolute highlight is Kumeu River being recognised and listed in people's favourite lists of Chardonnays. We are this little winery in a very unfashionable part of New Zealand.

'Chardonnay is really what put us on the map in the United Kingdom; not necessarily on the wine show circuit but with tasters and write-ups. The *Wine Spectator* has been huge on that, too, because they ranked the 1987 Kumeu River Chardonnay highly initially and then the 1994 made their Top 100 wines of the year, and, for me, that was the absolute epitome of achievement.'

While the early 1980s were the boom years for the first top Kumeu River Chardonnays, sadly this changed when Cyclone Bola struck, devastating the 1988 vintage. Thankfully, 1989 was a terrific year — 'small cropping but it made a very fine, elegant wine'.

TASTING GREAT BURGUNDY

'You get lucky, and I have been very fortunate in having had the opportunity to taste many great burgundies, and many great wines in general. I've had three occasions where I've been able to visit Domaine de la Romanée-Conti (DRC) and I know that while that is a rare privilege now, it's going to become even rarer.

'For most people these top wines are out of reach. That's one of the sad things, I think. Growing up in the wine business I had access to an incredible array of fine wines. At current prices you realistically can't get hold of those top wines now; unless you get invited to a tasting you're not going to go out and buy DRC, so it's been moved from the people who need to taste these wines or would love to taste them to a few elite rich who are perhaps more interested in the cachet or rarity than the real calibre of the wines. It's really sad.

'I know that the producers of those wines are very concerned about that aspect, too, because it doesn't take much of an economic change to lose that market completely and then where are you? You've lost your traditional market of punters who have moved on because they simply couldn't afford these wines, due to market pressures.'

WHAT'S NEXT?

Distinct characteristics are beginning to reveal themselves in the growing range of single-vineyard wines the Brajkovichs make.

'It started off with Mate's Vineyard, which was an old site that originally was just going to be blended into our Estate Chardonnay, until we saw what it

'AT A PARTY IN NEW YORK WITH WINE WRITER HUGH JOHNSON, HE LOOKED AT ME AND SAID, "HAVE YOU EVER THOUGHT OF MAKING BUBBLES?"'

---

had to offer as a standalone wine. More recently with Hunting Hill and Coddington Chardonnays we've started seeing really distinctive terroir-driven qualities. We look at them to decide what gets put into our own estate wine and what makes a single-vineyard wine.

'The wines taste so different each year and the vineyard sites are not that far apart, but it's the same differences in taste we see every year. If you were to line up all the Hunting Hills every year then the same characteristics are showing through. The favourite varies a bit from time to time and mood to mood. I think the Coddington is the richest style, but I'm a great fan of the Hunting Hill. I think it's the most Burgundian; the French talk a lot about the finesse of the acid, which affects the way the wine tastes. That's what I see in the Hunting Hill.'

UNCHARTED TERRITORY
Bubbles, Gewürztraminer and Verdejo are all close to Brajkovich's heart and, he predicts, all have the potential to be high quality from West Auckland. Not that there is any of the Spanish white grape, Verdejo, in New Zealand, yet. Verdejo comes from the Rueda region in Spain; it's an aromatic white, often blended with Sauvignon Blanc, and Brajkovich wants to trial it here.

More auspiciously, there is a bubbly on the way.

'At a party in New York with wine writer Hugh Johnson, I sat down and shared a glass of 2004 Mate's Vineyard Chardonnay and he looked at me and said, "Have you ever thought of making bubbles?"'

Now they are. It won't be big scale. The wine will spend a minimum of three years on yeast lees (a prerequisite in making high-quality sparkling wine).

'That's the absolute minimum. I remember trying these wines that had spent eight, nine and 10 years on lees and the results were incredible.'

'We've always been interested in sparkling, and we have some Pinot Noir vineyards from which we don't necessarily make very robust red wine, but making them into bubbles has always attracted us. The difficulty has always been the ability to disgorge it and do the dosage, but Soljans Wines [nearby] have all that gear for hire, so we're going to use that. We will start this year: 2012.'

Then there is Gewürztraminer. It's a tough sell, but it's an unsung hero of the New Zealand wine industry, insists Brajkovich.

'Gewürz goes with everything from pork to seafood and is especially good with Asian and lighter food styles.'

He is working on a small run of this wine — 100 to 200 cases a year — 'Which probably won't be released until a couple of years from now.'

'FOR THE FIRST TIME NOW WE'RE SEEING AUSSIE WINE JUDGES PENALISING A WINE FOR SHOWING TOO MUCH OAK. THAT'S A REVOLUTION IN ITSELF. THE SAME IS HAPPENING IN NEW ZEALAND.'

Not one to rest on his laurels, he and his family are planting two hot new clones of Chardonnay in the vineyard that was previously given over to Pinot Noir. He's also planning to trial the full-tank technique on a few high-quality batches of Chardonnay because lees-ageing of Chardonnay in stainless steel tanks is a technique without the use of oak that works wonders on Kumeu River Village Chardonnay, a cheapie that tastes anything but.

'It will be very interesting in terms of making full-bodied wine without oak using this technique, which is working so well for our Village Chardonnay.'

Ironically, for a winemaker focused more strongly on Chardonnay than any other variety, Brajkovich predicts this wine will change in style.

Australian trends show that.

'For the first time now we're seeing Aussie wine judges penalising a wine for showing too much oak. That's a revolution in itself. The same is happening in New Zealand.

'I think it's because they've gone away from judging very big line-ups of wine where it tends to be the oaky ones that jump out. Now that we're splitting classes of wine in competitions so that no one is judging more than 25 to 30 wines at a time, it gives judges much more of an opportunity to see the more elegant and refined wines which are showing up across the board. These wines are much more interesting, more restrained and, as a result, for the past two years a Chardonnay has been the top wine of the show at Adelaide.'

Stylistically, the same is happening with Riesling: 'Elegance, finesse, citrus characters, all those things that used to typify Eden and Clare Valley Rieslings are now qualities that we're seeing across the board, both in New Zealand and in Australia. Then there are the newer styles: lower alcohol, slightly sweeter — and, yes, they are valid expressions of Riesling.'

Why exactly are these flavours shining through now?

Earlier harvesting of grapes plays a part, as does 'better' (that is, 'gentler') handling of grapes all the way from the vineyard to the winery and, 'Dare I say it, the screwcap at the end helps things tremendously.'

Brajkovich was a longtime chairman of the New Zealand Screwcap Initiative when it was launched one chilly spring morning in Blenheim, in August 2001. He was one of the first 26 New Zealand wineries to use screwcaps, and as soon as their stock of bottles and corks had run out in September 2001, he and his family converted 100 per cent to the new seal.

Loath to claim any credit for his foresight in using screwcaps, he says, simply: 'Rather than an achievement, it's one of the biggest changes happening in the industry, and it will become much more mainstream, too.'

As will wine.

'In the future I think we'll see less of the sheer bulk of wine being made today. People will take on messages about their health, drink less and a bit better, but there has to be value. There will always be room at the top of the market for very expensive wine and we want to be in that area. We're also going to see some pretty good value. Even at a winery of our size, not everything you can make is going to be at the top of the tree. You need good-quality wines that people can drink every day.'

OAK CITY

Will oak become a thing of the past?

'Oak barrels are simply containers that are used because they are watertight. During the Second World War there had been so much neglect in the wine business that they had to replace very large numbers of barrels with new oak.

'Then you had this big hit of new oak in wines, which people liked and it became popular. It never was before. In recent times it has also become very popular in the New World and that saw a huge expansion in the amount of cooperage (cooperage is the industry of making wine barrels) worldwide. That trend has slowed, and in France in particular now there's a lot more emphasis on larger format oak containers, "cuves", which allow the slow ageing of wine, but without the big whack of tannin and vanilla character. There is less aroma impact, but it's a container that's more wine-friendly than stainless steel and more gentle.

'The larger format barrels give a softness to a white wine that you don't get with the stainless, and you can do things like lees-ageing, which also benefit the flavour.'

THE FUTURE

'There are too many grapes planted. It beggars belief that people planted so many grapes based on spurious research, but people are stupid when it comes to wine. They'll make emotional decisions that are not based on business reality and then it affects all of us. Common sense is the answer; better information.

'I know New Zealand Winegrowers is accumulating a much better picture of what the industry actually has, in terms of production capacity and vineyards planted. This information will allow people to make proper decisions, to allow banks to make lending decisions.

'You hear of so many instances of people borrowing 100 per cent of the funding to buy vineyard land and then the latest GV for Marlborough comes out showing that vineyard land has gone down 40 per cent: so many of these

---

'IT BEGGARS BELIEF THAT PEOPLE PLANTED SO MANY GRAPES BASED ON SPURIOUS RESEARCH, BUT PEOPLE ARE STUPID WHEN IT COMES TO WINE.'

people are now in negative equity and they just have to wait until things start to come right.

'The other thing that needs to change is excise. It's ridiculous the amount of money wineries are taxed because they produce an alcoholic drink. And in most cases, wineries — large, medium and small — absorb the cost because, unlike some sectors of the drinks trade, we are simply not in a position to be able to charge more for our wine.

'I think wine is becoming a very important part of our everyday lives. It's part of what we consume with food, and it's just part of having a bit more interesting and balanced life. The problem with the use of alcohol in the general sense — the abuse of alcohol — is a real worry to us, but we strongly believe that wine doesn't contribute very much to it. The government has to take a pretty blunt approach to it all and not tax us so heavily.'

MICHAEL'S GO-TO WINES

Verdicchio, Godello, Verdejo, Côtes-du-Rhône, Chianti and . . . Chardonnay all hit the spot in the Brajkovich household.

'For everyday tasting and drinking Casal di Serra Verdicchio from Umani Ronchi in Italy. When I was growing up in the industry, Verdicchio was the closest thing to battery acid, but the Italians have done a great job with that grape and style now, and it's never far from the table at home.'

Other favourites include Telmo Rodrigeuz Gaba do Xil Godello (Spain), Telmo Rodrigeuz El Transistor (a Verdejo from Rueda, Spain), Domaine Perrin Côtes-du-Rhône (France), Roche della Marcie Chianti Riserva (Italy) and Kumeu River Village Chardonnay.

TOP WINES FROM MICHAEL BRAJKOVICH
- Mate's Vineyard Chardonnay
- Hunting Hill Chardonnay

SIR GEORGE FISTONICH

VILLA MARIA ESTATE, SOUTH AUCKLAND

'I doubt there is a pioneering producer of the 70s and 80s who remains as passionate and committed to their founding business and the quality of New Zealand wine as George. To work for George in the period immediately after receivership in the 80s right through until the end of the 90s was a very inspiring time for me. In the face of almost insurmountable odds, he had great belief that he was going to not only survive, but create a great wine business.'

— Steve Smith, MW, Craggy Range winery

'George is a visionary with a perceptive mind. Once he has all the facts he will make a decision on the spot. His overriding aim is to make some of the world's best wines. He wants to employ the best people and really enjoys watching them grow to great heights in their field. His common phrase is "if you stand still you go backwards".'

— Ian Clark, export and PR manager, Villa Maria Estate

GREATEST ACHIEVEMENT
'Still being a New Zealand-owned private family company after 50 years.'

KEY ACHIEVEMENTS
- Founder (1961), former winemaker and managing director of a large New Zealand-owned winery.
- Received a knighthood in 2009, for services to the wine industry.

- Queen's Diamond Jubilee Medal for services to New Zealand wine, 2012.
- Induction into the New Zealand Wine Hall of Fame at the Royal Easter Show Wine Awards 2011.
- The first large New Zealand winery to commit 100 per cent to screwcaps in 2001.
- Opening New Zealand's first winery restaurant at Vidal's in Hawke's Bay, 1979.
- 'Most Impressive Winery of the Year 2007', Hubrecht Duijker, European wine writer.
- Winery of the Year 2006, *Restaurant Wine* magazine, United States.
- Kea World Class New Zealander Award in Manufacturing, Design & Innovation, 2011.
- Lifetime Achievement Award at the International Wine Challenge Awards in London, 2011.

TAKE TO A DESERT ISLAND . . .

'Château d'Yquem, a great drink to sip and savour and almost a feed. I could have it for breakfast, lunch and dinner — if I was lucky enough to have dinner on a desert island — and I'd take my wife.'

THE STORY

It is a bright sunny day when Sir George Fistonich and I meet to talk about a topic he deftly avoids: himself. The year 2012 marks his fiftieth in business and he's planning a five-month world tour to spread the word about the wines he began making as a young man at his parents' home in South Auckland, in 1961.

The warm weather suits his buoyant mood, and both the travel and his winery are topics Sir George would rather talk about than how it all began. Focusing on the present and looking to the future are clearly key to the success of his winery, for a long time one of the top three in terms of size in New Zealand. Today it remains among the top 10 in size.

The winery is, of course, Villa Maria Estate. It was christened 'Villa Maria Wines' in the early 1960s. The name took Fistonich's fancy as it sounded European, like his parents' Dalmatian origins and the origin of all the world's fine wines.

At 70, Fistonich cuts a slender figure, has a twinkle in his eye and exudes an air of openness to new discovery; they are qualities for which he has become well known, hence his knighthood in 2009 for services to the wine industry.

'What do you think we should drink with lunch?' asks the man who has built a reputation around harnessing the talents of his staff to the needs of his ever-expanding company. Many a famous winemaker, grape-grower or Master of Wine has worked for Fistonich. Many still do. Master of Wine Steve Smith of Craggy Range, Master of Wine Kym Milne (now an overseas consultant winemaker) and winemaker Michelle Richardson are a mere sprinkling in the glittering pool of talented people who have worked for him. Master of Wine Alastair Maling is currently the general manager of winemaking at Villa Maria Estate. Asked how

he attracts, retains and fosters so many high achievers, Fistonich says, quietly, he just lets people be themselves.

Fistonich picks my brain about the many quirky European grapes and wine styles I enjoy while I gently attempt to steer the conversation back to his pending world tour to promote Villa Maria's three wineries, his pioneering adherence to screwcaps and the little-known grapes he and his winemakers are currently experimenting with at Villa Maria: Arneis, Grüner Veltliner, Verdelho and Viognier among them.

Until around 2002 Fistonich was actively involved in blending wines at Villa Maria. He continues to have a great deal of input into the vineyards and wine styles in a bid to ensure that wine quality is the number-one focus. His main job, however, is steering his business through the bumpy waters of recession, national wine glut and supermarket price slashing.

'I remember going away on holiday with George years ago and, while the rest of us were off on a trip for the day, he was busy planning, reading, thinking — and working. I find it hard to stop thinking about wine and work when I'm away somewhere but George is something else again,' recalls Ross Spence.

Which accounts at least in part for why Villa Maria Estate today is one of the few 'large New Zealand wineries' — those whose sales exceed 4 million litres — still in local ownership.

This is of burning importance to Fistonich — and to the wine industry in New Zealand, he says.

'The hardest thing this millennium has been watching all the New Zealand-owned companies disappear. We are a totally New Zealand-owned, private family company exporting wine with a worldwide reputation for quality, which sets us apart from other big New Zealand wine companies.

'Initially, the New Zealand wine industry beat the French at their own game, taking their spot on UK wine shelves by making such good quality wine that we commanded the highest per litre price of any country in the world. Now it has changed. We still command high prices in the UK, but also some very low ones. The largest wine company in New Zealand is now owned by a multinational. Other New Zealand wineries like Nobilo's, Kim Crawford Wines, Selaks and Matua Valley, which was a lovely little boutique winery with a family feel, are all now owned by multinationals.

'We hear all this press about New Zealand selling its dairy farms overseas, but we're talking about 1 or 2 per cent of farmland in that respect. What I find upsetting is looking over the mass of vineyards in Marlborough — 19,570 hectares — knowing most of it is now owned outside New Zealand. More important than profits from those companies disappearing overseas is the fact that the owners of those companies no longer have a direct connection with the land. They will never have the same passion for the unique New Zealand identity.

'Some of them see wines simply as brands in the marketplace. There is a real danger of New Zealand wine becoming a commodity.

'I'm a passionate New Zealander and I'd like to see those companies and that land in New Zealand hands.'

'WHAT I FIND UPSETTING IS LOOKING OVER THE MASS OF VINEYARDS IN MARLBOROUGH . . . KNOWING MOST OF IT IS NOW OWNED OUTSIDE NEW ZEALAND. . . . THEY WILL NEVER HAVE THE SAME PASSION FOR THE UNIQUE NEW ZEALAND IDENTITY.'

THE ANSWER

Fistonich would like to see more support for New Zealand-owned companies with their own vineyards and cellar door sales. Currently, the tax system and regulations work against the smaller family-owned operations. Yet it is the owner-operated winery that is crucial to the identity of our wine and tourism industry. This fact seems to be ignored in New Zealand, yet in other wine-producing countries there is a lot more support at government level for locally owned wineries with cellar door operations that provide jobs and support tourism.

Identity is about having real personalities behind the bottle of wine, not just a brand dreamed up in the marketing office of a foreign country with the wine being made at a mega-factory winery.

'It is hard to turn back the clock, but there needs to be more scrutiny on further sales. We are better off to have the vineyards and the wineries owned by New Zealanders where we can control the identity of the wines and keep the added value component and the jobs in New Zealand.

'Long term we will have a shortage of land for expansion, unless we find new areas in which to plant grapes.'

And does he think such areas exist?

'You never know; 40 years ago people said you couldn't grow grapes in the South Island. There may not be large areas like Marlborough, but there could be promising pockets.'

One such pocket, which is currently over-delivering, lies about 500 kilometres north of Marlborough. It's a 120-acre vineyard in Hawke's Bay, planted 10 years ago and producing Chardonnay grapes which make wines that keep winning awards. Constantly.

The Keltern Vineyard is 3 kilometres south of Sileni Estates winery east of Maraekakaho in Hawke's Bay. Dry, warm, inland and protected from coastal winds, Keltern Vineyard is home to a number of grape varieties, but it's the Chardonnay which is taking the accolades.

Keltern Single Vineyard Chardonnay won five trophies in the year leading up to this book's publication, all of which follow on the heels of its former wins. The first vintage was the 2002 Keltern Vineyard Chardonnay, which won Champion Chardonnay at the annual Hawke's Bay Wine Awards in 2004. It has since won 12 'Champion Chardonnay' trophies, five of which have been in the past two years.

Among the wins are: 2011 Villa Maria Estate Keltern Vineyard Chardonnay won Champion Wine of Show, Champion Chardonnay and the Sustainability

Trophy at the 2011 Romeo Bragato Wine Awards; Champion Wine of the Show at the 2011 Hawke's Bay Wine Awards; Champion Wine of the Show at the 2011 Air New Zealand Wine Awards.

PASSIONATE ABOUT NEW ZEALAND WINE STYLES

It's not the grapes from the Keltern Vineyard nor even the medals the wine wins that make Fistonich proud. Making Chardonnays that are a natural expression of New Zealand fires him up.

Gone are the days of big buttery Chardonnays, says Fistonich, who wants to distance himself from wines he sees as inelegant expressions of a teen-like wine culture. In his quest to make the ultimate white wine, Fistonich hopes to build on the company's already incomparable record with a Villa Maria icon Chardonnay. It's a work in progress right now, but Fistonich has never been one to rest on any laurels, despite winning more than any other New Zealand winery.

He is keen to see how far he and his winemakers can push the reduction of new oak in full-bodied white wines. 'If your site selection is right and the grapes are ripe in the first place, the wines don't need lots of new oak. In fact the aroma and taste profiles can be far better without all the oak, which became a trend in New World wine countries a couple of decades ago,' he says.

The name, launch and exact details of his top new white have yet to be revealed, but if it can be another 'first', Fistonich will be happy. He has something of a reputation for being 'first' in wine circles.

In 1979 he was the first to open a winery restaurant in New Zealand at Vidal's Wines in Hawke's Bay. In 2001 his was the first large winery in the world to commit to sealing 100 per cent of its wines under screwcap. In the last wine glut, in 1986, he was the first winery to go into receivership, too. Something else he will come back to in this discussion.

More important are the new wine styles that Villa Maria and a number of other New Zealand winemakers are pioneering.

The Villa Maria Private Bin Riesling (a sub-$20 wine), which won a trophy at the Air New Zealand Wine Awards in 2010, breaks with tradition by being dry in style. It is also a readily available, everyday affordable premium wine, and good enough to win a top award for its high quality. 'Riesling is incredibly underrated in New Zealand and to be able to make a dry style at this price and have it awarded so highly speaks volumes about the potential of New Zealand for this wine. I would like to see more Riesling made in New Zealand, especially from North Canterbury, which has an outstanding climate for it. It's important we don't just stick to the wines we know and do well, which is why we're experimenting with new ones, too,' he adds, citing the fresh dry white made from the Arneis grape (originating from northern Italy), a Grüner Veltliner (from Austria) and a Viognier (from the Rhône Valley in France).

Fistonich would like to find other grapes to trial as well: 'What do you think we should look at?' he asks, part-way through our interview.

Of his work in pioneering new wine styles — both from well-known grapes and from those not known at all — Fistonich says it is part of evolving the New Zealand wine industry.

'INTERNATIONALLY, WINE DRINKERS SEE NEW ZEALAND AS SAUVIGNON BLANC AND AUSTRALIA AS SHIRAZ. THERE IS MORE TO IT AND I'M PASSIONATE THAT WE SHOW WHAT THE "MORE" IS.'

'It's important to me that we don't just sell our New Zealand Sauvignon Blanc to the world. We've got to sell our Rieslings and Chardonnays, too. Internationally, wine drinkers see New Zealand as Sauvignon Blanc and Australia as Shiraz. There is more to it and I'm passionate that we show what the "more" is.'

SCREWY DEBATE

Making and bottling the best wine possible is of paramount importance to Fistonich, who wanted to move completely to screwcaps as soon as they were available in New Zealand, in 2001. But it wasn't only his decision at the time; it was his board's.

When the idea of using screwcaps reared its contentious head, Fistonich had to persuade the management board at Villa Maria Estate that they were the best wine closures to use.

The previous year had seen unprecedented success with screwcaps in Australia, where a bunch of Clare Valley Riesling producers had successfully joined marketing and winemaking forces to pioneer the use of the screwcap. Some of those Australian wineries sealed 50 per cent of their wines under screwcap and 50 per cent under cork. The screwcap-sealed wines sold out first, begging the question: why bother with a fault-prone closure at all?

'For me it was about wine quality. I always knew they were better than corks for quality wine because 25 years ago I had seen that, so there was no question in my mind that screwcaps were more reliable.

'We have done experiments with corks for a long time, taking them out of bottles and soaking them in neutral water or in wine and finding a huge variation in their quality, and they seemed to be going from bad to worse. I was getting quite angry about the whole thing. We were rejecting up to about five out of every 10 bags, so I always found it quite illogical to talk about imagery and marketing because it goes back to our wine quality,' he says.

'There is no romance in a faulty bottle of wine. The cork people had done such a great job of building up this imagery, and I suppose some wine writers were sucked into it. New Zealand wine writers in general supported the change.'

QUALITY FIRST

The change came when Fistonich suggested that all board members at Villa Maria Estate read their constitution, him included.

'It says wine quality comes first. As soon as we read that, we decided

unanimously on the 100 per cent use of screwcaps. They were controversial, but they always represented more consistent and higher quality — and therefore better value — wine than any other closure currently available to winemakers.'

It might have been an easy and obvious transition for the winery, but the waters were choppy in the marketplace, particularly in the United States.

'We got delisted out of the 30 seafood restaurants in America and we got a lot of abuse. I remember saying to our suppliers in the US that if they wouldn't take our wine under screwcap, they wouldn't be able to have any at all. So eventually our distributors did take it, but not without a few battles.'

One of those was a 'filthy letter from a member of the American public saying that they were proud of New Zealand wine and are now ashamed'.

Nasty letters emerged from closer to home, too. One from a wine drinker in Palmerston North read that its writer had drunk Villa Maria wines for years but would never drink one again now they were sealed with screwcaps.

'We had a letter we sent out, thanking everyone who wrote in and saying: "You're obviously passionate about your wines; so are we . . ." We kept it to a very well-executed one-page instant reply, which was very courteous, and we turned just about everyone who was anti-screwcaps into missionaries for screwcaps.'

Fistonich is no stranger to battles. Over 50 years in business means there have been a few, but the biggest one was being forced into insolvency on 18 November 1986 or, as Fistonich puts it, 'voluntary receivership'. It's a period in Villa Maria's history which he prefers to forget, although he admits it carried with it a few hard lessons.

'I wasn't going to sit down and die, but it was a hard comeback,' he says, recalling the events of an oversupply of grapes in the 1980s, which led to a national wine glut, a reduction in prices and a financial crisis in the industry. Not unlike what is happening in 2012, in other words.

'The oversupply we see today has happened before, only last time we were the victims of some large corporates, who basically tried to force us out of business in order to have the market all to themselves at the time. I wasn't going to let that happen, and even though we went into receivership, it wasn't for long,' says Fistonich.

His trump card on the eve of going into receivership was being tipped off that he had won several gold medals and trophies at an Australian wine show.

'I organised Ian Clark [the company's PR and export manager] to go over to Australia and pick up the trophies, so he arrived at the airport on the same day that we were announced to be in receivership. That morning Ian Clark and I were on the front page of the *Herald* with a beautiful headline: "Trophy-winning

winemaker forced out of business". The timing was perfect because it planted seeds of doubt in the public mind about why we had been put in receivership. They bought our wines and we worked our way out of the problems.'

It was the perfect wake-up headline for all the staff Fistonich had flown to a joint meeting in Auckland the previous day: Sunday 17 November.

'I wanted to tell the staff, not just send out a letter to them. I was initially told flying them up to a meeting wasn't a responsible use of money, but I was determined to do it in person and make sure everyone had the same message. Peter Howell, the receiver, saw the logic of this and gave his full support so I organised a sales conference on the Sunday afternoon, and we also decided we'd have a few drinks afterwards. People donated crayfish and champagne, and then Peter Howell made an announcement that we had been forced into receivership. We ended up having quite a few drinks that day.'

A month later he started receiving phone calls from fellow winemakers who were facing the same financial difficulties during the grape and wine glut of the day.

Fistonich always felt his receivership had been forced as part of a calculated plan by larger corporate wineries which were selling below cost in an attempt to rationalise the industry.

'I told Warren Berryman of the *National Business Review* at the time that's how I felt and he did a two-page story saying Villa Maria had been bulldozed out of business. That and the trophy wins in Australia helped get us back on track.'

In the late 1980s the New Zealand wine industry was constituted largely of cask wine, which accounted for 55 to 60 per cent of production. Due to a grape glut sales of casks fell below the cost of production. 'A case of six casks which would normally sell for $42 fell to as little as $13 when it had cost $28 to produce,' wrote Jan Corbett in a *Metro* magazine story, published in 1987. The worst part of the receivership involved the months leading up to it when the company couldn't pay its bills. The more discounts it gave, the more wine it sold, the greater loss the company made.

'It was a tense and frustrating time,' Fistonich said at the time.

Today, as he recalls the situation, he remembers losing two stone in weight, walking a lot and encountering a lot of unsupportive phone calls.

'People would phone up and say, "You're stuffed now. You've had it." I was told I had to lose half my staff and I said, "Which half?" because I didn't want to fire anybody.'

In fact the company was running so tight that once the receiver had reviewed the business he agreed it could not afford to part with any of the employees.

Fistonich has always looked after his staff and there are a number, including long-serving and amiable Ian Clark, who are still present more than 20 years after the receivership.

'It was quite interesting because even though the receivership meant we didn't have to pay our creditors, we decided that if we were going to grow a long-term business, we needed to do the right thing, and pay back the money to all those people that were our suppliers. Because of our big wins at that wine competition in Australia almost instantly our sales went up 30 per cent. The grape-growers who worked for us took a full-page ad out in the *New Zealand*

'I COULD NEVER HAVE DREAMED THAT CREATING VILLA MARIA WOULD TAKE ME ON SUCH AN INTERESTING AND EXCITING JOURNEY OVER SO MANY YEARS.'

Herald saying they were growing grapes for us and wanted to keep on growing.'

Within five months, Fistonich had a new business partner, a new trading name — Villa Maria Estate — and within a year, after paying back his creditors, he had acquired a new winery. One of the casualties of the wine glut in New Zealand in 1986 was the Glenvale winery in Hawke's Bay, which was suffering trading difficulties. In 1987 Fistonich bought it, and building on Glenvale's Esk Valley Wines brand turned it into the jewel in his wine crown.

JEWELS IN VILLA MARIA'S CROWN

It wouldn't be fitting to talk about jewels in the Villa Maria crown without mentioning medals. They are big in Fistonich's winemaking book. For a start, he has won more medals and trophies at wine competitions for Villa Maria wines than any other producer in New Zealand for more than 31 consecutive years. Secondly, it's what these awards represent that's important to him.

'In the late 1980s we began working with contract grape-growers on a new basis. Instead of paying them blanketly for whatever grapes they could produce — as was the norm at the time — we set up contracts with them to pay for grapes based on quality not quantity. The whole point was — and is — to discover what vineyards are capable of, in terms of flavours, then to work with those growing the grapes on those vineyards and make the best wine we can, wines that really turn people's taste buds on.'

MOVING ON

Ask Fistonich what the next challenge for the New Zealand wine industry will be, and the names Chardonnay and Riesling come up.

'I think the overall average quality of New Zealand wines is among the highest in the world. Our maritime climate and long growing season give us the ability to retain amazing fruit flavour in our wines. I think our Chardonnays are totally outstanding, especially at reserve level. We can almost taste the flavour of the grape in the wines. The same could be true for our Rieslings, but we have a problem in that we have confused the public by making sweet styles of Riesling and not differentiating them from the dry wines. I think if everybody made dry Rieslings and sweet versions (in appropriately labelled bottles and packages), and just left it at that for at least 10 years, the wine-drinking public would understand that Riesling makes a lovely dry wine.'

After 50 years of making, marketing, exporting, tasting, talking and pioneering wine in New Zealand, Fistonich's glass is still overflowing with ideas on how to push quality upwards. His journey around the world as this

book was going to print is just the beginning of telling his story — 'People feel they can capitalise on the fact that it's unusual to have someone who started as a one-man band 50 years ago who's still there now. There's really good PR in that, and it's a competitive industry. This trip is not going to be a big party. It's got to have a return on it.'

His journey from boutique winery founded in Auckland in 1961 to global brand today has also provided a return. In talking with Sir George Fistonich, there is more than a hint of the boy who began selling wine at the family gate, when he says, in typically understated fashion, sounding surprised at himself: 'I could never have dreamed that creating Villa Maria would take me on such an interesting and exciting journey over so many years.'

GEORGE'S GO-TO WINES

'Funnily enough, when I come home normally I'll have a glass of Chardonnay pre-dinner, and when I was highly involved in blending — up until about 10 years ago — I'd bring home whatever I was blending: a Riesling or Gewürztraminer. My social drinking was very much around what I was working with at the time. For dinner now I normally drink Pinot Noir, Syrah or a Bordeaux blend.

I have a lot of French and Italian and some South American wines in the cellar and periodically I buy some of the lesser known Australian cool-climate wines, but there are so many great wines coming out of this country now, particularly from the Family of Twelve wineries, that I tend to drink a lot of New Zealand wines these days.' (The Family of Twelve is an export-focused marketing alliance of New Zealand wineries, comprising Fromm Winery, Pegasus Bay, Ata Rangi, Villa Maria Estate, Kumeu River, Felton Road, Lawson's Dry Hills, Nautilus Estate, Neudorf Vineyards, The Millton Vineyard, Palliser Estate and Craggy Range.)

TOP WINES FROM GEORGE FISTONICH
- Villa Maria Reserve Chardonnay
- Villa Maria Reserve Cabernet Merlot

CLIVE PATON ONZM
ATA RANGI, MARTINBOROUGH

'Ata Rangi's success is a testament to Kiwi determination, integrity and bloody hard work. Clive and Phyll were presenting benchmark wines to the world when others were wondering if New Zealand could even produce Pinot Noir.'
— Baxter Fagan, Scenic Cellars, Taupo

'In the international wine world Clive and Ata Rangi are considered icons in the wine industry. The status of the wine, coupled with Clive's natural humility, continues to pave the way for other quality New Zealand vineyards.'
— Ruth Pretty, chef-caterer, Te Horo, Kapiti

'Clive is a true pioneer; he has passion, determination, single-minded vision and a deep connection with the land. He's my pick for a gorgeous dinner party guest.'
— Cath Hopkin, director of Le Cordon Bleu New Zealand

The words Ata Rangi are Maori for 'dawn sky' or 'new beginning' and were chosen by winemaker Clive Paton in 1980 when he traded in his career as a sharemilker in southern Wairarapa to follow his heart into winemaking. He has since been joined by his partner in wine and life, winemaker Phyll Pattie, and also by his sister, Alison Paton. Today Clive's focus is on conservation as much as wine, and Ata Rangi's winemaking reins are now held by Helen Masters.

GREATEST ACHIEVEMENT

'Building from scratch a successful international business with a family-friendly work culture and making one of the New World's leading Pinot Noirs. Playing a part in the revitalisation of Martinborough has also been pretty satisfying, as has establishing the Aorangi Trust [a conservation trust].'

KEY ACHIEVEMENTS

- Awarded an Officer of the New Zealand Order of Merit in the Queen's Birthday Honours, 2012, for his contribution to conservation in the Wellington and Wairarapa regions.
- Awarded the inaugural Tipuranga Teitei o Aotearoa, Maori for 'Grand Cru of New Zealand' and presented by the wine industry in recognition of the long-term consistency of Ata Rangi Pinot Noir.
- Winners of the Bouchard Finlayson Trophy for Champion Pinot Noir at the International Wine and Spirit Competition in London, in 1995, 1996 and 2001.
- The Wellington Regional Conservation Award in the Business category in 2007 for 'an outstanding contribution to conservation'.
- Winner of the Supreme Award from the Ballance Farm Environment Awards; as well as the Innovation Award, the Habitat Improvement Award for work at the Bush Block and the Hills Harvest Award for soil and water management, 2006.

TAKE TO A DESERT ISLAND . . .

'My wife, a corkscrew and a bottle of 1990 Comte de Vogüé Musigny Grand Cru.'

ON MAKING WINE

'I made a mental note early on that I wanted to be in the top five red wine makers in New Zealand. If that sounds ambitious, maybe it was, but it seemed like the natural thing to aim for. I didn't say that to anyone. It was like making a mental note that if, in 10 years' time it hadn't worked out, I'd change tack. I couldn't see the point in trying if I didn't aim for the top,' says Paton.

BIGGEST RISK EVER TAKEN IN WINEMAKING?

'Lighting a small fire under a horizontal tank of Célèbre to keep it warm through malolactic fermentation.'

'I COULDN'T SEE THE POINT IN TRYING IF I DIDN'T AIM FOR THE TOP.'

THE STORY

Clive Paton describes himself as a quiet sort of bloke, but his determination speaks volumes.

From the second he set foot on his vineyard in Puruatanga Road, Martinborough, in 1980, he wanted to make one of New Zealand's top reds. Since then, he has three times won the trophy for top Pinot Noir at the world's largest wine competition — the Bouchard Finlayson Trophy for Champion Pinot Noir at the International Wine and Spirit Competition in London — but his thoughtful, quiet focus is on the grapes, the soil in which they grow and caring for the environment rather than oiling the wheels of the PR machine.

Like many who work in wine today, Paton grew up knowing its taste and he found that intriguing. It was his father's enjoyment of wine that first exposed him to it and made such a profound impact that, even with an entire farming career mapped out in front of him, the lure of making wine drew him in at a time when few others in New Zealand made it, drank it or gave it so much as a passing thought.

He was a sharemilker in the southern Wairarapa when he first heard a fledgling wine industry was under way half an hour's drive up the road in Martinborough, so one weekend he went to investigate. It was 1980. He liked the piece of land he'd driven to look at, decided to buy it and, within a matter of months, he had moved there to plant grapes.

'It was fast. It was one of those moments in life when I knew it was the right thing. It was exactly what I wanted to do.'

He arrived debt-free, momentarily. By selling the cows he owned in the Wairarapa he was able to buy the property without any initial debt.

A report by scientist Dr Derek Milne of the Department of Scientific and Industrial Research (DSIR) stated that Martinborough had the potential to be prime wine country because of the similarity it bore to Burgundy, France, in terms of climate and soil conditions. This affirmed Paton's gut feeling that the decision to buy land and join the only other grape-growers in Martinborough was the right thing. Not that it was easy. It was, he says, a highly unusual thing to do in that environment at the time — and the locals certainly made that clear to him.

The small town of Martinborough was relatively run down around 1980. Forget the characterful restored buildings, cafés and wine community which exist there today. Back then, the hotel's exterior was boarded over, there was one pub and the only place to buy food was a lone fish 'n' chip shop. Today the fish 'n' chip shop has been joined by a string of restaurants, including a French-style bistro, a cheese shop, a wine centre, boutique cinema, two boutique hotels and an eclectic fashion store which stocks many of New Zealand's top designer labels. While these trappings of success appear to thrive in this once little-known country town, Paton's aim has remained constant: making top-quality red wines.

When he planted his first vines, Paton also grew vegetables between the rows as a back-up to earn a little income while he established the vines — and tried to figure out how to derive an income from them.

As things panned out, the reality of trying to establish a new vineyard while

'THE MAKING AND DRINKING OF WINE WAS STILL A TOTALLY FOREIGN CONCEPT IN THE REGION. NOBODY REALLY DRANK MUCH WINE IN THE WAIRARAPA BACK THEN, SO WHY ON EARTH WOULD ANYONE MAKE IT?'

running a market garden of pumpkins and garlic, albeit a small one, proved too much for a one-man band. The vegetable-growing venture was really a way of making enough money to pay for petrol to get to rugby practice and games, because at the time the locals weren't exactly familiar with wine.

'The making and drinking of wine was still a totally foreign concept in the region. Nobody really drank much wine in the Wairarapa back then, so why on earth would anyone make it? It just didn't sit easily with most people living here.'

Despite the sceptical local farming community, there were three other wineries in the region at the time: Chifney, Dry River and Martinborough Vineyards.

'All of us felt we were up against the New Zealand beer-drinking culture which wine really wasn't a part of. It was difficult tapping on that door when few people could relate to what we were doing,' he remembers. 'But it still felt like it was the right thing to do.'

EARLY LIFE

Wine first appeared in front of Paton when he was a child.

'My father loved wine and we often had it at home, growing up in Tawa, an outer suburb of Wellington city which sprawled across the hills and was semi-rural when I was a child.'

His father was stationed in Italy as a soldier during the Second World War and he had fallen in love with the country and its wines. The experience left an imprint on his life which he couldn't shake. The idea of a glass of wine always appealed more than a beer.

While red wines were often on the table, it was the northern Italian Piedmontese grape, Moscato, which left the strongest impression on Paton's young taste buds.

'I remember the reds, but I particularly remember Asti made from the Moscato grape, which I still love. When you're drinking Asti, you can feel the grape in that wine. It opened my mind to the power of wine to transport the taste buds and mind to another place.'

When Paton left school, he first took on farmhand work for a few years before studying at Massey University in Palmerston North. The plan was to complete a Diploma in Agriculture, gain practical experience and then move north to the Waikato to manage a family-owned dairy farm. But even in his student days, he would slink off from beer-drinking mates at the pub, in search of red wine.

'There wasn't much on offer, usually just a very basic red available by the

glass in a hotel bar somewhere, something none of my mates at the time would have related to — they would have laughed. But I just had this desire to seek out and taste and learn about red wine. I felt a connection with it.'

That connection remained with him when he later graduated and then found himself in the southern Wairarapa farming community, a place in which he felt ill at ease.

'It wasn't that I'd grown up in anything other than a semi-rural environment, it was just that I had this longing in me to drink wine, to be around it and to be involved with it somehow. Perhaps that's why it was so easy to make the decision to move when I saw that land in Martinborough.'

PIONEERING AT PURUATANGA

While his first six to seven years were spent working largely alone in Martinborough, Paton did work a couple of vintages further north — one with the late Malcolm Abel, the other at Delegat's. Both stints helped gain much-needed practical winemaking experience in his early days.

The first grapes he planted in Martinborough included Gewürztraminer, Cabernet Franc, Malbec, a mystery red he nicknamed Super Siebel and over the years he has also experimented with the Italian grape varieties Nebbiolo and Sangiovese.

Part of his plan was to make a red combining the best of both Bordeaux and the Rhône Valley in France; Ata Rangi Célèbre is that wine. Originally Cabernet-dominant, Célèbre has become Syrah-dominant and remains a relatively unusual wine for Martinborough in that it combines an unconventional blend of red grapes in a region where most winemakers have hung their red hats entirely on the Pinot Noir hook.

When he decided to plant Pinot Noir, he asked neighbour Dr Neil McCallum (now retired) from Dry River Wines for advice. This led him to the late Malcolm Abel, from whom he bought the 'Abel' Pinot Noir clone, often referred to in wine circles as the 'Ata Rangi clone', or 'Gumboot clone'. This clone has remained the mainstay of Ata Rangi Pinot Noir.

Is this legendary clone, widely regarded as having originally been obtained from a Romanée-Conti vineyard in Burgundy, the reason behind Ata Rangi Pinot Noir's consistent success and high quality?

'Partly yes, but I think there are a lot of factors that go into making any wine really good. We've worked hard to get consistency with Pinot Noir, especially in the vineyard,' says Paton.

It helped meeting the woman who was to become his future partner, too. In 1986 Paton met winemaker Phyll Pattie at a visiting winemakers' social weekend in Marlborough. She had a food technology degree from Massey University and had worked in the dairy industry before falling for wine, when working in a ski village in the north of Italy on her own overseas travels. When she returned to New Zealand she found a job at Montana Wines (now Pernod Ricard New Zealand) in Auckland where she worked as cellarmaster — a daunting role at the start. 'I couldn't tell much of a difference between white wine varieties initially, but within just a couple of weeks I was hooked.'

The job involved organising transport of wines from the company's Marlborough and Gisborne wineries as well as blending, cold-stabilising, filtering and preparing wine for bottling.

Within two years Pattie was working in the laboratory and cellars at harvest time in each of the company's Gisborne and Marlborough wineries. In 1984 she transferred to Marlborough to take on a role as winemaker at Montana's Blenheim-based winery. It was here that she and Paton first met, and they immediately clicked.

They kept in touch and Pattie moved to Martinborough the following year, selling her Blenheim house to buy out the shares of John Stephen, a friend of Paton's who had helped keep the business going, in terms of cash flow.

'It was a leap of faith and something of an adjustment moving from a 12,000-tonne winery in Marlborough to a 10-tonne one in Martinborough with a few barrels in an old shed,' she says.

By now Paton had won Martinborough's first gold medal for his 1986 Pinot Noir, but there was still no net income, so Pattie took on a product-development role at the New Zealand Dairy Board in Wellington. She commuted daily for more than three years, travelling to the Middle East and South America for market and product research, while setting up the labobatory at Ata Rangi in Martinborough, making the white wines and looking after marketing and finance.

'It was a crazy, madly busy time, but I was able to leave the Wellington job and focus full-time on Ata Rangi by the middle of 1991.'

It was that year that she made a Chardonnay which the couple still regard highly. As Paton says, while his winemaking 'street cred' comes predominantly from Pinot Noir more than any other varietal, his Chardonnays have also received consistently high praise.

'Both Phyll and Helen [Helen Masters, the present winemaker] have a great feel for the variety. Phyll made the early Chardonnays; the 1991 is still an amazing wine. And Helen's gentle touch with Chardonnay is legendary.'

MARTINBOROUGH'S TRUMP CARDS

Unlike other nearby towns in the Wairarapa, Martinborough lies in a rain shadow, sheltered by the Rimutaka and Tararua ranges to the west and the Aorangi Range to the east. A stony, ancient riverbed meanders through the region, defining the Martinborough Terrace appellation with its alluvial gravel deposits, providing reliable drainage for vines grown there. Wind is a factor and it comes from two main sources: drying winds come from the north-west and cold winds blow in from the southern coast. The latter are often accompanied by rain. While this can inhibit the number of grapes which set on the vines early in the season, the cold wind also contributes in a positive way by creating the large temperature variation between day and night, also known as a wide diurnal range. Cool night temperatures help preserve the grapes' acidity and fruit characters. Martinborough is the driest grape-growing area in the North Island, with an average of 700 millimetres of rainfall a year being one of its trump cards for grape growing. This dryness means fungal disease pressure in the region is relatively low.

CRIMSON

The Ata Rangi team's passion for Pinot Noir is now beginning to pay powerful new dividends in the environmental arena, thanks to a wine called Crimson.

Launched in 2005, Crimson was named in honour of Paton's association with Project Crimson, a charitable conservation trust focused on the protection and restoration of rata and pohutukawa, two of New Zealand's best-known red-flowering native trees.

Pattie suggested to the Trust that they create Crimson; a portion of the proceeds from its sale would go towards the Project Crimson Trust each year. The trustees liked the idea, not only because they already knew of Paton's commitment to conservation in the region but because the message carried on each bottle would help to spread the word of their work.

Paton estimates he has planted 50,000 trees at the Ata Rangi bush block in the past decade, and he also works closely with the Project Crimson Trust on its tree-planting work. The trust is helping to slowly but steadily transform the Tinakori Hill in Wellington city, progressively removing aged pine trees and replacing them with the red-flowering northern rata that once graced the area.

LOOKING AFTER THE LAND

The dry air and cool nights in the Wairarapa region meant that vines growing in and around Martinborough didn't need to be sprayed as often as many of Paton's counterparts in West Auckland, Gisborne or Hawke's Bay suggested.

'The first sprays I used were recommended and supplied by a stock and station agent and were based on what was then used in Auckland and Gisborne, but it didn't take long to figure out that we didn't need to do the same amount of spraying here. It started me on the sustainability path, which we're now strong advocates of.'

Paton has never used insecticides at Ata Rangi but does use sulphur, allowed under organic regimes and used to control powdery mildew.

'We've changed shelter belts into mixed native plantings to encourage biodiversity in what is otherwise essentially a monoculture. One of the reasons that Ata Rangi has more trees around the vineyard than probably any other vineyard I know of in New Zealand is so that there is a lot more activity in terms of the natural environment, so everything keeps itself in balance.'

The two key environmental factors are the dry air in Martinborough and the timing of rainfall.

'Most of the weather comes from the west, so it drops any rain on the mountains and ends up in Martinborough as warm, very dry wind. When it does rain, the air is usually very cold; there's really only risk of botrytis when there's warm rain. For temperatures below 10 degrees, which is typical when there's a southerly, we don't have problems.

'The nature of Martinborough is that it naturally produces low-cropping vines, so you have to make sure you get the best from the little they produce. Maybe money's never been that important to us, so we set a goal to be a quality

'WHY TRY TO MAKE SOMETHING THAT'S MERELY "GOOD" WHEN YOU COULD MAKE SOMETHING GREAT?'

operation rather than saying, "We want to be millionaires." My feeling is that if you can stay afloat and become a top winery, then the financial benefits will hopefully follow,' Paton says.

One of his joys comes from making the decisions to care for both the vineyard and the environment in their own way. 'It means we take the pluses and the minuses on our own shoulders. It's the same with the winemaking to a degree. We end up making the wine we want to drink ourselves because it's our business and the decisions don't have to go to a committee; they are ours to make and live by.'

The winery today is run by three equal family shareholders. In July 1995, the Paton–Pattie partnership was replaced by a private company, incorporating two more family members — Clive's sister Alison Paton and her then-partner, the winemaker Olly Masters. Ali Paton had purchased a 5-hectare adjoining block of bare land in 1984 before moving to the United Kingdom to study for the Wine and Spirit Education Trust Diploma and work in the London wine trade. In the meantime, Clive planted her vineyard and it is now leased to Ata Rangi. Ali Paton returned home in 1989 and she is now the Ata Rangi business manager while Pattie looks after export marketing.

Despite changes within the business structure and Paton's passion for conservation initiatives, his wine aim remains the same: to make one of New Zealand's top five red wines.

'Why try to make something that's merely "good" when you could make something great?'

CLIVE'S GO-TO WINES
Aged German Riesling and the best of Kiwi Rieslings, Italian reds, local Pinot Noirs, and burgundies for special occasions.

TOP WINES FROM CLIVE PATON
- Ata Rangi Pinot Noir
- Ata Rangi Craighall Chardonnay

LARRY MCKENNA

ESCARPMENT VINEYARD, MARTINBOROUGH

A life in wine, for some winemakers, means they come to virtually embody their wines and their place, shaped by their craft and reflecting the surrounds in which they toil. Larry McKenna is one of these. His pioneering role in establishing Martinborough as a jewel in the crown of New Zealand Pinot Noir is an act of vinous national service and his ongoing commitment to making wines of longevity and authenticity is a gift to Pinot lovers the world over.'

— Nick Stock, wine writer and author

GREATEST ACHIEVEMENT

'When I first came to New Zealand, the mountaineering I did in the South Island changed me permanently; it gave me determination, commitment and those sorts of qualities.' And down on the ground? 'My family is my biggest achievement.'

KEY ACHIEVEMENTS

The unofficial wearer of the crown 'New Zealand King of Pinot Noir', first at Martinborough Vineyards; since 1999 at Escarpment Vineyard in Te Muna, 5 kilometres (as the crow flies) west of Martinborough's tiny township.

TAKE TO A DESERT ISLAND . . .

'Burgundy, both red and white.'

'WE COULD HAVE PLANTED THE WHOLE PLACE IN SAUVIGNON BLANC AND WOULD HAVE BEEN IN DEEP SHIT. LUCKILY WE DIDN'T DO THAT. PINOT IS PAYING DIVIDENDS.'

THE STORY

It's April and it's warmer than it has been in months. If this was the northern hemisphere, it would be a time to celebrate the end of another cold winter, but in New Zealand it's autumn: harvest time for wine grapes. This year the vintage is so late and so small, thanks to cool temperatures over the past half year, that many winemakers are less than ecstatic. Mother Nature has taken the country's wine glut in hand. This year (2012) she refused to supply conditions to allow plentiful fruit set in spring — the time that determines how many grapes will develop on each vine. Larry McKenna is not complaining that the wine glut is being somewhat rebalanced in this way.

The veteran Martinborough winemaker — he has made wine in the region since 1986, one of the first there — is happy with the quality of his grapes in 2012. Quantities are down, but they need to be, nationwide, in order to get the wine industry back into balance.

'I am focused on quality more than ever and must admit I feel extremely focused now, all things considered.'

All things considered being the news that the Escarpment Vineyard, which he and three others started in 1999, is now on the market.

The small vintage doesn't bother him. The winery being put up for sale does. It's a step he's not happy about taking but which he says is 'one of those things that has to happen — it's for health reasons'.

He began Escarpment with his wife Sue McKenna and Robert and Mem Kirby, in 1998. He had left Martinborough Vineyards where his Pinot Noirs played a major role in the development of New Zealand's high-quality red wine production.

McKenna began work in New Zealand as a young Australian émigré in 1980. He was the assistant winemaker at Delegat's Estate to his old school friend, John Hancock, a fellow ex-pat Australian. When Hancock left Delegat's, McKenna took over and stayed on as chief winemaker until 1986 when he went to Martinborough Vineyards. It was 'an easy start' to Martinborough back then, he says.

'Let's say we had the right district, the right place, climate and soils. We had the opportunity of selling everything we made within months of bottling it. It was all too easy so the businesses were pretty profitable really. People made some money and it was very exciting establishing ourselves.

'We were lucky to be in on the ground floor in Martinborough in the early 1980s. Others started planting Pinot Noir here before I arrived and it was an extremely good decision, in my mind. We could equally have been planting the whole place in Sauvignon Blanc and would have been in deep shit now, but luckily we didn't do that. The Pinot plantings are now paying dividends.'

A GOOD TIME AND A LONG TIME

The easy time lasted, too, seeing him through to a buoyant beginning at Escarpment Vineyard in 1999. At the time, plantings of all grapes were spreading like wildfire throughout New Zealand; or like Sauvignon Blanc, as the case usually was back then. Even small new vineyards, such as his, were championed for sticking new grapes in new places; in 2000 he planted Pinot Noir, Chardonnay, Riesling, Pinot Blanc and Pinot Gris at Te Muna, 5 kilometres west of Martinborough township. The first wine was made in 2001 and, thanks to his reputation for making top Pinot Noir, he built another high-quality wine brand with relative ease.

Unfortunately, when the global financial crisis hit, the exchange rate turned and the overplanting of Sauvignon Blanc and Pinot Gris in particular began to affect the wine market with much of the industry beginning to crumble.

For McKenna, he plans to continue business as usual, either at Escarpment Vineyard with a new owner or on his own. Either way, 'There is a lot of work to be done to see the potential of Pinot Noir reach what it can in this country.'

There is infrastructure to be completed at Escarpment, but, more importantly, says McKenna, there is vine age to achieve. Vine age, soils and weather all determine wine quality, he adds. 'But vine age comes first for me. I'm a great believer in it. When it comes to saying which one makes more of a difference to vines between soils and weather, I'd have to say the climate, though. There are attributes in soil that are required, but if you've got those broad outlines, it doesn't really matter; you'll make good wine. If the climate's too hot, too cold, too wet, then it's not going to work.'

STICKING TO THE KNITTING

While the wine scene in New Zealand is in a bit of slump right now, due to oversupply, McKenna keeps coming back to one of his mantras: commitment.

'I think the most important thing is that there are a number of us who are sticking to our knitting: Martinborough Vineyards, Ata Rangi and Palliser Estate, among others in this region. When I left Martinborough Vineyards, I could have gone to Central Otago or to Victoria in Australia, but I believe in this district. It's a tough place to grow grapes and while we hear it said that being on the edge is the place to grow great Pinot, I don't know about that. It sounds like the sort of thing some wine writers might say. I believe in this region because the wine quality we get from it is consistent.'

Some would say (though not this writer) that he did plant grapes on the edge of Martinborough, geographically at least. At the start of the 2000s, Te Muna was considered an untried sub-region of Martinborough, slightly cooler in climate but with similar soils.

'THE MISTAKES WE'VE MADE WITH SAUVIGNON BLANC ARE REALLY BIG. IT'S REALLY STUPID BECAUSE THE PROBLEM OCCURRED DUE TO TWO WORDS: NO VISION. THERE WERE TOO MANY GRAPES PLANTED. NOW WE'RE ALL LIVING TO PAY THE PRICE.'

'I don't see anything different between us and Martinborough. It's the same. The same alluvial soils, the same area and the same free-draining alluvial gravels on which we have our grapes planted.'

Conversely, it has proven to be easier culturally than being in the heart of Martinborough.

'There's a lot of pressure on some Martinborough winemakers from those in town, who don't necessarily understand the wine industry and its need to make noise to get rid of birds from ripening grapes at certain times of the year. At least everybody out here has got a vineyard or a farm around them, so life's a little more straightforward from a political point of view.'

There is also more space at Te Muna. The land prices have not yet reached the lofty heights of some in Martinborough, created thanks to top winemaking on the part of people such as McKenna, Clive and Phyll Paton at Ata Rangi and those at Palliser Estate, whose managing director Richard Riddiford has done an enormous amount to champion the region and its wines overseas.

That's not to say that Te Muna is identical to the rest of Martinborough: 'We pick marginally later in the season than in Martinborough, but at the end of the day I defy anyone to tell me they can tell the difference between Martinborough and Te Muna, so it is effectively the same climate and soil types.'

CHALLENGES

Ask McKenna what the biggest challenge is in the New Zealand wine scene right now and he reels off a raft of difficulties: the global financial crisis; what he sees as over-regulation; the challengingly cool weather leading up to the 2012 vintage; and the Sauvignon Blanc glut. And the country's drinking culture also warrants more than a passing mention.

Of these, it is the overenthusiastic planting of Sauvignon Blanc that has caused the most damage.

'The mistakes we've made with Sauvignon Blanc are really big. It's really stupid because the problem occurred due to two words: no vision. There were too many grapes planted. Now we're all living to pay the price. There's too much wine on the market, and we're all too keen to dump it at prices that aren't profitable. It's all tied up with exchange rates. We would be doing very nicely if we could go back to 55 or 60 cents to the US dollar, but for us to export to the US at the moment just doesn't stack up. We have to pull out of that market and we have to plan.'

Another big challenge is that people in New Zealand don't understand wine well, he says.

'A lot of people still treat wine as alcohol. I can understand why so many

people are still in love with Sauvignon Blanc because they haven't tasted other things. We need another generation brought up with wine and food before they understand it. If it's something they've never heard of, they're not prepared to go there right now, which is a real shame because there are some great wines made in this country which are not just Sauvignon Blanc and Pinot Gris.'

That said, he will continue to make Pinot Gris, though only in relatively small quantities.

'Pinot Gris was only ever small for us and it can be extremely good but only when it's produced with an eye to quality, which means low yields in the vineyards so that the flavours are concentrated, and there has been work done on the phenolics of this grape, which can be awful, if handled badly,' he says.

Even when it is handled well, Pinot Gris, for McKenna, is just not the most interesting tool in the box. He sees New Zealand as heading in the same way with Pinot Gris as it has with Sauvignon Blanc. 'There's too much of it and too much ordinary wine made from it. We don't need what we've got, and we need to stick to what we do well. We very proudly call ourselves a Sauvignon Blanc-free zone and I'd like us to stay that way, too. We'll leave that to Marlborough.'

There are diversions from his prime winemaking passions of Pinot Noir and Chardonnay, however. In his case they are Pinot Blanc and Riesling.

'It always amazes me that the public don't embrace Pinot Blanc as easily as Pinot Gris. I prefer the complexity I see in Pinot Blanc and in Riesling and plan to stick with those, although they are relatively small. The focus at the Escarpment Vineyard is firmly on Pinot Noir and Chardonnay and will stay that way. Small quantities, high quality. I think it's important to stick to what we do best and keep on pushing ourselves to better heights with it.'

IN THE VINEYARD

Speaking of what he does well, McKenna plans to replant 5 to 10 per cent of his vineyard every year. It's part upgrade, part discovery. The replanting programme he plans allows him to replace and renew not only grapes but also the rootstocks on which they are planted.

'We are still changing the clonal and rootstock mix for Pinot Noir, Pinot Blanc, Riesling and Chardonnay, which have a strong influence on flavour,' says McKenna, whose passion for growing things is ingrained; he grew up knowing he would work outdoors.

'I've never had to decide what I would do for a living. I always knew I would be involved in the agriculture sector in one way or another so, yes, it was a logical step to go to Roseworthy Agricultural College when I left school. My first option was veterinary science, but I applied and didn't get in. So a dryland farming degree, including horticulture, vines and wine happened instead.'

When he graduated from Roseworthy in South Australia, his old school friend John Hancock offered him his first job, which tied in nicely with something more important to McKenna: his girlfriend, Sue, who became his wife.

McKenna wine fans regard him as something of an honorary New Zealander since he has lived on this side of the Tasman and made Pinot Noir for the best part of 35 years now.

THE PINOT NOIR CROWN

Asked how he feels about wearing the unofficial 'King of New Zealand Pinot Noir' crown, McKenna deflects the compliment by falling back on another of his frequently quoted mantras: 'I'm a believer in sticking to my knitting,' he says.

'I did my background winemaking at Delegat's, but ever since I've really been focused on one variety and one district and built up a reputation from there. No one gets it right all the time, but there's a lot to be said for continuing to build the reputation that you work on with something. I've worked on that with Pinot Noir in Martinborough since the early days of this region and that grape in it.'

Venturing outside the region has helped too. In 1990 he worked a vintage in Burgundy at Domaine L'Arlot and Dujac; in 1994 he made Pinot Noir at Saintsbury in Carneros, California; in 2000 with Gary Farr at Bannockburn in Geelong in Victoria, Australia and in 2001 with John Hancock at Trinity Hill winery in Hawke's Bay, 'just for the fun of it'.

MAKING PINOT A PRIORITY

When he first began making Pinot Noir, McKenna's focus had a paradigm shift, he admits. Like other Martinborough winemakers in the 'early days' — 26 years ago, in his case — he knew he had to make a serious red from Pinot Noir grapes, not just another drinkable one.

'That was a major shift for me. I'd made Pinot before coming to Martinborough, but it was always the last priority. Every other variety came first. Nobody cared about it. Everybody said, "You can't make good Pinot outside of Burgundy", so that was a challenge and a priority when I moved to Martinborough.'

THE WHITE QUEEN

Chardonnay. The mere mention of the word frustrates McKenna. Not because he can't find good ones, but rather that so many New Zealand Chardonnays are good but are rarely rated as highly as he thinks they deserve to be.

'We make some of the world's best-value, high-quality Chardonnays in this country, but they are not seen in that light by most wine drinkers. You just don't get any better than what Michael Brajkovich is doing at Kumeu River with Chardonnay; what John Buck and Peter Cowley are doing with Elston Chardonnay at Te Mata; and Tim Finn at Neudorf. We have to pay our dues and get more track record.'

'WE MAKE SOME OF THE WORLD'S BEST-VALUE, HIGH-QUALITY CHARDONNAYS IN THIS COUNTRY, BUT THEY ARE NOT SEEN IN THAT LIGHT BY MOST WINE DRINKERS.'

For McKenna, Chardonnay is a totally oak-driven affair; only 30 per cent of which is new, however, with the balance being old oak.

When making Chardonnay, McKenna dabbles with wild yeast fermentations, allowing the grapes to engage with whatever yeasts are floating about in their vicinity. It is as risky as it sounds. The grapes and the yeasts might get on; they might not. When they do, the results frequently create more interesting-tasting wines than those made with inoculated commercial yeast strains tend to.

THE FUTURE

'You get three-quarters of the way up a mountain and there's no getting off. Whatever happens you have to deal with it. You're risking everything there is to risk. You can do it in other ways — sailing, perhaps, which I've done in the past — and it's the same thing. If you're in the middle of the ocean and something goes wrong, you have to fix it and work it out.'

In the same way he talks about his experiences of mountaineering, McKenna speaks about winemaking.

The winery he set up 13 years ago with three business partners may now be on the market, but instead of letting it be the elephant in the room, he openly talks about it and the different possible outcomes it could mean for his future. He is committed to seeing through his dream of making top Pinot Noir.

Of mountaineering, he says, 'You're committed because you're risking the biggest thing you can risk and it's not anyone else's choice, it's your choice. I love wine for the same reason.'

ESCARPMENT PINOT NOIRS

Like nearby Martinborough winery, Ata Rangi, Escarpment Vineyard's Pinot Noirs pay homage to Maori names. In this case the names of the wines — rather than the winery, as in Ata Rangi's case — are drawn from Maori tradition and mythology.

The top wine, Kupe, is named after the Maori discoverer of New Zealand; the hills behind the vineyard being 'nga waka' — the canoes — of Kupe. Incidentally, Nga Waka is the name of another high-quality Martinborough winery, owned by Roger Fraser. The other wines are: Pahi, the twin-hulled canoe; Te Rehua, Antares — a prominent star in the southern hemisphere in the summer; and Kiwa, the god of the Pacific.

'These names locate us in Martinborough and in Wellington and are a useful way to tell the New Zealand story offshore. As much as we love burgundy and would love to be confused with Burgundy, we thought we'd better name our

'YOU'RE COMMITTED [TO MOUNTAINEERING] BECAUSE YOU'RE RISKING THE BIGGEST THING YOU CAN RISK, AND IT'S NOT ANYONE ELSE'S CHOICE, IT'S YOUR CHOICE. I LOVE WINE FOR THE SAME REASON.'

wines as New Zealand in identity as we are here and want to give the wines that feeling.'

LARRY'S GO-TO WINES

'It varies a lot but Friday night is when I turn off. I don't evaluate wines. I just enjoy wine for the hedonistic sake of wine and, partly due to my upbringing on McLaren Vale Cabernet Shiraz blends, these are the go-to wine when I just want to relax. They last almost forever and, I think, they become a very enjoyable drink. Bin 389 is a very good example of a realistically priced wine that is a great drink.'

TOP WINES FROM LARRY MCKENNA AT ESCARPMENT VINEYARD

* 2008 Escarpment Kupe Pinot Noir
* 1991 Martinborough Vineyard Pinot Noir

JAMES MILLTON MNZM

THE MILLTON VINEYARD, GISBORNE

'James is a winegrower — his term — who, in his role as 'challenger of conventional thinking', answers his sceptics with the perfect reply — beautiful, thoughtfully crafted wines of elegance and complexity — and Chenin Blanc.'
— Mark Young, Vintners New Zealand

'James' tireless commitment has been supportive and inspirational, and his guidance of organic and biodynamic winemakers has been outstanding.'
— Rudi Bauer, Quartz Reef winery

'James is a genuine and thoughtful person, who has consistently stuck to his guns. Rudi Bauer talks about him as the godfather of organics and biodynamics in grape growing in New Zealand. He is the one everyone goes to.'
— Simon Beck, colleague of Rudi Bauer, Quartz Reef winery

GREATEST ACHIEVEMENT
'That we are here today practising a biodynamic philosophy; that we have put our money where our mouths are; that Annie has stood beside me to make this an internationally successful brand; and that people enjoy the fruits of our labours.'

KEY ACHIEVEMENTS
- Awarded a Member of the New Zealand Order of Merit in 2012.
- Current chair of Organic Winegrowers New Zealand.

- New Zealand's first vineyard and winery to have BioGro certification, 1989.
- Gaining Demeter biodynamic certification for the vineyards in 2009.

TAKE TO A DESERT ISLAND . . .

'A desert island is a place I go to each day and find solitude, reverence and deep thinking for it is here that you find the elemental beings giving you all the answers to any concerns you are having . . . I would just wish to be by myself, with nothing else, and on the horizon would appear all the loaves and fishes I could ever ask for.'

ON WINEMAKING

'They say I'm a dreamer, but now I'm not the only one — similar to what John Lennon's great resonance was for me.'

THE STORY

'In the kingdom of Mother Nature it is not about achievement but about finding the place where you can see what she has to offer and finding happiness there. Each day we get closer to that point; some more easily than others,' says James Millton, when talking about being awarded a New Zealand Order of Merit in the Queen's Birthday Honours list for 2012.

He likened the official acknowledgement of his passion for wine and for the environment as being akin to walking in duck-down slippers; it was a feeling of unexpected luxury for his work, which has gone under the radar for the past three decades. Wine has always been a passion for Millton, ever since his first sip when he was a youngster, which reminded him of ink.

'I wonder who knows what that smells like any more,' he says, remembering its intensity and the feelings it evoked in his young mind.

Exactly how young he was is anyone's guess. He says he was about 10 years old when he first tasted wine because he estimates the wine was a 1966 Corbans Claret.

'God only knows what was in it, in terms of grapes grown back then to make "claret", but it tasted amazing . . . I had never tasted anything like it before. It intrigued me.'

There were many more intriguing wine smells and tastes for Millton during his childhood. He grew up in the remote community of Franz Josef on the West Coast of New Zealand's South Island. In this unlikely setting, post-Second World War when barely any wine was available in New Zealand, there was often wine on the Millton family dinner table.

'My father regarded himself as something of an exile from Canterbury after the Second World War, but he retained a close friendship with a wine importer back in Christchurch. Down on the coast they were only drinking beer and whisky, but Dad was a third-generation Canterbury farmer who, in protest from succession and inheritance within his family, had moved to the West Coast where he bred Black Angus cattle while everyone else bred Herefords.

'MY FATHER PASSED ON *THE BOOTS' HOME BREWING GUIDE* TO ME AND SAID, "I THINK YOU SHOULD READ THIS." THAT WAS THE BEGINNING OF THE END.'

He was an Anglican while everyone else on the coast was Roman Catholic. Everything he did seemed to run counter to the culture there at the time so it took him two and a half decades to be accepted there; just as it has been for me in Gisborne,' says Millton.

GROWING INTO WINE

By the time he was 14, he was picking all the fruit he could find from the scrubby blackberry bushes growing in the wild near where he lived; fermenting it because he was fascinated by the process. And yet it was a book, rather than a sip, that set him on the path to making wine. *The Boots' Home Brewing Guide* had been given to his father by a family friend visiting from the United Kingdom.

'My father passed the guide on to me and said, "I think you should read this." That was the beginning of the end. I believe now that you get one piece of information in your life, which becomes a major lead and that was mine.'

BEGINNINGS AND ENDINGS

The real beginning of the end — of his childhood at least — was being expelled from high school for fermenting fruit. He then became 'a pest' to wineries, writing to everyone he could find, asking to be taken on as a trainee or apprentice. The chief executive of Montana Wines was then Russell Gibbons, who relented and offered Millton a cadetship — after his fourth letter.

'By that stage he realised I was quite determined, I think,' says Millton, adding that 'I had written so many times and finally told him that "I got booted out of school for making wine — how about it?" that it worked. I was taken on as a cadet.'

The cadetship with Montana began in Marlborough with Allan Scott, now one of the region's best known, most experienced winemakers but back then a grape-grower, who now says it was Millton's passion which made him realise there was more to wine than he thought at the time.

'I heard an interview with Allan Scott on National Radio in early 2012 where he was talking about how he got into winemaking from growing grapes after he met a young guy who came and worked for him and had a car filled with wine paraphernalia. He couldn't believe there was someone who was totally absorbed in the subject of wine as an 18 year old like this: that was me.'

GRADUATING TO GISBORNE

Millton moved around in his early days as a cadet. His next port of call was a harvest in Gisborne where he met the girlfriend who was to become his future

'THERE SHOULD BE SOME HARDSHIPS AND CHALLENGES WHEN WE'RE IN THE FORMATIVE STAGES. WHEN WE FOLLOW THAT HARD PATHWAY IT PAVES THE WAY TO THE HIGHWAY WE ARE SUPPOSED TO BE ON.'

wife, Annie. The next couple of years were spent toing and froing between Gisborne and Auckland, working vintages in the former and bottling the wine up north in the latter, but a trip overseas with a school friend whose father was a wine merchant in Canterbury fanned the flames of his passion further. Visits to Champagne Bollinger, Rémy Martin Cognac, Château Palmer in Bordeaux and throughout Italy, Spain, Germany, Austria and Hungary saw him learn about the world of wine, not to mention enjoying the warm reception in each place along the way.

'We were treated like royalty, thanks to my friend's father's reputation. His company was called Fletcher, Humphreys & Co and the owner, Jum Kingscote, was a gentleman and he treated people as such. You don't find that necessarily these days. It was a lucky way to get to taste all of the first-growth Bordeaux.'

There was also a tasting at Château d'Yquem 'which blew my mind'. Less mind-blowing was the offer to carry on travelling to Scotland to learn about whisky.

'Instead I went to Germany to make wine in the Rheinhessen.

'We made Riesling and they had this cross-breeding programme of varieties, which were new in Germany at the time but have since fallen by the wayside. Müller-Thurgau was one and they had a whole string of other wine crosses, which I think would have confused the consumer. They were frivolous. They weren't classic. It wasn't necessarily great wine all the time, but it was experience,' he says.

While there, Annie would come and meet him in Germany to keep their spark alive, but the compromised winemaking, the hardship of travel and the distance from home were never easy for either of them.

'There should be some hardships and challenges when we're in the formative stages. We follow the pathway that hardship paves and it leads onto the highway we are supposed to be on.'

Moving back home, Millton decided to train formally for winemaking either in Germany or at Roseworthy Agricultural College in Australia. It didn't happen.

'I had decided I didn't want to learn how to make wine with the Germans, who were too rigid and organised, when my then-to-be father-in-law (Annie's father) suggested I come to Gisborne and work the harvest, and so I became an artisan winegrower by starting out as an apprentice there.

'I use the word artisan intentionally. It's a person who has learnt his trade from the masters, the same as being a stonemason or a butcher. It's not about going to university. It's about living it, tasting it, feeling it and being it. It's not about making bulk wine but about being in touch with the wine you are making. That's how I feel about it.'

'WE ARE CONTINUOUSLY HAVING TO PROVE OUR INNOCENCE BECAUSE OF OUR DEMETER AND BIO-GRO CERTIFICATION, WHEREAS PEOPLE CAN USE ARTIFICIAL INPUTS AND THEY DON'T HAVE TO PROVE ANYTHING.'

His and Annie's vineyard is at Opou Station, the oldest farm in New Zealand to be farmed by one family.

'We are now the fifth generation. I settled in Gisborne from the South Island primarily because of marriage and I have come to very sincerely love this region for all the aspects that make up the four quadrants of a sustainable lifestyle: economic, social, financial and, most importantly, cultural.'

BIGGEST CHALLENGE TODAY

What is the biggest challenge in making wine today? 'That we are continuously having to prove our innocence because of our Demeter and BioGro certification, whereas people can use artificial inputs and they don't have to prove anything. The ridiculousness is that we have to prove to people what it is that we don't do.'

The most important step forward for the New Zealand wine industry today, he considers, would be to see a significant proportion of it being certified organic, biodynamic or 'some other true and sincere method of production by 2020; much like us being Switzerland in the South Pacific'.

He and Annie began walking the organic and biodynamic path as an intuitive response. As an example, he remembers a grape-grower saying to them, '"No, don't eat those grapes because I've just sprayed them with a bird repellent", and I thought to myself, "What a total nonsense not being able to eat the fruit which we turn into wine."

'The wine industry has become so industrialised to provide consumers with a simple, consistent product, yet you see the advent of farmers' markets in England and Europe and the flow of real natural food and wine in those places, which shows that a good 20 per cent of people are getting sick of just being dealt to with whatever mass-produced stuff they get given.'

Which leads Millton into what he believes are the major problems in the global wine industry today, namely, greed, technology and fast turnaround.

'The predominance of the supermarkets selling wine is at odds with what we need to do to survive in the New Zealand wine industry, namely to create a new culture, one in which large quantities of wine do not sell regularly for $8 a bottle.

'The presence of wine sales under the cost of production has begun to destroy the geographical fabric of our rural society, for the want of gaining a better margin of profit for some. Another major problem is the industrialisation of the wine industry and the propensity of its overriding organisation to make such foolish and ignorant decisions in regard to marketing that will be the undoing of our very special place in the world of wine.'

The trouble with supermarkets being able to sell $8 bottles of wine is that it creates an expectation of ongoing low prices for a product which actually costs more to produce.

'People don't even stop to think what they're consuming when it's so cheap. I think people have to understand that they are being dealt to when they go to the supermarket. They're not getting a bargain. They're getting an unrealistic expectation.'

The answer?

'Drink less but pay a little bit more. It is the best investment to make in yourself.'

So how does someone who cares about wine and wants to learn more create their own culture around it?

'When you go to buy ingredients to make dinner from the supermarket, think not only about you're going to eat that night but think about what would be complementary to drink with it.

'The biggest problem for New Zealand wine today is that the consumer cannot understand what the taste of quality really is. It is about looking and seeing, feeling and touching, listening and hearing. Take the time. If you make wine, then lie under the vines and really look at what you see. If you drink it and enjoy it, then really taste it and think about that.'

FORMALISING THE FEEL-GOOD

The Milltons first qualified for formal BioGro certification in 1986 for a couple of their wines, reaching full certification in 1989. Today this is not the prime focus of their green ethos.

'Certification is a topic in itself as to whether you must follow the rule from the bureaucrats or not, but the thing about it is that, to be taken seriously, you need third-party endorsement. We got wooed by a chemical company making a synthetic insect growth regulator in about 1994. This was for the control of mealy bug. The interesting thing was that they said to us, "Here, you can apply a naturally derived product such as pyrethrum and yet the synthetic insect growth regulator is less toxic than common salt." So I applied it to two rows of the

'THE BIGGEST PROBLEM FOR NEW ZEALAND WINE TODAY IS THAT THE CONSUMER CANNOT UNDERSTAND WHAT THE TASTE OF QUALITY REALLY IS. . . . IF YOU DRINK IT AND ENJOY IT, THEN REALLY TASTE IT AND THINK ABOUT THAT.'

'WE NEVER WANTED TO MAKE ORGANIC OR BIODYNAMIC WINE. WE JUST WANT TO MAKE THE BEST WINE.'

vineyard and thought it was amazing because it worked quite well. Instead of taking those grapes away, we sprayed all of our Riesling — about 7 per cent of the vineyard — because we were encouraged to do so by this company, and as a result I said, "Well, if we're going to do that, I'll step away from being certified organic." Because we were the formative force for organic certification it didn't say anything to the consumer, who we were wanting to protect.

'Not only did we get wooed and screwed by the chemical company but also by wine writers and critics who just wanted to dwell on the fact that we had failed at our goal of being sustainably accredited to the best known green scheme of the day.

'I thought this was just terrible. We only used it once and then realised it actually worked against other insects with a siliceous exoskeleton; a ladybird is one of those types of insects. After that we stood down from BioGro for three years and hopefully kept our honour.

'We never wanted to make organic or biodynamic wine. We just want to make the best wine.'

CREATING A BIODYNAMIC ENVIRONMENT
Today it's the phone calls, the questions and the seeking of advice from fellow winemakers that keep Millton as busy as actually being biodynamic. Fielding phone calls about biodynamics is not his favourite pastime, but the questions he is asked fascinate him.

'Consultancy in particular is difficult because you are answering the questions of those who haven't figured out how to find the answer within themselves.'

When interviewed for this book, he had just taken several such calls from people in other wine regions asking how to use the biodynamic quartz crystal they had heard of as a spray for their vines.

'They all asked: "Where can I get it from and how can I put it on? It's obviously what we're meant to do." I'm intrigued they're asking this question. The practical response is that you have to get your household in order first before you put the finesse into it. I say: "You never really want to put icing on a cracker, do you? You put icing on a nice cake that you've spent time mixing and preparing. You have to prepare the land first before you do this as an extra."'

Today the Millton Vineyard's vines are all Demeter certified and have been since 2009. Demeter certification is considered the high altar of the biodynamic movement.

'It is the penultimate form of growing things. It's a shame it takes up so much headspace, drawing me away from actually looking after the land, but it's worth it.'

As is his membership of the Renaissance des Appellations; a French

'THE GLUT WE ARE EXPERIENCING TODAY HAS BEEN SEEN BEFORE IN THE OVERPRODUCTION OF WINES SUCH AS BEAUJOLAIS, CHABLIS, LIEBFRAUMILCH AND RIOJA AND IT WILL CHANGE, SO LONG AS DISCERNING CONSUMERS DO NOT RELY ON THEIR SUPERMARKET TO SUPPLY PRODUCE OF MEANINGFUL HEALTH-GIVING QUALITY.'

biodynamic group to which he has belonged since 2004. The aim is to give full expression to the appellations, which includes looking after the land rather than just taking what it provides.

'We started off with the first exhibition of our wines in Bordeaux with people like Anne-Claude Leflaive and Nicolas Joly (the organiser), Marcel Deiss from Alsace and Lalou Bize-Leroy from Domaine Leroy in Burgundy — people I just worship for their winemaking. It was a case of the French showing that the New World is making them reinvent themselves with wines that express what they do best. It was truly inspirational.'

In his own situation, Millton found Gisborne to provide rather a lot more than he bargained for, in terms of its desirable climate and soils. And in the 1980s it was renowned for delivering high yields of grapes from vineyards, eventually resulting in a wine glut similar to the one the country is encountering today, in 2012.

The boom and bust in the wine scene today is part of what Millton sees as a 30-year cycle: 'part of a continuous cycle of growth, decline and renewal'.

Which brings us to an important aspect of renewal for Gisborne: its image.

'When I hear about Gisborne's particular image I think, here we go again. We hear about our isolation, climate challenges, the current wine glut and so on, yet never the opportunities and pleasure of making wine here. When you farm biodynamically, as we do, our focus is about "life energy" (bio-dynamic), so we are not isolated, merely secluded. The glut we are experiencing today has been seen before in the overproduction of wines such as Beaujolais, Chablis, Liebfraumilch and Rioja and it will change, so long as discerning consumers do not rely on their supermarket to supply produce of meaningful health-giving quality.'

GISBORNE'S FUTURE

So what is the future for Gisborne wine?

For Millton it is in exploring the diverse, the interesting, the unusual and the high-quality grapes which he thinks will work in the region. For the most part these are white grapes, predominantly from France's Rhône Valley. His latest project is to explore these by producing a white wine made from a traditional Rhône Valley blend of Viognier, Roussane and Marsanne. Unfortunately, the dream was momentarily dashed, thanks to poor vintage conditions for the

2012 harvest, so it will have to wait another year. The inspiration is in creating a wine which is more than the sum of its parts, a wine drinkers will enjoy as much for its tactile appeal as for its flavours. In other words, a wine which has body and weight as part of its character, as opposed to being *mono-cépage* or single variety (as in, made from just one grape).

'We can see that in examples of co-fermentation of aromatic varietials such as Gewürztraminer, Riesling and Pinot Gris there are some amazingly delicious wines to be made. And, similarly, softening out Sauvignon Blanc with a little Sémillon can make it a more appetising and digestible wine. These styles actually do work. The challenge is in the name "other varietals"; that's where we have to be creative.'

EXCITING CHALLENGES AHEAD

'One of the biggest changes in the wine world has been watching the Italians and the French getting back to their true roots and becoming "terroirists",' says Millton.

By this he means they are exploring the potential of their land, climate and history in more depth than they were three or four decades ago.

'The French and other Europeans understand that they haven't got the monopoly on winemaking, and now they realise there are others doing it in the New World they are going back to their roots, exploring the wealth of their grapes (Italy), their top-quality wines (France) and their unique climate and wine they make; as in the originality of Riesling in Germany. It makes us all think about the wines we are making and how we make them.'

JAMES'S GO-TO WINES

'My go-to wines are like my children. I love them all, but I have a place in my heart for the Millton Clos Ste. Anne Chardonnay. Other wines I like include anything which sings of presence, purity, place and definition. For that reason, I love the Loire Valley . . .'

TOP WINES FROM JAMES MILLTON
- 2009 Clos de Ste Anne Naboth's Vineyard Chardonnay
- 2010 Te Arai Chenin Blanc

RUDI BAUER

QUARTZ REEF, CENTRAL OTAGO

'Rudi's passionate nature comes through in his philosophy of wine and winemaking. Each and every wine is like a child born for Rudi to guide through its development. These are words I have heard Rudi explain to wine amateurs: "Like children as they progress through infancy, having not yet developed a personality, one waits with anticipation as the 'children' reach adolescence, all arms and legs without coordination. When reaching maturity they are like women who get fuller and rounder and have a character that has lost its rough edges." When described as such, people find it amusing but Rudi continues describing his passion for the subject thus: "If one tries to tell an adolescent what the parent (or in this case a winemaker) wants that child to become, they rebel. If one tries to change what the woman has become, she will be resentful and bitter." This is Rudi's philosophy and one that I have imparted to all our winemakers and cellar hands who have been through a training at Rippon Vineyards, where Rudi first made wine in Central Otago.'

— Lois Mills, Rippon Vineyard, Wanaka

'Rudi deserves great credit for producing the first high-quality Central Otago Méthode Champenoise and introducing the world to sparkling wine from a region so obviously suited to its production. In my view, however, Rudi's wonderful Bendigo Pinot Noir is an even greater achievement.'

— Bob Campbell, MW

GREATEST ACHIEVEMENT

'Growing up as part of a very young industry and being able to create something with many other people for the next generation, which could be my children.'

KEY ACHIEVEMENTS

- Top sparkling wine maker.
- Champion Winemaker of the Year, Royal Agricultural Society of New Zealand Easter Wine Show, 1999.
- Driving force, with Alan Brady, behind the first Central Otago Pinot Noir Celebration, 2000, and Chairman, 2000 and 2002.
- International Pinot Noir Celebration Wellington, board member, 2004.
- *Der Feinschmecker* Wine Awards 'Winemaker of the Year' nominee, 2010 (one of six in the world and first ever from New Zealand).
- New Zealand Winemaker of the Year 2010, Royal Agricultural Society.
- Current chairman of Central Otago Pinot Noir Ltd.

TAKE TO A DESERT ISLAND . . .

'My family and my wine collection.'

ON MAKING WINE IN CENTRAL OTAGO

'I've always felt we hit the jackpot here.'

BIGGEST RISK EVER TAKEN WITH WINE?

'To have the guts and faith to plant a vineyard in the middle of nowhere.'

THE STORY

It mystifies me why the name Rudi Bauer isn't a byword for the best bubbles in the southern hemisphere, but there are lots of mysteries in the wine world. If Bauer is worried about not being acknowledged as the best bubbles maker Down Under, he's not letting on.

In his words, he hit the jackpot by planting grapes on top of New Zealand's biggest deposit of quartz in Central Otago. Now he just wants to make the best wine possible from his vineyard — and get better known for doing so.

His name deserves to be better known. In 2000 at a blind tasting with a group of Australian wine writers from Australia's *Gourmet Traveller Wine* magazine Quartz Reef Pinot Noir was our unanimous favourite. For several years after that, one of those writers — Peter Forrestal from Western Australia — asked me to bring bottles to Australia whenever I visited. No matter how convoluted the drop-off, pick-up and swapping of wines proved to be, it was a constant reminder of Bauer's great, yet strangely unsung, winemaking talent.

Quartz Reef Pinot Noir is not a big name when it comes to New Zealand's

best known reds — just like the wine itself; its immediate appeal comes from a subtle, silky, smooth, sensuous style, not from being an instant, juicy, tutti-frutti wonder. Not that there's anything wrong with those styles of wine. It's just that Rudi Bauer's winemaking encapsulates both the savoury elements of his European winemaking background *and* the fresh, upfront fruit that defines New Zealand's and the world's southernmost winemaking region. While his focus has always been on making top-quality wine, he wouldn't mind it if his wines were slightly better known, which is why he is focusing on marketing more than ever before.

Bauer was one of the first winemakers ever to make Pinot Noir in New Zealand's southern regions, having made some of the earliest reds at Rippon Vineyard on the shores of Lake Wanaka, when its founder, the late Rolfe Mills, was pioneering winemaking there.

As Lois Mills of Rippon Vineyard says of her late husband Rolfe: 'He was Rudi's mentor as Rudi is my son Nick's mentor.'

One of the big questions posed back then — mostly from those in the north of New Zealand — was: can Central Otago even ripen grapes properly?

Rather than dwell on this icy issue, Bauer wants to thaw the freeze on wine drinkers' spending right now and move them away from the cheap glut that saturates supermarket wine shelves. Instead of the mire of mediocrity, which currently defines so much New Zealand wine on sale at rock bottom prices, he wants to show wine lovers what great wine is by making and marketing it himself.

His philosophy has always been to make three individual outstanding wines. By keeping it to a simple trio — a red, a white and a sparkling wine — his focus on quality has never been diluted, even if critical acclaim for his bubbles has eclipsed his production of and passion for Pinot Noir — in the public's eye at least. Yes, he reluctantly agrees, 'Our sparkling wines have had a stronger run, but it will change when some of the younger vineyard blocks on the hillside go into the Quartz Reef Pinot Noir. My love is certainly Pinot Noir.'

In any case, both the Pinot Noir and the sparkling wine ultimately express what he describes as 'finesse and concentration', something most in the wine industry would agree with. Ever since he first arrived in Central Otago as a young backpacker from Austria, keen on using his European winemaking degree in New Zealand, Bauer has brought a much needed northern hemisphere perspective to the southern New Zealand wine industry.

His first vintage in Central was in the momentous year of 1989 — the year the Berlin Wall fell, the Tiananmen Square riots took place, Fine Young Cannibals were big in top 20 song charts — and he made some of the country's best early Pinot Noir from vines growing at the breathtakingly beautiful Rippon Vineyard.

He was well versed in quality winemaking, having landed in New Zealand in 1985 to work a vintage at Mission Vineyard in Hawke's Bay as an assistant winemaker. It was an interesting time to arrive there, he says in hindsight, because 'The Mission' — as it is known in wine circles — was still being run at the time by the Catholic Marist priests, who were 'extraordinarily well educated people who spoke four to five languages and had travelled throughout the world and could teach lots of things'.

'I THINK THE NEW ZEALAND CONSUMER STILL HAS TO GRASP THE CONCEPT THAT WE HAVE THIS AMAZING DRINK WE MAKE IN THIS COUNTRY. IT'S CALLED WINE AND IT'S PART OF OUR CULTURE HERE NOW.'

Among the things they taught Bauer was just how youthful most of the New Zealand wine industry was. And also where to find the most heart-stopping beauty in the country: down south.

'I must have done a good job because they were very helpful to me and gave me all the information I needed about where to explore New Zealand.' So once vintage, pruning, winery cleaning and bottling were all over for the year, he left to travel. From December 1985 to February 1986, he cycled the South Island and did 'a lot of mountaineering, too', which is how he arrived in Wanaka and Queenstown. It's also where he forged his first relationships with Central Otago winemakers, including Alexandra's pioneers Verdun Burgess and Sue Edwards, who famously blasted away schisty rocky hillside to plant vines in the area, which still has the highest and lowest recorded temperatures anywhere in the country.

While Verdun and Sue are planning to move on, the New Zealand wine industry is still in a youthful phase.

'I think the New Zealand consumer still has to grasp the concept that we have this amazing drink we make in this country. It's called wine and it's part of our culture here now. Our biggest challenge as a wine industry is to lead wine drinkers to quality rather than quantity.'

This is intrinsic to the success of New Zealand wine, says Bauer. 'We have to protect our wine industry by making great quality, especially with the generation, which is focused on not drinking too much, so if they can only drink a couple of glasses, then our job is to make sure those glasses are good ones.'

BAUER'S BEGINNINGS

Bauer's wine story begins at 11 years old when he moved with his parents from the district of Salzburg, Austria, where he was born and raised, to Baden near Vienna, where Beethoven wrote his Ninth Symphony. The move made him think about what he wanted to do when he grew up, and a year later he told his parents he wanted to be a chef. They advised against it because they said he'd have to work weekends. 'So I decided I wanted to work in the theatre (medical theatre, moving on to be an anaesthetist, but at that stage I was too young). That also seemed to involve a lot of weekend work, along with unsteady pay. So then I became interested in working outside in viticulture, horticulture and agriculture.'

Growing up in a rural environment in Baden, he remembers lots of mostly small farms where grapes grew alongside grain and cattle farms.

'Most of the farmers needed an additional income to the livestock they raised, so they were allowed to sell wine from their farm gate for limited

periods, four times a year. When it was the permitted time, people would come into the farms, sit down at the farmers' tables, drink their wine and buy their food. It's part of Austrian culture. Normally those wines are bone dry, very high in acidity and go extremely well with food. As a youngster to have fresh bread with a spread of pork fat with onion on top with wine, it was heaven.

'That experience was quite complete. The atmosphere, the simplicity and the people all coming together in an environment which was quite noisy and very entertaining — it was great. What I most liked was the simplicity. There was a lot going on from a visual, sensory and emotional point of view.'

FIRST DRINKS

The first wine he remembers drinking was at the age of about 14 or 15 — 'quite late in the piece'.

When he finished high school at the end of 1974, Bauer went straight to study winemaking and viticulture in the ancient Roman town of Gumpoldskirchen, in Lower Austria. Graduating in 1979, he then studied further in Krems, following that experience up with a diploma in wine management in Bad Kreuznach, Germany, in 1983–84. And still hungry for more knowledge, he wanted to travel. 'South Africa was out of the question for political reasons; I couldn't possibly support them. I couldn't get into Canada or North America, and Australia wasn't on the radar for me; I didn't think of it. I was wondering where to go and what to do next.'

KIWI CONNECTION

The 'what next?' question was answered by a chance meeting between Bauer and the late German viticulturist Dr Helmut Becker, a key expert at the Geisenheim Grape Breeding Institute in Germany, who had collaborated with many in the New Zealand wine industry — as well as others in Canada, Australia and Japan, among other countries — to improve the variety of grapes and grape clones in these countries.

'He suggested I go to see the New Zealand ambassador in Bonn so I met him and he gave me a little booklet about New Zealand wineries, which led me to write in my broken English to a couple of wineries about possible work opportunities.'

Two wrote back, inviting him to work a vintage: Mission Estate and Ngatarawa, both in Hawke's Bay.

GETTING HERE

That was the easy part. Getting to New Zealand without a work permit was the hard bit. All his wine qualifications had to be translated into English, there was a full police check, a full medical check and an interview with the New Zealand Consul in Vienna before Bauer was granted a six-month visa, which finally arrived in 1985. So in April that year he hot-tailed it out of Austria, arrived at Mission Estate and, apart from a couple of vintages he

has worked in Oregon, California and Burgundy, he's effectively been in New Zealand ever since.

STAYING PUT

'It's funny how things fall into place,' says Bauer, who met his wife, Suellen Boag, one day at Mission Estate. A photographer, she was working on an advertisement at the winery when he was working there and they started seeing each other regularly. But their early days proved to be far from smooth sailing, due to an unusual stroke of bad luck. But first, Bauer went off in 1986 to Simi Winery in Sonoma, California, to do research work on colour extraction for rosé production, then worked a vintage making Pinot Noir in Oregon before returning to Mission Estate in New Zealand. The plan was to go between hemispheres, taking Suellen with him on the next trip. Instead, they both were involved in a hit and run accident in Auckland on 21 May 1987.

'We were very badly injured. Suellen was four months in hospital; I was six weeks in hospital. She had a massive femur break and my knees were destroyed. I remember it very clearly; I was there but not really there. We were just thrown into the ambulance and my first reaction was "This is a really bad dream", and then I realised it wasn't a dream. You don't feel the pain; you just know something's not right. The nice thing was they put us together in intensive care.

'We stayed together for six weeks, then I went home for two weeks to Austria. When I came back I went to see Suellen every day in hospital. I think both of us being hit by that car changed a lot and, truth be told, I still don't know the meaning behind the accident and why we had to go through that.'

Two years later, Bauer went back to work in California, again at Simi Winery as a small-lot winemaker. When he returned to New Zealand in 1989, he took over the reins as viticulturist and winemaker at Rippon Vineyard at Lake Wanaka, where he stayed until 1992. His earlier work at Simi with colour extraction in rosé helped him work with the relatively delicate Pinot Noir grapes he pressed into service as top red wine at Rippon. And the following year a vintage at Méo-Camuzet in Vosné-Romanée, Burgundy, added to his experience with and understanding of the Pinot Noir grape; by now he'd worked with it in southern New Zealand, in Oregon in the United States and in its rightful home, Burgundy.

'WE KNOW NOW THE HUGE GROWTH IN NEW ZEALAND WINE HAS BEEN TOO FAST.'

BIG CHANGES

Ask Bauer to name the biggest change in the New Zealand wine scene since he's been part of it, and he says massive rates of unplanned growth. 'We know now the huge growth in New Zealand wine has been too fast.'

Since 1992 the national producing vineyard area has grown nearly six-fold, from 5800 hectares to 33,600 hectares.At the same time the number of wineries has grown from 166 in 1992 to 698 in 2012.

'In hindsight, it would have been good to avoid such massive and fast growth, but you can't put restrictions in place in a country where the whole idea is about free markets. This type of growth wouldn't happen in Austria because we know there we're not allowed to grow that fast. In 2012 the vintage might be smaller than expected, which is the opposite of the massive 2008 vintage, and it's equally as challenging. So we have to watch this space.'

CHALLENGES AHEAD

Lack of collective winemaking experience, lack of data on climate and soils and lack of vine age all make New Zealand a challenging environment in which to make wine. The answer for Bauer is collaboration, something Central Otago winemakers have been doing ever since they began in the 1980s.

'In Champagne, for instance, the winemakers all have a consistent story about their winemaking, their region and their history. For us in Central Otago we are still creating our own story and it's important to make this a real one; not based on myth but based on true stories. We all need to have the same story so we end up helping each other as a region to move ahead with the same message.'

GOLDEN HILLS

'My gut feeling about Central Otago was always that it could work, and I had this strong belief in the region, so I always knew I wanted to come back here,' says Bauer, referring to a temporary move slightly north to Canterbury, where he worked for the Giesen family when their wines were based there (they are now based in Marlborough).

Before moving to Canterbury, Bauer had met a visiting French winemaker, Clotilde (changed from Clothilde) Chauvet, from Champagne Marc Chauvet in France. The pair clicked instantly in their winemaking philosophies. Both loved bubbles. Both could see the potential for top-quality sparkling winemaking in Central, so they decided to collaborate on a joint bubbly project. In 1994 and 1995, Bauer and accountant Peter Alexander put together a partnership between John and Heather Perriam of Bendigo Station, Clotilde Chauvet and Bauer. Then, in 1996, they formed Bendigo Estate Partnership:

'At that stage the thinking was that Bendigo would be on the label. When it came down to the crunch we realised there was also a Bendigo in Australia and thought it might not be such a clever idea to put it on the label. Hence, the name Quartz Reef came up because it all links into Bendigo itself, the place in Central Otago — as well as being descriptive of the massive quartz deposits lying underneath the vineyard.'

SPARKLING FUTURE

The adage that good things take time definitely fits Bauer well. He felt frustrated knowing about the land he had fallen in love with in Central, but not being able to establish it. Things finally began to fall into place for him in 1996 when he returned to Central to get started.

Clotilde Chauvet worked with the late Mike Wolter with the first vintage, in 1997, at the Central Otago Wine Company, before returning to Champagne. Unfortunately, Wolter passed away in July 1997, which was when Rudi came down to complete all the wines for the Central Otago Wine Company (this job as winemaker there helped him to survive while he was setting up Quartz Reef winery). And aided by the Giesen family, he made the first Quartz Reef bubbly in 1996 from Marlborough-grown grapes, supplied by them, which he aged for two years on lees (dead yeast cells, post-fermentation). It was a staunch nod that he was doing things the French way; all non-vintage Champagne must be legally aged on lees for at least 15 months and vintage bubbles from Champagne for far longer.

In the early days at Quartz Reef, the bubbles was called 'Quartz Reef Chauvet', but since Clotilde is no longer a partner in the business, her surname has been removed from the label. It was an instant hit, but nowhere near the style that Bauer envisaged. He saw the Marlborough grapes version of his bubbles merely as a transition, until the grapes he had begun to plant in Central could yield fruit.

'My initial thought was to produce still wines from Pinot Noir, Pinot Gris and Pinot Blanc as part of a Pinot Trilogy, but at that stage I never had any plans to make sparkling wine.

'Going back to 1991, to go to an unproven site in Bendigo with the vision to make a great Pinot Noir still wine, I realised that I needed a Plan B as a back-up, which was the birth of sparkling wine for Quartz Reef. I was wrong on both counts, that not only was the Pinot Noir very successful, but the sparkling was also. This is the reason that we at Quartz Reef have the Bendigo Estate vineyard hillside committed to Pinot Noir still wine and the Quartz Reef Loop Road vineyard committed to Pinot Noir for sparkling wine.

Calling his bubbles méthode traditionnelle is code to champagne fanatics that he was using two of the three classic Champagne grapes: Pinot Noir and Chardonnay. The third grape, Pinot Meunier, hasn't featured, but then it doesn't always in Champagne either.

'The most satisfying part of making the sparkling wine is that it gives me a good understanding of what's going on in the vineyard from an acid point of view. It's very much a cool-climate sparkling wine, which really suits us so well in

'I WANT TO DRILL DEEPER ... AND SHOW WHAT WE'RE DISCOVERING IN OUR WORK ON THIS VINEYARD BY MAKING WINES WHICH REFLECT THE PLACE IN THEIR TASTE.'

Central. You can see that you are improving this sparkling wine in a similar rate as you understand more; it is Pinot Noir and Chardonnay; two-thirds and one-third, and it has always been 80 to 100 per cent Chardonnay for the vintage wine.'

FUTURE PROOF
'I would love to consistently make more distinctive wines from our vineyards here at Quartz Reef because everything we do is now single-vineyard expressions of the place. I want to drill deeper into the expression of that and show what we're discovering in our work on this vineyard by making wines which reflect the place in their taste.'

'I also want to put in place a more sophisticated sustainability practice for our vineyards and winery.'

Bauer became biodynamic-certified with Demeter in November 2011, joining the other five New Zealand vineyards to have achieved full certification to date.

'I think it would be nice to see this vineyard pass to my children to take over after me, but time will tell whether they want to. I know that I have been quite a later starter in my life overall, so maybe that will happen with the children, too.'

The Quartz Reef Wines partnership now is equally owned by Trevor Scott [a former accountant/businessman from Dunedin] and Rudi, with John Perriam a minority shareholder. In 2010 Bauer was nominated for the German *Der Feinschmecker* Wine Awards as Winemaker of the Year nominee, one of six in world and the first person in New Zealand ever to be nominated.

'It was the combination of making wines from various wineries in Central Otago awarded with gold medals and trophies, as well as recognising the contribution I made to Central Otago over the years which got me the nomination,' he says, explaining that the nomination is threefold: having an outstanding portfolio of wines; being a visionary and leader; and being respected for making an outstanding contribution to the local and national wine industry.

AIM HIGH
'My aim for the future is to be part of creating Central Otago as the Burgundy equivalent of the south. More importantly, I would like to show wine consumers the world of Pinot Noir; to be able to line up these wines for people regularly and show them the story that the taste of these wines tells. Our story is most likely to be the most compelling one because the climate is on our side. It's the

'IT'S THE CLIMATE, VISION, KNOWLEDGE AND THE RIGHT SITES THAT MAKE PINOT NOIR GREAT. THERE ARE ONLY A FEW AREAS IN THE WORLD THAT CAN ACHIEVE THIS COMBINATION, AND I HAVE ALWAYS FELT THAT WE STRUCK THE JACKPOT HERE.'

climate, vision, knowledge and the right sites that make Pinot Noir great. There are only a few areas in the world that can achieve this combination, and I have always felt that we struck the jackpot here.'

While so many Central winemakers see their pot of gold as Pinot Noir, Bauer has tapped into a brighter-coloured golden hue with with his sparkling wines. If Quartz Reef Méthode Traditionelle is not the greatest Champagne lookalike in the southern hemisphere, then I have yet to taste what is.

RUDI'S GO-TO WINES

Bubbles tops the list. New Zealand and France are the first ports of call when it comes to bubbles. Favourites include Taittinger — 'My absolute favourite is Taittinger Comtes de Champagne Blanc de Blancs, which is absolutely stunning, and I'm also fond of Billecart-Salmon Brut Rosé. I've been tasting more Champagne Jacquesson to try to understand the house style, too.'

Not that bubbles is the only wine in Rudi's glass. Austrian and German Rieslings and Grüner Veltliner are also high on his list of must-have-at-home wines. As are New Zealand Pinot Noirs and any burgundies he can find. 'I also enjoy good wheat beer.'

TOP WINES FROM RUDI BAUER
- 2002 Quartz Reef Bendigo Estate Pinot Noir
- 2006 Quartz Reef Bendigo Vintage Sparkling

KEVIN JUDD, GREYWACKE, MARLBOROUGH

WITH IVAN SUTHERLAND MNZM AND JAMES HEALY, DOG POINT VINEYARD

'Three industry pioneers, not being satisfied with individually creating an iconic new world wine brand, namely Cloudy Bay, have taken their skills and expertise to now produce their own highly successful wine styles.'

— Gerry Gregg, national wineries, Brancott Estate

'These three have taken the whole Marlborough Cloudy Bay thing to another level by going away from that commercial version of Marlborough, and I think have really hit the region right on the head with some high-end, terroir-reflective wines of the region.'

— John Hancock, founder of Trinity Hill

GREATEST ACHIEVEMENT

'A lot of people these days refer to me as the founder of Cloudy Bay, but I cannot lay claim to that. It was David Hohnen from Western Australia who founded the company; it was very much his brainchild and he employed me to make the wine and manage the winery. He had amazing foresight, a precise focus on quality wine production, a natural intuition for marketing and a dry sense of humour. I learnt a huge amount from him. I was, however, responsible for the winemaking at Cloudy Bay for 25 years. The greatest achievement for me was

building a sense of integrity and trust within the business — something that was hard to walk away from and something of which I will always be proud.'

KEY ACHIEVEMENTS

Publishing *The Landscape of New Zealand Wine*. 'I was interested in photography before wine, but it was just a hobby for many years. In the 1990s I started shooting wine images professionally, and it has now become part of what I do in my everyday life. The book is the culmination of over a decade's work and seeing it in print brings great satisfaction.'

TAKE TO A DESERT ISLAND . . .

'Kimberley and Dixie, my camera, my computer and, if I was only allowed one wine, it would have to be a Chardonnay. There are great New Zealand Chardonnays and I don't drink enough French Chardonnay to give a sensible selection of names, but I love the more savoury styles, which are yeasty, nutty, oily and rich, while still retaining good acid. My favourite New Zealand versions include Neudorf, Fromm, Dog Point and Kumeu River's.'

ON MAKING WINE IN MARLBOROUGH

'The incredible intensity of flavour. I'll never forget the first time I ever tried Sauvignon Blanc from New Zealand. It was a complete eye-opener; the intensity is not just in the wine, it's in the grapes. It's a serendipitous mix of grape variety and climate, high sunshine hours and low rainfall, with sufficient heat in most years to achieve full ripeness, but an extremely maritime South Pacific climate where maximum temperatures rarely exceed 30 degrees. The grapes ripen in a cool, sunny environment and the flavour and natural acid retention is extraordinary.

'However, the climate that provides the ability to produce these potent levels of fruit aromatics and flavour comes with its challenges; being so maritime it is sometimes susceptible to climatic extremes. I'm old enough to remember some tricky vintages, like 1995, which was looking like a great vintage until it started raining and didn't stop, and then in 1993 it was so cold that we didn't finish picking until late May. In 1990 we had a minus-5-degree frost that defoliated the entire valley mid-vintage. These are all classic examples of Marlborough and New Zealand; in terms of the extremes we can get growing grapes on two little islands in the middle of the South Pacific. On average the growing and ripening seasons are ideal for the variety. We've had a smooth run lately.'

BIGGEST RISK TAKEN WITH WINE?

'Setting up Greywacke the vintage after Marlborough moved into an oversupply situation and in the middle of a global financial crisis.'

THE STORY

Even before I tasted Cloudy Bay Sauvignon Blanc, I could conjure up its fresh lawn, lime zest, fruit salad flavours, all rolled into one, leap-out-of-the-glass white wine. I wasn't disappointed when I finally got a sip, even if it did take three plane rides, two buses, a train and two underground Tube trips to get hold of a bottle, in the early 1990s, having travelled to the UK with backpack, boyfriend and high hopes of finding the wine there. It was nigh on impossible to get in New Zealand at the time. There were many great wines from other places in our glasses, too, but the first sip of Cloudy Bay was worth travelling so far to find.

Like its evocative label, the wine in its early days was refreshingly vibrant and intensely different to most other Marlborough Sauvignon Blancs at the time. Whether it was the improvement of other competing wines, the focus on creating a new great Sauvignon Blanc — which Cloudy Bay Te Koko most definitely is — or something else, there are now many other wines to rival this still great white. And for those who have followed the journey of the wines, the region they come from and of course, the Sauvignon Blanc grape in New Zealand, it is no surprise to discover that two of Marlborough's newest top Sauvignon Blancs are made by former members of the Cloudy Bay team.

Not that this story is about comparing and contrasting one winery with another. It's not.

This story is about the trio of men behind many of Marlborough's top wines; namely Kevin Judd, Ivan Sutherland and James Healy. And since Judd was the original winemaker at Cloudy Bay, this chapter is predominantly about the journey that led him first from Australia to New Zealand and, secondly, just around the corner to a new winery. From the moment before he set foot in New Zealand, he had high hopes of making fresh, vibrant aromatic white wines here because he always loved those styles — even when making big reds in Australia.

After 25 years at the iconic Cloudy Bay winery, first as winemaker, then as chief winemaker and, by that time, also a successful part-time commercial photographer, Judd began a new wine brand called Greywacke. The first vintage was 2009 and from the start, he found himself working alongside Sutherland and Healy, all over again.

'There are many of us working here who have worked at Cloudy Bay together at one time or another,' says Judd, who makes his wines at the Dog Point Vineyard winery.

Judd says he always imagined he would work out his days at Cloudy Bay but when the luxury global giant, Moët Hennessy, decided to restructure the management of Cloudy Bay in 2008, the job as he knew it was in jeopardy. With a mixture of uncertainty about what to do and clarity about what not to, he found himself uncomfortable about the offer made to him: to be a roving global ambassador with the title 'Founding winemaker'. It was, he says, the last thing he wanted.

'It was not the role for me. I'd always wondered where I might go from Cloudy Bay. It has such an extraordinary reputation. I never thought I would set up my own label — it seemed like a hard act to follow.'

But just in case the opportunity, courage and timing did coincide one day, he registered the name Greywacke in 1993. It was not for another 15 years that he'd be using it.

NEW WINEMAKING PASTURES

It all seemed more plausible after a chance meeting Judd had with Sutherland and Healy one day in the nose of a 747 from Hong Kong to London. 'We had a chat about the fact that I was contemplating setting up my own label. The timing was fantastic in retrospect because Ivan could see the writing on the wall with the impending oversupply, he'd need another home for some of his grapes and they also had spare room in the winery, while I needed a place to make wine.'

From there, things moved swiftly. The chat with the Dog Point duo was in October 2008; by April 2009 he was crushing grapes at Dog Point, while simultaneously working out a six-month handover period at Cloudy Bay. His exit was gradual, dignified and on good terms, which were all important to him, says Judd. But best of all, he moved straight into a situation where he was working with people he knew and trusted.

'It's great. We all know each other's good and bad points and we know when each other's bullshitting, so it's a smooth coexistence.'

It also enabled Dog Point Vineyards to grow from a small, category three wine producer to a larger, category two New Zealand winery, giving some economies of scale. The categories are set by New Zealand Winegrowers. Size is determined by the number of litres of wine produced annually by a winery or wine brand.

Judd buys most of his grapes from the Sutherland family's vineyards and also from two other growers he knows in Marlborough, one from the Brancott Valley and one from Rapaura.

'It's handy having stuff close,' he says, when asked about his thoughts on using grapes from the Awatere Valley, south of and cooler than Blenheim. While not entirely sold on the idea of having to truck grapes from there, he wouldn't rule it out but, for now, convenience and long-term knowledge of the grapes he works with define his wines. The notion of sticking with what he knows is a formula he, Sutherland and Healy all adhere to. That's the beauty of doing their own winemaking.

For the Dog Point Vineyard pair, sticking to their knitting means making the wines they enjoy best: two Sauvignon Blancs, one of which is barrel fermented (in old oak barrels), as well as Chardonnay and Pinot Noir.

'Nothing else,' says Sutherland, adding that they would 'quite like to make a great Riesling but we need to focus on what we're doing right now.'

DOG POINT AND THE DOGMOBILE

The entirely original metallic green 1971 Holden, in which Healy drove his family down from Auckland to Marlborough during 1990 — to take up his winemaking role at Cloudy Bay — is now used as the 'Dogmobile', Dog Point's

marketing vehicle. It bears the words 'Dog Point' and a painted image of ti kouka (cabbage tree — the winery's logo) on its sides.

James Healy and Ivan Sutherland, the owners of Dog Point Vineyard, worked closely together running the vintages at Cloudy Bay for 12 years. Healy's pioneering work with Sauvignon Blanc, using natural ferments (rather than introducing commercial yeasts, which is generally the norm in winemaking) was the catalyst for the establishment of Cloudy Bay's Te Koko wine.

James and Wendy Healy first met Kevin and Kimberley Judd in 1983 after they had recently moved to New Zealand from South Australia. Their friendship led to Healy working at Cloudy Bay, where he met Ivan and Margaret Sutherland, which, in turn, led to the relationship all three couples enjoy today through Dog Point.

Sutherland and Healy set up Dog Point Vineyard as their own winery in 2002. The vineyard has always been the source of Sauvignon Blanc grapes for Cloudy Bay wines and is one of the oldest private vineyards in the district with vines (actually Müller-Thurgau) planted in 1979. Ivan and Margaret added Riesling in 1980, Chardonnay in 1981, and Pinot Noir and Sauvignon Blanc in 1983.

'In those early years of Marlborough the wine industry was mostly focused on producing bulk wine, but time spent in Europe as a rower and visiting vineyards in France, Germany and also California opened my eyes,' says Sutherland.

'In the early days I was doing viticultural consultancy work in the development phase of Marlborough and occasionally elsewhere, at the same time growing grapes for Penfolds New Zealand, providing them with Müller-Thurgau, Riesling and Chardonnay, but my role dramatically changed over time, thanks to practical experience. The French say "terroir" and definitely the understanding of climate and soils, along with the seasonal variability of a cool-climate region, such as Marlborough, has been invaluable to understanding the entire regionality, which also includes rootstocks on which grapes are grown and grape varieties.

'The good thing about this region, even though it was economically damaging, was phylloxera. It made people think about the variety, the aspect and which varieties were best suited to a particular soil type. For example, our hill slopes with the more water-retentive clay soils certainly give a nice evolutionary and even development of fruit over summer, ideally suited to Pinot Noir. When it was found here in the 1980s, we had to replant the majority of the vineyard on rootstock, but we couldn't afford to do it all at once. However, in those early years we did manage to plant some Pinot Noir, Chardonnay and Sauvignon Blanc on rootstock.'

This vineyard is now the source of grapes for Dog Point Section 94

Sauvignon Blanc; a barrel and wild yeast-fermented, full-bodied white, it has broken the mould of tutti-frutti Kiwi 'Savvy' with its medium to full body, rich savoury flavours and floral aromas.

Sutherland no longer refers to himself as a viticulturist these days, either. Like Healey, he eschews any single description of his role. 'When you're creating your own very hands-on wine label, everything is totally integrated and you've got to be all things and you certainly, I think, need to have an understanding of the entire process. That's how James and I have worked since starting our own label. If you want to be hands-on, as we do, you can't be too big. We're pretty adamant that what's important to us is being involved all the way through every aspect of the production from growing the grapes to making the wine, to selling it, to understanding the markets it goes to and explaining to the people in those markets what our wine is all about.'

As is teamwork. While Sutherland and Healy are the faces of Dog Point Vineyard, their partners work steadily behind the scenes: Margaret Sutherland and Wendy Healy are both actively involved in and an intrinsic part of the winery team.

Having an understanding of wines of the world, as well as of New Zealand, is close to both Sutherland's and Healy's hearts.

When he first planted grapes in the 1970s, Sutherland was also an Olympic rower, winning bronze for New Zealand at the 1976 Olympics in Montreal; it's a part of his life he rarely talks about in wine circles, but which proved to be pivotal in his wine journey.

Since then he has been the rowing team manager for New Zealand at the 1988 Olympics in Seoul through to the 1992 Olympics in Barcelona. But it was in his early days of travel with rowing that he got exposure to many of the great wines of the world and also to wines which were infinitely higher in quality than most New Zealand wines back then.

'Because of the extensive travel internationally and considerable research at the time, I gained an appreciation of quality wine, in terms of grape varieties, the soil they grew in and climate suitability, and I really couldn't get my head around Müller-Thurgau, hence the plantings in those early years of Riesling, Chardonnay, Pinot Noir and Sauvingnon Blanc. Some people in the industry told me that I was mad, but it was clear to me that these grapes were our real future,' says Sutherland, who was awarded a Member of the New Zealand Order of Merit for services to rowing and viticulture in the Queen's Birthday Honours in 2011.

He and Healy also make very small quantities of top-quality sparkling wine, made along the same lines as champagne.

'It's hardly a broadening of our small repertoire because we really make it for ourselves and for guests at our annual Dog Point Vineyard Picnic to enjoy, all 200 or so of them each year,' says Healy, adding that since it is made from Chardonnay and Pinot Noir, it remains within the realms of their tight focus.

If they did broaden the net and include another grape or wine into their mix, Riesling may be added. For now, however, benchmarking themselves against the best in the world is a higher priority, as witnessed in tastings and in their personal wine cellars. At the 2012 Dog Point Vineyards Picnic, for instance, they brought out 20-year-old bottles of Ornellaia, decade-old Vega Sicilia (current release, for the record), eight-year-old Domaine de la Romanée-Conti Échézeaux, among other great wines of the world. These wines are but the tip of the iceberg that this exacting duo taste, cellar and taste again.

'We think widely and taste widely, putting our own wines in line-ups with the identities blinded, because we want to be careful not to have a cellar palate. James and I work together all the time and we eat a lot of meals together with our wives; the wine's important to us in terms of matching it to the food. We believe that helps you to produce wine people want to drink, as opposed to wine that just tastes amazing in a line-up for one or two sips.'

The Dog Point pair describe themselves as artisan wine producers. All their grapes come from their own vineyard. All are low-cropped, hand-picked, run under an organic regime and the winemaking process is also very hands-on for both Healy and Sutherland.

'Thankfully, there are a few wine labels around New Zealand like that,' says Sutherland, 'and long may it continue.'

EARLY DAYS

Judd first came to New Zealand with his wife, Kimberley, in 1983 to work at Selaks Wines, then still a family-owned West Auckland company, as opposed to being absorbed into the large global wine company it is part of today.

Born in England, Judd and his parents emigrated to Adelaide when he was nine; he was raised there and he went to Roseworthy Agricultural College to learn winemaking, working for Château Reynella under Australian winemaker Geoff Merrill.

'We used to make everything from bag-in-the-box wines to amazing Australian takes on vintage port wine styles and great Coonawarra reds. Then Hardys bought the company. By then I was 22 and keen to take on more winemaking responsibility. What they offered me — being in charge of tank-fermented sparkling wine — was not what I had in mind, so I started looking around for another job and couldn't find anything in Australia.

'I was really interested in making aromatic white wine and really impressed with some of the Sauvignon Blancs being made from South Australia at the time and also Coonawarra Rieslings. I figured New Zealand would be a new frontier in which to make cool-climate white wines, so I applied for two jobs that were being advertised at Delegat's and Selaks.

'WHEN THE 1986 HIT WINE GLASSES IN THE UNITED KINGDOM, A LOT OF JOURNALISTS THERE WENT CRAZY OVER IT.'

'The first New Zealand white wine I ever tried was a bottle of Delegat's Müller-Thurgau, which I tasted with Jim Delegat when he interviewed me in Adelaide. Another winemaker was appointed at Delegat's and never turned up, but by then I had accepted the job at Selaks and we moved across the Tasman pre the 1983 vintage.

'I remember a long late night with Larry McKenna and John Hancock (both of whom had moved from Australia to make wine in New Zealand) and Hancock was telling Kimberley that she would never go back to Australia and that we were both here in New Zealand for good. It comes up in discussion from time to time.'

After three years in New Zealand the couple were planning to move back, when a phone call from West Australian winery owner David Hohnen stopped them in their tracks.

Hohnen liked New Zealand Sauvignon Blanc and was raising funds to start a winery in Marlborough. He had twice won Australia's highly regarded Jimmy Watson Memorial Trophy and now needed to find a good winemaker in New Zealand; Judd had impressed him. So, in 1985, they bought 40 tonnes of Marlborough grapes and made their first wine at an existing Gisborne winery. It was a similar transition to Judd's departure from Cloudy Bay 25 years on. He was still working for Selak's while making the first vintage of 1985 Cloudy Bay Sauvignon, giving instructions by proxy (well, down the phone, actually) to winemaker Dave Pearce.

'It was a pretty unromantic start,' says Judd, 'but it did get us under way in a hurry.'

The first Marlborough grapes they used came from the now well-known Stoneleigh Vineyard.

'To my knowledge the 1985 Cloudy Bay Sauvignon Blanc didn't go further than Australia but when the 1986 hit wine glasses in the United Kingdom, a lot of journalists there went crazy over it. I don't think we were expecting that to happen. From there on it just seemed to always outsell itself.'

TROUBLE IN MARLBOROUGH

Greed, profiteering and overzealous planting characterise the main problems in Marlborough today, says Judd.

'Marlborough is a victim of its own success. It has attracted a lot of greedy people who are focused solely on making lots of money. To quote David Hohnen again; he used to say that financial reward should be the result of a job well done, not the force that drives all your decision making. It's a pity that more people didn't have that attitude in the wine industry. There are so many stupid decisions based on numbers and graphs that appear to keep going upwards forever.'

As to how this can be rectified, Judd says the lucrative bottom line has disappeared for many winemakers: 'Hopefully it'll sort itself out.'

GREYWACKE

'Having been part of Cloudy Bay, I've also always seen the world as the market for Greywacke. I've certainly aimed to create a business that is very much international in focus and we are already in 25 markets, which is keeping me pretty busy.'

The company is only going to grow to about 40,000 cases; 50 per cent of which is likely to be Sauvignon Blanc, with the remainder split between Pinot Noir, Pinot Gris, Riesling and a late-harvest wine, the first of which was a Gewürztraminer — 'I wasn't intending to make a sweet wine the first year, but I found some beautifully botrytised fruit which had been left hanging in a vineyard for the birds to eat; it was too good for them so I bought the fruit.'

The grape he intends to use for his late-harvest wine in the future is the unsung queen of white grapes, the one winemakers love and many wine drinkers struggle with, the one which Marlborough has great potential to make and the one with which Germany already has: Riesling. It is the bittersweet hope of winemakers to see Riesling become one of the favoured darlings of wine drinkers; Judd doesn't hold quite such high hopes for it, but he does plan to keep making top Rieslings which gently woo wine drinkers into its fold.

KEVIN JUDD'S GO-TO WINES

'It is usually something handy and often bearing a Greywacke or Dog Point label; these days it's often a glass of wild ferment Sauvignon Blanc, and Coopers Sparkling Ale remains a long-time favourite.'

IVAN SUTHERLAND'S GO-TO WINES

'Generally, Chardonnay and Pinot Noir from small New Zealand and Burgundy producers and occasionally German Riesling from the Mosel, particularly JJ Prum.'

JAMES HEALY'S GO-TO WINES

'Mosel Riesling, especially the sweet ones. Chardonnay from anywhere, provided it's not overwooded, syrupy or dead. Sauvignon Blanc that goes beyond a one-dimensional expression of fruit. Pinot Noir — anything perfectly ripe and perfectly extracted from New Zealand, France, the US or Australia. No prune juice, please.'

TOP WINES FROM KEVIN JUDD AT GREYWACKE

- Greywacke Wild Sauvignon
- Greywacke Pinot Noir

TOP WINES FROM IVAN SUTHERLAND AND JAMES HEALY

- Dog Point Sauvignon Blanc
- Dog Point Pinot Noir

TIM AND JUDY FINN

NEUDORF VINEYARDS, NELSON

'Tim and Judy Finn are two of my favourite wine people. They have created Nelson's best wine estate and one of the southern hemisphere's great names. They have proved that a small family winery can compete with the big boys, bringing style, creativity and consistency to the creation of world-class Pinot Noir and Chardonnay.'

— Tim Atkin, MW

'Tim and Judy have aimed from the beginning for perfection and have achieved it by expressing through their wines the place that they call home.'

— Warren Barton, wine writer

GREATEST ACHIEVEMENT

'Rosie, our lovely daughter.'

KEY ACHIEVEMENTS

- Pioneering winemaking in Upper Moutere, Nelson.
- 'Creating terroir-driven wines of international repute from virgin fields and a dream.'

TAKE TO A DESERT ISLAND . . .

'We will plump for the power and finesse of Domaine Anne Gros Richebourg.'

ON WINEMAKING IN NELSON

'Making wine is constantly scary and stimulating. We survive on hard work, high hopes and a dollop of common sense.'

THE STORY

It was 1978 when Tim and Judy Finn started their winery. Or rather they started building the foundations of their vineyard from a humble, ramshackle home that was thrown into the deal when they bought land in the Moutere hills in Nelson to begin a winery.

Unlike anyone who ends up with a small fortune in wine from starting with a large one, they began with literally nothing but each other, a desire to move to the country and a clean slate after paying off Tim's Master of Science degree. Throw in five years of journalism experience (Judy's), a lot of optimism, and relative youth, and they found themselves in sunny Nelson.

'There was this wonderful hangover from the 60s of getting back to the land, to live off it and to explore new horizons. It was an incredibly innovative time and you thought you could do anything,' says Judy Finn, of their move to the South Island.

The wines they have since made set a new benchmark not only for Nelson — an often overlooked corner of the country — but for New Zealand, from their debut, in 1981.

Tim's quiet, thoughtful approach comes through in his wines, particularly Neudorf Chardonnay, the roots of which are now settled several metres deep in the Moutere clay soils where the 33-year-old vines grow.

The vines come first, Tim says, when asked about his winemaking philosophy. 'It sounds trite, I guess, but my aim and belief is to make the best wines from our land; which goes right back to choice of grape varieties. We find that Chardonnay and Pinot Noir do particularly well on these clay soils. Right from the start, it has been about looking at the quality of grapes, for us. That was the major push and always has been. Every year you learn more about the different seasons and how to work with them.'

Of late, he has been moving towards organic vineyard production, focusing on and trying to relate to what's happening under the ground, by digging three and a half metres down to the roots of the vines.

'It's absolutely amazing down there. What we're finding is that we've got roots there that have colonised whole micro-fauna areas where there are worms that weren't down there before, and an interaction between the roots and the

---

'RIGHT FROM THE START, IT HAS BEEN ABOUT LOOKING AT THE QUALITY OF GRAPES, FOR US. . . . EVERY YEAR YOU LEARN MORE ABOUT THE DIFFERENT SEASONS AND HOW TO WORK WITH THEM.'

'OUR WINES REFLECT THEIR MOUTERE ORIGINS; THEIR TEMPERAMENTS REFLECT OUR SEARCH FOR COMPLEXITY AND FINESSE.'

virgin clay soils,' says Finn, recalling not only the recent work but relating it back to when he and Judy first moved to Upper Moutere — a time when they also dug deep, quite literally, to see what type of earth they were going to grow grapes in.

Since then, the changes in colour and pH in the soil have been profound. While the native pH in the soils in which they grow vines was incredibly low — 'They're pretty acidic soils' — the older vines have built up organic matter, which now acts as an interaction between the soil and the grapevines.

'You can immediately see why old vines are good vines because they reflect the particular soil type they are growing in. Topsoil is just topsoil. It's only when you get down to what's underneath that you get to the uniqueness of a particular site.

'When we very first came there were very few worms, but now there are worms everywhere and we've been composting so we can see a tangible difference that's made. As growers of grapes, we play our part by encouraging this organic relationship, helping the vines to maintain their own health, keeping vigour and crop levels down. As winemakers we prefer to be light of hand, employing wild yeast fermentation and minimal pumping, fining or filtration. Our wines reflect their Moutere origins; their temperaments reflect our search for complexity and finesse,' Finn says.

While they treated wine as a business from the moment they bought the land, it took six jobs shared between them to get the funds together to start things running; all the while they lived in a house with no hot water, no indoor toilet and inadequate electricity.

'We were interested in wine and there wasn't much great wine around, but New Zealand wine was starting to be made from better grapes. New varietals from Cooks and other progressive companies were coming on the scene, and interest was high in exploring new regions. Meanwhile at Te Kauwhata Viticultural Research Station Dr Rainer Eschenbruch was having a really hard time convincing New Zealand's winemakers not to put water in their wine,' says Tim.

'He was a bit ostracised by the industry, which left him plenty of time to share his knowledge with newcomers like ourselves.'

MOVING TO NELSON

When they moved from Waikato to Nelson to plant grapes, Tim was 32, Judy was 27 and winemaking was considered pretty unusual in New Zealand at the time.

'We figured Tim's Masters along with my unimpressive journalism career would be beneficial. His approach as a scientist to everything helped us succeed — and still does.'

'EVERYONE WAS A LITTLE BIT INTERESTED IN WINE IN THOSE DAYS, SO WE WERE, TOO . . . TO TAKE IT FURTHER INVOLVED A BIT OF RESEARCH AND A LOT OF BEING PROACTIVE.'

They met at Massey University in Palmerston North, a couple of hours' drive south of New Plymouth, where Judy grew up, and three hours' north of Lower Hutt, where Tim did. After he finished his science degree at Massey, they moved north to the University of Waikato so he could complete a Masters degree at the Ruakura Research Centre.

Since both staff and students at the centre worked in agricultural science and had close links with fellow researchers and students at the nearby Te Kauwhata Viticultural Research Station, opportunities to learn about wine were inevitable.

'At Ruakura I was doing animal behaviour research for my Masters at a time when the dairy industry was expanding. My research related to large herd behaviour because herd sizes were growing and farmers were having a lot of problems relating to stress and disease. It was a really interesting area to be working in. We were all part of the same research chain.

'At Te Kauwhata they would present discussion papers and you would go along at lunchtime and listen to them talk about new grape varieties, and taste the experimental wines. Everyone was a little bit interested in wine in those days, so we were, too. A little later Dr Richard Smart [a viticultural expert] became involved at Te Kauwhata, transforming the way we grew grapes in this country. We got involved at Te Kauwhata through studying and personal interest. To take it further involved a bit of research and lot of being proactive.

'We looked at all of New Zealand and chose somewhere we wanted to live that looked like it had potential to make great wine in,' says Tim, who gathered every shred of information he could find on climate, soils and annual heat data.

So they moved. The land they bought came with a run-down house, which had been a commune, thrown in for good measure — or bad, depending on your perspective. Built in 1910, it had since had a pretty rough life, prior to Tim and Judy arriving.

PLANTING THE FIRST GRAPES
Like many young vineyards, Tim and Judy's first was a fruit salad from which they quickly discovered which grapes worked well and which were a no-go, despite the temptation to persevere.

'You can force a grape into growing in a place by exceptionally great viticulture, but at the end of the day someone else will do it far better in a better suited area. We were doing our best to learn which grapes would thrive. We had Gewürztraminer for a few years and we didn't have enough viticultural knowledge about it, so it went,' says Tim.

Now there are many great Gewürztraminers in New Zealand but, back then, Tim and Judy didn't like the over-the-top, heavily perfumed style they

were getting from the Gewürztraminer grapes they grew.

'It lacked balance between crispness with intense flavour, which good Gewürztraminer needs. Now that we know how to handle it in the vineyard and in the winery, we might reinvestigate this grape,' says Judy.

When they began, very little was known about basic viticulture in New Zealand. Everything was trial and error.

Merlot and Cabernet Sauvignon both came and went. It was too cold for both these reds, which need more heat than Nelson can provide to ripen well.

White grapes trialled included Chenin Blanc, Sémillon, Gewürztraminer and the alarmingly insipid Müller-Thurgau. All made a passing appearance; all eventually were rejected. It was too cold to ripen Chenin Blanc grapes properly; it proved too acidic in Nelson's climate. Müller-Thurgau didn't work because Tim and Judy couldn't see the merit in it. From the start, Chardonnay proved to be well behaved and a high achiever.

'I remember the guys visiting us from Te Kauwhata, coming and sampling it and looking at it in a very positive way from year one: 1981.'

Pinot Noir, Pinot Gris and Sauvignon Blanc all appeared in the mid- to late 1980s, when it was challenging to get good clones.

'The biggest and earliest change was in viticulture rather than in winemaking. To make basically pretty good wine, New Zealand could do that quite early on and we could as well. What we had to learn an awful lot about was growing good grapes. We really didn't have that knowledge at the early stage of the industry, and I've got to say, Te Kauwhata with Dr Richard Smart really played a huge part in that.'

WELL-BEHAVED CHARDONNAY

Chardonnay has always been the white queen at Neudorf Vineyards and is grown in relatively heavy clay soils, threaded with gravel throughout, which aids drainage. The soils and the climate help Chardonnay to thrive in Nelson, says Tim.

'We have a sunny maritime climate with long warm summers, but few really hot days. Every now and then we might reach 30 degrees, but really we'll only get a few days like that a year, and there is a marked difference between day and night, especially in autumn, which draws the season out and gives us what is called a high diurnal variation — that's the difference between day and night temperatures. In fact we have that in summer, too. Nelson has few really scorching days but a large amount of very warm ones.'

This may also account for the freshness found in the winery's famous Chardonnay, which won trophies in New Zealand and Australia in the early 1990s, for its outstanding weight, elegance and taste. It was constantly and consistently likened to white burgundy. Finn says today that he and Judy have always been 'quite Old World in terms of our preferences in wine styles', yet determined to make the best of the grapes that Nelson gives them.

Their aromatic white wines have also grown in stature — and sales. Of Riesling, Pinot Gris and Sauvignon Blanc, the Sauvignon is particularly growing in appeal, says Judy.

LARRY MCKENNA

Pinot Noir king — Australian-born Larry McKenna at the Escarpment Vineyard, 9 kilometres west of Martinborough township, a slightly cooler area on the same soil types as the Martinborough Terraces.

JAMES MILLTON

First city to see the sun — and, in the 1960s, Gisborne was one of the few places in New Zealand to have vines; here Annie Millton's mother plants her family's first grapevine in Opou Vineyard in the late 1960s.

The wine flows — Garry Millton, Annie Millton (née Clark), James Millton and John Clark at the opening of the Millton Vineyard winery and release of their first vintage, October 1984.

Challengers of conventional thinking — Annie and James Millton with late family members, Si Si the cat and Digby the dog.

A labour of love — winemaker James named his hillside vineyard of Viognier, Syrah, Pinot Noir and Chardonnay vines after his wife, Annie: this is the Clos de Ste. Anne Vineyard.

RUDI BAUER

Under the Central Otago sun — as well as under the radar and on top of all aspects of his winemaking from the vineyard to the bottle: Austrian-born and educated winemaker, Rudi Bauer. He first arrived in New Zealand as a backpacker in the 1980s, when he walked, tramped and made wine in the South Island, and met New Zealand-born photographer Suellen Boag; they and their children now live in Central Otago. Bauer is at the forefront of biodynamic grape growing in New Zealand.

KEVIN JUDD

Knowledgeable noses — Cloudy Bay Wines founder David Hohnen with Kevin Judd (right). Photograph by Jane Adams

A dog's life — Dog Point Vineyard founders and modern wine pioneers Ivan and Margaret Sutherland and Wendy and James Healy with their 1971 Holden Dogmobile, still in use to take Dog Point wine and its message around New Zealand. It is here at Dog Point Vineyard winery that Kevin Judd now makes his Greywacke wines.

Expert winemaker — and talented photographer, Kevin Judd with faithful winery friend, Dixie.
Photograph by Jim Tannock

TIM AND JUDY FINN

From commune to vineyard — Vinous gold in the Moutere Hills sees these vines (top left) sprawl down Tim and Judy Finn's Neudorf Vineyards sloping site. Standing on their land in Nelson (top right), with their late dog, Nick. Their move to a ramshackle house in the middle of the paddock they turned into their vineyard was driven by a desire to move away from the city and get back to the land: 'It was part of this wonderful hangover from the 1960s, the idea of living off the land, and we were determined to do it successfully,' says Judy Finn. She and Tim converted a former commune into a home and a hillside in the Upper Moutere area in Nelson into one of the country's most respected Chardonnay and Pinot Noir vineyards. Their proudest mutual achievement is their daughter, Rosie, pictured with Tim and Judy, below.

BLAIR WALTER

Mr Optimism — being irrepressibly positive is one of Blair Walter's greatest qualities; it is rare to see him without a smile on his face, as friend and fellow winemaker Steve Davies notes in the chapter on Walter. And like most New Zealand winemakers, Walter is involved intimately in all aspects of making wine, from the vineyard — which he and Felton Road owner Nigel Greening are converting to be fully biodynamic — to the winery to sales and marketing.

PATRICK MATERMAN

Marlborough Man — his move to Marlborough in 1994 sparked a passion for the wines, countryside and sea surrounding New Zealand's largest wine region. He planted his own vineyard at his home in the Awatere Valley, pursued his love of yachting and has built his career from assistant winemaker to chief winemaker of the largest wine company in New Zealand. While Materman still loves the vineyards, winemaking and blending aspects of creating wine, his job is now more focused on overseas marketing. The Brancott Estate Visitor Centre (below) opened in 2011 and sits on 'Rob's Knob', among a sea of Sauvignon Blanc vines; home to the first grapes planted in Marlborough in 1973.

ALAN BRADY

Brady's Bunch — In 2012, journalist-turned-wine pioneer Alan Brady celebrated 25 years of the first commercial production of Central Otago Pinot Noir. The first vintage was in 1987 at Gibbston Valley Wines; he then pioneered the smaller Mount Edward Winery, which has since been sold. Brady is now officially 'retired' and makes his own Wild Irishman Pinot Noirs. He appears here with daughter Susan, and her partner, Terence Vallelunga (the name is of Italian-American descent).

TERRY DUNLEAVY MBE

Island adventures — Terry Dunleavy was a one-time actor in a Gary Cooper film shot in Samoa, where he lived in the 1950s.

Tenacious leader — Terry Dunleavy was founding editor of *New Zealand Winegrower* magazine, the first CEO of the Wine Institute of New Zealand, and a former journalist, working on newspapers in New Zealand and Samoa. Dunleavy has been involved in every aspect of New Zealand wine from the moment when, as a printer, he helped sort out label-adhesive problems with Montana wine bottles in the early 1970s.

'Because we're not in Marlborough, we're benefiting a bit now, particularly in Australia where sommeliers are quite sniffy about Sauvignon Blanc because it has gained a reputation as a bulk wine rather than something special. If they are offered something other than Marlborough Sauvignon Blanc — perhaps a more complex dry style like Neudorf Sauvignon Blanc from Nelson for instance — some of them will leap on it. In some ways there's a little bit of an up for us, but I think the future is plateauing for Sauvignon from New Zealand.'

PICKY PINOT NOIR

The Pinot Noir road is a harder one to travel than Chardonnay because Pinot varies greatly from one region to the next. Even the types of Pinot Noir grapes — clones — vary greatly.

'It took a while for us to get all the better clones of Pinot Noir. We had what we considered was "Gamay Beaujolais" in those early days, but found it was an upright clone of Pinot Noir. If you wanted more, you got Clone 10/5 — not the greatest clone in the world. The big step forward was when Clone 5 (Pommard) came onstream in the early 90s, closely followed by the Dijon clones,' says Tim. 'It was the early 90s before we had any material that gave us the basis of making balanced and great Pinot Noir.

'At the same time the annual Southern Pinot Noir Workshop was instigated, based on the Oregon Steamboat event. New Zealand Pinot Noir owes an immense debt to our friends in Oregon for taking us under their wing over that period.

'We see our climate as a positive, enabling us to produce sensuous sophisticated Pinot Noirs,' says Tim.

'Clay soils tend to give you good density and tannins, but you then have to work on the finesse of the wine as well, and with clay it becomes more important because you really have to tie in more strongly with clones that give you greater finesse.

'Where Chardonnay so obviously suits the area we're in really well, and we don't have to make too many sharp decisions for it to do that, it's pretty hard to make a great Pinot Noir anywhere.'

In his bid to make a Pinot Noir which equals the quality of their highly acclaimed Chardonnays, Finn has focused more on clonal selection than anything else. Vintage variation is also more pronounced in Pinot Noir than Chardonnay.

'The winemaker's and viticulturist's challenge is to understand that and to compensate for the years that are not going to give you the great grapes.'

Which brings Finn back to clones, since a variety can help in this regard by mitigating different climatic variations in a country where vintage is as marked as it is in New Zealand. 'We find a range of different clones work well here, but they are all so different that while clone 777 works well in some years, the Pommard clone is better in others. Everyone will find that, depending where they are growing grapes. Our challenge is to master what does best here.'

And then there's oak.

OAK AND PINOT NOIR

Less is more where oak and Neudorf Pinot Noir are concerned. And Finn has progressively reduced the amount of oak he uses in Neudorf Moutere Pinot Noirs from 50 per cent about 15 years ago down to 30 per cent new oak these days. Not that it was an immediate step down.

With about 25 different blocks of Pinot Noir grapes from which to make components of the final wine, Finn says the overall reduction in use of new oak has been tailored around the types of clones of Pinot Noir used and what best suits each one.

'Some years we might have 25 different wines to work with to come up with our final blend. We match the oak to each particular cuvée — or component wine, in other words,' says Finn.

With this in mind, Finn says only about 18 per cent of the grapes that make up Tom's Block Pinot Noir spend time in new oak barriques. 'There are younger vines which contribute grapes to that wine and, in general, those that didn't make the cut at the top end go into that wine, whereas we only make 500 to 600 cases of the Moutere Pinot Noir and it's the most structured wine, so it receives more oak.'

That said, good Pinot Noir does not benefit from having its tannins built up with oak, says Finn. 'It's just the support of oak that we want. We tend to keep away from sweet oak; it's not something I like. We don't want wines that taste of and are dominated by oak flavours.'

As to the future, Finn says he likes the level of oak as it currently stands — on average about 30 per cent new oak — but it will always be tailored to the grapes, the vintage and the taste of the wine as it is being made.

'We currently have a lot of young Clone 5 Pinot Noir, and it has lovely silky tannins. We don't want to see them fighting with the oak tannin and losing because that would destroy the elegance in the wine. We're always progressing and looking ahead and also looking back, and wanting to do better.'

DEAL JUNKIES

'Everyone's a deal junkie. It's not about the best wine you can buy but the best deal you can get,' says Judy, whose heart sinks 'every time I see piles of beautiful, well made wine dump-stacked in the supermarket'.

Once upon a time, wine was something people respected, admired and collected, but now it's become a commodity, with an upside — and a downside.

The upside is that people treat it as part of their everyday life, enjoying wine without it being a binge-drinking experience because it's available, it's affordable and a lot of the time it has a local feel-good factor.

The downside of the present situation is that it's a disaster for the wine industry: unsustainable, uneconomic and creating long-term unrealistic expectations. 'The rise of the supermarket has been a double-edged sword,' says Judy.

'We have been round long enough to have an incredibly loyal client base and not have the pressure of the bank telling us to sell at a loss. It's one of the nice things about having been around for so long, but it just makes me weep

sometimes to see dump stacks of beautiful wine in a supermarket aisle where nobody makes any profit at all. In a funny sort of way I think that in some cases the small winemakers are better positioned to survive the storm.'

SAVING SAUVIGNON

'Sauvignon Blanc will never be the fashionable wine it was 10 years ago. I think those days are gone. It will continue to be a very good wine, which will sell well, but a great tragedy has happened with massive bulk discounting overseas. I don't think it's recoverable,' Judy says.

Tim agrees. 'Once you've lost the mana or respect for a grape variety, it's very hard to get that back. The United States wine buyers see New Zealand Sauvignon Blanc today as a numbers game, and it really doesn't matter whether it's yours or anyone else's. The States in general is about moving volume and getting money in the hand, so even though they may like your wine, a small winery can't be there supporting the brand all the time — you haven't got the spare time. And there is no particular allegiance to you. The States has been a huge disappointment to most small and many larger New Zealand producers.'

TWO TYPES OF WINE

New Zealand wine has grown up at the same time as a huge move in the Western world towards drinking more wine, says Tim, so there is a growing acceptance of wine as part of everyday life. However, wine tastes are increasingly dividing into two camps. The first is the fruity kind of wine where riper flavours are seen as king and sweet fruit is championed. Second, there are wines with relatively more complexity and interest.

'I'm aware that with Pinot Noir we in New Zealand are not always getting the complexity of flavour that we could. Even pretty ordinary burgundies tend to be more interesting than many New Zealand Pinot Noirs. I'm not sure that Pinot Noir should be a sweet-fruited red and that's it. It's costly to make well, and we need to move on from cheap, simple, fruity Pinot Noirs to something a little more cerebral and rewarding.'

With the exception of Pinot Gris and Grüner Veltliner — and the thankful decline of Müller-Thurgau (which every winemaker, marketer,

writer and critic in the New Zealand wine industry unanimously agrees was a dire grape) — the same grapes dominate in New Zealand: Sauvignon Blanc, Pinot Noir and Chardonnay are the big three.

The second tier comprises Pinot Gris, Riesling and Merlot, with smaller amounts of others being Cabernet Sauvignon, Syrah, Viognier, Sémillon, Malbec, Gewürztraminer and Cabernet France.

'We had to plant a few more grapes to make the whole thing work. While it was great fun when we were younger, we were constantly exhausted and had absolutely no money when we started. It was all done on the smell of an oily rag, but our focus was always on quality rather than big quantities, even though we have increased to about 12,000 cases.

In future the focus is on improving their Chardonnay further and on experimental grapes; among them are the northern Spanish white, Albariño. Not that he's convinced Albariño will be a star, but it is worth investigating.

'I guess I was drawn to it because it seems to suit exactly what Nelson is — a maritime climate. It goes with all range of fish dishes, and it seems part of what we do here. Climate-wise it will ripen nicely, as it does in a similar climate in north-west Spain.

'In the end it's like bringing Sauvignon Blanc into New Zealand. Who knew what would happen until we planted it here? It's the great unknown. It's been seen as a very fresh wine from northern Spain and does a very good job. There might be great potential in it, which we won't know until we try. We want to make a special wine, otherwise why bother?'

Other possibilities they have tried included the Spanish white grape, Godello. As soon as it was discovered that Godello is susceptible to botrytis, it was sidestepped. 'You could spend an awful lot of your life bringing in varieties not suited to New Zealand's climate.'

Novelties and fads aside, the Finns have joined the Grüner club — Austria's great claim to white wine fame, Grüner Veltliner, that is.

'We're still searching for that wonderful magic moment when we tasted this gorgeous line-up of Grüners from Austria at a wine masterclass 15 years ago. We had that experience once, and I certainly haven't seen it replicated, but there's still time and it's still possible. That tasting convinced us to try it.'

'There are a lot of grapes out there that make very good wines. I don't want to make very good wines. I want to make great wine. You can end up with a great avalanche of very good wines, but that's not what we're about here,' says Judy Finn.

THE WHITE PINOT

The birth of Pinot Gris in New Zealand has been painful for many, Tim Finn included: 'Right from the start demand outstripped supply, and people were tempted to overcrop. So we have ended up with these amorphous Pinot Grigio styles which lack flavour and have been damned as being "that ubiquitous white", and often too sweet. We can do a better job of Pinot Gris. Because we have a warm climate with cool nights we retain the acidity with good ripe fruit flavours and excellent texture. It has the potential to age better than some whites, too, because it will evolve in the bottle with some complexity but without herbaceous characters, especially if it's made from grapes that are not overcropped.'

WHAT LIES AHEAD

'We never feel we have it all sorted, but we are still learning and not just about viticulture and winemaking but about exporting, currency exchange, the internet, human resource issues, distribution, yeasts and barrels, grape clones and crop levels in our vineyards,' says Judy Finn.

In 2012 the Finns exported about 50 per cent of production, as they have for the past 15–20 years. Their shared and unwavering vision to make great wines has seen Neudorf Vineyards not only survive but thrive in the minds and mouths of wine lovers all over the world.

TIM AND JUDY'S GO-TO WINES

'Premier Cru Chablis such as Pinson, but there are so many reliable producers. Love that mineral second-glass appeal of Neudorf Nelson Chardonnay, a Chablis style made from New Zealand grapes. Or something from our cellar full of Riesling.'

TOP WINES FROM TIM AND JUDY FINN

- 2010 Neudorf Home Vineyard Pinot Noir
- 2010 Neudorf Moutere Chardonnay

BLAIR WALTER

FELTON ROAD, CENTRAL OTAGO

'Blair is a relentlessly positive guy with energy reserves to match and it's part of Central Otago's good fortune that he's both done a lot of work for, and helped inform the culture of, Central Otago winegrowers.'

— Steve Davies, winemaker and owner, Doctors Flat Vineyard

'Felton Road is not a collector of silverware — or goldware for that matter — and Blair follows suit. He is a winemaker who never enters wines into shows and doesn't garner "winemaker of the year" type awards. Yes, lots of critics say flattering things about him but, in truth, only one accolade counts: the superlative wines that have brought Felton Road to iconic status among fine wine enthusiasts worldwide. He made every single one. You could take every review of a Felton Road wine in the last 15 years and apply the praise to him personally. He wouldn't like it, but he'd deserve it.'

— Nigel Greening, owner Felton Road

GREATEST ACHIEVEMENT
'See what Nigel Greening says, above.'

KEY ACHIEVEMENTS
- Bachelor of Horticultural Science with First Class Honours, Lincoln University.
- Deputy chair of Central Otago Pinot Noir Limited.

'WE'VE KEPT OUR FOCUS ON HIGH QUALITY ALL THE WAY, WITHOUT EVER RISKING THE DILUTION OF THE PERCEPTION OR THE REALITY BY MAKING A LOWER PRICED "SECOND LABEL".'

- Tramper, mountain biker, sailor, Messerschmitt (microcar) enthusiast, amateur pilot.
- Winemaking experience at Giesen and Rippon in New Zealand; Saxonvale and Tarrawarra in Australia; Newton Vineyard in California; Sokol Blosser in Oregon and Domaine de L'Arlot in Burgundy.

TAKE TO A DESERT ISLAND . . .

'My wife Erin, our Burmese cats and a few grapevines. After having tasted delicious wines from vines grown in all sorts of climates and soils around the world, I'm sure I'd be able to coax something fun from them to sustain us.'

ON WINEMAKING IN CENTRAL OTAGO

'It's interesting. There's a perception that Central Otago is a challenging and difficult place to grow grapes and make wine. Everybody further north thinks it's marginal, frosty and cold, yet if you look at the records, Central has fewer problems with frost and poor flowering than most other regions.'

BIGGEST RISK EVER TAKEN WITH WINE?

'Relying 100 per cent on indigenous yeasts and making totally unfiltered wine from a relatively early stage in our winery's short history. Risky but necessary to help establish our identity.'

THE STORY

Perhaps it's because he's a hard-working perfectionist — who is also an extrovert who loves music, climbing and biking up mountains, sailing, flying and driving microcars. Or perhaps it is because he is the perennial early bird who catches the worm — as well as the last one standing at the party after the tasting, too. Whatever the reason for his success, Blair Walter is a high achiever with masses of humility.

More to the point, to what does Walter himself attribute his success with Felton Road Pinot Noirs, Rieslings and Chardonnays?

'We've kept our focus on high quality all the way, without ever risking the dilution of the perception or the reality by making a lower priced "second label". We put all our effort into selling our best wines. It's more work but it's also a lot more rewarding.'

As is the daily grind of routine winery work: 'Winemaking is not all glamour, 95 per cent of it is cleaning — just get on with it,' he was once famously quoted in the British magazine, *Decanter*.

There is no doubt he hits the high notes for Central Otago Pinot Noir more often and with more international acclaim than any other winemaker from the world's most southern and New Zealand's most controversial wine region.

Walter has been the winemaker at Felton Road since day one: 1996, to be precise.

The winery was founded and begun by Stewart Elms, who bought the land now under vines at Felton Road, Bannockburn, in 1991. Elms was Walter's significantly older lab partner at Lincoln University and retired to Wanaka in 2000 when he was in his sixties, but the two were among the earliest winemakers to spearhead top-quality wine from Bannockburn, Central Otago.

'Stewart invited me to become a partner at the start, so I am a shareholder — a very small one. Stewart knew that you either employ somebody and they work for wages or you get somebody passionate about the business and you'll get all that extra out of them — that's me.'

The duo made their first wines in 1997, garnering immediate international success from a gobsmackingly wide range of quarters: New Zealand, Australia and the UK — where the future owner of Felton Road, Nigel Greening, fell immediately for the bright, bold, big-bodied Bannockburn Pinot Noir style.

The early accolades included *Winestate* magazine's Wine of the Year in 1998; *Cuisine* magazine's Best New Winery of 1998 and, also from *Cuisine*, a five star and 93 out of 100 points for the first Felton Road Pinot Noir Block 3, from the inaugural 1997 vintage.

The accolades have never stopped flowing.

Speaking about Felton Road's Pinot Noirs, Australia's most revered wine writer, author, judge, critic (and former lawyer and winemaker) James Halliday says: 'These wines anchor Felton Road's position as the greatest Pinot producer in New Zealand.'

Halliday is not talking about that white usurper, Pinot Gris, which rides on the coat-tails of Pinot Noir's success; this is a one-Pinot winery — and it's red.

'Walter has established Felton Road as one of New Zealand's hottest producers in near world record time,' according to wine retailer, writer and collector Philip Rich, writing in the *Australian Financial Review* in April 2001.

A STEEP NEW PATH

By this stage, Elms had sold the winery to British wine lover, Nigel Greening. Not content to rest on the high praise already flowing towards the winery, Greening and Walter embarked on a steep new wine path together: converting their vineyards to biodynamic certification.

The year was 2002. Progress was slow, but the wine quality has benefited no end — and continues to, says Walter.

Felton Road Wines has just over 32 hectares of land, all of which is now biodynamically certified; 10 hectares of it is the Calvert Vineyard, which Felton Road has leased since 2001.

'We initially started with organics and moved towards biodynamics as a gradual conversion.

'You don't want to go cold turkey because that's quite risky. It takes time to figure out how to manage the soil and the vines' vigour. You can really shock plants, which are vulnerable when their growing environment changes dramatically. It has to be gradual.'

Walter knows more than a little about working with the land, having grown up in the rural Waikato on his parents' farm. It was always his intention to find a career in which he could work at least part of the time outdoors and so, when he left school, Walter decided to study horticulture. In a roundabout and unexpected sort of fashion, this led to viticulture and winemaking while he was studying for a four-year degree at Lincoln University in Canterbury.

The exciting bits happened in the third year. He was offered a student exchange in either California or Oregon. He accepted the latter, moved there and inadvertently became involved in what has proven to be a highlight of his learning journey: being part of a wine sensory evaluation panel.

'Wine wasn't really on my radar until I got to Oregon where there was a professor who was looking for panellists for sensory evaluation, so there was me and a couple of other Kiwis on this panel. We'd meet three times a week and then socially to taste wines and that's how I first started,' he says.

He recalls a lazy Susan in the middle of the sensory evaluation table, packed to its retro gills, so to speak, with a bunch of 'samples' of grass clippings, jam, spices, pepper and other aromatic examples of everyday 'smells'.

'You'd smell all these aroma samples, then they would bring the wines out and you would evaluate them. We had to say, "In that wine it's blackberry or raspberry", and identify exactly what was the predominant aroma in the wine.

'If there was an outlier on the panel they would have to explain themselves, and then the person leading the panel would be essentially calibrating everyone. After the sensory analysis we met socially on Friday afternoons, and a lecturer would buy different wines. We knew over the series of the term that there would be an expensive wine. One day there was a bottle we knew cost a couple of hundred bucks.

'It was Domaine de la Romanée-Conti La Tâche, 1985. It really threw me

'IT REALLY THREW ME THAT YOU COULD HAVE THIS WINE THAT WAS SO MUCH MORE EXPENSIVE AND A LOT OF PEOPLE IN THE ROOM DIDN'T THINK IT WAS ANY BETTER.'

that you could have this wine that was so much more expensive and a lot of people in the room didn't think it was any better. It was my second wine, but it wasn't one of those moments which really blew me away because I had no reference point. It did pique my interest and made me completely intrigued by the diversity of wine.'

Returning to Lincoln University for his final year, Walter began a sensory evaluation panel based on the same model he had learnt about in the States. It set him up as a technical expert on wine sensory evaluation.

When he returned he completed the postgraduate oenology classes while finishing an Honours degree in horticultural science. During that final year his professors allowed him to specialise in wine science and sensory evaluation. They liked what he had told them about the quantitative descriptive analysis panel in Oregon and helped him to set one up based on the same model.

Part of those studies included making four experimental wines: all Pinot Noirs, two from Larcomb Vineyard and the other two from St Helena Vineyard in Canterbury. At Larcomb he was looking at the differences between grapes grown under bird netting and those without the netting.

'I looked at the properties this had on the sensory taste of the wine, and I also separated different clones of Pinot Noir from St Helena Vineyard. While I wasn't able to obtain any significant differences within the two vineyards, I did manage to get significant results for Larcomb and St Helena.

'There was a large ripeness difference between the two wines. One was 11 per cent alcohol; the other was 14 per cent, but I couldn't get my panellists to pick up the difference, so I gave them neutral alcohol samples at 5, 10 and then 15 per cent and immediately I got a significant result. They were then able to give me a statistically significant result that the St Helena Vineyard wine tasted lower in alcohol than the Larcomb one. It was coming at wine technically and it was quite geeky, but, for me, I view it as a nice basis to train your palate and think about being statistically significant about what you're tasting.'

His analytical approach lasts to this day.

'When I do tastings at the winery now, we always blind taste and when I'm tasting with Todd, my assistant, we'll always refer to our notes about how we saw the wine last time so that we can see if we're consistent and can reproduce ourselves.'

It's key to the evolution and understanding of Central Otago Pinot Noir, he says.

'We know from all the blind tastings we do that we can't identify clonal characteristics of different Pinot Noirs, so we'll admit to that.'

It's one thing to see and taste marked flavour and character differences between clones, but pinpointing them in a blind tasting is another thing

---

'IT WAS COMING AT WINE TECHNICALLY AND IT WAS QUITE GEEKY, BUT, FOR ME, I VIEW IT AS A NICE BASIS TO TRAIN YOUR PALATE . . . '

altogether. Some say they can; Walter would like to 'at some point'.

Practice makes perfect and he's certainly dedicated to that at work tastings and in his leisure time, when he enjoys a personal wine collection consisting mostly of burgundies, because it's the best way to look at the types of wines he aspires to make.

THE GEEKY APPROACH

Has Walter ever been tempted to study for the Master of Wine qualification?

'Never. I completely admire everyone who attempts it and especially those who succeed. I think the challenge would be astronomical. I'm not tempted at all because I'm just not into the academic side of it that much. I spend so much time with wine, I'd rather be learning to fly or restore my little car in my free time than to have to spend more time on wine.'

The car certainly is little. It's a 1955 Messerschmitt, created by the German aircraft makers at a time when a push was on to construct cars which used less fuel, due to the Suez Crisis. Originally his dad's, the Messerschmitt sat in the shed at home on the farm while Walter pestered his father to repair it. Eventually, he caved in. Rather than fix the car, he passed its tiny reins on to Walter.

With long hours during vintage each year and extensive travel in winter months, the bubble car is a long-term project. As is Walter's love of great wine.

His first taste of the world's most expensive Pinot Noir — Domaine de la Romanée-Conti, when he was in Oregon — may not have set his fledgling wine taste buds on fire at the time, but it wasn't long afterwards that top wines did.

The first mind-blowing tasting moment he recalls was with fellow winemaker Marcel Giesen, who has been something of a mentor.

'Working for Marcel Giesen was really formative in terms of tasting wine because he was very generous with his cellar. In my early days of winemaking, he shouted me to go to a fancy-pants tasting in Christchurch, of 1990 Bordeaux reds, so I got exposed to the great wines of the world early on and have great respect for them.'

The fancy-pants tastings continued the next year when he went to California to work for Newton Vineyard, where he regularly drank — and enjoyed — Coche-Dury, Leflaive and Lafon. These top white burgundies are regarded as being among the greatest Chardonnays in the world. He also took regular road trips up to Oregon, where he got better acquainted with his favourite wine, Pinot Noir.

Ironically, the first Pinot Noir he fell for was from Central Otago, but the first time he tasted it was in Oregon when winemaker Rudi Bauer brought it to him there.

'Rudi brought the 1990 Rippon Pinot Noir over when I was living in the States; I remember tasting it with my friends in Oregon and being completely blown away by its clarity and brightness. I was astounded. When I came back to New Zealand, Rudi regularly brought out the 1991 and 1992 Rippon Pinots to taste; those were really landmark wines.

'They're made from a unique vineyard site on the shores of Lake Wanaka, and they take a lot of careful farming. Rudi was approaching the viticulture —

growing the grapes — and the winemaking with a European attitude, which was quite rare in New Zealand at the time. It's like a respect for the vineyard and what it's capable of, not trying to push the wine to something that might fit in with the ideals of a New World winemaker. At that time most New Zealand winemakers were probably largely influenced by Australian winemaking and took a trophy-focused approach, whereas Rudi looked at things differently.'

THE FELTON FEELING

It's similar to the approach at Felton Road winery today, where Nigel Greening understands the fine wine business of the world, having been born and bred in the United Kingdom, before moving out to live permanently in New Zealand in 2009.

'Nigel's not coming to wine with a big business model in mind and saying something along the lines of, "Well, if we buy 10 tonnes of grapes we can make a large amount of wine and it's going to give me a certain amount of profit. He wants to make the best wine we can, doing what we need to in order to achieve that.'

Naturally, high quality all the time is a challenge, given that in some years the spring or autumn in Central Otago can reduce the crop — and therefore the profit. That's not the most challenging aspect of the winemaking for Walter, though, who says the focus of aiming for the top presents the greatest work and the greatest rewards.

'We don't have a sales or marketing manager; it's all me. That's how a fine wine estate is run. I get a real kick out of the whole sales side of it, making sure our wines are going to the right places around the world. Being on the ground and putting that time in is the biggest challenge, purely because it's a lot of work.'

Both the winemaking and the selling of it on trips around the world stand in stark contrast to Walter's upbringing, where wine was an absolute rarity.

He only recalls a bottle of wine ever appearing on the family dinner table at Christmas time or perhaps another special occasion. Even then, the only discussion about that wine would turn to how to pronounce it; Gewürztraminer was a particularly tricky case in point.

Then there was his teenage experience of wine: Marque Vue, 'Which would have been lucky if it had any grapes in it!'

'My folks would have cask wine with their friends for barbecues but never bottles. Now I look after them; I always make sure I send them a ton of wine, so they are never short of good wine to drink.'

COLLABORATING WITH CENTRAL'S WINEMAKERS

Blair Walter's role as deputy chair (and a founding director for 10 years now) of Central Otago Pinot Noir Limited (COPNL) is a chance for him to play second fiddle to fellow winemaker Rudi Bauer, who is chair of the winemakers' association.

COPNL was formed 10 years ago to host wine events in the United States, the United Kingdom and around the world where Central Otago wines are sold.

'Our aim with the Central Otago Pinot Noir Celebration is to bring

leading influencers of the wine world together and we wanted a joint entity of winemakers in Central Otago who would work closely together. That collaborative approach of sharing information and resources defines our region. I am deeply passionate about our region and remain firmly committed to Central Otago maintaining and building on its premium image.

'There's a spark that ignites every time we bring people here, and the results are that people see us working together rather than being competitive with each other.

'We're somewhat unique in Central Otago in that we're all similar-sized businesses here. Almost all the winemakers are also the decision makers. Largely, it's the young guys who are inspired by great wines and we've all worked in Oregon, Burgundy and California, so we're all coming at it from the same angle. We're not trying to downsize big operations by making them sound cutesy; we've only ever known small and cutesy.'

WHAT NEXT FOR CENTRAL?

Vine age springs to mind, for Walter, who says most of the region's successful wines have been made from vines that are relatively young — generally 10 years old and even less, with few exceptions.

'We don't know yet the quality differences we're going to get off 20-plus-year-old vines, which will still be a few years away, but it's coming.'

More importantly, viticultural expertise and commitment finally exists in the region.

'Until the last few years, the grape-growers tended to be farmers rather than dedicated viticulturists with expert knowledge, but now there's a real cross-pollination with overseas winemakers and grape-growers bringing new ideas, years of experience and a great deal of knowledge into our region.'

Walter predicts there'll be an increasing emphasis on small top-quality brands in the region. In early 2012, examples already included the relatively new wines from Burn Cottage, Doctors Flat, Charteris and Sato, among a small clutch of other experienced winemakers focusing on making relatively minuscule amounts of high-end wines. These are labels to capture people's attention and encourage them to take the next step up in their wine drinking, not only by paying more but by drinking more interesting wines as a result.

CENTRAL OTAGO'S SUB-REGIONS

Ask Walter if there are still unexplored areas in the region for successful grape growing and his immediate answer is: 'Not really.'

There are, he adds, probably still some great sites that are tied up in a greater land ownership situation where it's difficult to separate off a great little 4-hectare patch of prime grape-growing land. In time, such special slivers of land may become available. But in terms of finding a significantly large-sized new area, he doubts it.

'I don't see another Bannockburn or a similar-sized promising sub-region on the horizon anywhere around here. The chances are slim, at best.'

GEOGRAPHY OR FLAVOUR?

The Gibbston Special Character Zone was registered in May 1988 with the Queenstown Lakes District Council as a region with special character. The Gibbston is relatively well defined because it is so easy to do so; geography being the dramatic rocky feature it is in Central, this special character zone begins just after Lake Hayes on the Queenstown side and ends at Nevis Bluff. The trouble is, should Gibbston include vineyards and wineries on the margins of these areas — or not?

Walter is adamant that boundaries need to be drawn on maps before flavours are defined in wine.

'We don't need to spend too much time saying a Bendigo wine is different from a Bannockburn wine from a Lowburn wine and so on. Not yet. I think we need to define the boundaries first. We call our Felton Road Pinot Noir 'Bannockburn'. We are calling it that to give it a name, to tell people where it's from, not what it tastes like.'

TWO PRINCESSES — WHO WILL BE QUEEN?

Two white princesses vie for the crown of queen wine in Central Otago. They are Chardonnay and Riesling. Which is more likely to sit on the great white throne?

'Chardonnay,' says Walter.

'Without a doubt. We can do some good Rieslings and the style that we champion, which is lighter bodied and intensely flavoursome white — verging on the German *spätlese* style — is lovely. There's always interest in those wines and there are dry versions, which are probably more sellable and easier for most people to understand. The Rieslings of Central Otago are of world class. They are recognised widely, but in the long term I think Chardonnay is a hell of a lot easier and more pleasurable to have on the dinner table.'

It's also easier for most wine drinkers to identify with, having a reputation for being consistently dry and full bodied, as opposed to Riesling's roller coaster of bone dry, medium, verging on sweet and then intensely sweet; its extraordinary versatility is both its calling card and its Achilles' heel.

'Yes Chardonnay is more popular but it also has the ability to stand out as a world-class white wine from Central. I just don't think we've been putting the effort into it as a region, so Chardonnay is a more difficult sell because it's a more competitive market with so many out there.'

'THE RIESLINGS OF CENTRAL OTAGO ARE OF WORLD CLASS. THEY ARE RECOGNISED WIDELY, BUT IN THE LONG TERM I THINK CHARDONNAY IS A HELL OF A LOT EASIER AND MORE PLEASURABLE TO HAVE ON THE DINNER TABLE.'

BLAIR'S GO-TO WINES

'Chablis because I can afford it. It probably sounds boring, but it's fun to keep track of what white and red burgundies taste like and the evolution in their flavour and style.' Even after-hours, at night when he pulls out a bottle of wine, Walter says it's not nearly as relaxing as it used to be: 'It is work for me.'

And yet, he does drink wine every day: Rhône reds such as Châteauneuf-du-Pape are also regulars on Blair and his wife Erin's table. 'I'd like to drink more Spanish wine, and I know very little about Italian wine, but I'm keen to drink more. I taste widely when I'm travelling overseas and have made a lot of somewhat random but special friends all over the world, due to the wine thing. It's a surprising fringe benefit.'

TOP WINES FROM BLAIR WALTER AT FELTON ROAD

- 2010 Felton Road Pinot Noir Block 3
- 2010 Felton Road Chardonnay Block 2

PATRICK MATERMAN

PERNOD RICARD NEW ZEALAND, MARLBOROUGH

'For the 10 years I have known Patrick and seen him rise from trainee winemaker to assistant winemaker, senior winemaker and now chief winemaker, the one common thread is that he still gets his hands dirty each vintage and not just with pen ink. Regardless of the increasing business responsibilities over the years, Patrick remains a winemaker at heart.'

— Philip Bothwell, former national wine ambassador, Pernod Ricard New Zealand

GREATEST ACHIEVEMENT

'My greatest personal achievement is becoming a dad for the first time; never been so proud! My greatest professional achievement is working for New Zealand's number-one wine company for over 22 years.'

KEY ACHIEVEMENTS

- Chief Winemaker for Brancott Estate from January 2010, being promoted from Marlborough regional winemaker.
- New Zealand Winemaker of the Year in 2001, *Winestate* magazine.

TAKE TO A DESERT ISLAND . . .

'I've had the good fortune to visit a few desert islands and there's something pretty magical about visiting those white sand beaches with their palm trees.

I'd say Marlborough Sauvignon Blanc because it's fresh and uplifting. The practicality of the screwcap would make sending a message in a bottle more likely to make it there dry.'

THE STORY

You can take winemaker Patrick Materman out of Marlborough but you cannot take Marlborough out of Materman. Since he moved to Marlborough in 1994, his heart has found its home in New Zealand's biggest wine region.

His job is one of the most marketing-driven winemaker roles of any in New Zealand, a role removed from the hands-on side of winemaking where you get to don a pair of gumboots one minute and use the lab kit the next. These days his role is as much about promoting wine as it is about defining its taste.

He moved to Marlborough to work as an assistant winemaker for Montana Wines and in 2010 he accepted the new challenge as chief winemaker for the company (now Pernod Ricard New Zealand). The shoes he had to fill were a large, well-respected pair previously belonging to Jeff Clarke, who was chief winemaker for 20 years.

Although in his new role Materman is less involved with day-to-day winemaking, he is actively involved in blending finished wines; he is keen, though, he emphasises, not to micro-manage those in the winemaking team. He has enough to keep him occupied with the work of educating new and existing markets about New Zealand wine, and in particular Marlborough Sauvignon Blanc, with the aim of helping build export markets. Materman is on a quieter mission, too: to demystify wine for those who consume it.

SEA OF SAUVIGNON BLANC

'Oversupply has been our biggest challenge in recent years. There's no doubt the last two or three years have been challenging, affecting profitability for growers and winemakers. Oversupply has created an element of bulk wine being sold offshore supplying private labels. There has been very little price erosion with our branded wines in export markets despite competing against other private labels, but essentially what's created the whole thing is not so much the scale of the industry but the rate of growth in the past decade. The rate of production growth was not matched with expanding existing export markets or developing new markets.

'Because New Zealand is not regulated the way places such as France are, supply and demand have easily gotten out of balance. We've come a long way in a short period of time and regulations haven't hampered progress. The

'THE RATE OF PRODUCTION GROWTH WAS NOT MATCHED WITH EXPANDING EXISTING EXPORT MARKETS OR DEVELOPING NEW MARKETS.'

downside, however, has been that supply and demand were not aligned.'

Supermarkets have been well placed to capitalise on industry oversupply, but their wine sales are a double-edged sword, says Materman. On one hand they have spoilt the consumer for choice and grown wine sales. On the other, supermarket wine sales have created an unrealistic long-term expectation for wine drinkers. 'I would like to see more stable pricing of wine. So many sales are driven by promotion; 90-odd per cent of all wine in this country is sold on promotion, and to me that's not realistic. I can't think of any other country in the world where you expect to see 50 per cent off the recommended price of wine.'

NEED FOR INNOVATION

With the industry back in balance after the 2012 vintage, Materman wants to see less complication in the wine world.

'We alienate some consumers because of complicated wine labels, unimaginative wine packaging and traditional wine closures. I'm bored with wine packaging where there are pretty much only three bottle shapes and only one main wine bottle size: 750 ml. I'd like to see more creativity, perhaps 500-ml wine bottles and far more innovation in design.'

He's right, of course, unless you're talking about Italy's traditional Verdicchio di Matelica or Castelli di Jesi, or Moscato di Scanzo and its enormous range of *passito*-style wines, the best of which generally stay within Italy. In the wine world at large, there is rarely any variation in bottle shape, size or design. The original 750-ml bottle was the result of a lungful of air. Now that bottles are no longer mouth-blown by glassblowers, why stick to that size?

Alternative closures on sparkling wine bottles are also important to Materman, whether in a form of screwcap — which works on sparkling at full pressure — or something altogether new and innovative to replace cork.

PLAYING TO NEW ZEALAND'S STRENGTHS

Another market opportunity is style, says Materman. He is a long-term fan of medium-dry Rieslings, which he knows consumers enjoy when they get to drink them — despite the unfashionability of Riesling. And it's not only Riesling that can capture people's taste buds in an off-dry wine.

'Many wine drinkers think they don't like sweet flavours. In reality there's a big part of the market which does like wine that is slightly sweeter and softer than traditional dry wines. We have the ability in New Zealand to make

'WE'RE ONLY AT THE BEGINNING OF THE JOURNEY WITH PINOT NOIR.'

intensely aromatic wines and there is the opportunity to make wonderful blended aromatic wines, both whites and reds.

'They won't always be off-dry, but the whites especially lend themselves to that, at times.'

As a red case in point, Materman suggests Ata Rangi Célèbre, a red blend which is happily more than the sum of its individual parts — Syrah, Merlot, Cabernet Sauvignon all get along quite nicely together in Célèbre but fare less well as standalones from Martinborough, where the wine comes from.

Since aromatic grape varieties grow best in pretty cool climates, Muscat and Gewürztraminer are also grapes that Materman would like to work with to create sophisticated blends — 'not overtly sweet wines, but wines which carry good balance and acidity, which our climate in New Zealand delivers'.

In a drier fashion, he loves the perfume of Central Otago Pinot Noirs, a factor that comes from the cool climate they grow in. 'We're only at the beginning of the journey with Pinot Noir. We planted Pinot Noir at the same time as Sauvignon Blanc, but it obviously took longer to catch up'.

He remembers being impressed by an early example of Gisborne Pinot Noir, in the 1980s, although admits that 'I didn't know then what I know now. My first real experience with Pinot Noir was visiting Martinborough in 1989 and being seduced by its charm.'

It wasn't until 1996 that Materman had the opportunity to work with Pinot Noir himself. In doing so he discovered a red variety that worked wonders in Marlborough's cool climate where Bordeaux red varieties struggle.

All of which highlights the infancy of the New Zealand wine industry.

STEPS INTO WINE

Materman was six when he decided to grow flowers for a living; it was the result of a Dutch father's influence, he jokes. He studied horticulture at Massey University after secondary school, but changed focus from flowers to wine partway through his degree.

'It was only after university that I wrote to every winery in Western Australia looking for work. This was largely spurred on by my love of windsurfing, and it looked like the perfect place for that! I didn't get a job in WA, but door knocking at Montana Wines landed me a two-month job as a cellarhand in 1990.'

That job held him as a trainee in Auckland till 1994 when he moved to Marlborough. At the time there were just three winemakers, compared with six today — and a team of assistants. Müller-Thurgau no longer rules the vineyard roost now, as it did then, and Chardonnay is no longer in second place either. Sauvignon Blanc is numero uno in the New Zealand vineyard and still growing in its percentage share of the vineyard, and Pinot Noir is number two. Materman wants to see the vineyard become slightly more mixed.

WHAT'S NEXT?

'I'm backing Sauvignon Gris in a major way; it plays on Sauvignon as a name and people know "Gris" from Pinot Gris, but in terms of taste, it's distinctly New Zealand — and it offers a good export opportunity that's slightly different.'

In terms of production scale, there are no other significant new grape varieties, but he's keen to see more variation. Grape varieties from the cooler northern Italian regions appeal due to their potential compatibility with New Zealand's climate. New Zealand has looked largely to France for grape varieties, but Italy also has numerous suitable strains. One of interest is the red grape, Refosco, from the north-east. Its ability to yield a high crop makes it commercially useful and it has high acids and fruity flavours, all of which have easy appeal for New Zealanders. And it has good resistance to autumn rains and rot, potentially perfect for 'the land of the long white cloud'. The most respected variation of it is known as Refosco dal Peduncolo Rosso; named after its red stem.

Three warmer climate, more noble Italian red grapes that have already been tried — and not thrived — in Marlborough are Nebbiolo, Barbera and Sangiovese.

'When we tried these grapes here we struggled to ripen them, and the acid levels were 18–20 grams rather than a desired 7–8 grams. It's a shame but it seems too cold here for those grapes.

'Syrah might have a future in Marlborough, if grown on the right soils and at appropriate crop levels with a view to making high-quality wine,' says Materman.

'There will always be some fringe varieties. I think it's good to be adventurous and we need that. But there's no doubt that Sauvignon Blanc will continue to lead the charge with Pinot Noir.'

BUBBLES

Fizz began as a top-shelf French collaboration with Champagne Deutz from France. Now the massive Marlborough sparkling winemaking facility is finding new expressions. Well, one mainly: sparkling Sauvignon Blanc.

It has been a massive success, surprising even Materman, who spearheaded it three years ago. It began as an add-on. Now it's bigger than Deutz.

So what's the future for Marlborough sparkling wine?

'Although we produce a very good méthode traditionnelle with Deutz, it's harder to create an international point of difference with that style. That's why we developed a sparkling Sauvignon Blanc. With its freshness and vibrancy it captures the essence of New Zealand wine. Under Brancott Estate, we believe it will drive future growth in sparkling wine for us.

'Sparkling Sauvignon Blanc gives us a unique New Zealand story, which is really well received internationally. We've created a sparkling Pinot Gris, too, under the Brancott Estate label, but I think there's a stronger story with Sauvignon Blanc.'

SELLING NEW ZEALAND

Selling strong stories is part of Patrick Materman's role as chief winemaker at Pernod Ricard New Zealand. In a time when the industry has been oversupplied, the need to build strong brands and create a point of difference with your wines has never been more important. The year 2010 was a hell of a time to take over as chief winemaker when oversupply was at its peak.

'Having to contend with the supply–demand balance has been quite a focus in the past couple of years. I wanted to make sure that the passion wasn't lost while industry balance was restored.'

PINOT NOIR MYTHS

Part of building New Zealand's wine reputation has been through launching New Zealand Pinot Noir to wine drinkers in countries where Sauvignon Blanc is the byword for Kiwi wine. It's a steep learning curve, both in marketing and back in the vineyard, where the wine is made.

'We're continuing to learn about Pinot Noir and the vineyard sites where we're growing it. Some sites haven't performed for Pinot Noir and have been replanted in varieties better suited to those soils.'

There have been big changes in canopy management with more intensive hand work rather than relying on less precise mechanisation.

The company is also putting more money and time into getting the grapes ripe by shoot-thinning vines more vigorously to lower crop levels, and it means more leaf removal; this is good for disease control and evening out the ripening process so that all grapes get to see the sun evenly.

HIGH- VERSUS LOW-PRICED PINOT

At the top end, quality is rising, thanks to more meticulous hand work in the vineyards. Better quality at the peak of the pyramid trickles down to lower-priced wines. But Pinot Noir at ultra-low prices is pretty much impossible. Cropping levels with Pinot Noir vary season to season, and they depend on the temperature and weather at flowering — at times cropping levels can be uneconomically low.

To make good Pinot Noir, cropping levels need to be low and the viticulture meticulous, but that all comes at a cost. That's why it's rare to see super cheap Pinot Noir in supermarkets. Like all New Zealand wineries and producers, Materman struggles to deliver a premium Pinot Noir with robust flavour and body for less than $15 a bottle. 'We've tried and found it very difficult at that price.'

It's a different story for Brancott Estate's Letter Series 'T' Terraces Pinot

Noir, first made in 2002. The Terraces Vineyard in Marlborough is an east-facing, sheltered hillside site in a region which traditionally has had few elevated vineyards, though the number is now growing.

The higher daytime temperatures on this site are due to it being sheltered rather than its elevation, which accounts for the cooler night-time temperatures. There is a wider day–night temperature difference or diurnal range. In theory, this means the grapes will have more pronounced flavours when grown this way. In practice, too, Brancott Estate's 'T' Pinot Noir sets a new high for the company, rising to join the steadily growing number of top red Pinots made in Marlborough.

'There's no reason to have a bad year of Pinot Noir, generally because it ripens so early, but it's about deciding whether the quality is there. If we have a bad year, we'll make less volume than we would have. We won't compromise on quality.'

NEW AREAS

Materman moved to the Awatere Valley in 1994. Today the valley has more planted vineyard area than the entire Hawke's Bay wine region, and Pernod Ricard's Triplebank Vineyard is sheltered from the wind, which winds its way around a bluff in a howling southerly, blowing straight over the top of the vines. Treelines have been established along the riverbank nearby to add more shelter in this rather windy valley. Planted on three levels, the Triplebank Vineyard has a range of soils, the areas with higher clay content targeted for Pinot Noir. It also has the longest growing season in Marlborough, mild winters giving early bud-burst, but cool summer temperatures created by its coastal location slow ripening.

'Awatere grapes add another layer of flavour to the wines we make, if we blend between sub-regions in Marlborough. Some of the most expressive wines come from areas where you push the extremes of the season. A long growing season builds intensity of flavour, and cooler regions yield higher natural acidity which, if balanced, can give an extra vibrancy to the wines. We like the flavours we get in wines from here, and they have a real brightness to them.'

The company first planted grapes there in 1999. The Sauvignon Blanc, Pinot Noir, Riesling and Pinot Gris first planted have now been joined by a smidgeon of Sauvignon Gris. And the valley is also where Materman has his own Sauvignon Blanc vineyard to manage. Materman, his partner, Leona, and their 18-month-old daughter, Zoe, have moved to a larger home in the Wairau Valley. As Materman spends at least 40 per cent of his time on the

road, he has precious little spare time, but his family — and the region — keep him grounded.

As well as his yachting hobby in the Marlborough Sounds, the knowledge he can drink a glass of Sauvignon Blanc while looking out over the vines and valley is one of the best things about living there. It's Materman's antidote to a busy life where work is increasingly outside of the winery these days.

'I love Marlborough; it's where the wine industry has really boomed, and it has changed the face of the region in a very positive way.'

PATRICK'S GO-TO WINES

'I drink according to the season. Summer is about Sauvignon Blanc to me, and that's what I drink most often. In winter, I enjoy Syrah — not Shiraz. I'm loving the Hawke's Bay Syrahs and really like the spice-driven expression. I also have a lot of respect for Church Road and Trinity Hill wines from Hawke's Bay. To me, there are good Syrahs emerging from other areas in Hawke's Bay, not just off the Gimblett Gravels. I'm liking what I see off soils a bit further inland from our Redstone vineyard, the grapes of which go into Church Road Reserve. I like Côte-Rôtie Syrah and the likes of Delas and Chapoutier, but in general I tend to drink more New Zealand wine than anything else. My year-round wine is Pinot Noir: it's a toss-up between Marlborough and Central Otago; the first one for its palate length and structure, the second for its seductive fragrance, which I love — but, of course, my first choice may perhaps be biased.'

TOP WINES FROM PATRICK MATERMAN

- Brancott Estate Letter Series 'T' Marlborough Pinot Noir
- Our yet-to-be-named ultra-premium Sauvignon Blanc

'The latter is near completion and is a new style of Marlborough Sauvignon Blanc with a focus on ageing potential and structural power. We need to continuously innovate and have a commitment and desire to create unique premium-quality wines that encourage differentiation and discovery, from the novice right through to the expert wine lover.'

ALAN BRADY MNZM

WINE PIONEER, CENTRAL OTAGO

'I worked with Alan both at Gibbston Valley and Mount Edward wineries. His winemaking was exacting in a belligerent, Irish sort of manner. He wanted perfection and wasn't afraid to tell you when he wasn't getting it — and there was always a beer at the end of the day.'

— Steve Green, Carrick winery

'While Alan's tenacity, determination and unwavering belief in our cohesiveness as a wine region is his most obvious legacy, it is the sense of pride he has instilled in Central Otago wine growers for which we owe him the most thanks.'

— Duncan Forsyth, Mount Edward co-owner and winemaker

In the spirit of going against the grain, the softly spoken Irish-born journalist Alan Brady was a key pioneer in creating the world's southernmost wine region, Central Otago. He arrived in New Zealand aged 23 to work at the *Manawatu Evening Standard* before moving to Dunedin to work at the *Otago Daily Times*, then worked at the New Zealand Broadcasting Corporation, where he later held the reins of news and current affairs when it became TVNZ.

He fell under wine's spell when he was looking for an escape from work, inadvertently creating more work for himself than he ever could have imagined. He remains the only person to date to have founded and built two wineries in Central Otago: Gibbston Valley and Mount Edward.

GREATEST ACHIEVEMENTS
- Made a Member of the New Zealand Order of Merit, 1996.
- Being around for the entire modern history of a new wine region.
- Establishing the first purpose-built winery in Central Otago (Gibbston Valley) in 1989–90, and 10 years later founding a second winery (Mount Edward) and being involved at the development phase of other new wine brands.
- Heart of the District Awards Civic Award 2006 for Outstanding Voluntary Service in the Queenstown Lakes District.

KEY ACHIEVEMENTS
- Sir George Fistonich Medal 2011 for services to the wine industry.
- Founding member and past president of Central Otago Winegrowers' Association.
- Board member of New Zealand Wine Institute, 1994–1996.

TAKE TO A DESERT ISLAND . . .
'A winemaker's worst nightmare is being condemned to a desert island with just one bottle of wine, so I'd have to take something to evoke nostalgic memories as I sat on the beach and prayed for rescue. I'd take a Pinot Noir, of course, one with age, which I could savour, lingeringly. It might be a 2000 Gibbston Valley Reserve Pinot Noir, the first in a line of Central Otago wines to win a major international trophy in London (Champion Pinot Noir London International Wine Challenge). Grant Taylor built those reserve Pinot Noirs to last and this one, with a high proportion of Gibbston grapes, would remind me of home. I'd probably also take a few vine cuttings, just in case I got stuck.

'And I might take my friend Ed Lamont, owner of the Mt Soho winery and event centre near Arrowtown. We did vintage together once. Ed wanted to reinvent everything and I decided I'd rather be his friend than his winemaker. He's an incredibly talented engineer and it wouldn't be long before we were living in some comfort, using things he'd invented from flotsam and jetsam. And we'd have a lot of laughs.'

ON MAKING WINE IN CENTRAL OTAGO
'Sharing the successes and failures, trials and tribulations of the early days with a bunch of passionate people who were determined to realise their dreams when the odds seemed against them.'

BIGGEST RISK EVER TAKEN WITH WINE?
'Standing on a plank atop a 3-metre-high fermenter to do punch-downs at the age of 75. Back in 1981, winemaking was an exciting step into the unknown, but I never considered I'd taken a risk planting those first vines or going solo as a winemaker when I built Mount Edward. Every season is an adventure and some risk goes with the territory.'

THE STORY

Central Otago. A name which conjures up stinking hot summer camping holidays, rugged mountain walks and brave swims around edges of chilly lakes rather than a wine region with nearly all its eggs in one precarious basket: the Pinot Noir one.

The intense scent of wild thyme carries on the air in Central's summer months, casting its aromatic spell over visitors hoping to relax in the region's wild beauty. For journalist Alan Brady, it held another hope: a change of lifestyle when he moved to Central to make wine in 1980.

Like any Dunedinite who drove to Central for regular weekend breaks, he was just looking for a change of pace. Burnt out with churning out news for TVNZ, based in Dunedin in those days, he was able to regain his sense of sanity and equilibrium on weekend trips to Central with his wife, Denise.

The jaw-dropping natural beauty of Central, its quiet solitude and the fantasy of a different way of life ensured the weekends gradually grew longer and the working weeks shorter. Slowly but steadily the Bradys moved away from even wanting to be in the city. The only trouble was: how would they survive in that environment?

Two wineries, a job in local journalism at the *Mountain Scene* newspaper and a book later, and Brady can finally answer the question: 'By taking the plunge and getting into a whole new industry and way of life.'

He was one of the first to plant grapes in the region and is the man behind one of the largest wineries there today — *the* largest for quite some time — Gibbston Valley; it's home today to an underground wine cellar (his idea also), a cheesery and a large restaurant, visitor and tasting centre.

'People say to me all the time, "You must have had such great vision to see all this," as they wave their arms towards the massive wineries, the small wine brands and all the vineyards and restaurants,' says Brady, adding, 'But I didn't see all this. Not at all.

'After starting Gibbston Valley Wines, I did believe Gibbston Valley would be full of vines one day, but at that early stage I didn't have any vision of Central Otago as a wine region. We were just peasant grape-growers who knew very little about what we were doing and found out as we were going along.'

The 'we' he speaks of is the small cluster of early winemakers who pioneered wine in the region. They include Lois and the late Rolfe Mills of Rippon Vineyard in Wanaka; Rob Hay, founder and still at the helm of the iconic Chard Farm winery; Sue and Verdun Burgess, who established Black Ridge Winery (now sold); the Grant family at William Hill winery; and Brady. None had grown grapes, made wine or even consumed much of it before they began doing all three in Central. What they had in common was a love of the stony beauty of the rugged region.

'The thing that's defined Central Otago is that we are a very collaborative bunch. We have been since the beginning because we had to be. We knew we were isolated, so we had to share ideas. We celebrated our successes and cried over our disasters together. That ethic, which Rolfe Mills and I were very strong about at the start, has seen Central develop as a region of winemakers who get along together and get things done by cooperating.'

'THE THING THAT'S DEFINED CENTRAL OTAGO IS THAT WE ARE A VERY COLLABORATIVE BUNCH. . . . WE CELEBRATED OUR SUCCESSES AND CRIED OVER OUR DISASTERS TOGETHER.'

HOW IT HAPPENED

Brady and his second wife (also called Denise) bought a characterful and dilapidated former stone staging post in 1977. Originally a place where coaches once changed their horses on their way to the goldfields in the 1800s, it was full of dust, rodents and dead possums. They planned to clear out the possums, hook up running water and create their own weekend asylum in a place of their own, four hours away from city life in Dunedin. There was never a plan to live there permanently, much less to make a living off the land, but each weekend as they began to feel less like leaving to go 'home' to the city and more like living on the land, they began looking for work in Central. It wasn't exactly easy, says Brady, because neither of them had made a living off primary production before, so many ideas came and went, gooseberries and grape-growing among them.

And since the grapes sounded more promising than the gooseberries, by 1981 they had planted their first experimental vines. They planted more the following year, 1982. It was one of Central Otago's first vineyards in the Gibbston Valley and, a year later, these vines were history. Parched and dehydrated, they died an arid death on the unirrigated rocky landscape.

VINOUS BEGINNINGS

The irony of this loss was that it cut the dire Müller-Thurgau out of the picture early on. Never a grape to set the world on fire, Müller-Thurgau was not one which would have given Central winemakers the same wow factor they later gained from Pinot Noir — not least because Müller-Thurgau is a cross rather than a pure *Vitis vinifera* grape, belonging to the wine grape family. Also known as Rivaner, Müller-Thurgau was created in the 1880s by crossing the noble Riesling grape with the ignoble Madeleine Royale. The aim was to come up with a high-cropping Riesling style, which tasted great and gave good profit margins through large yields. The result was insipid, bland and confused in taste. It was the backbone of the New Zealand wine industry throughout the 1980s — climbing to 20,740 tonnes in 1986, the country's biggest tonnage for any grape — but thankfully by the early 1990s it was in decline as Chardonnay took over at number one. It is now Sauvignon Blanc, of course, which is another story told in these pages.

Müller-Thurgau wasn't the only interloper that Brady tried in those early days. There was the relatively bland Chasselas grape, also known as Edelzwicker in Alsace, France, where it's pretty much dying out. And the experimental initial cocktail of grape varieties also included Cabernet Sauvignon and Pinotage — 'Thank goodness that's gone. It never ripened properly and was even worse

than the Cabernet in this climate!'

There was also Syrah/Shiraz and Merlot. More recently, Tempranillo has been trialled: 'Not bad, but certainly not Spanish in style.'

An eternal optimist, he also planted later-ripening grape varieties that would have a chance of surviving in a climate with searing hot summer temperatures which lasted only a relatively short time, stretching the entire season out to a late-ish one, in terms of ripening. The successful grapes he planted included Gewürztraminer, Riesling, Pinot Gris and Pinot Noir.

'I think we were very fortunate back in the 1980s that Pinot Noir was one of those varieties that put its hand up, not through any expertise or vision of ours but because we had to try everything.'

Riesling was almost lost because it seemed untameable in the vineyard, until winemaker Grant Taylor came along, demonstrating how to prune it to deliberately take a lower crop. 'We didn't know what to do with Riesling and its acids were horrendous when we first planted it because it grew like a weed. Once we knew how to prune properly, and manage for lower yields, we could reduce acid levels and get a much better balance of sugar, acid and phenolics. Riesling could easily have been written off as a no-go variety whereas it's one of our best.'

SEARCHING FOR IDENTITY AND NEWCOMERS

Like Pinot Noir, Pinot Gris has always ripened easily in Central, although Brady suggests it's still searching for its regional identity: 'It's made in a range of different styles from rich and opulent to Grigio-like in style, lean and mean, but it has a market.'

Not so Gewürztraminer, which struggles to sell, so has never become big in Central Otago, despite the high historic notes it hit from the likes of Black Ridge, William Hill, Rippon Vineyard and Gibbston Valley wineries.

Along with an increasing focus on high-quality sparkling wines, newcomers today include Pinot Blanc, and also the Austrian grape Grüner Veltliner (also gaining ground in many Marlborough and North Island vineyards). The Austrian winemaker Rudi Bauer of Quartz Reef is a champion of Grüner Veltliner, but of New Zealand's early attempts at it, he says emphatically that nothing stands out, yet. 'We are really just playing with it so far, and it's way too early to say we can do it well as a country.'

FIRST VINTAGE

Brady's first vintage was 1985. He harvested a modest 60 kilograms of Pinot Gris and Chasselas, hardly enough to make a living from, but enough to bottle an experimental first run.

'We learned the hard way, by trial and error, and in the end that's not a bad way to learn when you are pioneering grapes and winemaking in a new region. We learnt that what works elsewhere may not apply in our conditions, we had to watch and observe what nature and our specific environment told us. That process should never stop; and we learned to work with nature and live by the rhythm of the seasons.'

That first vintage in 1985 might have been tiny, might have been a step off the shingly vineyard into the great unknown of winemaking and might not have been stellar, but it was made in consultation with Dr Rainer Eschenbruch, a scientist at the wine research centre at Te Kauwhata. And he was impressed enough by Brady's land and first wines to encourage him further into his new winemaking hobby.

By then Brady was smitten anyway. Winemaking was fun. That it also happened to be costly, time-consuming and a steep learning curve was part and parcel of life in Central. The challenges were not to be dismissed, however, as the death of his first few thousand vines attests to. Another spectacularly unfortunate near-loss occurred due to a visitor's accidental blunder, which set fire to the hillside on which Brady and his family lived. Thanks to the active volunteer fire brigade, it was quickly extinguished, but it served as another reminder of the importance of water in a place where there simply isn't much.

Lack of water is an ongoing issue in Central, as anybody who has ever tramped across its hillsides knows, let alone those trying to coax a living from plants growing on it.

STEP INTO THE VAT

By the end of 1984, Brady had written a proposal to plant a commercial vineyard, build a winery and create a tourist wine bar as part of the whole big plan. The next step was to take his proposal to a bank, get financial backing and begin a new business in late 1987. By the mid-1990s, the new business was thriving; and in that decade Gibbston Valley Wines became the biggest cellar-door operation in the country.

ROMANCE VERSUS REALITY

'Our whole industry is often driven by romantic notions of what wine is, whatever perspective you come into it from. The hard reality is marketing and it's the tough end of the process. It takes a lot of time creating a market. You've got to walk the walk, talk the talk and do the dinners. The winemaking season is followed by the travel season; it's part of what we do, part of the vineyard cycle. Most of us enjoy it. It's very rewarding to go out and meet the consumers around the world.'

What was the biggest challenge of pioneering winemaking in Central Otago?

For Brady there is no shortage of candidates to take the number one spot in the difficulty stakes: isolation, lack of capital, lack of knowledge, cynicism from wine experts further north are all among the tribulations, as is the lack of water in the region.

'We were down there at the bottom of the wine world; people coined phrases to describe us like "vineyards on the edge" and "the southernmost in the world", and few people in the north of the country gave us much chance of succeeding at the time,' Brady remembers.

And Central Otago did seem to be an awfully long way from the rest of the grape-growing world. But it was the first place Brady felt at home in New Zealand.

In his own book, *Pinot Central: A Winemaker's Story*, Brady describes gazing across the rocky blue vastness from Alexandra to the distant Hawkdun Mountains and feeling a stronger sense of belonging than at any time since he had left Ireland's emerald shores several decades earlier.

That sense of connection to place was something all of the region's pioneering winemakers shared. Their common love of the region spilled into their collaborative way of working. Together they learnt about winemaking. Together they shared ideas, equipment and knowledge. And in this strangely uncompetitive and collaborative fashion, they began to unlock the secrets of growing grapes in the stunningly beautiful but challenging environment in which they found themselves. Despite what the soothsayers further north said, getting enough heat to grow grapes wasn't the problem. Getting enough water in this extremely arid region most definitely was. The geographic remoteness from the rest of the wine industry was both a help and a hindrance.

'We never let it bother us particularly. We had determination and stubbornness to plow on regardless.

'Many in the north were a bit patronising because they thought it was too cold down here — most of them had never been down here.'

In hindsight, Brady says the region would have benefited from not growing quite as quickly as it has. It would also have benefited if there had been more emphasis on growing winemaking facilities as well as planting vineyards, he suggests.

BRADY'S EARLY WINE LIFE

Brady's earliest experiences of alcohol erred on the dry side; he grew up in a teetotal household where alcohol's evils were regular proclamations. Not that such a trifle stopped him being just as compelled as most teenagers to discover the truth for himself.

It was in the 1960s and 1970s that he got into wine, and this meant exploring the liquid delights of Cresta Dore, Bakano, Blue Nun and Liebfraumilch, with the odd bottle of Chianti in a *fiasco* (basket) or Mateus Rosé thrown in for good measure.

'Back then you thought you were pretty sophisticated if you drank wine at all, but I don't think we really tasted it, and we certainly didn't know much about how it was made or where it came from.'

'I SUDDENLY GOT WHAT GREAT PINOT WAS ABOUT: THE ELEGANCE, THE SUBTLETY, THE INTRIGUE. IT SEARED ITSELF ON MY MEMORY.'

His first serendipitous wine moment came in the late 1980s, by which stage he was already immersed in making the stuff.

In those early days of Central Otago as a wine region, the small group of winemakers and enthusiasts met regularly for tastings at Treetops restaurant in Sunshine Bay, Queenstown — which, yes, in fact had a tree growing through it. It was owned and operated by Leon Udy, who ran a good restaurant, had an eclectically stocked wine cellar and a wealth of wine knowledge, but didn't suffer fools gladly; if anyone arrived at the restaurant and Udy didn't like the look of them, they were swiftly turned away.

It was on a Sunday afternoon at Treetops when a wine stopped Brady in his tracks and led to 'a fatal obsession for Pinot Noir' — that wine was Domaine de la Romanée-Conti Échézeaux, a member of the world's most expensive stable of burgundies. 'I don't remember the vintage, but it would have been 12 or 15 years old at the time, making it from the early 70s.

'That wine triggered senses in me which had never been used before. It was like an awakening. I suddenly got what great Pinot was about: the elegance, the subtlety, the intrigue. It seared itself on my memory.'

BURGUNDIAN COMPARISONS

'Over the years Central Otago has developed links with Burgundy, regarded by most of us as the historic birthplace of great Pinot Noir. But I'm uneasy about making comparisons. We're on a different latitude, we have different soils and climates, and these two factors alone ensure our wines will be different.

'We have learned a lot from Burgundy about their traditions, their passion, their viticulture and oenology. But essentially we make Central Otago Pinot Noir not red burgundy. We must always remember that.

'Having said that, we should go on learning from Burgundy and the other great Pinot-producing regions of the world, just as they are now learning from us. One thing we need to focus on in the future is the development of more small to medium winemaking facilities, which are linked directly to the vineyards — family or small company-owned operations on the Burgundy model, where you get a total commitment at both ends of the cycle, from growing grapes to marketing and selling the wine.

'Our region would not have grown as quickly as it has without contract winemaking, and the big operations in Cromwell, the Central Otago Wine Company and Vinpro do a superlative job. But while we have over 100 producers in the region we still only have about 25 wineries, and I would love to see that imbalance corrected.

'I believe it will happen. Already we have a second generation of Central

Otago winegrowers. Nick Mills has taken over from his parents at Rippon Vineyard, and he has sons of his own. Mount Difficulty is another example, it's a big company, but the Dicey family now has two sons in key positions. Chard Farm is also probably destined to become a family dynasty, and it might even happen with me, with my daughter and son-in-law perhaps picking up where I leave off.'

FUTURE CHALLENGES

'There's no room for mediocre wines.

'I've never been a great crystal-ball gazer. I've been more focused on personal goals rather than making predictions, but we will continue to see the development of sub-regions in Central Otago. I just don't think we can draw definite lines around those areas at this stage.

'If we start drawing definite sub-regional lines we will start getting involved in the infighting that characterises Burgundy. We don't want that.

'Burgundy expert and Master of Wine Jasper Morris said two years ago, "It's time to have that discussion but it's not time to draw the boundaries." I agree with him. I believe the vines and wines will tell us where the boundaries are. There are one or two exceptions to that, and one of them is Gibbston because we are already a geographical entity, and nobody can dispute where it begins and ends. Wanaka is also clearly defined because there are only one or two vineyards there, but in other areas it will be the wines that speak more clearly than people drawing lines on maps.'

BRADY'S BUNCH — THE WILD IRISHMAN

So what is Central Otago wine pioneer Alan Brady doing now?

Aside from being on the board of Felton Road winery and a shareholder at both Gibbston Valley and Mount Edward wineries, he makes two small single-vineyard Pinot Noirs; one from a block at Gibbston which is 480 metres above sea level and the other from a Felton Road vineyard, which sits at some 250 metres above sea level.

Both are branded with his Wild Irishman label and currently he makes them at the Coalpit Winery, 500 metres from where he lives. It's a personal, hands-on operation where he takes all the decisions and gets to indulge his interest in exploring the individuality of Central Otago's sub-regions.

'In the future, just as they have always done in Burgundy, I believe people will buy Central Otago Pinot Noir based on their preference for the characteristics of Gibbston, Cromwell, Wanaka and so on.'

ALAN'S GO-TO WINES

'Pinot Noir is at the top of my list because it has teased and tantalised me all my life. It's got me out of bed in the morning and woken me in the middle of the night worrying about frosts or what's happening in my barrels. Burgundy occasionally, when I can afford it, finds its way onto our dinner table, as do Cabernet Sauvignon, Shiraz and other reds, as well as Riesling from the Mosel, Alsace, Clare Valley and Central Otago. Our favourite Chardonnays are likely to come from Kumeu River, Te Mata, Neudorf, Felton Road, Chablis and Burgundy.

'I would love to have all the great examples of Pinot Noir from all the notable regions in the world, but I can't afford to. I have some good burgundies, some good Pinots from Martinborough and Canterbury, some Californian and Oregon examples.

'Do I have a favourite Burgundian sub-region? Volnay and Gevrey. I like Volnay because I think that Gibbston wines at their best can be similar in style: floral, elegant and supple. I love Gevrey because it makes more powerful wines but still very linear and elegant.

'I also enjoy Felton Road Block 5 and a wine that's made from the old vines at Gibbston Valley, the vines I planted 27 or 28 years ago. The old vines from this single vineyard deliver a wine that doesn't have to shout at you. From the oldest-producing vineyard in the region, it's a wine that has a sense of age and wisdom.'

Just like Brady, in other words.

TOP WINES FROM ALAN BRADY

- 2008 Wild Irishman Three Colleens Gibbston 2008
- 2008 Wild Irishman Bannockburn

'These were wines that delighted because of their purity and simplicity. I'm on a single-vineyard bent because I believe the purest expression of Pinot Noir is captured in wines that convey the essence of a specific site and year, which 2008 did effortlessly. What we got was charming wine reflecting the innocence of young vines and a year that was much better than most of us thought. Four years on they have hardly begun to age.'

Note: Mount Edward Wines was purchased by John Buchanan and Duncan Forsyth in 2004. Alan Brady retained a small shareholding until late 2011.

TERRY DUNLEAVY MBE

WINE VISIONARY, AUCKLAND

'From the mid-1970s Terry Dunleavy believed fervently that New Zealand could succeed in global markets at a time when very few others did. In his position as executive officer of the Wine Institute he was a one-man tour de force, cajoling and corralling a sometimes diverse winemaking community into coordinated investment into our key markets. He has left a legacy of co-operation and self-belief which remains an intrinsic part of our marketing to this day.'

— Philip Gregan, chief executive officer, New Zealand Winegrowers

GREATEST ACHIEVEMENT

'A toss-up between the May day in 1988 on the roof garden of the Kensington Events Centre in London when New Zealand was featured nation at the London Wine Trade Fair at only our second appearance; or the February day in 1990 when I was given the honour of proposing the toast to Her Majesty Queen Elizabeth at the Viticultural Field Day lunch, an event that I had been quietly working to achieve for the previous two years; or July 2009 when our exports topped $1 billion for the first time.'

KEY ACHIEVEMENTS

- First executive officer of the Wine Institute.
- Honoured as a Member of the British Empire (MBE) in 1990.
- Fellow of the Wine Institute of New Zealand in 1996.
- Awarded the George Fistonich Medal in 2007.

- Inducted into the New Zealand Wine Hall of Fame in 2009.
- Founding editor, *New Zealand Winegrower* magazine.
- Awarded Honorary Life Membership of the British-based Circle of Wine Writers in 2012.

TAKE TO A DESERT ISLAND . . .

'To stay the time distance, with a daily taste that would linger long and remind me of Godzone, a bottle of Mazuran's Port, circa 1960.'

THE STORY

Terry Dunleavy was a beer-drinking journalist when he joined the wine trade in 1971.

Fresh off the boat from living in Samoa for seven years where he had edited the weekly *Samoa Bulletin*, starred in a film with Gary Cooper and helped revive rugby football there — not to mention having five children while away — he was back home in New Zealand, managing a printing factory in Hawke's Bay. One of the factory's clients was Frank Yukich, founder and managing director of Montana Wines, who was unhappy about the fact his labels were not sticking to his wine bottles. Dunleavy came up with a solution; Yukich was impressed and offered him a job, selling Montana's 'finest' from Northland to the Bluff.

However, when we talk about 'finest', we are not speaking here of Marlborough Sauvignon Blanc, Hawke's Bay Merlot or West Auckland Chardonnay. Müller-Thurgau was barely out of diapers, Pinotage was in its absolute infancy and fortified wines ruled the roost the length and breadth of New Zealand — for anyone who drank local wine, that is. Few people did. The wine scene was mostly based in Auckland with a burgeoning number of grapes grown in Gisborne. Most New Zealanders drank beer, with the occasional 'sherry' or 'port' (New Zealand-made lookalikes) being consumed. Those who did drink local wine either made it or tended to live near to where it was made.

There was no Central Otago Pinot Noir. No joint wine marketing body. There were no wine exports. There were few licensed restaurants at which to drink wine. BYO was carefully concealed before being decanted into a teapot under the table at those restaurants whose owners understood their customers might want a glass of wine with a meal while they dined out.

There was wine in New Zealand, but not as we know it. And while Dunleavy's contribution to this country's wine has not been in making it, he brought his aspirations in journalism and politics to bear at a time when New Zealand wine was in dire need of change, growth and offshore marketing. Not that he had any idea his role was to be so pivotal to New Zealand wine when he accepted the job offer of national sales manager for Montana Wines, in 1971.

A MAN OF MANY CAREERS

It wasn't the first radical change in Dunleavy's career. His third career change happened after one morning tea break when he was just 20 years old and

working at the State Advances Office in Auckland, in 1948.

'I looked around the room at the miserable faces, listening to everybody complain about their jobs and realised they were all twice my age and I didn't want to be like them, so I left,' he says, recalling the epiphany which led him to walk out one day. His first career was a brief stint at welding — 'a disaster, definitely not me' — followed by a short time in the Royal New Zealand Air Force. But after leaving the State Advances Office, he says he knew exactly what he wanted to do: work as a newspaper journalist.

So he applied for a job he saw advertised as a reporter at the *Manawatu Evening Standard*. Two months later he was offered a less auspicious role as reporter at the *North Wairarapa Herald* in Pahiatua. The editor there had just lost his only reporter to the *Manawatu Evening Standard*, whose editor had poached him for the job Dunleavy applied for.

It was a long way from Queen Street, but after three years it led straight back to Auckland, where he began working as assistant editor of *New Zealand Sportsman*; 'I was lucky enough to work with the late Sir T. P. McLean, whose sports writing had earned him a knighthood. It was my dream job to work as a sports journalist.'

Then one night in a bar after work, he discovered there was a job going editing a newspaper in Samoa, so off he went with his wife Margaret and their eldest and only child at the time, Michael. They departed Auckland on 1 September 1951, returning home seven years later with another five children and a keen interest in politics. The island state, then known as Western Samoa, was in the run-up to independence, which was granted in 1961, and the chairman of his newspaper and printing company — effectively his boss — was prominent in Samoan politics. Dunleavy wrote parliamentary speeches and helped plan political events there.

BACK HOME

When he arrived back in New Zealand, Dunleavy moved to Wellington in 1958 to become the branch manager of a major print supply and ink manufacturing company, from which he was head-hunted two years later to become the Wellington representative of a Napier printing firm, Martin Print. This was where he first encountered wine and print together. Or not together, as the case may be, because in a campaign to increase the firm's involvement in the printing of bottled beverage labels he ended up winning the contract to print all labels for Montana Wines, on its way to becoming New Zealand's largest wine producer at the time.

'The contract was won after negotiation with Montana's dynamic managing director and wine visionary, Frank Yukich,' says Dunleavy.

'These were the days before self-adhesive labels and he was having trouble avoiding labels from curling with the wet glue which was being used on a variety of different paper stocks. I suggested to Frank that we switch to a wet-glue-compatible matt paper, with the grain running across the labels. I also suggested cost economies by standardising the label design, which enabled the company to save money by making product name changes only rather than

'THE CHALLENGES WERE HOW TO TURN THE MINDSET OF THE MAJORITY OF NEW ZEALANDERS AWAY FROM BULK WINE CONSUMPTION TOWARDS SEEING WINE AND FOOD AS NATURAL PARTNERS.'

---

having entirely different labels for its range of products. The consistency of label presentation also enhanced the company's brand on shop shelves because it made it easy to identify Montana wines.'

The solution worked, then Yukich offered him a job and in December 1971, the Dunleavy tribe shifted from Napier to Auckland, where he took up the position of national sales manager for Montana Wines.

WINE OFF TRACK

'The whole industry was living with the hangover of near prohibition earlier in the century and wineries like Corbans had been hamstrung with restrictive regulations on wine sales. In the case of Corbans, the company was able to make wine on one side of a railway line, but was only permitted to sell it on the other side of the tracks. Wine was tarred with the same brush as spirits and beer and the binge-drinking, six-o'clock-closing pub culture of the time,' says Dunleavy. 'But the New Zealand wine sector back then was one in which I could see first-hand both great potential and great challenges.'

The potential was the quality of some of the wines.

'The challenges were how to turn the mindset of the majority of New Zealanders away from bulk wine consumption towards seeing wine and food as natural partners, which could be enjoyed together without necessarily over-excessive consumption.'

Long after work, meetings with Yukich were regularly held over a glass or two of wine and this, says Dunleavy, was where 'our decisions were really made because it was more relaxed and we'd had time to think about what needed to be done'.

'I still have pages of notes I took at those meetings about the structures of the wine wholesale and retail trade as it was in the early and mid-70s. Large wineries had master agents and licensing trust shareholders to whom they sold, who in turn sold to smaller wholesale merchants; hotels and wine resellers could buy only from or through a merchant,' he says.

The margins between each level were fixed, as was the 20 per cent sales tax; paid at the wholesale level and a worry for wineries only on the odd occasions they sold direct to consumers.

'One of my jobs during my five years at Montana was revising the company's price-lists. There were always two: a wholesale list and a retail list. Pricing was a mixture of Frank advising me that prices needed to increase by a certain percentage followed by a close look at the lists of other wineries' prices. Wine lists from Corbans, McWilliams, Penfolds, Cooks and Villa Maria were

all compared line by line from the sherries, ports, sparkling wines, hocks, moselles, sauternes and burgundies to the clarets and, occasionally, an actual varietal wine made from a particular grape.'

PEARL AND COLD DUCK

Fortified wines made up more than half the volume of New Zealand wine in the 1970s, and two Montana products were especially popular: Pearl, an unashamedly off-dry sparkling wine in a voluptuous, heavy-bottomed bottle, and its subsequent follow-on sensation, Cold Duck, labelled as a mix of champagne and burgundy, which was an instant success because it was red, sweet and easy to drink, says Dunleavy.

'Those were good times. Competition was relatively gentle, wineries could make profits to finance their growth and keep shareholders happy; but three unrelated developments changed all that. The free marketeers in Dunedin and Christchurch began discounting and bypassing the wholesaler–retailer structure. Then there was the emergence of varietal table wines made from classical *Vitis vinifera* grapes, such as McWilliams Cabernet Sauvignon and Pinot Chardonnay, Corbans Pinotage and Riverlea Riesling, and one of the earliest of the cold-pressure-fermented varietals made from Müller-Thurgau, all of which rapidly revolutionised wine drinking. As did Montana Bernkaizler Riesling, which was slightly sweetened by the addition of unfermented Muscat juice.'

THE 1970S

There were three winery organisations in New Zealand in the early 1970s, none of which had any formal allegiance to any of the others, although their aims overlapped at many points.

'The Viticultural Association was headed by the revered George Mazuran and comprised virtually all small and medium-sized wineries, mostly Dalmatian. Then there was the New Zealand Wine Council, which comprised Corbans, Montana, Penfolds, Cooks and a few relatively small wineries, such as Collards, under the presidency of Alex Corban. And lastly there was the Hawke's Bay Winegrowers' Association, comprised only of McWilliams, which was ruled by the formidable Tom McDonald. Whenever wineries needed to engage with the government – which was frequent for any business back then — the three leaders would troop off to Wellington to confront whichever minister needed to be told of a wine-sector problem.'

Because of his close personal involvement with the National Party — including as a National candidate for Napier in 1969 — Yukich took Dunleavy to meetings of the Wine Council, held in the venerable Corban homestead at Henderson (now the Corban Estate Arts Centre). Yukich then handed Dunleavy the reins of Montana representation at the meetings.

At that time, Assid Corban (cousin of winemaker Alex Corban) was the council's secretary, but a year or so after Dunleavy's appointment, he stood down and, in default of anyone else, says Dunleavy, he was made secretary.

'This was just in time to become closely involved in finalising a submission to the government for an increase in import duties on overseas wines that Alex had initiated months before, which brought me in close contact with George Mazuran and his vice-president, Mate Brajkovich, as well as winemakers Tom McDonald and Alex.'

There was a deep desire for a single organisation at the time, says Dunleavy. Previous attempts had failed because of an inability to settle the key question of where the ultimate power would lie.

'As tariff meetings proceeded, Mate Brajkovich and I agreed we needed unification and could see the three organisations had much more in common than what members thought divided them. We spent days in Wellington attending a hearing before the Tariff and Development Board, then gave them plenty of evening time to talk about a single body and eventually it was agreed to canvass the proposal seriously.'

Corban and Dunleavy attended meetings of the Viticultural Association, but they were unable to dispel fears of some smaller wineries about dominance by the big companies.

'The breakthrough came when I suggested dividing members into categories based on size, allowing each to elect its own representatives, with key powers vested in the executive representatives. We talked it through to an executive of seven, comprising two members each from the small category, two from the medium, and three from the large, with the proviso that any decision to change the rules, confirm the budget, or fix the membership levy (based on volume sales) could only be made by the executive, and then only if there were six votes in favour. This meant any category could stymie any change against its interests simply by abstaining.'

A meeting held in the late wine maker, Peter Fredatovich's office, in Lincoln Road, West Auckland, saw representatives of the three organisations agree this was a workable solution. Then, in September 1975, a general meeting was held in the Henderson Borough Council to confirm the decision to form the Wine Institute of New Zealand Incorporated.

'We agreed to form a provisional executive immediately. Alex Corban was nominated as chairman by George Mazuran, who became deputy-chairman, and I was appointed provisional executive officer. It could never have turned out that way but for the good grace demonstrated by George in nominating Alex in recognition of his efforts and the realism displayed by Tom McDonald in acknowledging that the representational work of both Alex and George entitled them to the two top roles.'

FROM SALES TO CEO

Dunleavy spent most of 1976 working out the constitutional details of the new Wine Institute of New Zealand Incorporated, following which he was persuaded to apply for the job as permanent chief executive officer, which he got. He began as the first CEO of the Institute on 1 October, in a room made available by their accountants, Kendon Cox, at the 1 Blomfield Spa, Takapuna, branch where Graeme Chandler, accounts advisor and trustee, was also located.

Funding had been hotly debated. First it was agreed there should be compulsory funding to prevent free-loading. The basis was to be a levy per gallon of wine sold on the basis that this figure could be verifiable, if necessary, from official returns.

The then Labour Government was persuaded to pass the Wine Makers' Levy Act, which recognised the Institute and provided one of the preconditions for the renewal of a wine maker's licence as then required under the Sale of Liquor Act as confirmation the applicant had paid the required levy for the previous year to the Wine Institute. Verification was by means of a trustee (Graeme Chandler) appointed under the Levy Act, charged with receiving confidential returns of volume sales from each member and making known to the Institute only the total volume sold. Meanwhile, the Institute executive compiled a budget of anticipated expenditure.

'By dividing the dollars in that budget by the gallons of wine sold, the trustee was able to calculate a levy per gallon, which was then required to be confirmed by the minister of agriculture by notice in the Gazette. The system was put to all licensed winemakers, only one of which objected. So the Levy Act was passed in time for the Institute office to open on 1 October 1976.'

The establishment of the Institute gave voice for all winemakers to government departments, local bodies and other stakeholders. There was also general agreement that the regulations governing winemaking, then contained within the Food and Drug Regulations, needed tightening up, especially in relation to additions of water and sugar.

'The responsible officer in the health department, Jim Fraser, had an excellent grasp of the realities of winemaking, which enabled changes to the regulations to be phased in on a staged basis, in consultation with the Institute,' Dunleavy says.

The third aim of the New Zealand Wine Institute was promoting New Zealand wine.

In the early stages, this was confined to the Institute taking over from the Department of Industries and Commerce responsibility for the National Wine Competition, in association with the Tourist Hotel Corporation (THC). This carried on for 10 years until the demise of THC, when Dunleavy negotiated for the Institute to become sponsors of what has been for the past 25 years the Air New Zealand Wine Awards.

From the early 1980s, Dunleavy was the organiser and members who wanted to would participate at their own costs in the first export market ventures in Australia, the United Kingdom and America.

'In 1983 I spearheaded the country's first export foray into Australia, to Expovin in Melbourne. The Department of Trade and Industry reminded me

'THE DEPARTMENT OF TRADE AND INDUSTRY REMINDED ME THAT A SUBSIDY WAS AVAILABLE FOR WINE COMPANIES TAKING PART IN SUCH AN EXPORT VENTURE, SO I PERSUADED A FEW ENTERPRISING MEMBERS TO TAKE ADVANTAGE OF THIS GOVERNMENT BENEVOLENCE, AND OFF WE WENT.'

that a subsidy was available for wine companies taking part in such an export venture, so I persuaded a few enterprising members to take advantage of this government benevolence, and off we went.'

They travelled again to Expovin in Sydney the following year, then back to Melbourne in 1985 for the Victorian International Exhibition of Wine (VIEW), an official part of the state's 150th anniversary.

In 1986, Bryan Mogridge, then managing director of Montana, and chairman of the Institute, went to London for the London Wine Trade Fair (LWTF) at which Montana's wines featured on the stand of its United Kingdom agents, Seagram UK.

'Bryan came back and directed me to make sure New Zealand was at the next LWTF, preferably as the host nation, which Australia had been in 1986. I estimated such status would double its sales to United Kingdom in a short time. Bryan persuaded the Institute executive to allow me to organise a New Zealand representation and lead the group, provided participants chipped in to cover the travel expenses; which they did.'

KIWI WINE IN LONDON

As newcomers, the New Zealand stand was popular, making it easy for wineries to cash in on their newfound popularity and for Dunleavy to persuade organisers to make New Zealand the host nation for 1988.

'The main duty for the host nation was to put on a lunch for exhibitors on the first day of the fair. As one of the co-founders of the New Zealand Food and Beverage Exporters Council (an initiative that a venison exporter and I had cooked up in Sydney in 1984), I was able to persuade a range of food exporters to donate the necessary ingredients, and Air New Zealand provided the transportation.'

It was a sunny day in May when the New Zealand lunch took place on the roof of the Kensington Exhibition Centre. The cream of the United Kingdom wine trade were there and that was the day New Zealand announced its arrival on the United Kingdom wine trade stage, Dunleavy says.

The following year, en route to London, the New Zealand wine contingent detoured via New York for the first presentation of its wines in the Big Apple, and then by train to Washington DC, where wine writer Robert Parker was among celebrity guests who joined them for a wine tasting at the home of the New Zealand Trade Commissioner.

RETIRING FROM THE WINE INSTITUTE

When he retired officially in 1991 as CEO of the Wine Institute of New Zealand, known today as New Zealand Winegrowers, Dunleavy was retained for a year to help his successor, Philip Gregan, find the ropes.

He also worked to establish an export entity focused on the United Kingdom: the New Zealand Wine Guild, a voluntary organisation for members exporting there.

'I worked from his home in Takapuna as secretary of the Guild', says Gregan, 'communicating with the first UK appointee by fax in those far-off days pre-internet and email. This carried on until 1996, when responsibility for managing the New Zealand wine export effort went in-house to the Wine Institute office, and Louise Hill took over the reins.'

HIGHLIGHTS

'The highlight of my parliamentary lobbying career was the vote in 1989 to permit the sale of unfortified wine in supermarkets and grocers,' says Dunleavy.

During the committee stages of the debate on the Sale of Liquor Amendment Bill 1989, the proposal to authorise sales of light wine in supermarkets was narrowly defeated. Institute chair Bryan Mogridge and Dunleavy sat in the back of the House when that vote was taken.

'Mogridge said to me: "Well that's that until next time, whenever that will be." I suggested trying on his own to resurrect the issue. The following morning I ran into Jonathan Hunt who had honoured a much earlier promise to the licensing trusts movement to vote against wine in supermarkets. When Jonathan saw me coming he said: "I'm no longer the minister of wine and cheese . . .", to which I replied that the vote was against the weight of public opinion. Jonathan said if he could be convinced of that, he would see what he could do.'

So Dunleavy raced back to Auckland, consulted with Bryan and the boss of New World supermarkets, and persuaded them to mount a proper independent market survey of consumers exiting three supermarkets around Auckland, asking the simple question: 'Would you like to be able to buy table wine along with your groceries?' The response was overwhelming: more than 80 per cent in favour.

'There is a convention in the New Zealand Parliament that once a clause has been passed (or rejected) during committee stages, that's the end of the argument, unless there is an obvious miscarriage of legal drafting. I then had to win a vote to recommit the wine in supermarket clause. Fortunately, there had been a drafting error in a clause that disadvantaged the Porirua Licensing

'WHEN IT WAS AGREED THAT THE INSTITUTE NEEDED A NATIONAL MAGAZINE ... THE THEN-CHAIRMAN, JOHN BUCK, POINTED TO ME AND SAID, "WELL, THERE'S THE EX-JOURNALIST".'

Trust and Jonathan was able to associate it with the issue, so the recommittal of both issues were linked. Graham Kelly argued successfully for the Porirua issue and the late Fred Gerbic argued for wine, in both cases successfully. Both votes were won,' he says.

The first was for recommittal and then for the substantive issue of approval of sale of wines in supermarkets and dairies.

NEW ZEALAND WINEGROWER

Despite his dream job of working with the late T. P. McLean, Dunleavy says his most satisfying journalism role was founding and editing *New Zealand Winegrower* in 1997.

'It came into being during a meeting of the board of the Wine Institute early in 1997, by which time Kevyn Moore, president of the New Zealand Grape Growers Council, attended Institute board meetings by invitation. This was the first move towards eventual amalgamation of the administration of two organisations into what is now known as New Zealand Winegrowers. I was a member of the Institute executive as an alternate member for large, local wineries at the invitation of Nick Nobilo.

'When it was agreed that the Institute needed a national magazine to represent what was happening in New Zealand viticulture and wine, the then-chairman, John Buck, pointed to me and said, "Well, there's the ex-journalist".'

Initially, he sold the advertising as well, with the aim of covering the production and print costs so the magazine could be mailed free to all members of the Institute, Grape Growers Council, other industry organisations and desirable contacts in the political and departmental wings of the government. But it was a struggle doing it all. So the magazine was eventually contracted to Rural News Group, with Dunleavy retained as editor.

GRAPES THEN AND NOW

The inaugural issue of *New Zealand Winegrower* was Winter 1997. Its statistics show a marked difference between the New Zealand wine industry then and now. Marlborough had 2376 hectares of grapes (compared with 19,570 producing hectares in 2012); Hawke's Bay had 1980 (5046); and Gisborne had 1254 (2003). In 1977, there were 261 licensed winemakers in New Zealand; in 2011 there were 698. The leading grape variety in 1997 was Chardonnay with 12,683 hectares harvested nationwide; in 2011 there were 25,580 hectares of Chardonnay harvested nationwide, which was eclipsed by Sauvignon Blanc,

with 224,412 hectares harvested in 2011.

Then there are the reds. In the past decade alone, Pinot Noir has tripled in the number of grapes harvested, growing from 10,402 in 2002 to 31,156 in 2011. Cabernet Sauvignon has showed a significant decline. Merlot, Malbec and Syrah are all on the rise. It's not over yet. As I write the last words in this book, the first words are being put to paper by grape-growers around the country to fill in the latest statistical survey sent out by New Zealand Winegrowers, whose chief executive officer, Philip Gregan (Terry's successor) wants to make sure we all have an accurate picture of the number and whereabouts of grapes in New Zealand today.

Watch this space.

LEGACY

Dunleavy may have finished as editor of *New Zealand Winegrower* in mid-2011, after 68 issues, but his influence, thoughts and ideas for the future resonate with those working with New Zealand wine: making, marketing and exporting the stuff.

TERRY'S GO-TO WINES

'Whatever goes best with the coming meal, but for casual aperitif enjoyment, increasingly one of the excellent, dryish Rieslings we have started to produce in New Zealand.'

TOP WINE FROM TERRY DUNLEAVY
• 1993 Te Motu (from Waiheke Island)

Note: As this book was going to print, Terry Dunleavy was in Samoa for the country's fiftieth anniversary of independence, reporting for the *New Zealand Herald*.

❧ ABOUT THE AUTHOR

Joëlle Thomson is the wine columnist for the *Dominion Post*, *Christchurch Press* and *Waikato Times*. She also writes for *New Zealand Winegrower*, *Next*, *Off Licence News* (UK) and edits *Drinksbiz* magazine.

Her first wine column was in *Capital Times*, Wellington, in 1994. Two columns in, she immediately began attending the excellent tastings at Regional Wines in Wellington, where she fell for Riesling, which remains her 'desert island' wine. Her other great wine passion is Italian wine: 'The fascinating diversity, history and wildly varied flavours take me on endless lessons in geography and taste. Italian innovation is incredibly inspiring, too; it reminds me of what makes the New Zealand wine industry so exciting today.'

Joëlle is a member of the British-based Circle of Wine Writers, and teaches at the New Zealand School of Food & Wine in Auckland, New Zealand.

Joëlle Thomson's Under $20 Wine Guide (2002/03 edition, New Holland Publishers) was winner of the Best Wine Guides in English (Rest of World) category at the Gourmand World Cookbook Awards 2002. Her *Celebrating New Zealand Wine*, also published by New Holland, was a finalist in the 2005 Montana New Zealand Book Awards in the Lifestyle & Contemporary Culture category.

AUTHOR'S GO-TO NEW ZEALAND WINES

A go-to wine is like your favourite music, food or place: it's where you go to relax. For me, Riesling tops the list. And where New Zealand is concerned, Pegasus Bay Riesling, Framingham Classic Riesling and many of our top Chardonnays are my favourite go-to wines; refreshing, luscious and complex. For the same reasons I love Italy's Verdicchio and France's Chenin Blanc.

Just as the patient publishers of this book were trying to extract the manuscript from me, I flew to Vinitaly and discovered one of Italy's — and the world's — most forgotten, least known and incredibly age-worthy wine treasures made from the Timorasso grape in Piemonte. A 14-year-old Timorasso tasted like a fresh, aged Riesling — with acidity to burn, full body and fantastically intriguing flavours.

When it comes to red wine, Pinot Noirs from New Zealand are endlessly interesting. And I like the medium-bodied, fruity, silky Nero d'Avolas from

Sicily or a great southern Rhône red, for the reasons that winemaker Gordon Russell so eloquently puts it — they're earthy, warm, adventurous wines.

If I could drink them every day, I would love to pour great Barolo, Burgundy, Barbaresco, Barbera and Freisa into my glass. Thanks to Framingham winemaker Andrew Hedley — a fellow Riesling fan — it's possible every few months to buy one of this planet's least-known but most wonderful wines, Nerello Mascalese from the lower slopes of the fiery Mt Etna.

Great New Zealand wines that are taking my breath away include: Dog Point Vineyard Section 94 and Dog Point Chardonnay; Quartz Reef Pinot Noir and George's Road Pinot Noir; Fromm Chardonnay; Auburn Riesling; Craggy Range Les Beaux Cailloux Chardonnay, and, of course, the many Pinot Noirs around the country.

Even as I write these final thoughts, talented winemakers turn up to taste their latest wines with me; Steve Skinner from Elephant Hill, Paul Pujol from Prophet's Rock, Max Marriott from Auburn, Guy Porter from Bellbird Spring and Kirk Bray from George's Road . . . among many others. They may be small wineries on a world scale but thanks to their global outlook — and international winemaking experience — what they produce is as world class as the large Kiwi companies' wines. And here I think of Church Road Merlot, Cabernet Sauvignon and — the wine that outsells them both at the cellar door — Marzemino.

These go-to wines make me feel the way I do when standing on top of a South Island mountain, absorbing a breathtaking view; they are a reminder of the natural beauty of the world.

AUTHOR'S ACKNOWLEDGEMENTS

While there's no time like the present, I must admit the historic stories of Ivan Donaldson, Nick Nobilo and Peter Babich made me wish I'd been involved when they were planting the first grapes in Canterbury, pioneering Pinotage in West Auckland and trying to change the legal minimum 2-gallon wine retail sale in New Zealand. Not that the Canterbury Plains, Pinotage or law change are close to my heart. Nor are they burning issues in today's wine scene.

But the drive of these blokes to push cultural change away from laws that encouraged binge drinking; to have the courage to plant grapes that would make table wine; and to venture outside the accepted norm in winemaking is incredibly inspiring.

Not that I'm singling these three out for any special reason. Every story in this book gave me pause for a 'what if . . .' moment. What if we all pursued our passions with as much focus as they have and do? How much would we all achieve then? Their stories are just the tip of the adventurous iceberg of wine pioneers in New Zealand today.

My first big thank you goes to all those who have shared their stories here. Thank you for making wine come alive for me and, all going well, for everyone who reads this book.

The partners, parents, brothers, sisters and other family members of those profiled here also deserve a big thank you for their help in rustling up research, sourcing photos — historic and new — and assisting with advice. Special thanks to Edward Donaldson, Fabian Yukich, Ian Clark and Terry Dunleavy for going beyond the call of duty to make sure these movers, shakers and groundbreakers have been well represented in these pages.

Thank you to my friends and family, who have taken the risk and not only listened to my Riesling ramblings but actually encouraged them — especially thank you for great friendship and great books to Douglas Wallis; to my beautiful, intelligent and inspiring daughter, Ruby; to my family: Jacqui, Susan, Dad and Mum.

Thank you to Stephen Bennett MW for the wonderfully challenging, eye-opening blind tastings and great friendship. And thank you to all who have been quoted in these pages, friends and colleagues in wine: Tim Atkin MW, Nick Stock, Paul Brajkovich, Michael Palij MW, Bob Campbell MW, Phyll Pattie, Cath Hopkin, Ruth Pretty, Baxter Fagan, Ian Isaacs, Celia Hay, Steve Smith MW, Steve Davies, Steve Green, Duncan Forsyth, Nick Lewis, Tessa Nicholson, Mark Young, Simon Beck, Gerry Gregg, John Hancock, David Babich, Hattie Thodey, Angela Clifford, Andrew Hedley, Guy Porter, Philip Bothwell, Philip Gregan, Warren Barton and Nigel Greening and many more in the world of wine. Apologies if your name is not here and should be.

Thank you to all those in the winemaking, selling and tasting trade, both in New Zealand and internationally, who have patiently taught me about wine over the past 18 years since I began writing about it. Thank you for your time, for the tastings, for the many wine samples and for having the faith in me, a journalist wanting to understand wine and impart that understanding in a digestible fashion. If and when I achieve my aim — to make wine as stimulating and fun to read about as it is to drink — thanks are as much due to the great minds within the industry as to any of the words I string together.

There is no time like the present but it's a great privilege to be shown a little of how we got here too. Thank you to all those who have made that possible in this, *The Wild Bunch*.

FURTHER READING

NON-FICTION
A Hedonist in the Cellar by Jay McInerney, Vintage Books, 2007
Biography of a Local Palate by David Burton, Four Winds Press, 2003
First Big Crush by Eric Arnold, Scribner, 2007
Judgement of Paris by George M. Taber, Scribner, 2005
Pinot Central by Alan Brady, Penguin, 2010
Questions of Taste, the philosophy of wine, edited by Barry Smith, Signal
    Books, 2007
Riesling Renaissance by Freddy Price, Mitchell Beazley, 2004
To Cork or not to Cork by George M. Taber, Scribner, 2007
The Juice by Jay McInerney, Bloomsbury Publishing, 2012
The New France by Andrew Jefford, Mitchell Beazley, 2002
The Oxford Companion to Wine, edited by Jancis Robinson MW, Oxford
    University Press, 1994
The Wines of Italy by Cyril Ray, George Rainbird, 1966
The World Atlas of Wine, Sixth Edition by Hugh Johnson & Jancis Robinson,
    Mitchell Beazley, 2007
To Your Good Health by Dr Thomas Stuttaford, Faber and Faber, 1997
Waugh on Wine by Auberon Waugh, Fourth Estate Ltd, 1986
Wine & War by Don & Petie Kladstrup, Coronet Books, 2001

FICTION
A Soldier's Tale, by M K Joseph, 1976 (republished by Godwit, 1995)
Brideshead Revisited by Evelyn Waugh, Penguin, 1945
Perfume (first published as *Das Parfum*) by Patrick Suskind, Penguin, 1985

Many of these books are out of print but thanks to the internet it is possible to
track them down in minutes. If it takes longer, these inspiring tomes are worth
the time, the search and the read — for those interested in matters of taste;
fact, fiction and the in-between bits.